THE WHITE ARROW

BOOK 3 OF THE BOW OF HART SAGA

P.H. SOLOMON

TABLE OF CONTENTS

Copyright & Credits	v
Other Books by P. H. Solomon:	vii
Thank You	ix
Northeast Denaria	xi
Western Auguron	xiii
Chapter One	1
Chapter Two	16
Chapter Three	31
Chapter Four	51
Chapter Five	62
Chapter Six	77
Chapter Seven	91
Chapter Eight	97
Chapter Nine	109
Chapter Ten	116
Chapter Eleven	131
Chapter Twelve	138
Chapter Thirteen	148
Chapter Fourteen	157
Chapter Fifteen	169
Chapter Sixteen	178
Chapter Seventeen	191
Chapter Eighteen	204
Chapter Nineteen	218
Chapter Twenty	233
Chapter Twenty-One	254
Chapter Twenty-Two	265
Chapter Twenty-Three	278
Chapter Twenty-Four	292

Chapter Twenty-Five	309
Epilogue	321
Dear Reader	331
About the Author	349

Copyright & Credits

Thank you for purchasing The White Arrow. I hope you will enjoy the story as much as I've enjoyed writing it. Feel free to visit me at http://phsolomon.com for more information about my writing or to sign-up for email alerts of upcoming release, events and more. Once you've finished this book please share how much you liked it with a rating or review.

Published by P. H. Solomon at Amazon.

The White Arrow is a work of fiction. Names, characters, places, and incidents either are the product of the author's imagination or are used fictitiously. Any resemblance to actual persons on the cover or in the text of the book, living or dead, events or locales is entirely coincidental.

Copyright 2017 by P. H. Solomon

All maps are the property of the author, Copyright 2015 by P. H. Solomon

This eBook is licensed for your personal enjoyment only. This eBook may not be re-sold or given away to other people. If you would like to share this book with another person, please purchase an additional copy for each recipient. If you're reading this book and did not purchase it, or it was not purchased for your use only, then please return to your favorite eBook retailer and purchase your own copy. Thank you for respecting the hard work of this author.

Print Edition ISBN: 9798673020036

Cover image licensed/commissioned through/by Chris Rawlins. Special thanks also goes to Chris Rawlins whose artistic vision produced such an excellent cover art.

Credits

This is the end of a long journey that covered several decades so I want to thank all my family and friends for their support and encouragement over the years including my wife and daughter. I also want to thank the many writers I've met in recent years who have been so helpful, generous and encouraging. You've all been amazingly helpful.

I want to especially offer my thanks to my editor, Jessica Barnes, without whom I wouldn't have made it this far. Jessica, you are truly a gem of an editor and you've taught me a great deal through your work.

OTHER BOOKS BY P. H. SOLOMON:
THE BOW OF HART SAGA:

Trading Knives (prequel novella)
What Is Needed (prequel novella)
The Bow of Destiny
An Arrow Against the Wind

THANK YOU

Thank you for purchasing The White Arrow. When you are finished, if you have liked this book, please consider leaving a review.

If you've enjoyed reading the other books in The Bow of Hart Saga, you can subscribe to my newsletter for more information about my other books, fun updates about the series and news about upcoming releases at: https://phsolomon.authorreach.com/lead/5a9927e5 and receive a gift.

MAPS OF DENARIA
Northeast Denaria
From the Sigoth Range to Dragon's Maw

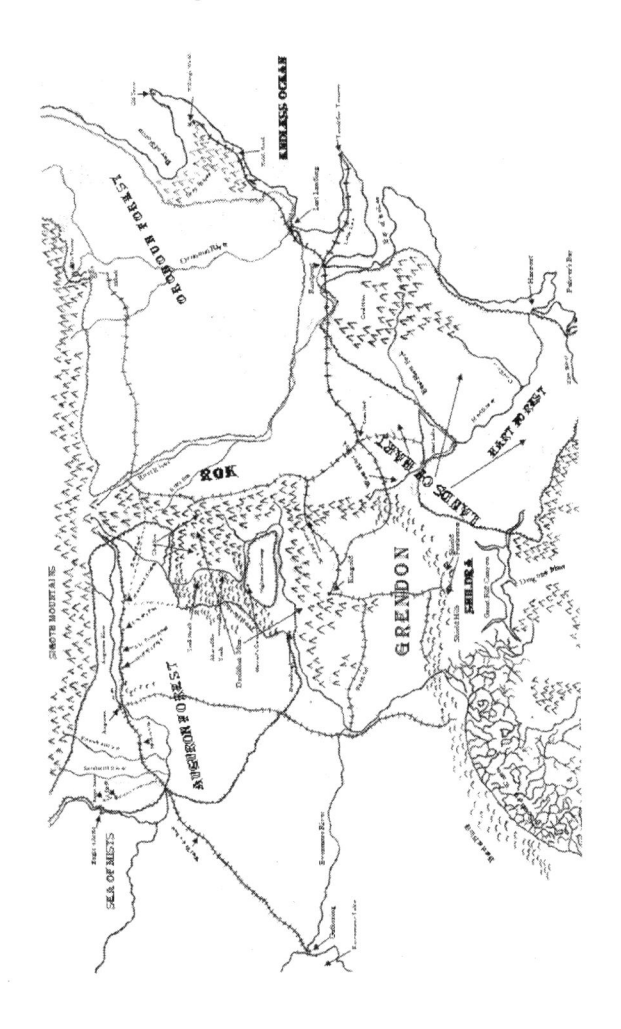

Western Auguron

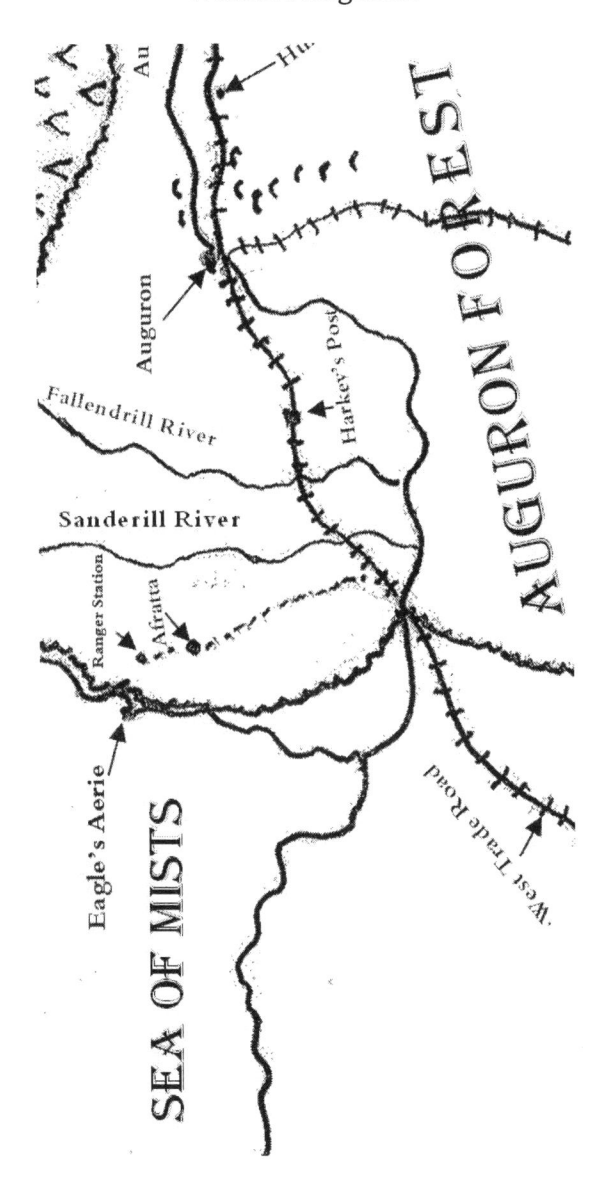

CHAPTER ONE

Events spun out of Magdronu's grasp like a whirlwind. He had gathered more useless wood as Gweld than magic since that incident at his shrine in the mountains. How foolish of him to challenge Eloch's will back at Howart's Cave. Most of these fools would have been out of his way by now were it not for that mistake. Magdronu-as-Gweld dropped wood near the fire and turned to retrieve more for Hastra. He resisted clenching his fists. A careless mistake against Eloch was one thing, a minor event the others deemed a miracle instead of a reaction between powers. But events had turned against him since whatever Withling—Apeth Stellin or someone else—had denied him at his own shrine with Eloch's blessing. Yet there remained the Bow of Hart and hostages on the bluff. If only Corgren could complete a sacrifice to transfer magic. If only there was some signal.

Behind Magdronu, Ralda gasped. Magdronu-as-Gweld wheeled about. Was it a body? He'd felt nothing of a sacrifice. The giant leaned past a sheer corner, his arm outstretched, and Hastra stood just behind him. Hastra spoke, but her words were lost amid the roar of water among boulders and the moaning wind.

Ralda heaved a white body from the water by an arm. Magdronu-as-Gweld gaped at the sight of Limbreth, sodden and limp, as the giant gathered her and set her by the fire at Hastra's gesticulations. The Grendonese woman shivered, and blood discolored her white leathers on the right side below her ribs. Not a sacrifice. Magdronu-as-Gweld stepped around the fire and displayed his false concern.

"Ralda, grab my blanket but have a care for the fire." Hastra touched Limbreth in several places.

The young woman's eyes rolled in her pale face, and her teeth chattered.

"Withling Hastra, I must go now and try to—to find Athson." Magdronu-as-Gweld wheeled away.

"Not yet and not alone. Let's have the tale from her lest we step into some trap ourselves." Hastra uttered her healing prayer, the words pitched softly and lost in the noise of the nearby river.

Ralda hovered close, ready with the blanket. The dwarves and Danilla gathered beyond the fire and watched, eyes wide.

Magdronu-as-Gweld leaned close. Another hostage lost and no passage of power from either member of that traitorous Hartian family. Possession of the Bow of Hart appeared in jeopardy. He restrained his anger with effort and watched the Withling at work.

Limbreth's trembles eased as Hastra murmured and touched the young woman in various places. The gash bled freely. Hastra covered it with one hand, and Limbreth squeezed it with another, her groan of pain lost in the noise of the river. The blood began to course less after a few moments, and Limbreth lifted her left hand to Hastra's shoulder, her eyes wide but alert to her surroundings.

"Withling, the lights! Did you see them?"

Hastra continued her prayer, and the others murmured among themselves.

Limbreth's jaw worked, and her breathing steadied. "Hurry! Athson and his father fought Corgren. The Bane. It was there too. Stabbed me and shoved me over."

Danilla knelt beside Limbreth, her face intent. "I only know of you, Limbreth but I'm Danilla, Athson's mother. What do you know of them? Are they safe?" The woman's voice wavered with restrained emotions.

Limbreth gasped for air and offered her hand to Danilla who grasped it. "I'm pleased to see you safe. But I know nothing for sure." Limbreth's gaze drifted to the faces of those gathered. "You must hurry and help them if you can." She tried to rise but her body didn't respond.

Tordug advanced and knelt beside Limbreth and Hastra. "You're in no condition to go yet. We'll find them. Tell us more."

Limbreth shook her head where she lay, and a sudden sob burst from her throat. "Couldn't fight it off. Didn't see much. I don't know much." She focused her gaze to Hastra as the Withling ended her prayer and lifted her blood-covered hand from Limbreth's side. "Spark—did you see him? All the colors. I didn't think he was real, but he—he fought the Bane and leaped after me. Light like a rainbow surrounded me, and the wind carried me—so strong, it blew me sideways. Stronger than that storm in the mountains. Remember? But Spark, he was there, really there."

Magdronu-as-Gweld stood. "What? That imaginary dog again. She must've seen things when she was injured."

Tordug gazed between Hastra, Magdronu-as-Gweld, and Limbreth in turn. "Who is this Spark?"

Magdronu-as-Gweld heaved an exasperated sigh. That guardian of Eloch's at work again. "It's a dog Athson's seen since he was a child. But it's not real. Instead of talking about mind-tricks, we need to go find Athson and the bow."

Makwi's voice rumbled over the noise of the river. "Athson mentioned that name in the mountains when his head was injured. I thought it was nonsense. He mentioned something about being helped then."

Tordug motioned to Limbreth. "She's seen something."

Limbreth tried to sit up while nodding vigorously. "It's true. He saved me when I failed against the Bane! Hastra, you know about it, don't you?"

The Withling braced herself and attempted to gain her feet. Danilla scrambled to Hastra's aid, and the Withling stood with the help. She patted Danilla's hands. "Thank you, dear. Spark is real and has been more active of late. It's a guardian who has aided Athson since he was a child."

"Really? We're standing around talking about this imaginary dog while we need to help Athson? I'm going." Magdronu-as Gweld whirled about. He'd heard enough. He suppressed the heat of his anger. *Easy, now.* He needed this disguise yet, it seemed.

"He's right about helping Athson." Hastra stooped toward Limbreth. "Can you tell us more? No? Tordug, I suggest you and Makwi accompany Gweld."

Magdronu-as-Gweld paused and spoke to Makwi. "Get your things but hurry. It's a long climb on the trail. I fear we're too late already."

Danilla released Hastra and went for her things. "I'm going too. That's my son and husband up there."

Hastra shrugged at a questioning glance from Tordug. "Uh, Ralda, can you stay and stand guard?" She extended her hand, palm down and flicked further along the defile. "Let Limbreth change, though." She turned back to Limbreth. "Let's get you dry and steady on your feet first. What was needed was given for you, but narrower than the eye of a needle. There is much to come for you, I think."

Magdronu-as-Gweld scrambled back along the defile ahead of the others. Let the laggards come at their own pace. He needed to see what had happened. Atop the crevice, Magdronu closed his eyes. *'Corgren!'* He waited, but there was no answer. Not good.

As the others arrived, he strode away. No one just escaped from him. Eloch played many strings, it seemed. Magdronu-as-Gweld shook his head with a scowl the others could not see from behind him. He'd misplayed his hand several times to let this much spin out of his grasp. That whirlwind not the least. He quickened his pace. Time to see what remained in his grasp.

∼

LIMBRETH SHIVERED BY THE FIRE, her limbs weak, as Hastra unfastened her leather armor to change into another set of clothing. Ralda climbed higher in the cleft and stood guard with his back to them. She needed to thank him, thank them all. "Hastra, thank you for saving me. You've even brought my pack. How did you know to be here?"

Hastra pulled spare clothing from Limbreth's pack. "What was needed was given. Eloch led me to this spot, though I was surprised we caught such a fish as you." She patted Limbreth's pack. "You've Danilla to thank for bringing this. We found your weapons discarded in Howart's Cave and brought them too."

"I—I didn't expect to see those again or my other belongings." Limbreth touched the swords, and tears formed in her eyes. "I hoped Athson would catch us, but—but I tried to escape. But the Bane, its touch froze my thoughts and my limbs —except for my arm. You brought Danilla out of Rok?" She rubbed her left arm.

"Here, let's get you out of the rest of that armor and dry it as fast as we can. The others will be waiting on us or coming back with news. I'll tell you my tale as I remember it." Hastra helped Limbreth out of her things and recounted what she remembered of her capture and captivity in Rok as well as her escape and the whirlwind. "But that wasn't a regular storm. I suspect it came from Magdronu's magic, though I don't know where he was or why it occurred."

Limbreth fumbled out of her leathers and into her spare clothing while Hastra laid her things by the fire to dry some. She closed her eyes, and the Bane loomed from her memory, the dagger falling. Her breath came in short gasps. *Open your eyes and don't think about that.* When Limbreth opened her eyes, she saw her blood-stained leather armor and the rent in its right side. She stood on unsteady feet with Hastra's help and finished dressing, but her boots were soaked. She wrapped her fur cloak from the dwarves around her shoulders, and her chill subsided. "Good thing I wasn't wearing this. I doubt I'll be able to move soon. The others may return before I'm ready."

"We'll do what we can here and get there soon enough." Hastra offered Limbreth food and finished setting her things out to dry. She then produced her Withling book and thumbed through it.

Limbreth chewed the ration as she lay on her side by the fire and stared. How had she lived? It must have been Spark. Athson must've sent him to help. "Hastra, what is Spark? Is he some spirit?"

Hastra paused with her book. "A guardian from Eloch, I should think. But why the form of a dog, I don't know. Since he's been with Athson so long, I can only guess that Eloch has had a deeper purpose to guard Athson all this time." The Withling peered over her book at Limbreth. "And now you, it seems. I need to ask Athson more questions about Spark, but I think there was some foreknowledge that this guardian would be needed against such as the Bane, since it is beyond physical might alone to defeat." She pointed a finger at Limbreth. "But you are a different matter. It saved you for a reason, and you should consider that, since I asked you to guard Athson too."

Limbreth swallowed the last of her ration of dwarven travel-meat. "I should have done more, but I couldn't with the Bane. I guess Spark takes care of Athson, and he wasn't with me when they captured me in the cave. But at least I'm here now. I'll do what I can for Athson regardless. I'm glad he came for me and his father. I hope they're both alive." Surely they had made it. Athson had the Bow of Hart and his blessed sword. Ath could have broken free of his chain. Maybe they had met the others by now and were coming back.

"You did your best with what you had. From what you say, that death-grip came in handy with the Bane."

"More than once, it seems. But it wasn't enough."

"No, I suspect dispelling the Bane will take more than swords and such. Now, let me see if I can figure out who else is helping us." Hastra thumbed through her book as she held it out of the breeze.

Limbreth closed her eyes again. The terror of falling brought her heart thumping into her throat.

The wind threw her sideways. Pain seared her side. The helpless certainty of death seized her. Color surrounded her and slowed her fall until she splashed like a skipped stone into the water. She gasped at the frigid rush and struggled to stay afloat with her wound. She slammed into a rock with a grunt. Stunned, she almost sank under the river. But the current yanked her around the rock, and she bounced off others as cold drained her awareness. A hand appeared from the sheer rock side of the river. Was it real? She lifted her left hand with effort and caught the hand.

Limbreth opened her eyes. She still lived by some miracle. She took deep breaths and slowed her heart. And her friends still lived. Hastra's observation returned. It was for a purpose that they were all alive. But why? The Bow of Hart and helping Athson were the only reasons she settled on that made sense. A thought arrived with Limbreth's conclusion: *Be ready.* She moved her boots and other wet gear closer to the fire.

Hastra muttered to herself as she read her book. Her eyes flicked to Limbreth's movement. "Careful you don't burn them." She returned to her reading.

"I just want to help now that I'm free of Corgren and the Bane." Limbreth touched the bloody gouge in her leather top. So much blood lost; no wonder she was so weak. She lay down by the fire again. When she closed her eyes, the Bane loomed over her. She gasped, opened her eyes, and lay trembling.

Hastra touched her face. "Eloch bless your rest. Ralda is guarding the ravine, so we're as safe as possible for the moment."

Limbreth relaxed after a moment. She needed rest after her trek to the Funnel. She rubbed her wrists. The binding rope still chafed her wrists, if her mind. She caught her breath and lay still.

A sudden thought seized her mind. She scrambled to her feet and almost fell into the fire. *Cursed weakness!* "Athson, he'll think I'm dead!" She should be. "I hope they find him fast, or he'll think he lost me too."

"They will find him and have news of what happened. But rest before you fall over."

"I wish they were back." Limbreth sat again.

The Withling touched her face. "You need to sleep and rest."

Limbreth lay beside the fire again and rolled onto her side. Ralda's broad back filled the upper end of the ravine where he stood watch. The giant had saved her. She needed to thank him. Beside her, Hastra muttered at her Withling book. "What has your attention?" Weariness dragged at Limbreth, but her need for news of Athson left her wakeful at Hastra's restless musings.

The Withling peered at Limbreth, her head cocked sideways. "Yes, I think you should know these things."

Limbreth raised herself on an elbow. "Know what?"

"Athson, the Bow of Hart, and the arrow to come. What is written in the Book of Prophecies from my order."

Limbreth sat all the way up. "Arrow? He mentioned that."

∼

ATHSON SCRABBLED AT LOOSE STONE. His head ached and spun, even lying down. Not the head injury again. But sweat drenched his brow, and Spark lay nearby at a fire that danced. Athson groaned and thrust a blanket from his body. He burned and shivered at the same time. How did that happen? He got to his hands and knees on hard rock, and his head spun anew. Darkness surrounded the fire, but his groan echoed. A cave? He held his head. What had happened? There was the Funnel and his scramble through the storm afterward.

The trapper. Athson lifted his head. Where was he?

"Spark, what's going on?" The mountain hound stirred and sighed, his gaze toward the mouth of the cave.

Athson squinted. Snow blanketed the heaths outside the cave. There was his mule and the tack for it. He needed to find his mother. Mother? That was right, they had her captive in Rok. His father...

He choked back a sob at the memory. He'd finally found him, and now he was dead, killed by Corgren while trying to save Athson. And there was Limbreth, gone over the side of the Funnel.

Athson watched Spark a moment. "Did you get her?"

Spark wagged his tail.

Athson looked away. The mountain hound had done more than he had. Shame rose with sour bile in his stomach. How could he have failed her? The wrong choice. Corgren had goaded him into that worthless shot into the wind. The Bow of Hart lay nearby, and he spat at it. Could he have even made the shot to save Limbreth with it? No telling after that poor choice.

But now he needed to find his mother. He'd leave the bow, but he could still bargain with the useless artifact. He cast around, half-blind in his fever, for all his things. He dragged them over near the mule before he collapsed. Athson rolled over and found Spark lying next to him. Maybe he'd fainted. He closed his eyes as weariness dragged at his arms.

Athson scrambled away from the kobold in the dark amid the howls of trolls hunting the night. Too late he remembered the edge of the Funnel and fell. He slid along a steep slope.

Limbreth fell too, her cry as sharp as that eagle when he'd met Zelma. He might catch Limbreth. No, she was gone. She fell at a different place.

Athson couldn't stop himself. He slipped into darkness and landed on a ledge. He bounced with a grunt and almost rolled into the darkened depths where the Deep Run gushed. He found a rough crack on the ledge and held it so he could scramble farther onto it. His breath came in rasping gasps.

Light waved above him. Trolls sought him, and he pushed away from the edge and slithered backward into a small hole of darkness. A little cave. He lay there until light glowed from far away and grew brighter until he saw a dog. Spark! The dog was friendly and nudged him farther into the little cave, where he lay down beside Athson and warmed him.

Later, the dog tugged Athson to his feet, and he walked beside the glowing animal, deeper into the cave.

Athson groaned. Spark had leapt after Limbreth but couldn't save her. But the mountain hound had saved Athson that night when he fell on a ledge. He got to his feet. Had Limbreth fallen on a ledge? No, he hadn't seen one below the Altar of the Trolls. He ground his teeth and gripped his pounding head. Sweat drenched his clothing from the fever. When had he caught a fever? It came on him after leaving the Funnel.

He grabbed his pack and leaned against the mule awhile. *Just load your things and go find your mother.* If he could stand. Athson fumbled with the tack for the mule.

Spark nudged at his legs and whimpered.

"Stop. None of that. I need to go."

He squinted over the mule's back at the storm. It was getting dark outside already. He ran his hand through his sweat-soaked hair, coughed, and shuddered before he fell on the hard rock of the cave's natural floor.

Spark stood on his chest.

"Cut it out, Spark. Let me up. I have to find her." Athson tried to push the mountain hound away but finally lay still by the mule, which stared at him and flicked its tail. He groaned and covered his face at his sudden tears. Why had he let her fall like that? He was no good. He let his father and Limbreth die. He sobbed until he fell asleep.

Someone gripped Athson and pulled him into a sitting position. His eyes fluttered. He found strength in his limp neck and lifted his head. The indistinct face of the trapper hovered in his blurred vision.

"Not you again."

"Here, put your arm around my neck, and I'll get you over by the fire." He got Athson to his feet and half dragged him toward the dying fire. "What were you trying to do?"

"I'm going to find my mother." Athson pushed at the trapper, a feeble resistance that got him nowhere. He sat hard as his legs gave out.

"Hey, watch that broth. You almost knocked it over." The trapper moved Athson's feet away from the fire. "You'll burn your boots if you're not careful."

Athson lay back with a heavy gasp followed by a cough. "How'd you get in this cave with Spark and me? I don't remember you when we left the ledge. He saved me that night."

The trapper shook his head. "Don't know what you mean. I brought you here in a snowstorm on that mule of yours. You'd have died by now out there with this fever you caught."

Athson frowned and shook his head. "I don't think so. Spark led me out of that cave. I was there."

The trapper patted his hands. "Just lie still. You must be remembering something else. Let me get some broth in you, and maybe I can get that fever down."

"No, I have to go find my mother. You can't stop me from that. I let all the rest of them die. I can't let her die too." He reached for his sword, but it wasn't at his side. He sat up and twisted his head in several directions, his breath heaving. "Where is it? Did you steal it?" He gripped the trapper by his coat. "I need that sword."

The other man pried Athson's hands away. "Relax. It's there beside you. And don't pull that on me. I'm trying to help you."

"You can't keep me here!" Athson rolled over and got to his feet, stumbled away, and retched. He finished and groaned.

The trapper helped him back to the fire and put a blanket over him. "Guess broth's not such a good thing just now." He held Athson by the head. "Listen to me. You're sick with a fever. You can't travel just now. You aren't even thinking straight." He tucked the blanket tighter about Athson. "Now you just lie still. I need to make my dinner. It don't make itself."

Athson faded in and out of sleep for a while as the trapper worked on his meal. He noted Spark lying by the fire again, panting and watching the cave entrance.

After a while, the trapper hummed a tune and spoke a prayer. Then he ate his meal. "Hits the spot." He smiled at Athson. "When you're better, you'll see just how good my cooking is."

"Yeah, sure." Athson laid his arm over his eyes. After a

while, he lifted his arm away, feeling clear-headed. "Hey, what's your name?"

The trapper paused as he ate. "Oh, we haven't been properly introduced, I suppose. We've met enough times before, but now we should get to know one another." He stuck out his hand and shook Athson's weak grip. "Name's Apeth Stellin."

~

MAGDRONU'S WINGS of magic enfolded Corgren as the wound seared with pain. In moments, he would arrive at help in Paugren's camp. Corgren's brother would help him.

But the spell flashed with daylight, and the encircling darkness threatened to break. Magdronu's power was weakened. His master had mentioned some trouble spreading his power among his servants.

Corgren stretched his mind for what power remained to him. His concentration fragmented with pain. Like the wound was cursed. Corgren released a choking gasp of effort and whispered the spell, strengthening his hold. Darkness solidified, and the grasp of magic roared like many voices of wind. At the last of Corgren's strength, the spell fell away, and he fell facedown. Was he there? Had his failing power taken him there or dropped him somewhere else due to the lack? "Help me." His ears roared.

Voices whispered around him. Corgren trembled. Not the dead wastes of the underworld ruled by Magdronu! He blinked and felt a rug beneath him. No, it was somewhere in the living world. Pain seared the deep wound in his back. Just like a Rokan dagger.

Hands grasped Corgren and rolled him onto his side. The Bane loomed in the tent, and the guards shrank from it even as they assisted him.

Corgren ground his teeth at the pain. "M-must have P-

Paugren." The wound felt like flame in his body. It had to have been a Wolfshead dagger. Of course, Athson had one.

An officer, by his crossed sword insignia, barked an order. "Go find Paugren! Now!" Someone left shouting. "Here, help me staunch the bleeding. He'll be dead unless Paugren gets here."

The edges of Corgren's vision faded to shadow. The Bane drifted closer, and Corgren heard its moan of hunger. Ah, in his fading moments, nearing death, he heard its true voice. Cursed creature hungered for any life affected by those traitors.

"What's happened?" The familiar voice sounded shocked. Paugren's face invaded his dwindling eyesight. "What happened to you? Get back, away with you. Here, you hold him still. Stabbed in the back. You're lucky to be alive, brother." He spoke a spell that Corgren barely recognized as healing.

Corgren's vision grew stronger, but his wound seared even more, and he shrieked. The pain remained even stronger, if that were possible. "Finish it, brother!"

"I can't, brother, my powers are limited. The high shrine is damaged somehow. I've healed you enough not to bleed to death, but the rest I have no power for from our master. We've been unable to reach the shrine. The dwarves created a slide that blocks the path." Paugren grabbed his brother's hand. "What happened?"

Pain tore another cry from Corgren before he spoke. "Stabbed by the traitorous father. The Grendonese woman fell from the Funnel. Athson remains alive with the bow. I've been stabbed with a Wolfshead dagger."

"Come, you men lift him and bring him to my house." Paugren stood as they lifted Corgren. "I'll tend you as I can, brother. This is ill news. Our master won't be pleased, since I've lost the other hostages to Eloch's wily efforts."

Corgren groaned and fought back tears against the

dagger's effects. "We've no further leverage. Magdronu must gain possession of the bow."

As they crossed from the tent used for spells, Paugren gripped Corgren's hand. "It's much worse."

Corgren ground his teeth. "It can't get much worse."

"Oh, but it can and has, Corgren. The sign of the prophecy spoken by the Withlings has arisen. Our doom lies before us with our master weakened."

As they entered the home, Corgren writhed amid the helping hands. Pain tore at him. Their master's weakened magic was cut off from them in their hour of need. Corgren rolled his eyes and stared at Paugren as they set him on a bed. "All our plans and those of Magdronu can't have come to naught after all this time."

Paugren grabbed his brother's hand as the soldiers left the room. "I fear the dragon asks too much of you, of us. But we will fight on."

Corgren squeezed his brother's hand. "It's not too much to ask. We will fight on." Another wave of pain forced a shriek from Corgren's throat and thrashed his partially healed wound. At least he lived, and that was something. "Curse those traitors, we will fight." His face twitched as he fought the pain.

CHAPTER TWO

Danilla's presence galled Magdronu. To think she'd been rescued after all these years from his clutches in Rok. Another mistake. He should never have let Hastra be taken near his prized hostages. Without Danilla, he lost control of Athson and the bow unless Corgren had taken it.

Magdronu-as-Gweld climbed toward the heights of the Funnel ahead of the others. He called for Corgren again. Nothing. He'd have to contact Paugren after he checked for Corgren at the Funnel. Magdronu-as-Gweld halted for the others to catch up. He'd pause for them often but then rush ahead. He didn't need to feign anxiety about what had happened. If only Corgren had the bow, Magdronu could discard the ruse.

The dwarves and Danilla slowed the climb considerably, but they finally crept into the notch overlooking the Funnel. Magdronu glimpsed nothing upon the rock shelf of the Funnel. No one there. Where were they? He sniffed for magic. Too far away, with the wind. He tapped his companions each in turn and said, "Let's wait and see if anything moves."

They waited, but no one revealed themselves. Makwi bent low and crept along the slope of the path. The others followed, and so did Magdronu-as-Gweld, feigning his part as a ranger. But no one was there.

He spotted bloodstains on the rocks as they gained a better view and pointed them out to the others. "There's been a fight here, and a body was dragged." He pointed to another stain. "Someone was injured, and then the trail just ends." He stared a moment. That trail was consistent with Corgren spelling himself away due to an injury. His servant had gone to his brother, Paugren, for help. Magdronu-as-Gweld trotted toward the altar stone and found a newer dried splash of blood. That was Limbreth. Where was the Bane? Where was Athson? Who was dragged away?

A shout on the wind drew Magdronu-as-Gweld's attention to Makwi, who waved him over to a pile of stones. That was new. So someone had buried someone else. Magdronu-as-Gweld hurried to the dwarves and Danilla.

The woman's eyes welled with tears. "It's one of them. I know it."

Makwi removed a stone from the cairn and set it aside. "This looks like where the head is. We'd best see who it is to make sure." He glanced to Tordug, Danilla, and Magdronu-as-Gweld, his gaze finally fixed on the woman. "We need to know, you understand."

Danilla nodded, her face drawn into a mask of restrained sobs as tears trailed along her cheeks. "Do it." She turned away, hugging herself. "But where did the wizard and the survivor go?"

Magdronu-as-Gweld pointed back to the largest stains on the rock shelf. "That abrupt ending makes me wonder if Corgren was wounded and used magic to escape. He did that back in the mountains more than once when he threatened hostages."

Tordug removed a stone from the pile. "One body and one person disappeared, at least. If I recall, Corgren had Ath on a chain and took him when he left with a spell. Is that right, Gweld?"

Magdronu-as-Gweld nodded. "Yes. He did." He removed a stone from the pile. Had Corgren killed Athson in a fight and received a wound for his trouble? It looked likely. Magdronu-as-Gweld restrained a grin. Then Corgren likely had the Bow of Hart. He needed to contact Paugren soon.

"Then this is probably..." Tordug's words trailed away, having reached the same conclusion.

Danilla wheeled back to them, her jaw set. She pulled at two large stones as Magdronu-as-Gweld and the dwarves continued their work. In short order, Makwi lifted the last stone away that revealed the face they were all certain was Athson. Cheeks protruded from the gaunt face which bore a tattered beard, the head topped with greasy hair. One ruined eye revealed who it was: Ath.

Magdronu-as-Gweld slouched. "Then it's not Athson. But where is he? And the bow?"

"Let's check Ath's hands for the chain. Athson got him away somehow." Tordug lifted another stone.

A long wail erupted from Danilla, and she collapsed into a weeping huddle over the grave, her words lost in her sorrow.

Magdronu-as-Gweld backed away and motioned the dwarves to him. When they approached, he said, "I think we should leave her to her grieving for the moment. Let's check for more signs of what happened."

Tordug nodded but knelt beside Danilla and touched her shoulders as she lay weeping across her dead husband. "Lady, your loss is heavy, and we are near if you need us."

Danilla nodded, her response lost in her tears.

Magdronu-as-Gweld led the dwarves away. He needed to

find out about the bow. He searched the area near the bloodstains with the dwarves.

"Here, a link was cut." Makwi lifted a half-link from the rocky terrain. He eyed the metal. "Looks like someone used a small file. Probably took a while, so that was Ath who did the work."

"And here it is." Tordug lifted a small piece of broken-toothed saw. "It's been heavily worn. He's been using that a while."

"So he got free suddenly and likely helped Athson." Magdronu-as-Gweld rubbed his chin as he squatted by the dwarves. "Maybe he attacked Corgren, who killed him."

Tordug extended a hand toward the bloodstains. "That would explain what happened. If you're correct, Gweld, then Corgren got away wounded, which left Athson to take care of his father." The Chokkran lord pointed to the grave. "Too bad we were so far away we couldn't help. Took far too long to get here as it was." He stroked his beard. "But where has Athson gone?"

Makwi stroked his beard. "And why leave?"

Magdronu-as-Gweld stood and crossed his arms. "Well, we assumed Athson wondered if we were all dead and left to rescue Limbreth and Ath. Based on that reasoning, he now believes he's alone, so he's gone after something else. But what?" Certainly not the prophesied arrow, since he knew little of it. Magdronu-as-Gweld knew nothing of how it would appear either. He turned partially away.

Makwi stood and spoke. "I can think of several things he would be after. If Corgren survived and took Athson prisoner, then he wouldn't have waited for the burial, so we can assume Athson is free. If he's got the bow, he could be after Corgren or his mother." Makwi motioned to Danilla, who still lay across her husband's grave. "He wouldn't know her fate. He would certainly want to find her, maybe Corgren too. If he still has the bow, then he might bargain with it."

Magdronu-as-Gweld paced away and back to the dwarves and paused. The dwarf made sense. Corgren wouldn't have cared about Ath and likely would have thrown the body over the edge otherwise. Athson was free. He peered between the dwarves. "I think we're clear who has the Bow of Hart."

∽

Hastra stuck her finger in the Book of Prophecies to mark her place and narrowed her eyes at Limbreth's attentive expression. Good, Limbreth was finally alert. Hastra needed a listener at the moment, and Withlings were in short supply.

"You've found something?" Limbreth pointed at Hastra's book.

"Only a few references, but understand, everything that has happened revolved around finding the Bow of Hart." Hastra stroked the old binding of the book, writings of her order saved from the fall of Withling's Watch. So much in it, but so little added in the long centuries since that time.

"Such as?"

"For one, there's my return." Hastra lifted one finger. "I was sent to Rok of Eloch's will and returned to face magic at need. It has happened to me before, but it is unusual, at least in my own experience. That happened around the bow. It was needed, but there was magic in that storm. Where did it come from?" She shrugged. "Magdronu was near, but how close?" She showed another finger to add to her count. "Which leads to the next part. The others were saved by that magical storm, not by Eloch. You weren't there, but it should not have happened."

"I thought they were dead." Limbreth wiped a dry cheek as if it were a memory of tears.

"Yes, well, it is portentous, but I cannot say why, nor can I yet speak to my own appearance." Hastra lifted a third finger. "You were saved from this fall, which is another event around the bow. That means something for you too. I'm thinking these three events should not have happened but did. They mean something. But it all revolves around the bow."

Limbreth pursed her lips. "That makes since, then, the miraculous around an item meant to do the miraculous."

"Spoken like a Withling, but yes. We find the bow—Athson, really—and things happened to us. That means events around the bow will be important in the future, but I cannot say how just yet. But there's more to it. There's the prophecy. It was miraculous when it was given at the time when Withling's Watch fell. We were..." Hastra touched her old wound through her clothing, and emptiness spread in her stomach at the memory. So many dead that day. And she should have been.

"Tell me about it." Limbreth touched Hastra's hand that marked the book. A rare tender gesture from the Grendonese woman.

Hastra opened the book and stared at the words that blurred in her sight at sudden tears. So many friends lost that day. "We were brought in to face Corgren and Paugren, the Beleesh sisters too, and told to join them or die. The prophecy then started with the elders. We would call it a concert of prophecy, where pieces are spoken in turn. With each piece, someone was slain, Howart, my sister, and myself included."

Limbreth stirred at that information, her eyebrows raised, eyes wide, and her mouth open to speak.

Hastra lifted a hand and forestalled Limbreth's words. "I know, shocking to see a dead person alive, and that for centuries. But it happened. I saw myself lying at Corgren's feet beside the others. Five parts were given, and three remained. We three surviving Withlings were offered the chance to return by Eloch. At least I was. None of us have spoken of this since.

Zelma rose, then Howart, then me to speak the last." She opened the book and read a line of the prophecy aloud: "The bow shall be hidden from heart." She smiled at her initial misunderstanding. Not heart, but the country, Hart. She cleared her throat and read the entire prophecy.

The false one begets betrayers, but he shall not have his way.

The Hidden Dragon may usurp kingdoms with deceits, but his ways shall not last, and he will not ascend.

A bow shall be made in defense.

To break the binding curses.

His prey shall be snatched from his fangs.

The bow shall be hidden from Hart.

The eagle will guide the heir.

The bow shall be found at need.

And the arrow shall Eloch prepare.

Silence lay between the two women as Hastra ended, broken only by the rustle of wind and the crackle of fire. Hastra let a sad smile display itself on her quivering lips. "The elders, Soren and Margen, died over those first lines." *Pools of blood spread across the floor from their bodies that day.* Hastra cleared her throat before she spoke again. "'The bow shall be found at need,' that was spoken by me, and I was part of it, guiding Athson. These words have been on my mind often during our travels, especially the last few days."

Limbreth's mouth worked several times before she finally spoke. "So you were intended to be there regardless?"

Hastra fed more wood to the fire, still marking the book with a finger from her other hand. "It would seem so."

"And now comes the arrow. But how? We've seen nothing of it."

"I do not know, other than it is planned. We all three spoke that line in unison, so it is..." Hastra's eyes narrowed. She reopened the book and stared at the page. "Of course, we all spoke it, and we will all be present somehow."

Limbreth lay down again and pulled her blanket over her body. "When?" She yawned. "Is it soon?"

"Undoubtedly. This isn't over, and the bow must be used." Hastra tapped her fingertips along the last line of the prophecy. "The arrow will come to us like to a target. But for now, I will think about all this. You sleep until the others return."

The young woman's face relaxed as her breath settled into the steady rhythm of sleep.

Hastra stared at the prophecy. Soren. Margen. They were a long time ago. She missed them still, and many others. She looked over the last lines again and gasped. She started to speak, but Limbreth lay asleep. Of course, it was as Soren once said about prophecy: when three things are predicted in conjunction with one big prophecy, events often unfolded much the same way. There were three unusual events around finding the bow, all involving those associated with Athson. That definitely meant something further to come. And around this coming arrow.

Soren's instruction on these matters further shook her memory. The dead elder had taught that wisdom, which he'd learned from another Withling. Who was that? She flipped farther back in the book and searched for similar prophecies or commentary about the subject. She supplemented her search with her fingers, running them along pages. Ah, there, from Apeth Stellin originally. Hastra tapped her lips. He was well-known. Went alone to the old tower and never returned, so long dead.

Her head rose with a sudden thought. Hastra stared at the stone side of the ravine. Never returned. She, Howart, and Zelma had never returned from the old tower, but they were alive. Why not him? She muttered to the wind, "Yes, maybe that was who the unknown Withling was. Someone presumed long dead. Hastra watched the flames of the fire dance. It was consistent. The teacher of this principle still alive amid such very things. Apeth Stellin. She closed the book. There was much to consider.

Voices drifted along the narrow ravine. Hastra watched Ralda, who spoke with Tordug and Danilla. Athson's mother was distraught, by the look of her face. Where were the others? Ralda led those two alone into the ravine. A lump formed in Hastra's throat. Athson was not with them, nor the bow.

∼

ATHSON'S STOMACH roiled and his head ached, but he narrowed his gaze at Apeth Stellin. This man knew things about Athson he shouldn't. Athson didn't recognize him from anywhere before their first encounter in Afratta, after Zelma presented Athson with the inheritance. However, she'd achieved that in a dream. Athson's head spun more, and he settled back and spoke with a weak voice, "Thank you for pulling me out of this storm. But I don't understand. Have we met? I mean, before Afratta. That was you who spoke to me then?"

That warning drifted across Athson's memory. "Careful of trolls on the trail." The old man smacked his lips and fidgeted.

Athson whirled and glared at the old man. "We've done well." He turned away.

A wheezy chuckle erupted behind him before Athson took two steps. "You should ignore neither warnings, dreams, nor visions—nor gifts."

Athson froze mid-step. Moments passed like a day as he turned. Shock filled him anew when he saw no sign of the trapper on the porch.

Apeth offered the same smile as back at Afratta. "Good of you to remember." His eyes twinkled from beneath his hat, and he wagged a finger at Athson. "You should have listened to me closer then—and at Marston's Station."

"So it was you." Athson coughed and groaned before he continued. "Why have you been following me?" He frowned as he recalled their encounter at Marston's. After his disagreement with Limbreth.

"You should trust her," a gravelly voice said.

Athson recognized who it was even before he whirled. The trapper from Afratta sat at the far end of the porch, leaning in a chair against the log wall. Athson's belly fluttered at the sight of the wide-brimmed hat pulled low over the wrinkled face, cheeks still covered with an unruly salt-and-pepper beard.

Athson took a tentative step. "You! Why are you here? How did you get there? *The porch was empty."*

"Just getting some rest after all that excitement last night."

"I don't remember you from last night. But I remember you from Afratta. Have you been following me?"

The trader let his chair rest on four legs, pushed his hat back, and shrugged. "I get around, I suppose."

Athson strode toward the old man. "Who are you? How did you know about the—that gift?"

The trapper spat over the rail. "You should worry less about your friends and more about your enemies."

Athson stopped short. "Are you a Withling? How do you know about my enemies?"

"Count me a friend."

"Really? Been helping me, have you? Last night, you say."

"Sure did. You wouldn't be here without my help."

Athson sighed and steadied himself against a post. This old man should marry crazy Zelma. These were worse answers than a Withling's. A horse whinnied and Athson turned away, watching one of Marston's men calm the animal.

"Here's more help. Remember, use one sword edge for justice, the other for mercy. You'll know which one to use when."

Athson turned. "How did you know about my—"

The trapper's chair stood empty. Athson gaped and his heart lurched. The same as at Afratta.

The same as at Afratta. "How did you move so quickly?"

Apeth was older and should not move so fast. Athson chewed the inside of his cheek. He had never answered that question. "You must be a Withling. Hastra thought you were Eloch but then thought better of it."

Apeth tasted his broth and tested the progress of his cooking venison. "I get that a lot, the last part about Eloch." He chuckled. "I'm not sure why."

Athson's face flushed more from irritation than fever. So he was a Withling. He didn't deny that. "It seems there are Withlings everywhere. I thought there were hardly any left."

"You're right on that point, and a sad tale too." Apeth paused his cooking and cocked his head. "I guess Hastra hasn't spoken of it, then?"

Athson pulled his blanket to his chin as he shivered. "No, she's been rather mysterious about that."

"Well, as you should know, a Withling only speaks what is given."

"I know that too well. It seems a little too convenient for me sometimes. An excuse to avoid sharing information."

"Humph. So it may seem, but it saves a lot to speak appropriate to Eloch's will, as we all learn." Again, Apeth cocked his head as if both listening and considering Athson at the same time.

"Why do Withlings do that?"

"Do what?"

"Act like you're listening."

Apeth shrugged. "Because we are. It's part of what we do, listen for Eloch's guidance."

Athson coughed, cleared his throat, and spat off to the side. That explanation still felt too convenient. "Yeah, seems to give me all kinds of trouble."

Apeth tipped his hat back and pointed at Athson. "You ready for some broth? Your stomach seems settled now, since you're talking so much."

"Yeah, I guess I'll try some." He needed strength to travel as soon as possible. He doubted he could reach his mother in time, but he had to try.

"Good." Apeth handed Athson a small bowl of broth that warmed Athson's hands well enough. "While this venison finishes and you eat your fill, I'll tell you what you want to know. If I can."

Athson suppressed a sarcastic laugh. Best not offend this Withling or he might never get more answers. "Well, for starters, how old are you?"

"Really, like that matters?" Apeth chuckled and shook his head. "I'm far older than Hastra and the other surviving Withlings."

"How old?"

"I started the order with some other like-minded people of that time, people who realized we were gifted by our devotion to Eloch."

That old? Athson stared at Apeth. He doubted the old man's age. He didn't look past his late fifties or early sixties. But he'd let the tall tale slide for the moment. He sipped his broth. It was too hot, so he waited before trying again. "Why have you been following me?"

Apeth shrugged. "Somebody has to keep an eye on a hard-headed youth that Magdronu tracks. The Bow of Hart has been a shadow across your path since before you were born."

"Is that right?" Athson doubted that statement too.

"It is."

"So you've been following me, or watching me, for years. Why didn't you help my family, help Depenburgh?" The last question left Athson's lips with a choked sound as he held back sudden sorrow.

Apeth shook his head. "I wasn't watching you then. Sad doings, that."

"So Eloch didn't care to watch out for us? People died."

"Not to belittle your sorrow, Athson, but people die. There are slaves in Rok and Hart who suffer all the time. Eloch cares for them and forbears with patience to let things work in his plans." Apeth checked his venison again. "Death is a part of this life, Athson. Everyone you knew from your village would have died sometime or other. It's what we do with the daily living that matters. How we live with others matters more than the dying."

Athson looked away. "Yeah, whatever. Easy for you to say." He suddenly felt no need for the broth and almost poured it out.

Apeth frowned at Athson, opened his mouth as if to shout, then shut it. After several moments of silence, he spoke. "You aren't the only one who suffers, Athson. You won't be the last. We're given choices. I watched a lot of good people die at Withling's Watch—murdered except for those three who survived. Them and me. Corgren and Paugren were sent to deceive the entire order. They even recruited some of the order to their cultic worship of Magdronu. They murdered everyone when they let trolls into the Watch that night while everyone slept. No, we're not told when we're to die—or live on, same as you and everyone else." He shrugged and drank from his canteen. "Like I said, living's what's important."

Athson drank his cooling broth and let it sit on his stomach as he stared at the flames. The Withlings suffered at Magdronu's hands too? "So how did Hastra and the others escape?"

Apeth stared into the flames. "They helped give the prophecy, even died for it, and were sent back to finish it and help other people." The Withling shot Athson a sidelong glance. "Yes, they suffered and still do now. Corgren stabbed all the speakers of the prophecy, one given in concert, and they died and came back to deliver the balance. When Corgren couldn't kill them, he imprisoned them. I was sent to get them out and help them escape. They had more service to perform, and they've done that faithfully for several centuries despite their losses."

Athson sucked at his teeth as he stared at the dancing flames through blurred vision. "I'm sorry to hear that. I didn't know."

Apeth cut some venison and set it on his plate. He licked his fingers. "You've had a bit of tunnel vision, if I might say so. But then, it's part of what's going on with your family." The Withling set about eating.

"So I've heard, but I never got the whole story about that either." Athson sipped more of the broth. It settled his stomach. "Thanks for the broth. It helps some."

The Withling nodded and continued eating in silence for a while. He drank some water and wiped his mouth with his sleeve. "Your family got caught up in Magdronu's cult back in Hart after the Watch fell. But as I understand it—and mind you, I wasn't present—your ancestor Thayer broke from that after a few generations. At least the best he could. He made the bow and fled as a traitor to the agreements his family had made several generations earlier. He passed the bow to his son along with the package, and so it's been. Sometime along the way, Zelma got the inheritance and protected it, but your family members always did their best to hide the bow. But they always suffered the curse of their betrayal to Magdronu. It comes out in anger, vengefulness, all ways that the houses of Hart behave now even though your ancestors wanted to be different. They couldn't help it. Your father meant well, but he couldn't resist. Magdronu plays on this, doing things to you, killing your people, your family. He gets power for his magic from your actions."

Athson swallowed a sudden lump. So that was the curse and the whole tale. "I didn't know that. What do I do about it?"

"Do your best to live well with others. Anytime you let the emotions get the best of you, you're giving Magdronu more power, more magic." Apeth cut a second helping of venison.

"So what about the rest of everything that happens to me? My fits, if you know about them."

"More of Magdronu working to keep you confused." Apeth paused his eating. "Why, what all happens?"

"Nothing more than you said." Athson paused. Should he tell Apeth more? Maybe not, he didn't trust him yet. Or was that his curse leading him? "Just fits sometimes. My blessed sword helps that, though."

Apeth fixed his gaze on Athson for the passage of long moments. "Yeah, you keep that sword handy, then. If you need something more, let me know. Confused thinking works to keep you off-balance so don't just suffer through it. You can live differently if you choose to. You finished that broth yet?"

Athson nodded and handed Apeth the bowl. "I think I'll sleep now. Thanks for all the answers." His eyes fluttered, but his head had stopped spinning. Now to find his mother. And Corgren.

CHAPTER THREE

No one knew the answer regarding the Bow of Hart. They confirmed Ath's hands were still bound by his restraints, but the chain was indeed cut. Magdronu-as-Gweld wanted to flay Corgren when he saw him. The fool had let himself be tricked by a half-blind prisoner. They reburied Ath at the end of Danilla's weeping. He eyed the woman. It was a pointless reaction to a traitor's death. "I suppose we need to inform Hastra and the others."

"Yes, either they are on the way or not, but we need to share this news with them." Tordug scratched his beard and hefted his ax. "Best be on our way, then."

"Not me. I'll scout and try to find Athson's track." He scanned the sky as storm clouds threatened from the northwest. "There may be snow soon. I need to find what I can before that. Maybe I'll see if trolls are in the area or bring in some game." Magdronu-as-Gweld tapped his bow. Good cover for him, as usual. He needed to shift forms and gather information near and far. He shrugged. "Maybe I can find Athson and bring him back. He can't have left that long ago."

Danilla's face lifted, her cheeks still tear-stained. "I should go with you."

Magdronu-as-Gweld feigned a consoling gesture by holding the woman's hand. "I don't think you're in any state to travel fast as I will. It's best you take word back to Hastra. If I can find Athson or sign of his trail in these heaths, I'll do what I can to bring him in." He motioned to the sky. "But you'd all better be ready for that storm. I'll be as fast as I can."

"We should be on our way, then. We'll need to move that camp before nightfall, and I saw a few likely places if there's no bears or trolls in them." Makwi propped his ax handle on his shoulder, the curved head shining in the dull light. He headed away without further words.

Tordug offered his hand to Magdronu-as-Gweld. "We'll look for you in the evening, then. Be safe." He turned Danilla toward the climb to the notch in the slope-rim farther up the trail on which they'd arrived and followed Makwi.

Magdronu-as-Gweld watched the dwarves and the woman as they climbed away. *'Paugren!'* He sent the magical call for his other trusted wizard. He waved to the others, trotted away north, and watched for signs of Athson's passage. He crossed over the craggy heights that bordered the northern edge of the Funnel along another trail. He'd gather information about Athson and consider all the events while he waited for Paugren's response. And there was the shrine in the Drelkhaz to be inspected.

The trail twisted among the windswept hills toward the darkening sky. The wind rose as Magdronu-as-Gweld descended into a ravine between natural walls of worn rock. He arrived at a patch of soft sand deposited by long years of weather. He knelt by a boot-print. *Definitely left by Athson.* He stood and climbed north out of the ravine onto a rolling flat-top of rock that lay between higher hills of stone dressed in thickets. He halted and turned in a circle. No one had followed him. Good. He climbed a slope, leapt off it, and changed into his dragon form.

Wind snapped his wings like sails, and Magdronu rode the currents northeast and passed over the gorge of the Long River, flying low over the eastern heaths. He banked into the northerly wind and rose toward the heights of the Drelkhaz Mountains. The swift winds on high carried him farther in moments than his elven form could travel in a day, and Magdronu soon rose toward the familiar summit of his hallowed shrine, where he landed in the heat of fire in his anger. Lost! All his hostages and plans foiled!

'Paugren!'

Magdronu paced the flat rock, which lay empty of fresh sacrifices. He sniffed the broad, flat shelf of rock and roared fire into the wind. His shrine lay devoid of magic since that encounter. That was the purpose, then. Breaking his shrine and weakening the transfer of magic to his followers. They would need weeks to repair this one or create another with spells. Magdronu crouched and—

'Master, I've come.' Paugren's reply danced along the magic spell with weakness, anger, and worry.

'Is Corgren with you?' He sent the heat of his wrath along the spell and felt Paugren bend to his will.

'Master, he arrived barely alive with the Bane hours ago. I've barely enough magic to keep him alive.'

'Never mind his foolish life. Does he have the Bow of Hart?'

'No, he arrived—'

Magdronu roared and spewed flame among the charred bones of former sacrifices that lay about the shrine. Paugren's mind quivered along the communication spell when Magdronu calmed himself with slow snorts. *'I'm done with you and your brother's failures. We've lost every hostage and all the leverage on Athson. He escaped with the bow, then. Corgren failed to be vigilant and let that pris-*

oner nearly kill him. And this shrine is empty of sacrifices and magic. What else have you to report?'

'Great lord, all our efforts are broken. Dwarves caused an avalanche across the approaching road after they escaped their village. The way is blocked. What shall we do if the shrine is broken and blocked? How shall I save Corgren?'

Magdronu snorted. If that one died, then it served as punishment. But he needed his servants supplied with magic. A growl rose in his chest. *'He suffers, no doubt. Let him suffer until magic is restored, then heal him.'*

Paugren replied after hesitation. *'Master, there is more news. It has been cloudy for weeks on this side of the mountains. Last night, the sky was clear, and I have seen a wandering star that has appeared at some point over these past weeks. I believe it will cross west over the Drelkhaz soon.'*

Magdronu crouched and peered north along the mountaintops of the Drelkhaz Mountains. *'Will it be north or south of this shrine?'*

'North of it.'

'This changes my plans.' Magdronu's anger cooled. The sign of the arrow prepared. But where and when would it appear? How long did he have to intercept Athson? *'Send one of the Beleesh sisters to the capital. She's to use what magic is available to travel with a spell. She is to round up any criminal, beggar, or other useless persons for sacrifice at the shrine there. With the flow of magic restored, you'll have your magic renewed from me. But we'll need a new shrine elsewhere. For now, do as I wish, and we'll plan from there. The arrow comes soon, and I'll have it and the bow as payment for my long suffering in this form. We shall meet soon.'*

He ended the spell and launched into the air. He needed what blood he could get now. He found a herd of mountain goats along a nearby cliff and roasted them with flame before he landed among the carcasses to feed. A distant shrine required more of his time for the most magic. But sacrifices alone at the distant shrine would provide some magical transference to his servants. That at least was needed now to heal Corgren to handle his trolls.

He belched fire and fed. This first. Then he'd return to the others with an appropriate meal for them to round out his disguise so he could search for Athson, and overcome his losses again. There were his plans for Auguron and the dormant ones laid there for contingency. Now he needed those plots activated to suit his needs when Corgren attacked. But his servants needed magic, and before Eloch's prophesied arrow arrived. Magdronu launched into the air and winged his way back to the Troll Heaths. He crossed over the entrance to the Troll Neath and inspected the camps where the trolls were staged for the invasion of Auguron. That, at least, was well done on Corgren's part.

For now, he needed to find Athson and the bow, since the sign of the arrow had arrived.

As the storm rolled over the heaths, Magdronu turned south and winged toward the place where he'd shifted from Gweld's form. Near there, he spotted three horses. Of course, Corgren's mounts lost from the Funnel and wandering. Greater haste was needed to find Athson, and these horses were useful. He descended and twisted his form to Magdronu-as-Gweld, approached the horses, and gathered them. He mounted one as the wind from the approaching storm increased. Now for a little hunting before he returned to his companions and his ruse.

∼

VOICES DREW LIMBRETH FROM SLEEP, and her eyes fluttered open. Hastra stood beside her and watched the others approaching, her book forgotten and lying on her pack. Limbreth rubbed her eyes and watched the others. Just Tordug and Danilla with Ralda trailing them from the upper ravine. Limbreth rolled out of her blanket and stood by the Withling. "The others must be up there." She squinted and shifted her position for better vantage past Ralda. Nobody there. Her stomach fluttered and yawned empty.

Hastra's reply barely touched Limbreth's ears. "I see no one else."

Tordug frowned, and by the tense mask on Danilla's face, they bore ill news. Sorrow. That emotion best fit Danilla's expression. The three of them climbed down closer.

Limbreth crossed her bare feet and glanced at her boots. Were they dry yet? She might need them. But she waited for the others and dragged her blanket over her toes. A bit of undisturbed sleep had left her stronger than earlier. At least she'd had no dreams of the Bane. Limbreth let that dark memory fly.

Tordug, Danilla, and Ralda approached, and the dwarf saluted them and motioned back along the ravine. "Makwi's searching out a new campsite. We need to move. Storm's coming."

Hastra crossed and uncrossed her arms, then brushed her skirt with her hands. "Where are the others? With Makwi?"

The dwarf shook his head and warmed his hands over the fire. "No. They aren't with us."

Limbreth unclenched her jaw. She didn't realize she'd done that. "They are hunting?"

Danilla wrung her hands as sudden tears welled in her eyes and trickled along her cheeks. "Ath's dead." Her body shuddered with a sudden wail. Hastra stepped close and embraced her.

Limbreth stepped closer to Athson's mother, lifted her hands, and then dropped them by her side. She turned to Tordug. "What happened? Where's Athson?"

Hastra patted Danilla's back. "And the bow? What of it?"

Tordug shook his head and raised his hands, palms up. "We don't know. We pieced together what might have happened. We found Ath under a hastily set stone cairn." The dwarf related the tale of the scene at the Funnel for several minutes while Ralda squatted at the fire. When the Chokkran lord completed the tale, he added, "So Gweld's out scouting for Athson's trail, but I fear snow will delay us and cover it for now." He gave Danilla a sympathetic pat on the back. "We'll find him yet. But we don't know anything about the bow, so we can assume he still has it."

Hastra sighed. "Well, please gather some of our things, and we'll get moving." She turned her head to Limbreth. "Are you able to go now? The afternoon is getting on, and I suspect it's a good walk."

"Yes, I must be, regardless." With arms crossed, Limbreth bit back angry words toward Hastra. She sighed her anger away and grabbed her boots, sat and pulled one on her foot. Dry or not, she needed them now. "I'm going to find Athson."

Ralda stood and gathered his pack and several others. "Need go camp. Storm come."

"Just stay with us. He's hours gone." Tordug glanced at Hastra. "Let's not argue again. We'll track him down after the storm. He'll have to take shelter too."

Limbreth got the other boot on and stood. She stomped the boots into a comfortable position and reached for her sword straps. "But he's out there alone and thinks we're all dead." She pointed to Danilla. "He probably thinks he can find his mother."

Hastra released Danilla. "Much as I want to find Athson, Tordug's correct. The storm will stop us, along with night. Please, help us move camp. We'll do what we can to find him when the storm has passed."

They were right. Limbreth hated to admit it, but they were. She crossed her arms and stared at the water surging past the end of the ravine. The choice between bad and worse. "Fine, let's go find Makwi. Maybe Gweld will catch him, but I don't want to delay any longer than necessary."

Danilla touched her arm. "Neither do I." She bent and handed Limbreth her blanket. "We'll talk while we go."

"That—that would be good, I think." Limbreth busied herself with her things while the others gathered packs and put out the fire. She strapped her swords on her back. Good to have them again. She'd thought they were gone for good. Her friends were good to her. She paused. "Uh, just so you all know—thank you for coming for me, and for these." She touched a sword hilt, then sniffed, wiped a tear, and found a smile. "Thank you, Hastra, for your prayers, and you, Ralda, for your big hand." Best to get that out of the way now.

"We come you." Ralda grinned. "We come you. You come us." His fingers flicked many words further. "We go far to here, far to end. You friend us."

It was more than she'd ever heard out of the giant. "You're right, Ralda. We have far to go and we must stick together."

"Besides, I spent too much time teaching you about dwarves, gell." Tordug hugged her. "Glad you made it back to us." He slapped her on the back like a warrior, then whispered in her ear. "You had us all worried, but me most."

They shouldered their packs and climbed toward the high end of the ravine. Limbreth grunted. Her weariness lingered, but she trudged ahead. She'd see to her leathers later.

Danilla walked beside Limbreth once they gained the trail. The older woman's face bore drawn lines. "Tell me of my husband and my son. How long have you known Athson?" She sniffed and her voice sounded hoarse. "I've missed them these past years. I was so close to finding my husband after all the years we were captives." She paused and slouched. "I wish I'd seen him just one last time, instead of this." Danilla mustered a smile. "But, there's Athson, isn't there?"

Limbreth adjusted her pack straps. "Well." What to tell her about Athson? "We are close. I met him when we started this journey. In the cemetery." She related how they'd met, their pursuit of the Bane, and Hastra's recovered book. Limbreth let the tale of their long journey and adventures unroll on her tongue as they climbed the trail.

Danilla halted when Limbreth related how she and Athson had fought trolls on the road near Marston's Station. "You fought them alone? You returned for him?"

"Yes, and the others came for him too. We drove them away that night. It's—it was then the dwarves named me an ax-maid." Limbreth leaned closer to the other woman. "I thought they were crazy, talking about the death-grip and how they like to talk up my exploits. But that's just how they are, and it helped back in Ezhandun."

"Now you're skipping ahead. How did you get there from the eastern forest?"

Limbreth brushed her hand along her braid. Her trinkets were still there. "That's a long tale, if there was any—"

Danilla squinted at Limbreth's trinkets. "Those are interesting. Where did you get them?"

"These were given to me by the dwarves. They are status-tokens in their society, and I wear them as someone honored among them." She felt her cheeks flush with heat in the cold evening wind.

"For when you saved Athson?"

Limbreth nodded.

"I'd give you a bag of gold and more for that. Thank you." She hugged Limbreth abruptly and released her. "I can see why he's fond of you like the others say. But tell me of my husband in his last days."

Limbreth swallowed hard, not sure where to start. "We were thrown together as hostages. He—he helped me when—when I was afraid. The Bane, you know. He had a plan to break his bonds. He must've been able to do it, from what Tordug said." She told Danilla of her fearful trip with Corgren and the Bane to the Funnel.

As Limbreth finished her tale, they found Makwi. The dwarf champion waved to them from a ledge nestled above the western side of the trail. Danilla fought back sobs again at the end of Limbreth's story. They scrambled among loose stone and found footing farther up along a narrow lip that slanted toward the ledge.

Makwi greeted them as they arrived and exchanged words in dwarvish with his father. "Greetings. I found this one high above the trail, with a defensive approach. Out of the wind, and I got a fire going. Snow may be bad."

Tordug answered in the common tongue. "It is well. A warm enough end to a harsh day. Perhaps we'll take these hills and build shelters among them for travelers. But it beats sleeping in the snow, eh?" He slapped Makwi's shoulder. "What of Gweld?"

They all turned into the high cave and clambered deeper in, where a fire of heather bows burned, the smoke gathering into a higher vault farther back. Limbreth peered into the darkness and imagined the endless depths of the Bane's cowl. She shivered and wrapped her arms around herself.

Makwi brushed past her and offered a wink. "Don't worry, ax-maid, there's no bears in this cave."

She shrugged her pack from her shoulders and forced a grin. "Good. I shouldn't like to wrestle with more than you for food or hear any snores louder than yours, champion."

Makwi laughed. "Taught her too well, Tordug!"

Tordug dropped his own pack. "Bah! Her wit is her own."

"Settle in, and I'll stand watch for a while. Won't be long until that snow comes. You all took your time, but you made it." The dwarf wove his way over patches of dirt and gravel among slabs and outcrops of rock.

Limbreth resisted a gaze into the dark recesses of the cave. *Face the light and forget the Bane.* She shivered anyway.

They settled and warmed water for tea at the fire and ate what rations they bore. Snow soon fell on a swirl of wind that rose and fell. Limbreth ate some travel bread. "Sounds like the high Drelkhaz."

Tordug sipped his tea. "Aye, it's a raucous song, but not the right notes and a different language here." He eyed Limbreth with a gleam in his eye.

Limbreth grinned at the old dwarf-lord. "It's a woman's song, maybe a—" She almost said *a dirge* but stopped herself in front of Danilla. She cleared her throat. "Sounds a bit sad."

"That it does." Tordug stared into his cup. "Storms have their own mood, betimes."

Makwi trilled a whistle and motioned an alert to them all. Limbreth went with Ralda and Tordug while Danilla and Hastra stood waiting. The dwarf pointed into the driving snow as dusk settled along the trail below their refuge. "Someone's coming."

"Gweld is due back. It's likely him. But that's three horses."

Limbreth covered her mouth with her hand a moment. "Corgren had three. I suppose he didn't take them, and they wandered."

Makwi strode along the ledge from the cave. "I'll check on him. Could be tough getting them in here. I didn't expect to house horses. But there's another cave nearby if we need to stable them elsewhere. Better than smelling dung if this storms settles in for a day or two." He motioned Ralda to follow, and the giant edged after the dwarf champion.

Tordug crouched, and Limbreth followed his lead as they watched their companions. They approached the stranger with the horses, and Makwi waved the *all's good* signal. Tordug exhaled. "So I guess it is Gweld with Corgren's horses. Those will help us travel faster. If Athson still has the mule, we have a chance to catch him now."

Limbreth stroked her braid. "Yes, if we can find his trail in all this snow. It's thick now and likely won't be gone soon. And we have little enough fodder for the horses." She stood and walked back into the cave to inform Danilla and Hastra they had horses now.

The horses couldn't be brought up the narrow incline to their cave, so Makwi and Gweld stowed them in another nearby cave. They would all take turns guarding the horses, and that meant gathering extra fuel for a fire as the storm gained intensity.

Several days followed as they huddled about their meager fires, guarded the horses, and waited out the storm. Limbreth shivered the days away but had time to repair the rent in her leather armor with trembling hands.

The storm ceased on the fifth night as clouds rolled away southwest and revealed a waxing moon amid the vast star field overhead.

Makwi stood guard with Gweld down below with the horses. The dwarf returned to their cave as they bedded down by the fire and touched Hastra. "Withling, come see this wandering star."

Hastra frowned at the dwarf champion. "Wandering star? We've not seen it before now."

Makwi shrugged. "It appears to have risen over the Drelkhaz during the last several days."

Limbreth followed the dwarf and the Withling to the mouth of the cave. A very bright star with a bit of a tail rose over the distant mountains that lay in the shadow of night. Tordug and Ralda gathered behind them.

Hastra gazed at the scene for several minutes, her mouth agape and her eyebrows arched. The Withling shook herself and pinched her lower lip as she muttered to herself.

"It's beautiful, isn't it, Hastra?" Limbreth smiled at the novelty and drew her pale dwarven cloak of fur closer around herself.

The Withling glanced at Limbreth and spoke to everyone gathered. "Someone go down to Gweld and tell him we must leave early in the morning. He should be prepared, as well as our horses." She turned toward the fire.

Limbreth's gaze drifted between the others, who all shrugged their confusion. "Hastra, what is it?"

Hastra whirled back to face them. "It's the prophecy, the last part. The arrow comes, prepared by Eloch. We must find Athson if possible. But I must attend a meeting and soon."

Tordug shifted his stance and nodded Makwi away to tell Gweld the news. "I'll stand watch for you until you return." He faced Hastra. "Where is this meeting to be, and with whom?"

Limbreth's heart surged at the thought of finally finding Athson after the snowstorm. "Yes, and how soon. Shouldn't we have Athson with us?"

Hastra shook her head with a frown. "I'm afraid we must hurry north. If we cannot find Athson soon, we must trust that he will go that way too, maybe to Marston's Station. But we must hurry. If we've seen that sign, then Magdronu and his servants have as well. The arrow comes, and we must be prepared. Athson will come. Or so we must trust Eloch. But the arrow must be protected."

Danilla spread her hands in pleading. "But what of my son? Is he not important?"

Hastra laid a comforting hand on Danilla's shoulder. "Eloch has all this in hand, but we are needed north as soon as possible. I cannot say more now."

Limbreth stowed her belongings in her pack beside Danilla. "I hope we find him."

Danilla offered a wan smile and touched Limbreth's hands a moment. "You are loyal beyond most. I hope you are right.

But I'll trust the Withling. She brought me out of captivity with her addled faith. I'll leave him to Eloch's care, as he has had for the last years."

Limbreth's doubts warred with any trust built by recent events. "I hope so. Hastra can be so mysterious, it's hard to trust."

Danilla squeezed Limbreth's hand. "I have little else now. I'll follow the Withling's lead."

Later, when Hastra roused Limbreth for her watch, the Withling beckoned her to the cave mouth again. There the wandering star rose much higher in the waning night sky. "What is it, Withling?"

Hastra gripped Limbreth's hands. "I know more about what I shared several days ago." The Withling glanced toward the sleeping figures of their companions about the fire, her face drawn with care, perhaps worry. "It concerns us all."

"Go on." Limbreth held her breath and stole a glance at the wandering star. Its message revealed this much to Hastra.

Hastra swallowed hard. "Those three events—the whirlwind I stopped, the others' survival, and your fall—they all mean something to each of us." She clasped Limbreth's hands tightly. "You must not tell the others, but I feel you must know. I do not know if I... Well, I must tell you so you'll know."

Limbreth's heart thudded with the palpable weight of the Withling's mystery. "I'll hold your confidence until you say so."

Hastra nodded and lowered her head. "You'll know when to share it if necessary. First, I must face Magdronu's magic again." She lifted her gaze to Limbreth. "Directly. It—I don't know if I..." She didn't finish her words, but her hands trembled.

"You mean you're uncertain of the outcome?" Limbreth's breath left her. By Eloch's light, what would happen if Hastra fell in the conflict to come?

The Withling's jaw worked, and she hid sudden tears. "The others must face death again. I do not know their fates either."

Limbreth covered her mouth and restrained her gasp. "You're sure?"

"They survived for no other reason than because of magic released in an untimely manner. The event is portentous, as is your survival. As I said, three events together point to more that will come to pass. It all revolves around the Bow of Hart." She paused and pointed to the wandering star. "And the arrow to come."

"Me? What of me?" She bit her lower lip and gripped Hastra's shaking hands. Ill news for them all traveled in threes. She nodded. "Tell me. I'll do what I can regardless."

Hastra's lips quivered. "There's not much to go on. I don't know the meaning, so we must wait for it." She took a breath. "You must return again as if from death."

Limbreth's heart skipped. Death. She lived because of a miracle. What lay ahead for her? For them all? Her vision blurred, and she staggered away with a whisper. "I see." She turned back to Hastra. "What is needed will be given."

This went beyond just Athson. Now she understood that, after all the travel and fighting.

∼

VOICES SPEAK IN A DIFFERENT LANGUAGE, rising and falling in volume. Cadence varies with intonations. Figures wave and dance as light rises among them—three figures cloaked, hidden. Athson moves closer. These people are not dancing. Instead light flickers and shifts in their midst first one way, then the other. The speakers lift their hands in supplication, their voices rise and implore. The light intensifies with the rising cries. The light wavers and slowly fades to one figure.

A woman stands before Athson, her back to him as single

braid of dwarven variations knotted along her white armor. Limbreth turns and faces him. Tears roll down her freckled cheeks. She extends her hands to him, palms up, and offers him something. He looks at her hands, and blinding light flashes in his face as he receives it. Again, the light fades.

Light flickers above him, shadows pass between him and the light. His vision clears, and shafts of sunlight pierce smoke and cloud as a shout of despair echoes. Cloth ripples in a breeze, and a banner stands out from a pole for a moment. Ten-tined antlers flutter with a bow below them, and the edges of the banner smolder, seared by fire. Weariness descends in Athson, and darkness encroaches on the scene until it covers all.

Athson gasped awake and squinted into the dim glow of the fire. Where was he? The cave. He groaned softly as Apeth snored away across the fire. Dreams again. The plague of things to come. His head spun, and weakness forced him down. He frowned. He had dreamed of Limbreth. His dreams always interposed into his life. That one was all wrong. She was dead. By his inaction. "No more dreams."

Apeth sputtered a moment, then resumed a rhythmic buzzing like bees around flowers.

Athson rolled onto his side and struggled to his knees. He gathered his belongings and dragged them toward the mule. He touched the animal, and it snorted, then flicked its tail. He leaned against the animal. So weary. But he must go, sickness or not. There was his mother to find. "I'm tired of dreams ruling my sleep and my life."

"Dreams, eh?" Apeth stepped beside Athson. "Don't you think you should be resting?"

"I need to find my mother." He motioned to the cave entrance. "It stopped snowing. The storm's passed."

"You're still sick. You won't make it far, even with the mule." Apeth squeezed Athson's shoulder. "I can appreciate your sentiments. But come back to the fire. Eat something and tell me of your dreams. You can go then, if you like, though I suspect our way lies north for days together."

The cave tilted in Athson's vision, and Apeth steadied him. "Need to go." He caught sight of a star beyond the upper edge of the cave opening. It was bright. He stumbled away from the Withling, his mouth agape. He leaned against a rock as he gazed east in the star-clad night sky. One big star rose over the distant Drelkhaz Mountains, a tail extending in a haze below it. "That looks just like an arrow."

Apeth gaped at the scene as well. Then he muttered, "An arrow shall Eloch prepare."

"What?" Athson wheeled toward the old Withling and almost fell over in his weakness. If he had the energy, he'd be angry. Heat rose on his cheeks at the words he'd heard back at Eagle's Aerie from Zelma. "Where did you hear that?"

Apeth stared at the sight a moment longer, then turned to Athson. "I was there when the words were spoken by Zelma, Howart, and Hastra." He motioned toward the sky. "This marvel, this wandering star, foretells the coming of Eloch's arrow for the Bow of Hart."

Athson tucked his chin. "That bow is worthless." It hadn't saved his father, hadn't killed Corgren. No, he'd chosen the wrong target. "That's nothing. Just something in the sky. Dreams and prophecies don't work unless it's ill fortune." He grabbed his head. Maybe he should lie down. No. Time to escape Withlings and help his mother. He stumbled toward the mule and his gear but veered sideways.

The Withling grabbed Athson again and steered him back to the fire. "At least eat some venison. You're still fevered."

At the fire, Athson sat and struggled to keep his balance while Apeth threw wood on the flames. He shut his eyes as the cave spun slowly around him. The memory of another dream rose:

A figure steps from foggy shadows, but not the cloaked Bane. Instead, he sees a familiar floppy hat that shades the face from clear sight.

The trapper from Afratta offers the sword, hilt first. In the slim light, the edges gleam crimson and blue. "Remember what the edges are for."

Athson grasps the hilt.

The mysterious man turns to leave and pauses. "Remember, it's not for him."

"How did you know about the edges of my sword?" Athson opened his eyes and swayed with his dizziness. A coughing fit erupted, and when it cleared, he said, "I dreamed you told me to remember what the edges are for..." He trailed away for a moment. Should he discuss his dreams? He plunged ahead. No reason to hide anything anymore. He had the Bow of Hart now. "Then you told me how to use it back at Marston's Station. It—something spoke to me about when, how, to use the sword. I dreamed about it before I got it back, and the edges were the same as I saw. I was told then that they are for justice and mercy. I dreamed you told me the same thing, and then you did. How did you know?"

Apeth handed him some venison. "Athson, I didn't know what to speak. It would seem you have gifts from Eloch. Tell me, have there been other dreams, maybe visions?"

Athson slouched. This discussion was getting personal. He didn't want a Withling knowing it. He shrugged. What did it matter? It was all done, and the bow was useless to him except as a bargaining piece. He ate the venison, and his stomach rumbled in answer. "Uh, yes. I have. They come true. The details are so precise sometimes, either words or what I've seen or heard."

The Withling leaned back on his bedding. "Please, tell me more. I'd like to hear it."

Athson's eyes narrowed. "Now, why don't I trust you?"

Apeth sat up and leaned close to Athson, his gaze intense but not threatening, his voice steady. "Why wouldn't you?"

"Because..." But no others words formed in Athson's mind. Did he really have a reason? He took another bite, chewed, and swallowed. Why not? "Alright, I'll tell you." He related all he remembered from Eagle's Aerie or visions and dreams, all that had happened on the trail, the sword at Harkey's Post, other dreams along the way. He spoke of Limbreth and how she appeared in his life out of the vision. He spoke of how they were so distinctly accurate. He included his other dreams outside of Chokkra and how they came true in vivid details.

The Withling merely listened, his eyes fixed on Athson throughout the wandering tale of his prescient dreaming and their accuracy.

Athson finished and ate in silence, and Apeth spoke no reply. The fire crackled in the silence between them.

Apeth pushed himself to his feet and then knelt before Athson. He touched Athson's head and whispered a word Athson never heard clearly, but it echoed across his mind in a moment that passed like hours.

Wellness covered Athson in an instant like a raincoat donned in a sudden downpour of rain. The cascade of sickness rolled from him. The fever fell away. The dizziness ceased, and his vision snapped into clarity along with his thoughts. Weariness clattered from his limbs like chains from a prisoner. He gasped in delayed reaction to the Withling's healing.

Apeth Stellin withdrew across the fire and rolled his bedding. "I was wondering why I was withheld from healing you. And now it's clear."

Athson stood. "I don't follow you."

"We need to move." Apeth pointed toward the cave entrance past the mule. "That wandering star is a sign. We aren't the only ones to have seen it. You can bet Magdronu is seeking the arrow. North is our way, but choices lie ahead for you."

Athson shoved the last of his venison in his mouth and chewed. In his mind, there was but one choice. "I see one way ahead."

Apeth tugged at the brim of his hat, and his blue-eyed gaze twinkled at Athson. "Oh, you have choices. What to do with the bow. Whether to finish this quest and find the arrow."

With his arms spread wide, Athson lifted his gaze to the darkened cave roof rising above them. "Don't you see? There's no need for choices. Everyone's dead that matters to me. My father. Limbreth. My companions. I can only see my way to one thing now, and that's bartering for my mother."

"That's a choice to let the curse on you continue to grasp your life, Athson, continue to let Magdronu's evil control you. You have a choice to stop it." Apeth stepped close again, intense but not threatening. "As for Limbreth, by your dream, I wouldn't assume anything about her fate. But there are choices ahead. Will you go as far as Marston's Station with me before you make your final choice with the bow?"

Athson nodded. "I'll go that far. I need supplies. But there's no other choice for me."

"Oh, but there is. Your dreams indicate something you must face." Apeth gathered his things and paused in front of Athson.

Athson crossed his arms. "What must I face?"

"That you are gifted to be a Withling, asked to serve Eloch with everything you've been given." The Withling strode toward the mule.

Athson's head spun anew, but not from fever. Light from the wandering star shone in the entrance of the cave and lit the Bow of Hart where he'd left it near the mule. His anger rose in a sudden shout. "No!"

CHAPTER FOUR

Corgren lay with agony twisting in his stab-wound. It was said the Wolfshead dagger of his people bore the hungry flame of Magdronu. He groaned at the searing pain that gnawed at his body and mind. "Heal me."

Paugren stood close. "We cannot heal you yet, brother. The mountain shrine is broken. We are activating the old one in Rok."

"Water." Corgren's body burned, and sweat poured from his skin. His tongue dried and shriveled in his mouth.

Water touched his lips but did little for his thirst. He drank in gulps, choked, and drank more. Paugren spoke the words of a spell, and Corgren drifted in half-dreams, unaware of his surroundings. Darkness snuggled him, but fire burned his awareness into mindless mutterings as the wound of the dagger tore into him. The passage of time slowed and its weight withdrew, though not the pain.

Corgren woke once, lying on his belly. Someone washed his injury with cool water and changed his bandage. But his limbs quivered with fire. His mind slipped into gray awareness. Voices rose and fell around him, sometimes with anger.

Paugren's face loomed close at one point. "I must use some power or you'll die. It will hurt anew, but magic from our master is still scant." He spoke the spell. "You'll soon bleed out without more healing—enough to keep you alive."

Corgren writhed anew as the spell worked into his damaged back He screamed, and the pain subsided with the spell. If he didn't know better, Paugren had stabbed him again. The stab seared his back, and his eyes rolled. "Curse that traitor. If he still lived, I'd kill him slowly." Corgren's body twitched, and his voice sounded both weak and hoarse in his ears. "Just heal me or kill me." He lost feeling in his body as his limbs lay limp. Consciousness rolled away with a sigh, his final realization that there may be little magic, but the spells the dragon did allow tortured him for his failures.

Light blinded Corgren after an undetermined time. The fire of his torture no longer seared him mind and body. He lay cool upon the bed—on his back. He inhaled without pain and squinted at daylight through the windows. "Where am I?"

"Still in Rok, at the camp within my cabin."

Corgren's head rolled toward the sound of Paugren's voice. He sat in a chair, his face drawn with concern, if not withheld anger.

"How long since I arrived?" His body felt lifeless, his mind sluggish.

"We kept you alive with small spells while Magdronu rationed magic without a working shrine to send us his magic. The spells were unpleasant for you, no doubt. They kept the knife-wound from killing you, but the curse of the dagger remained without stronger magic. As soon as Esthria got the shrine fully functional and blood flowing, Magdronu allowed us to heal you." Paugren stood and walked to the window, where he stared at the distant mountains, his fists clenched behind him.

Corgren rolled onto his side. "I deserved my punishment

for failing at the Funnel." Good to know the dragon's wrath had subsided. "Now I can return to service."

Paugren's head shook as he watched the outside world. "It was senseless. Not everything works according to plan. Others work against us in ways we do not know until someone stabs us. Magdronu discovered there is, indeed, another Withling in play. He's powerful and is the one who broke the shrine, as surely as the dwarves blocked our approach to it. None of what happened was your fault. It merely happened." Paugren wheeled and loomed over Corgren. "You almost paid for your mistake with your life." He waved his hand. "Magdronu promised so much for our service. You'd think he'd reward sacrifices such as yours. Generals hand out medals for wounds, but you suffered his wrath until he confirmed Eloch worked beyond our plans."

Strength returned to Corgren's arms, and he rubbed his cheek. "Generals are weak. We must be strong to the end if we are to see the age of our master arrive. His ways are not Eloch's. You know that. I gladly suffer for what is truly needed." He flashed a smile at his reference to the Withlings, an insult to their faith.

"Of what use were spells to keep you alive but tortured?"

"I'm alive—chastened, but alive. I know I must rise to challenges more, think more."

Paugren sniffed and looked away. "I'll have food sent with fresh clothing. The dragon calls you to a meeting when your strength returns."

Corgren's brother left the room, and his servant entered with food. The woman helped Corgren sit up in the bed and brought fresh clothing while he ate.

"How long have I been here?" he asked her.

The slave bowed. "Eight days, great wizard."

"You may go." Corgren waved his hand dismissively. Eight days. What of his trolls gathered for the invasion? Magdronu still wanted that. He finished his meal, and with the weariness of a man returned from a long journey, he dressed. His ring flashed the dragon's summons. Best not delay. He knees barely supported him to the communication tent, but the cold slapped the coils of inactivity from his body.

Within the tent, he called for fresh blood, and a lesser mage soon brought him a bowl of blood gathered from some slave. Corgren chose to stand, no matter the cost, and cast his spell, expecting the oppressive presence of his master in his mind. Magdronu's essence groped across Corgren's thoughts, but not with the weight of his anger. The dragon's visage, his scaled and horned head, filled the aperture of the green spell in Corgren's eyesight. Corgren felt the restrained emotion, though not directed at him. "Master, I answer your call. I offer my apologies for my failure to gain the Bow of Hart."

'All is forgiven, my faithful one. You alone among my servants will take wounds for my cause. It is now clear to me that Eloch has worked for long years through this hidden Withling." Magdronu paused, and Corgren sensed cold anger. *'With the Bow of Hart in Athson's hands, Eloch's sign of the arrow to come has arisen in the sky. I'll watch for that, but I need you to command the trolls on their march. You are needed to direct the new shrine. You know my plans, long hidden, and they are to be activated soon. But first, there are many plans to set in motion. We lost one chance at the bow. Now we must strike according to my longer designs, and we shall gain all in victory. We have limits to magic, but we can still do much with what we have. You will command the others according to my wishes. Listen closely...'*

Corgren knelt and listened, a smile spreading on his face as his master revealed his schemes.

∽

WHEN THEY HAD PREPARED their departure, Tordug drew Makwi aside. "I want you to take Gweld and have him show you where he last tracked Athson. Then you search for him, see if you can find him fast." He pointed between himself and Makwi. "We know these hills better, so it's just you on the search ahead. We need haste, not mistakes. Gweld's taken a few risks, but we can't afford walking into a pack of raiders."

Makwi nodded and sketched a salute. "I'll find him if it can still be done after this storm."

Tordug lowered his voice. "Have Gweld wait. We need him back with us. Leave sign of your direction. With just three horses and low rations, we need to collect Athson and head for the elven forts. We can't get caught up in running from trolls just because he's taking chances."

Makwi frowned. "I guess he's just worried, but I see what you mean. He was pretty upset when Hastra stopped us to rescue Limbreth."

When Tordug broached the subject with the others, Gweld held his tongue and nodded, but he clearly disliked the idea. Tordug didn't care what the elf thought, he just wanted out of the hills without more trouble. Three horses, six riders, plus the giant left Tordug's stomach knotted. Maybe the snow would keep the numbers of trolls wandering the heaths lower than normal.

They set out with Gweld and Makwi trotting ahead on a horse they shared. The others followed with more care. Tordug wanted Athson safe with them soon. They might escape without trouble from trolls. He wanted honor restored, but not by acting foolish. He led their group with Hastra riding behind him. Limbreth followed with Danilla on their last horse, and Ralda trailed afoot.

They followed Makwi's marks, left in subtle spots where the rocky terrain lay bare, and soon met Gweld waiting with an impatient but disturbed expression. Still he voiced no argument. Thank Elokwi for elven restraint. They needed it now. If only Makwi could catch Athson still holding up in a cave.

They followed Makwi's trail until Tordug found a mark telling them to wait. That was bad. Likely trolls, and he hated waiting in the open while making no progress through the short winter day.

By Tordug's count, nearly two hours passed, and he worried for Makwi's safety. But Tordug found no indication where Makwi had headed from their location. He glanced along ridges and back the way they'd come. *Bad just sitting and waiting for trolls like this.* He tugged his knotted beard and muttered.

Nearby, Gweld stood by his horse and nudged a few rocks with his boot. He faced Tordug. "Maybe I should've gone with him."

Tordug ran his tongue along his teeth. "I think he can take care of himself."

Gweld patted the horse and seemed poised to leap into the saddle. "At some point I'll have to go look for him."

"Not yet."

A few minutes later, a shape edged out of a ravine up the valley and paused. Gweld nocked an arrow to his bowstring. The figure approached, avoiding snow wherever possible.

Gweld removed his arrow. "It's Makwi."

They waited several more minutes until the dwarf arrived with his brow furrowed.

Tordug saluted Makwi. "Something wrong?"

Makwi nodded and answered the salute. "Killed three trolls." He pointed toward the ravine he had left farther up the valley they traversed. "Left them hidden in a cave up there. I scouted for Athson farther north, but I found more trolls out scouting. Killed a few more and hid them away. We won't find Athson anytime soon, though."

"Why's that?"

"Every valley, dell, and ravine I scouted heading north is

filled with trolls marching west. It looks like Corgren has emptied Chokkra to invade Auguron."

Tordug's eyebrows climbed his forehead. That was very bad. He sighed and stroked his beard.

Gweld glanced between them. "An army between us and Athson." He shook his head. "They must have started marching in the storm to move that many trolls."

Makwi climbed onto the horse with a leap for the stirrup. "You can look for him, but you won't get past that army."

Danilla's brow furrowed like Makwi's. "Do you think he's safe?"

Makwi shrugged. "Can't tell. I never found sign of his passing, but there's snow so many places and rock everywhere else, I'd never know I passed his trail. Anything he left behind under snow has been trampled by trolls."

Hastra stepped to Tordug's side. "I was afraid of something like this with that sign in the night sky." She glanced at Gweld. "The elves have worried about the trolls for decades, haven't they?"

Gweld watched clouds a moment, then exhaled. "Yes. I'd like to find him, but I don't know how we can now."

"So we just leave him to the trolls?" Limbreth's tone sounded adversarial.

Tordug sidled alongside Limbreth. He didn't want another scene like in the Drelkhaz. Arguing didn't help matters, and he didn't want to draw the attention of any nearby goblins or kobolds. "Look, we don't want to abandon Athson, but if we can't reach him, then we can't."

Makwi adjusted his weight on the horse. "Chances are he's gone on north to get away from them. He can handle himself. And if Hastra's correct, he's got help from this other Withling."

Limbreth crossed her arms. "I don't like it at all." She seemed intent on having her say without making trouble, at least for the moment. "What if they have him?"

Ralda waved his inked hands. "We no help save. Not know too."

Tordug tugged his beard. "No, we can't know either way. But trying to find out might just get us all captured." He fixed his gaze to the Withling. "What do you think?"

Hastra kicked a pebble at her feet, glanced at Limbreth, and released a long sigh. "My heart tells me to find Athson. My head tells me to secure the Bow of Hart. Eloch tells me to ride for the elven forts and warn them. Athson's still safe with Apeth Stellin."

Limbreth pursed her lips, then glanced Danilla's way.

Athson's mother clutched Limbreth's arm. "Hastra, I'll trust your Withling's sense of this. It's more than we can guess otherwise."

Limbreth slouched, then squared her shoulders. "You were right before. I'll go with what you say."

Tordug held the horse steady for Hastra. "I guess we ride for the forts, then."

They all mounted up except for Ralda and turned to skirt the troll army at Makwi's direction. Tordug chewed the inside of his cheek and glanced around them for sign of troll scouts. One thing he knew—if Corgren's trolls marched, there'd be plenty of chances to regain the rest of his honor. Or die trying.

He chuckled at the thought.

∽

ATHSON WANTED to ride off alone past drifts of snow, but his sensibility held him back. He couldn't abandon someone else in the Troll Heaths. He knew little enough of the craggy hills except from his own travels, but he disliked the thought of leaving Apeth Stellin here amid the fallen boulders and heather-covered hilltops just because he had urged Athson to become a Withling. Maybe when they found the road or arrived at Marston's Station. Athson needed to send a report to Sarneth about the others, hard as that might be. He'd go that far. He sighed. With Apeth.

"You seem to be debating something in your head." Apeth strolled alongside Athson as he rode the mule.

"Just decided I really do need to go to Marston's. I need to send a report about the others being dead." He slouched at that thought. His heart twinged with sadness. Limbreth grieved him most of all, after his father. He looked east. But maybe there was a chance with his mother. That wandering star meant nothing now.

"You don't know they are all dead."

"Well, I can't go back and look for them. You saw all those trolls on the march." North was the best way now. Athson eyed the surrounding ridges strewn with crumbling rock and their back-trail. Troll scouts might hide anywhere among these crags and brush though he spotted no tracks in the patches of snow. "Anyway, *you* say they may not be." Word of a Withling.

"You doubt me, I get that." Apeth shot Athson a grin.

Athson's breath caught. How had Apeth known his thoughts? He sniffed and searched for scouts again. Lucky guess.

"But that doesn't change that you're called, and you know it."

Heat rose in Athson face even with the cold. "I don't know that."

"Where's Spark?"

"He's ahead of us, being a dog." Athson's back stiffened. Spark might be the only thing left that he trusted. "Why?"

Apeth chuckled. "You know why. You can run from it, but it's still there. You dream, you see Spark, you get instructions about handling that blessed sword."

Athson opened his mouth for a loud, angry retort, then

thought better of it. He shouldn't attract the attention of trolls. "I've been debating leaving you behind."

The old Withling strolled on beside the mule without glancing Athson's way. "Decided not to?"

"Trolls are behind us. It wouldn't be good to just up and leave somebody alone here." Even if he didn't know the heaths that well himself.

"So a moral decision?" Apeth grabbed the bridle and halted the mule. He faced Athson. "Maybe you're listening to Eloch more than you think, Athson."

"I doubt that. I'm a ranger, is all." He wrenched the reins free of Apeth's grasp and kicked the mule's sides with his heels. Maybe he *should* leave Apeth. He sighed. That wasn't right, no matter what. He halted the mule. "Why don't you get on, and we'll put some distance between us and the trolls."

Apeth mounted the mule and rode behind Athson. He urged the animal forward along the dell of stone that bent away northwest between craggy ridges. Withlings toyed with him and manipulated him at every turn, and now this one offered him membership in their failing order. If that didn't take the bit from the mule, he didn't know what did. At least Apeth held his tongue for now.

After a while, Athson halted the mule and listened. Apeth started to speak, but Athson held up his hand for silence. *Just be quiet for once, Withling. You don't know everything.* Athson listened. Maybe he needed the Bow of Hart just now. If it really worked. It hadn't on the Funnel. That thought tightened his chest. Had he chosen the wrong shot? He had let Corgren bait him and nearly gotten killed himself. He shook his head.

There it was. A rock rolled along the ridge near where they were stopped. Not good. Spark stalked forward. Really not good.

Athson reached for an arrow and touched his sword-hilt. *Run!* Athson hesitated. So he shouldn't fight?

He kicked the mule into a gallop. "Hold on." Somehow Apeth held on, and so did Athson.

The mule ran along the ravine and passed Spark. Arrows whizzed past them, and Athson leaned forward. Limbreth on her white horse near Marston's Station crossed his mind. "Don't fall."

Spark snarled, and a goblin squealed.

"Get 'em, Spark!" He chanced a glance over his shoulder. He didn't want to count the goblins trailing and launching arrows after them. Several flailed with Spark among them, snapping at their throats.

Apeth shouted in his ear. "How'd you know?"

He'd heard the rock tumble but not the number of attackers. He groaned. There had to have been thirty. "Sword told me."

The Withling grunted as if to say, *Told you so.*

Athson swore into the rush of frigid wind as Spark's snarls echoed in the ravine behind them. Withling. He was acting too much like one, and he didn't think he could avoid it. He didn't know if he'd make through the day.

He laughed. He bet the Withling behind him knew.

CHAPTER FIVE

Corgren left Rok within hours of his meeting with Magdronu and traveled to the Troll Heaths. There, he commanded his trolls into the action demanded by the dragon and the appearance of Eloch's Arrow in the sky. The trolls marched west in a grumbling mass and mirrored the path of the wandering star. Alone among the trolls at night, Corgren stared at the comet as it distanced itself from the Drelkhaz and headed west. He stirred from silent musing. Hastra's little band of travelers lurked in the Troll Heaths, and he should have already sent scouts looking for them.

His eyes narrowed in thought. When the arrow came, it would be around her or Athson. Magdronu reported Athson missing, but Corgren assumed he, too, traversed the Troll Heaths. Stop them, and he'd thwart the coming arrow, sign or no sign.

He snarled for his officers. With the passage of days, Hastra and Athson had likely already fled the area, but Corgren planned for Athson's path. His master sought the arrow with Hastra, but Corgren might capture Athson with the Bow of Hart.

Corgren spoke in trollish and commanded his scouts to find the dragon's prey and bring him to Corgren if possible. He questioned them about any reports. None of his scouts had spotted anything of Hastra or Athson. He snorted. Trolls often lacked direction and wandered at times, returning when they wished, likely causing mischief wherever they discovered opportunity.

The next day, he returned to Rok and called his fellow mages to a meeting. He dismissed the junior, less powerful mages to Rok to take care of the sacrifices there. Once those bumblers departed, he sat with Paugren and the Beleesh sisters in Paugren's office. The women stared at him, their lips curled in slight smiles of hidden cruelty. Their dark eyes, alert and perceptive, sought weakness like birds of prey. Their pretty features of high cheeks on oval faces with pouty lips fooled many a man who encountered them. Corgren glanced at his brother and arched an eyebrow. A far distance from the flirtatious lasses they'd recruited back during his assignment at Withling's Watch.

"I've been given command of our next operations as I announced earlier to the others." Good riddance to those weaklings. Better they handled the mundane tasks while their betters performed the difficult tasks.

"Long deserved, brother." Paugren stirred at his desk. "We are yours to command." He nodded.

Corgren searched the sisters with his eyes for any challenge, but they returned blank stares. Careful after this long, those three.

"We have several objectives. Begin the shrine in Auguron City." He'd laid plans there himself as an agent disguised as Domikyas, the Rokan merchant. "But we've a wrinkle in our plans. There's been a hidden Withling at work who has thwarted us over time but more openly these last weeks." Corgren paused to let that sink in. He lifted a finger. "We know our enemies, their goals, and Eloch's prophecy. There's no more tolerance for these surprises. We'll overcome them, and we will win in the end."

Ahmelia narrowed her eyes and sniffed. "Eloch has played even Magdronu for a fool. We're not to blame."

Esthria crossed her arms and lifted her chin. "You're the one who lost the Bow of Hart and got stabbed nearly to death. If it had been me making decisions, I'd have let you die for those mistakes."

Corgren stood and loomed over the desk, but Paugren spoke first. "I think you tread where the ice is thinnest."

Cass crossed her legs but left her hands noticeably resting in her lap. "We almost got killed by that Archer's blessed sword. It would have been nice for the warning."

Esthria laughed and stared directly at Corgren. "And we almost got charred by Hastra's little stunt in the mountains. But we didn't let a half-blind slave attack us."

Corgren slammed his palm on Paugren's desktop. "Enough!" He pointed to each sister in turn. "You fled in the mountains at the slightest problem. Then you never noted Hastra's escape, let alone the loss of Athson's mother—both of them valuable hostages."

Cass pursed her lips and stared out a window, but the other two merely watched Corgren like they were waiting for a slip from him. Like they could kill him. He suppressed a sneer of arrogance. That had gotten him stabbed by Ath and nearly killed.

Paugren stirred behind his desk. "What would you have us do now, brother?"

Corgren sat again and checked his fingernails as if in consideration. He'd made his choices of assignments for the others. He lifted his gaze to the Beleesh sisters. "Our third goal is moving trolls to Auguron City and attacking. I'll see to moving their numbers west and watching the rest of you. Our master keeps close watch for the appearance of the prophesied arrow so he can take it with the Bane. He'll also take the Bow of Hart when the time comes. We've bungled those tasks, so he'll see to them himself. That leaves the shrine and this other Withling."

Ahmelia lifted one side of her mouth in a deeper sneer. "Tell me where this Withling is, and I'll slip my knife into him."

"Not you." Corgren shook his head. She'd leave a trail of bodies. She and Esthria needed watching and their time taken with activities. He'd decided this several days earlier. Cass moved in disguise among crowds with ease. "You and Esthria are to go to Auguron City." He pointed to each of them. "I'll be watching you regularly, so no games. The shrine is the priority, not your little side-schemes. You each stay at different inns, keep low, and work on the shrine. There's a magical marker left at two graves outside the city. Below that is a flat field with a large, quarried stone the elves have left sitting for many years. We'll just use the space and the stone for making a shrine."

Esthria rolled her eyes. "It will take forever with just the two of us."

Corgren chuckled. "You'll do the work yourself if it takes a thousand lifetimes if that's what the master requires." He clenched a fist and toyed with his dagger with the other hand. *Just try and disobey, Esthria*. Her eyes fell to her lap as if she read his thoughts. Corgren's eyes shifted to Cass. "You'll go with Paugren, track down this Withling with Athson, get him alone, and kill him. Then you can help your sisters with the shrine."

Cass nodded, and her gaze flitted toward Paugren with a sly smile. "A pleasure to work with you."

Paugren rolled his eyes. "Whatever, Cass."

"Regardless, everyone keeps their presence a secret. We've traps to spring on the elves, and playing these tasks wrong will foul our lines." He motioned the Beleesh sisters toward the door. "Go and prepare yourselves."

They left with varying degrees of defiance in their parade. Cass paused and blew a kiss at Paugren, then laughed.

Corgren waited, then checked the hall, then stood by the closed door. He wanted to hear if anyone approached while they talked. "You'll keep a sharp eye on Cass?"

Paugren inhaled and released an irritated sigh. "She'll be a handful with her little games, but we'll get to him. The shrine would be better for her, make things faster."

Corgren shook his head. "No, it's best to split them up. They're good at what they do, but troublesome together. We have time for Esthria and Ahmelia to begin it. They'll start with the design by the stone they've forgotten near the bodies of those elves the Bane killed."

"A big task for two to move the stone with magic funneled to them all the way from Rok."

"You'll join them by the time they get that far." Corgren checked his nails again and grimaced at one. "They'll spend weeks just getting the design set with spells." He shrugged. "Moving the trolls will take weeks as it is." He lifted his gaze to Paugren's. "We deal with this other Withling, then you move to assist with completion of the shrine. That should be right about the time I arrive and get the gates open with what I left behind." His smile widened. "With our localized magic and trolls successfully taking the bridge across the river, we're sure of victory over the elves and Eloch's prophecy."

~

THERE FOLLOWED days of wary plodding out of the snowy Troll Heaths. More than once, Makwi reported he'd killed a scout and hidden the carcass. For Ralda, the tension of their escape from such a large force of trolls through barren ravines of crumbling cliffs wove into weary days and cold nights until they arrived in sight of the southernmost ranger-fort.

Shocked elves scrambled to evacuate the fort at the news of trolls approaching in such a massive force and sent messages to forts further north. But Gweld secured them extra mounts and needed rations for the following leg of the journey. Ralda and his companions continued their trek north for Marston's Station among growing numbers of elves since the total force of rangers garrisoned in the forts lacked numbers to withstand the forthcoming horde.

Ralda watched distant smoke in the south with his companions one crisp, blue morning which bespoke a destroyed elven fort. At least, they had gotten word to the escaping elves. Hastra pushed their little band harder in the following days, saying, "We've little time. The sign of the arrow pushes west."

Ralda breathed easier when they left the elven forts behind them. He and his companions traveled ahead of the bulk of the garrisoned forces that manned the various small forts intended for quelling raids on the road and scouting. Even though trolls marched after them now, Ralda relaxed in the company of larger numbers. Their search for the Bow of Hart and their desperate chase for Athson and Limbreth had left Ralda spent, ready for friendlier faces in more numbers.

They marched for three days into deeper forest of pine, cedar and hardwoods, though they still had days of travel ahead of them before they reached Marston's Station. Ralda hoped the elven messenger pigeons reached the station well ahead of them baring warning. He settled at their campfire that night with his rations and chewed as he hummed a tune of his people as the darkening sky revealed the glowing wonder of the wandering star overhead. He scratched his cheek as he ate. He didn't remember the last time he'd sung anything. Creeping through troll territory, caves, or in the Drelkhaz had kept him busy surviving. He shook his head. It was good to hum a tune.

Limbreth arrived at the fire from grooming one of their

horses and sat next to him with her share of food. She fanned smoke from her face, sighed and cast a glance at him. "Can't wait to reach the station, maybe sleep in a bed." She rubbed her neck and stretched her shoulders.

"Ground hard, cold." Ralda shivered further agreement and spoke with his hands. 'Wish they had beds to fit me.' She didn't understand, so he shrugged one shoulder and kept eating.

"Anyway, maybe we'll meet Athson at some point. He has to be heading there." Limbreth tore off a piece of travel bread and chewed it.

"Troll no catch." He remembered to shake his head for 'no.' "Athson good track. No catch, me think."

Limbreth stared at her boots while she ate in silence.

Ralda threw more wood on the fire. Still cold nights. He shivered at the memory of their frozen nights in the dwarven shelters. Limbreth ate in silence. Maybe he'd made her sad? "No worry. Athson come." He added with his inked hands, 'Athson's coming with the Bow of Hart. He'll be so happy to see us all.' Well, Athson confused Ralda with his moods, but maybe he'd be happy. They'd done it, after all, since he had the bow now.

Beside Ralda, Limbreth nodded as if she had arrived at some conclusion on her own. "You're right, Ralda. No reason to worry for him. We've made it this far through all the danger. He can make it to Marston's Station. You're always around, looking after us, so you should know. I mean, you pulled me from the river and all." She elbowed him. "Thanks again for that." Limbreth flashed him a grin.

"Help all Ralda can. Come from home, help." His fingers said, 'I walked weeks before I found Athson. The elders sent me to help so I'd feel better.' But she didn't understand his fingers.

Limbreth tilted her head. "Why did you come all this way to help?"

Ralda felt the eyes of his other companions on him. He wasn't sure he liked Gweld's stare anymore since he'd seen that odd reflection in the mirror. Maybe he'd talk to Hastra about it, but he wasn't sure yet. He didn't want to accuse the elf of something uncertain. Maybe elves could do things like that, though he'd never seen it over these last months. What did he know of elves otherwise, though? Best tell his story.

"Brother, Kralda, die. We climb mountain. He fall, me slide, we tied on rope. Me slide over, uh, cliff, both die." He kicked his feet like he had tried then to stop Kralda pulling him over the steep ledge. "No, uh, place for feet stop." Ralda motioned his hand like a knife. "Cut rope, Kralda die, me not." He shrugged one shoulder.

The others sat paused in their meal, except for Hastra. Ralda had told her why the elders sent him.

Limbreth put her hand over his. "I didn't know that, Ralda. I mean, I knew he was gone and you missed him, but I didn't know why."

Makwi wiped his beard. "Tough choice you made. But he was going to die. It's said never cut someone loose, but if you're going over and can't even tell if they're conscious..." He shrugged. "What can you do?"

Ralda jerked his head in a rough nod and swallowed the lump in his throat. He slouched some. "Me blame me, sad long time. Elders send me, go find Withling, go help. After, come help. Remember rope sliding away, see it when something wrong." He tapped his chest. "Help then. No let rope go again." He pointed to Limbreth. "Pull you out. Fight troll, help. No see rope go away here." He tapped his head to help explain that he avoided having the memory nag him when he could help someone.

Everyone around Ralda glanced at each other. They'd never realized what he was doing since he'd never spoken of it.

Makwi gaped, genuinely surprised. "You pulled me out of the river in the Troll Neath. No wonder." He stood and bowed with several hand motions dwarves made that befuddled Ralda. "You have treated me like your brother. As you wanted to save him, so you saved me. You are always welcome at my table."

Tordug stood and did the same, saying, "You have blessed my family with your safe care, and you are welcome at my table."

Ralda sat in stunned silence. He'd just done what was needed.

Limbreth nudged him. "Just stand and bow and thank them for the honor of their table."

Ralda stood, bowed awkwardly. "Thanks to you of honor with table. Just help. Uh, thanks." He sat, feeling a flush on his face.

Limbreth whispered, "Good job. You'll be a dwarf like me any day now."

Laughter rumbled from Ralda's chest.

The meal passed, and they stretched out around the fire while Gweld took his customary first watch. Later, Ralda stood his watch as the fire burned low, the embers hissing and snapping. He reached for more wood, but at that moment, Hastra sat up from sleep with a gasp and flung her hand out toward him.

"Don't bother, we're leaving." She rolled out of her blanket with a grunt and started packing. "Please rouse the others."

Ralda opened his mouth to ask about their sudden leaving. He remembered the Withling's inexplicable actions and how he had reached blindly into the river and pulled bloodied Limbreth from the water. He roused Tordug. "Hastra say we go." He visited the others and roused them too.

Makwi rolled over. "We've still another watch before morning. Why now?"

Hastra lifted her pack with a grunt and a grimace. "I've a meeting very soon. Because Eloch's Arrow approaches closer."

"With who?"

"Other Withlings."

The others asked more questions, but Hastra offered no more explanation, so everyone gathered their packs, saddled their horses, and set out on the elven trail to the road and Marston's Station beneath the sign of the arrow and fading stars.

Hastra pushed them long into the night and shortened the next night of rest until they reached Marston's Station well after dark on the second day. They were met at the front doors by a red-haired woman who looked like Hastra and a tall, thin man. The Withling hugged them both warmly.

Hastra dropped her pack. "Howart, Zelma, I've come as fast I could to meet you both."

Ralda still stood by the steps onto the porch. He took a deep breath and watched the night sky. What Hastra called Eloch's Arrow now stood over Marston's Station, its tail stretching away east.

The thin man, Howart, said, "It's here, so it's time. Where can we meet?"

Hastra called for Marston and left Ralda and the others to settle their animals. Limbreth snagged her pack.

Ralda gazed with his mouth open at the sign in the sky over the station. If the sign was here, where was the promised arrow? He shrugged and entered the station. That was Withling business. He was just along to help.

∿

LIMBRETH ENTERED Marston's Station with her companions, and the tightness across her body eased. The scent of cooked meat and the noise of nervous conversation in the room replaced the scent and silence of the forest. She had never realized the tension within her until now. How long had it resided in her muscles? She rolled her head and eased stiffness from her neck. Definitely looser. But her stomach still felt knotted. Athson wasn't there. Limbreth glanced outside and remembered a conversation about his lack of candor with her before they had departed for the Troll Heaths. Was he really safe, as Hastra claimed? She moved deeper into the common room, past tables where travelers babbled already about trolls. The messages had certainly arrived.

The others sat, except for Tordug and Hastra. The dwarf settled them in rooms while the Withling walked down a hall, escorted by Marston. A meeting with other Withlings? Had to be something about the prophecy of the arrow. Or the Bow of Hart. Both, most likely.

Someone put a mug in front of Limbreth, and she sipped. "Uh, thanks, Makwi."

"Just buying my favorite ax-maid a drink." He settled with a weary sigh into his seat which whispered a creak.

Ralda carried his pack and Hastra's upstairs while the others held their table.

Gweld downed his drink and soon followed Ralda. "Think I'll have a look around, just in case Athson comes in."

Limbreth watched the elf go. Why hadn't she thought of that? But the Withlings drew her attention. Maybe she should stand guard. No, she might miss Athson's arrival. If he came tonight.

Danilla stood and grabbed her few belongings. "Shall I take your pack to your room, Limbreth?"

Limbreth stared at the hallway, engrossed by the Withlings. "Huh? What? Oh, yes, thank you."

Tordug sat, and Makwi wrangled their packs upstairs and returned. Limbreth barely noticed.

A familiar shiver ran along Limbreth's spine, and she sat up straight, her eyes wide. Just as suddenly as it appeared, it left. She sat rigid, eyes wide. She hadn't felt that since the Funnel. So it was still out there and not after the Bow of Hart? Withlings met, and the Bane lurked.

"Something wrong?" Makwi eyed Limbreth over a tankard's edge.

She sipped and narrowed her eyes at the door, then watched the hallway. "No. Not yet, anyway." She smiled. "Good to be back in the safety of a regular place rather than the wilds. Haven't had a bed since Ezhandun."

Well, *relative* safety, with the elven garrison withdrawing not far behind them, trolls invading, and that bothersome Bane lurking near enough to set her teeth on edge. Suddenly she really wished Athson were there with his blessed sword.

~

ATHSON KILLED several scouts from hiding with the Bow of Hart as he and Apeth crept north through the Troll Heaths for days. He avoided lighting fires at night and rarely slept well as a result, nodding toward sleep often as he rode the mule with Apeth each day. Dried rations dwindled as they reached the road and traveled west for Marston's Station.

Conversation grew uncomfortable over the days of travel. Athson avoided the issue of being a Withling with prolonged silence as they rode the mule in growing weariness each day. Athson's chin dropped close to his head. He wanted more sleep.

"We're getting close to Marston's aren't we?" Apeth's energy never seemed to flag. He never pushed Athson about being a Withling either.

"Yes, sometime tomorrow. Haven't seen trolls for a while so we may be out of trouble for now." Apeth's' silence on the subject jabbed at Athson harder than discussing it. "Why?"

"Why what? Why do I care about Marston's Station?" Apeth slipped off the mule. "Think I'll walk a while."

"No, why I should be a Withling." He hated asking but the assertion that he was a Withling nagged his mind. Athson needed resolution so maybe he'd argue Apeth out of the notion. Athson nodded to himself. Yes, convince Apeth he wasn't Withling material, just a ranger with a bow. He ran his tongue across his teeth. At least the bow worked on trolls. He frowned at the Bow of Hart balanced across his lap as he sat astride the mule. Just not when he *really* needed the bow to work.

Apeth walked alongside Athson and the mule and glanced at him. "I suppose just saying that I know it to be so isn't enough. Very well, as I said back at the cave, you've got the talent for dreaming. Dreams that come true by your own admission. That's a Withling gift. You see things others don't and I've known Withlings that did the same."

"But I'm not magical or mystical or whatever." Maybe there was something but if he convinced Apeth otherwise all this would go away. But, somehow the notion fit. Worse than that, part of him desired it. He slipped off the mule to walk and crossed his arm, the reins gathered in the grasp of his closest hand. "Withling work has been trouble for me and my family all my life."

"That's not an excuse. It's more a reason to accept the truth." Apeth peered at Athson over the mule's dark, brown withers.

Athson reacted with a derisive laugh. "I should think not. It's killed everyone around me that I care about."

Apeth offered a patient sigh. "You lay that on the shoulders of Withlings, and Eloch. But the blame lies with Magdronu, and Corgren. They are the ones who have done you and your loved ones harm. Withlings have only tried to help you. Don't you want help?"

The *clop* of mule's hooves stood for Athson's answer for several minutes. Help from Withlings only brought trouble. Or did it? He scratched his ear. He grasped his sword's hilt and that belief faded, replaced by the desire to be a Withling. He let go of the sword. That couldn't be his true desire.

Spark trotted by, tongue out in his silent pant.

There was that dog. Athson trusted that. But seeing Spark didn't make him a Withling. He slouched again. Maybe it did. He'd known when the trolls were about to attack the night Limbreth rode to his rescue near Marston's Station. He perceived trolls laying in ambush for them just days ago. Was that mystical or just keenly developed senses as a ranger? "I don't know. The fight with the dragon and the wizard was never mine."

"Isn't it? And isn't the thought of being a Withling a fit in your real yearning? The curse confuses that. I'd guess that you think differently about all that's happened in your life. You can't let the negatives be your guide on this trail of decision." Apeth stepped ahead and peaked under the mule's head. "You can't hide from the truth, only deny it. Your enemies still want you whether you accept that fact or not. But Withlings aren't your real trouble."

Athson ran fingers through his hair and scratched the back of his neck. "Maybe you're right." He needed time to think about this choice. But what did he really need to think about? He'd been doing some Withling things. But still he resisted. Withlings surrounded the troubles of his life. He slouched. Athson didn't know what to think. "I'll think about it."

Spark paused and watched behind them, hackles raised and ears standing at an alert angle.

"Uh, maybe we'll make better time riding." Maybe trolls

weren't so far behind after all. He halted the mule and mounted, then pulled Apeth on behind him. Sensing trouble, either from Spark or listening when he didn't mean to, bothered him more than the thought of trolls tracking them. He nudged the mule into a trot with his heels.

Athson laid the Bow of Hart across his lap and rested one hand with the reins over it. His other hand rested on the pommel of his blessed sword. The doubt faded to willingness about being a Withling. He should be more disturbed at the thought of trolls, not being a Withling. He sighed and glanced over his shoulder. No trolls. He sighed again. The thought of being a Withling somehow felt both like a betrayal and a yearning. The latter notion he couldn't deny, not as long as he possessed his father's sword - and he wasn't about to give his father's sword up.

CHAPTER SIX

Hastra hugged her sister again once they entered one of Marston's private dining rooms, and Zelma wept with joy. Howart stood beside them, his arms spread and hands on each of the sisters. "It's been so long and I've missed you so much."

Zelma wiped her cheeks and sniffed. Her crooked grin beneath her unruly red hair bespoke the wildness of her existence upon Eagle's Aerie. She shuffled into a slow dance in circles as she spoke. "I gave it to him. He has the bow, and the prophecy progresses. And now..." She paused and glanced between Hastra and Howart.

"The arrow." Howart clapped and rubbed his hands together.

Hastra took each of them by the hand. At last, the long years bearing fruit. A smile bloomed on her face. "Have either of you seen it or found it? The sign has been in the sky for weeks now."

Howart shook his head and motioned with his other hand. "I thought perhaps one of you knew of it. I've held the bow this last decade."

Zelma answered with a brief cackle. "So short a time. I've lost count of the years I held the inheritance. But I know nothing of the arrow either."

Hastra pinched her lower lip. "We've each performed different tasks over the years, but the arrow we've left to Eloch to prepare." She spread her hands wide. "What are we to do? The sign is there."

Howart paced the room, his hands clasped behind him. "Yes, the sign for all to see. It's drawn us together for the first time in a very long time." He stopped and shook a finger toward the wall of the dining room. "There's never a lost reason, and this is no different." The gaunt Withling turned his deep-set eyes toward Hastra and Zelma. "We have come for Eloch's purpose at the time of his preparation of the arrow for the heir. We do what Withlings do best—watch and listen."

They each knelt on the floor and breathed to calm themselves. Then they began an old chant from their days in the order, one meant to still their thoughts to listen carefully. "Gracious and holy Eloch, we have come to serve you with our lives by listening and being with you, acting as your blessing. Grant that our thoughts, which stray in fear, worry, or other concerns, might dwell in your presence, that our words and hands might be your blessing."

At the end, Hastra waited in silence with the others as they listened for Eloch's guidance.

Zelma's voice sounded unsteady, as if she were unused to speaking much. "That our words and hands might be your blessing."

Hastra peeked at her sister, whose expression resounded with peace, her face aglow.

Howart peeked at Hastra, his words soft. "A word of guidance, those, I think."

Hastra's eyes widened. Yes, a blessing. Athson's sword was

blessed, even the Bow of Hart bore a blessing. Why not an arrow?

Zelma spoke, her eyes still shut. "Go and find one, sister."

Hastra's eyes widened further. "Of course. They're more plentiful than coin with all these rangers nearby. I'll be back." She swept out the door, leaving it ajar, and went looking for...who? Gweld had arrows. She practically bounded up the stairs and knocked on the door of the room he shared with Ralda.

The giant opened the door and stooped to gaze at her. He opened his mouth in greeting.

Hastra pushed past him into the room but found no sign of Gweld, but his gear, even his quiver, was deposited on a bed. She motioned to Gweld's belongings. "Where has he gone?"

Ralda shrugged. "Gweld go scout." He shrugged again, and his fingers danced in the air with more words. "Something. Talk to ranger friends."

"What, scouting? But his bow and quiver are here." Odd that he'd leave them, and there were plenty of rangers for that task. But she needed an arrow without delay. She should just take one? Yes, take...that one. If the elf needed more, he'd easily obtain them, so one was of no matter. She held the arrow in her fist. "Tell him I needed an arrow. If he needs it replaced, I should think there are plenty to be had from the stock Marston keeps."

She brushed out the door before Ralda could offer a reply and clattered down the stairs. She whisked back into the dining room where Howart and Zelma waited, still kneeling. Hastra displayed the arrow. "I have one."

Howart stood and patted the table. "Good. Now let's see what happens with a blessing."

Hastra placed the arrow on the table and helped Zelma to her feet. Her sister swayed, still in her meditative state. Hastra bowed her head and waited for instruction.

Zelma began speaking in the Withling prayer tongue, her words rising and falling while she touched the arrow lying before them on the table. In moments, Howart joined Zelma as Hastra calmed her thoughts. So easy, so obvious, so simple. It was there the whole time. She joined her fellow Withlings, their voices rising and falling in unison, her eyes closed.

As they chanted, Hastra saw light flare in the room beyond her eyelids, the brightness growing in the space of minutes. Then they each spoke in turn. The arrow lifted into the air at their blessing, and Hastra extended her hand toward it. She blinked, then squinted against the brightest white light she could imagine. The arrow glowed as it slowly rotated among their outstretched hands. Their blessing continued, though Hastra no longer had a sense of the passage of time, until their words halted as one and the arrow descended to the table and lay glowing.

A hush filled the room, and Hastra didn't dare speak in the presence of the holy item. An amazing blessing from Eloch. The arrow prepared.

Howart touched her and Zelma and beckoned them from the room. He turned to them after they had walked along the hall so others in the main room might not hear their conversation. "What do we do with it now?"

Hastra groped for a solid thought and landed on one. "Hold onto it for Athson until he comes."

Zelma brushed her hair from her eyes. "Protect it. It is not for the dragon."

Howart spread his hands. "Hide it? Where?"

Hastra pinched her lower lip. "Perhaps we could wrap it in something and take turns carrying it every day so it's not known who has it. We can't let just anyone touch it. These items are meant for a purpose, and in the wrong hands oddities happen. At best a holy joy for some days to come."

Zelma cackled. "That's not such a bad thing."

Hastra touched her sister's arm. "Yes, my dear, but you've a gift for that sort of thing. Others might not know how to handle themselves and become a nuisance."

Howart rubbed his cheek a few times. "Then it's settled. We'll hide it between us until such time as Athson needs—"

Wildly joyous laughter erupted from the vacant dining room. Hastra and her fellow Withlings stared at each other and then turned to the private dining room's door, which now stood ajar. Someone laughed in the throes of holy joy, which meant someone else held the arrow.

Hastra groaned.

∽

LIMBRETH SAT at the table in Marston's Station with Tordug and Makwi and picked at her meal amid the noise of gathered rangers in the room, mostly officers. Hastra entered the dining room farther down the darkened hall. Limbreth cocked her head. The Withling meeting about the arrow occupied her thoughts. What were they doing? Did they know where it was? She stared across the bustling room but ignored the buzz of chatter.

Tordug nudged her shoulder. "Right, Limbreth?"

"Huh, what?" She felt her face heat with a blush. She wasn't paying attention to her friends.

Tordug stroked his beard and drank his ale, then set his mug down. "I said, this is where it all began for us. And Makwi, here, hasn't finished that verse yet."

Makwi frowned and fiddled with his own mug. "She keeps adding to it with all her antics. How's a good dwarf supposed to compose while dodging trolls, magic, and dragons and add to a growing list like hers?" He belched.

"Uh, my list?" She hadn't thought about that. "Makwi, you don't have to make it an epic poem."

Tordug chuckled and slapped Makwi's shoulder. "She aims high. You'd better stay up later at night or take more watches on the trail to finish her epic."

Makwi crossed his arms. "Might be that long before all this is over." He scratched the back of his head. "Whenever this is over." He squinted one eye as he shifted his gaze between Tordug and Limbreth. "When will it be over?"

Tordug brushed his mustache. "Don't know. Prophecy and all that, you know. But I guess we're in it this far. Might as well see it through." He nudged Limbreth with his elbow. "You know, just in case you need an epic poem."

Makwi laughed.

Limbreth laughed and took a sip of wine, then winked at the dwarves. "Well, I am taller and prettier than you too, so I need a lot of lines to cover everything. I mean, I do everything for this group as it is." She leaned back and crossed her arms. "I expect my list will get long."

Makwi scratched his cheek. "Just like a woman to take all the credit and make it longer."

Limbreth glanced back at the door of the private room when Hastra bolted out of it. She arched an eyebrow as the Withling scurried up the stairs. "What's she up to now?" Always a mystery with Hastra. But then, they needed to find this prophesied arrow soon. "I hope Athson makes it soon, if he's coming this way."

"He must. He needs supplies." Tordug shrugged and sighed. "It's good to be out of the wild, at least for the night."

Limbreth stroked her braid and tossed it over her shoulder. "If he arrives soon, it will be just ahead of those trolls. Don't get used to a comfy bed. I doubt we stay in one place too long with that lot on our heels."

Makwi yawned. "I'd fight the whole army of them for a bed tonight. It's been since Ezhandun that we slept in bed."

Limbreth stretched her stiff left arm. "Or slept a whole night without standing watch."

Tordug raised his mug. "To a good bed and no watches in the night."

Limbreth and Makwi joined the toast.

Hastra slipped back down the stairwell, this time bearing an arrow in her hands. Her glance passed over Limbreth as she hustled into the secluded back room. What was that Withling doing with an arrow? "What's Hastra's sister's name? Can't remember." Wait, if she had an arrow...? Limbreth's eyes narrowed as she watched the doorway. Light shone with white intensity in the crack between the door and the floor. She gulped. Where they doing something...miraculous in there? Best not bring attention to it.

"What's that, gell?" Tordug set his mug down and tore a piece of bread to sop up the gravy on his plate. "I think it's Zelma. You remember, Makwi?"

Makwi sloshed ale in his mug. "Think that's right. Not much for names, you know."

Tordug chuckled. "Yeah, who's that other one we're looking for? You know, with the bow and all?"

Makwi snorted and scratched his head. "Can't recall."

Limbreth snorted. "Well, I wish Athson would find his way here." She had a view the dwarves didn't. Maybe no one else saw what was going on in that room. She swallowed. There were mainly elves here with the arrival of the fort garrisons, but a number of travelers stayed over at the station too. Any of them could be Rokan or serving Magdronu in some way. She resisted twisting in her chair to look over her shoulder and stroked her braid again. She ignored Tordug's chatter with Makwi, the latter answering with dour grunts or comments as he finished his meal.

Over the noise of the room, Limbreth heard wisps of voices from that room. It was undoubtedly Withling prayers.

She stared at the door and waited as a few minutes passed. Perhaps a guard was needed at that door. She pushed her half-eaten bowl of stew away and scooted her chair from the table to stand. She could do the job.

The door opened to a soft glow as Hastra and the other two Withlings left the room. They shut the door and stepped farther along the hallway, out of Limbreth's line of vision.

Limbreth's gaze locked on the door. Whatever they'd done, something the Withlings had blessed was left in that unguarded room. That wasn't good. She stood abruptly.

"You gonna eat that?" Makwi pointed to Limbreth's ignored bowl.

"Uh, no." She spared a short glance at the table. "I'm not hungry just now."

Makwi shrugged. "More for me, I guess." He pulled the bowl of stew close and spooned the contents into his mouth.

"Uh, yeah, go ahead."

Limbreth walked toward the darkened hallway and the dining room door. At the door, she paused and listened to the Withlings just around the corner at the back door of the station. Their voices rose and fell in discussion, but she heard none of the details. Instead the room drew her attention. Whatever was inside shouldn't be left unguarded. No doubt about it.

She opened the door and peeked inside. Her breath left her, and she gaped at the sight. An arrow, lying on the table, glowed with white light.

She glanced each way, stepped into the room, and pushed the door almost closed. The glow and the silence of the room left her speechless and with the desire to tread softly. She tiptoed across the room and gazed in silent wonder at the arrow. It must be the prophesied arrow. Limbreth swallowed a sudden lump in her throat. They'd made it with a blessing from a common arrow. Where had Hastra gotten it?

It didn't matter. What did matter was keeping this safe for Athson.

The arrow pulsed with light.

Limbreth reached for it. Was it hot? She felt no heat from it. She held her breath for some reason, touched the shaft, and took hold of it. She gasped, and her eyes widened as she held the arrow in both hands, afraid to drop it. Her emotions whirled before sound bubbled out of her.

She laughed. Joy filled her thoughts. It was so wonderful, this miracle, this blessing. She laughed louder.

"What have you done?"

Limbreth turned, her uncontrollable joy shaking her body. Hastra and her other companions stood in the doorway, their eyes wide and jaws slack. "It has come. It's so wonderful."

Hastra crossed the room to Limbreth and reached for the arrow. "Give it to me, Limbreth."

Limbreth snatched the arrow from Hastra's reach. "No, you must not touch it." Her sudden shift in seriousness surprised even Limbreth. What was going on? "I have to keep it safe."

The Withling's eyelids fluttered wider, and her nostrils flared. "You can't—"

"Shut the door." The gaunt man pushed the wild-eyed woman with unruly red hair into the room. "Hold on, Hastra." He moved and stood at the Withling's side. "What's done is done here. Nothing happens by chance with these items."

Hastra shook her head. "No, we have to protect it, Howart."

Limbreth pulled away. "No, you cannot touch it. Only Athson can have it. It's the prophesied arrow, the white arrow. I'm to hold it for him until he comes for it. His enemies must not get it."

The door opened, and the other woman flinched, startled as Tordug and Makwi peered into the room. They too gaped, wide-eyed. The red-haired Withling sighed. "Uh-oh. This is getting out of hand, fast."

Hastra groaned, then hissed under her breath. "Don't just stand there, Zelma. Get them in here. They're with me. Quickly, now, before the whole station finds out. Magdronu would set the place afire tonight with this news."

Zelma whisked the dwarves into the room and shut the door. "You two, stand guard on the door. Make yourselves useful while we sort this out."

Tordug lined up at the door with Makwi but stroked his beard. "What's going on?"

Zelma cackled and then whispered, "Prophecy. The arrow prepared as we foretold, as the sign in the night sky portends."

Limbreth held it out for everyone to see as a grin of joy spread on her face. "Isn't it wonderful?"

Hastra cleared her throat. "And Limbreth's taken hold of a blessed item of prophecy. It can have odd effects, like unrestrained joy." She reached for the arrow again. "But she shouldn't have it."

"It can also cause a strong sense of protectiveness." Howart motioned to Limbreth and the arrow but faced Hastra. "You see? It's done. She's the protector."

Hastra's eyes narrowed, and she spoke in a whisper, "But we planned how to handle this. Magdronu will try to steal it from her."

Limbreth drew one of her swords in an instant. "Then let him come. He'll get a taste of an ax-maid's wrath."

Makwi chuckled. "Another item on the list for my composition."

"Hush, while we sort this out." Hastra turned back to Limbreth. "Listen to me. What you feel, it's just a side effect, like drinking too much ale with these two." She thumbed over her shoulder at the dwarves.

Tordug huffed. "We don't drink too much. We haven't had

anything hard since Ezhandun." He belched and covered his mouth.

Limbreth backed away and lifted her sword. "You can't have it."

Howart crossed his arms. "You see, Hastra? It's decided. Eloch has chosen the protector." He gazed at Limbreth. "And by the looks of it, a good one, if she's an ax-maid." He turned to the dwarves. "Is that true?"

Tordug, still wide-eyed in the glow of the white arrow, nodded. "Yup. She's even got death-grip." He patted Makwi on the shoulder. "Makwi's composing all her exploits, and she just keeps adding to them." He shook his head. "Protector of the prophesied arrow? That's a good one, Makwi."

Zelma cackled again. "Sister, what's done is done. We need a plan to move."

Limbreth let her sword point drop a little. "Are we settled then?" She peered at Hastra.

The old Withling frowned, then sighed and nodded as she slouched. "I suppose it's out of our hands now. Literally."

"Good choice." Limbreth sheathed her sword. Sudden joy erupted from her in laughter. "It's so wonderful. What are we to do now? Go find Athson?"

Hastra shook her head. "No, he'll come here if he's smart. But I think we should get to the city as quickly as possible. We'll leave word with Marston for Athson to come to the city." She shifted her gaze between Howart, Zelma, and then Limbreth. "We'll need more than just us in case word somehow gets back to Magdronu's agents." She motioned to Limbreth. "We need to stay ahead of them. Let's find a way to hide that." She turned to the dwarves. "One of you, please find Gweld and Marston. We need to know if these elves can be our escort."

Makwi left in search of the two elves.

Hastra sat and rubbed her face with her hand. "This is just

a fine thing. We get the arrow and nearly have a fight over it."
She eyed Limbreth. "So it's the White Arrow, is it?"

Limbreth snickered, then answered with sudden seriousness, "It is. And I'll guard it with my life."

Hastra closed her eyes and held her forehead with a sigh, then eyed Limbreth. "It might just come to that."

∾

MAGDRONU-AS-GWELD TOOK a deep breath as he considered what he'd just seen. The prophesied arrow, this White Arrow as Limbreth had named it, created from the blessing of Withlings. He touched the quiver of arrows that lay on his bed in the room. They'd used one from his supply. How neatly and ironically done by Eloch. He should destroy Marston's Station this very night in fire. Magdronu-as-Gweld shook his head. He couldn't risk revealing himself. He needed Athson to give him the Bow of Hart. Ownership by blood permeated the nature of the relic from its creation. That much he'd sensed long ago. Mere theft of the bow transferred nothing to him so his magic wouldn't work on it. But the arrow had been his and that made all the difference.

"We go morning, eh?" Ralda's voice rumbled like thunder in the small room.

"Yes. Have you ever traveled on a boat?" Magdronu-as-Gweld glanced at the giant. He knew the probable answer. Best not to destroy the place tonight, but he needed a plan.

"No. River small at Ralda's home. Giants walk in them." Ralda's hands and fingers told more.

Magdronu-as-Gweld didn't care what Ralda meant otherwise. "Well, as you remember, the river is wide and deep through the forest. Boats will carry most of the ranger garrison back to the city. We'll go with them for the best speed. Boats don't get tired, you know." They didn't, but even trolls did. But what mattered now was the arrow. And the bow.

Magdronu-as-Gweld turned back to his gear. His eyes narrowed as he gazed at the quiver again. Hastra had taken the last remaining arrow he'd had when Athson had recovered the Bow of Hart. That was when that magic escaped him. He scratched his ear. Strange, that it should be used for the blessing. He stood and paced. No, it wasn't strange. Eloch twisted everything to his benefit all too often. Why had he not seen it coming? No matter. He just needed a plan to take it.

"Uh, Ralda?"

"Hmm?" The giant looked up from his packing.

Magdronu-as-Gweld wanted to laugh at the giant's deep voice. One day soon he'd show Ralda, and everyone else, the power and terror of his roar. "Mind if I have some time to meditate alone?"

The giant quickly finished stuffing his belongings into the expansive pack he carried. "Go hear elf song." He patted Magdronu-as-Gweld's shoulder with surprising gentleness and left the room.

Magdronu-as-Gweld sat on the bed and crossed his legs beneath him, assuming his feigned meditation, and called to Corgren and Paugren for the second time this night. He waited for their response to the summons, imagining their rings flashing his urgency. It was fortunate that they now had magic from the shrine in Rok. Without that supply, meager though it was compared to the lost one in the Drelkhaz, their power to act over such distances, to carry out his plans, would be far more limited. He needed them for the new shrine and more now.

"M-master, we answer," the brothers stammered in unison as their communication spell opened.

"We have a problem." Magdronu-as-Gweld let his displeasure at the situation flow along the spell. *"The arrow has come on the*

words of Withling blessing." He avoided telling them it was from his own supply. *"I have the Bane in position. Paugren, you and one of the sisters continue after Athson and this other Withling. Leave the other two sisters at work creating the new shrine. Corgren, bring the troll army with all haste to the city. We travel by boat."*

"We obey, mighty one."

Magdronu-as-Gweld felt the brothers' obedience over the spell, but still the wandering doubt from Paugren. As expected. His concern for Corgren, perhaps.

Corgren stirred in the spell. *"What will you do with the Bane?"*

Magdronu-as-Gweld opened his eyes and stared at himself in the mirror across the room. *"Steal the arrow."* He let part of his true form loose, and his eyes flared like flame for a few moments before he released the communication spell with a casual snap and summoned the Bane into the room.

The spirit, a manifestation tied to Athson's familial curse, darkened the room. He must move quickly in this, before the Withlings or Limbreth were alarmed. He whispered, "Go into the night. Follow the princess from along the river and steal the arrow she carries."

The Bane stepped through the outside wall into the night beyond. Magdronu-as-Gweld leaned against the wall. He'd still win. He'd still beat Eloch's prophecy, arrow or not.

CHAPTER SEVEN

Limbreth sat up in her bed and fumbled in the dark for a sword. It was close. The Bane. Darkness shrouded the room, so she snatched the blanket off the White Arrow. The blessed arrow's light lit the room in an instant. She drew a sword and stood, waiting for the Bane. But the presence faded. She whirled, lit a candle, wrapped the arrow in cloth, and shoved it into her pack. She needed to be ready to leave. Ready for anything. Somehow, Magdronu or Corgren knew it was at the station.

Voices sounded outside her door, and Limbreth's heart leapt into her throat. She stood on guard with her swords when someone knocked.

"Who is it?"

"Hastra. Are you well?"

Limbreth sighed at the muffled answer. She threw the bolt and opened the door, then stepped back into on-guard position again. Just in case something else was going on. "It was near."

Hastra motioned to Makwi, her face tight with concern. "Stand here and watch. Give a call if you see it."

Makwi saluted dwarf-style. "I know what to do and what not to do with it."

Hastra entered the room and shut the door behind her. "I know it was near. I woke Makwi to stand guard. At least a little warning will help. I should have stayed with you, but I wanted to see my sister." She sat on the opposite bed and cleared her throat. "Where is it?" Her eyes fell on Limbreth's pack.

Limbreth lifted her chin. "I have it safe." She sheathed her swords and turned back to the bed. "Thanks for coming." Protective, that was what she felt. That, and giddy from joy without the mention or feeling of threat. Even now, Limbreth wanted nothing more than to gaze on the wonder, such was the attraction. The arrow and protecting it, giving it to Athson, kept all her attention. She swallowed, opened her pack, and checked for the wrapped arrow. *Keep it safe for him.*

Hastra rolled onto the bed and crossed her arms. "Get some sleep. We'll leave early for the landing on the river and the boat trip to Auguron City. It will be a safer trip, fewer ways to get at us."

Limbreth rolled into her blanket and sighed, one hand upon a sword-hilt and the other touching the arrow in her pack. She watched the Withling in the waving candlelight. "You're angry with me for taking the arrow."

The Withling swallowed, then shrugged. "More of an issue that you weren't in the plan to be its keeper. But there is some disappointment after working all these years to see it come to fruition."

Limbreth gripped her sword tightly. No one but Athson should truly possess it. "Well, things happened differently, I guess."

Hastra crossed the room to Limbreth and laid a hand on her shoulder. "Limbreth, I'm not your enemy in this. I'm on your side and not a threat."

Limbreth sat up on the bed and shrugged Hastra's hand

away. "Agreed. But I'm the keeper of this arrow now, and you can't just order me about either. We'll have to work together. You know the most about this, you and the other Withlings, but you need to hear my thoughts too."

"That's what Howart said." Hastra laid her hands in her lap and blinked at Limbreth. "It is hard to listen, I suppose, when I've been responsible for doing so much." She crossed her arms. "Very well, then, do you have a suggestion?"

Limbreth ran her fingers along her braid and felt for the arrow in the pack where it was wrapped. So Howart spoke for her already. She liked him. A patient, kind man. She needed to stick closer to this Withling if Hastra listened to him. "Well, perhaps we should create a ruse. We can switch boats when we can, or act like the arrow is with a different person at times. If someone about is up to no good, it will keep them guessing. Also, the Bane won't know where to start, and that will keep it off me."

Hastra lifted one hand to her chin and stroked it. "A good idea, I think. We can get other arrows and wrap them up to carry out the ruse. The more packs to check, the better." She paused and pointed at Limbreth. "We'll pair up in different boats with the fake arrows on each one. It will be harder to find. Are you ready to face the Bane, since it's already been near?"

Limbreth swallowed the sudden lump in her throat. *The Rokan dagger descended and stabbed her.* She blinked at the remembered fear and pain. But then, she'd fought the Bane on the altar. Her death-grip was some defense against it. She grinned and narrowed her vision as one hand squeezed the arrow and the other a sword. She lifted her left hand into Hastra's field of vision. "I have the death-grip, and it helped me at the Funnel. I can fend it off until you Withlings come." She closed her hand to a fist. "I am the keeper, and I'll face this enemy again as necessary."

The Withling nodded. "Good. We'll play the ruse for the sake of confusion, talk openly about who has it at times." She raised her eyebrows and wagged a finger at Limbreth. "But just remember, you can't defeat it alone, only hold it long enough for assistance to arrive."

Limbreth grinned. "Let it come." She was the keeper of the White Arrow until Athson arrived. They'd keep moving and throw off the enemy, but she'd do what was necessary for Athson's sake and the prophecy.

Hastra went looking for more arrows, and Limbreth withdrew the holy arrow from her pack, unwrapped it, and gazed in wonder at it, as awe swelled in her chest and her breath accelerated. This was the hope of the prophecy. She'd die to protect it if necessary.

∼

THE ELVEN RANGER garrison of Western Auguron continued its retreat in the face of superior numbers by marching to the river landing north of Marston's Station. Magdronu-as-Gweld went with them and his companions. The Bane awaited well out of the way near the river. He watched Limbreth often. They played their little game with several arrows, but she really carried the one that mattered to him. He'd have the arrow sooner or later.

He rode with his friends along the line of troops to the river and considered his various moves. He'd recovered from the setbacks in Rok and at the Funnel. His magic flowed once again to his servants. As for the bow and Athson, he'd have to take that when the opportunity arose in Auguron, since he'd not arrived. But Paugren hunted the other Withling. That one had proved disruptive for a while now, and Magdronu would see the problem removed, permanently. This Apeth Stellin, long presumed dead, bore no chance against his servants now.

Of that, Magdronu was certain. The shrine and his growing power would tip everything his way in the coming days.

"You can see it this evening, dear." Hastra fended Limbreth away as a ruse that she held the arrow.

Magdronu-as-Gweld smirked as his gaze prowled among the others. Ralda might be watching again. Magdronu wondered if the giant suspected something since Ezhandun. He showed no sign of it. *Practice care with him. Just a while longer.* But Hastra's ruse didn't fool Magdronu.

Limbreth sighed. "Yes, Withling." She feigned being disappointed, but the Grendonese woman was a poor actress. She rode with her chin up, her eyes searching, and a hand ready to a sword. She carried the so-called White Arrow, if anyone. So protective and yet so vulnerable to the Bane.

Magdronu-as-Gweld roved the forest for several days, feigning his scouting duties. He needed freedom to shift forms, to hunt. He'd have precious little time on those boats. He couldn't attend sacrifices in Rok, but he needed blood regardless. Perhaps a few victims on the boats might help. There was always a bit of mishap among troops. He'd add his own quiet mayhem to the mix.

Several days passed until they came to the landing, a river wharf that extended into this wide section of the Auguron River gliding west. Several barges and larger transport boats lay assembled to ferry people escaping west. The rangers boarded in orderly detail. Limbreth and Hastra found one boat to their liking, large enough for them to sleep below the deck in the storage space. Their other companions took to other vessels as planned. Horses lined other barges for the trip.

One of the other Withlings, the man Howart, gazed at him, and Magdronu-as-Gweld nodded toward him. "Withling, I hope you like travel on boats."

"It's been a long while since I was on water. I think I'll spend a few hours gaining my balance." Howart shook his head. "Not like you elves. You seem to always have your balance in all situations."

Magdronu-as-Gweld offered a respectful salute. "Indeed, we are blessed with long life that gives us practice in many settings like this. Lean on a ranger's shoulder, if you need it."

The appearance of these other Withlings represented a slight change in Magdronu's plans, but he'd adjust for them. Kill them all in the end, and he'd be rid of the entire order. He cupped an elbow in one hand and raised the other hand for a speculative scratch on his elven-disguised cheek. He'd have them all soon. Not soon enough, but soon. Thankfully, Howart and Zelma boarded another craft with Danilla.

The barges and boats cast off and weighed their anchors as they were filled. Boatmen poled and guided the little fleet into the deeper current with the morning sun glistening off the dark blue water. The craft smelled of the river mingled with that of horse. The sound of water sloshing and lapping against the boats formed a cadence to the calls of the crewmen and the rangers. Magdronu grinned inwardly. A seemingly simple retreat from overwhelming numbers of trolls on the march. They never guessed their worst enemy stood among them. He resisted a snort of derisive heat and leaned against the rail while the crewmen did their work and Limbreth acted out her part of the ruse in another boat further back from his own.

Magdronu lost sight of Limbreth's vessel. A boat limited his prey's movement, but not the Bane's. He'd move his piece of the game and capture that important item soon enough. He almost chuckled at the despair the capture of the arrow was certain to cause. He'd run through his necessary act until that occurred. Necessary until Athson handed over the Bow of Hart, and then he'd reveal himself.

CHAPTER EIGHT

Athson and Apeth Stellin arrived late in the day at Marston's Station amid the hustle and scurry of travelers escaping the oncoming troll army. Within the station, Athson found turmoil as people barked demands for supplies and Marston's workers busied themselves with their own evacuation while also selling their supplies.

"Panic's setting in." Apeth Stellin stepped out of the doorway before two scrambling merchants and other travelers trampled them. "I wonder if you can make it east now."

Athson hid his irritation for the moment. He'd head east, trolls or not. "I can swing north through the forest, maybe take a boat upriver."

A Grendonese merchant paused in passing. "There aren't any boats to be had now. The ranger garrison took most downriver to the city. Most other vessels have fled or withdrawn in either direction at the command of the rangers, lest the trolls get their paws on them. They want to hold them up in the forest so they have to forage and travel slower."

Athson regarded Apeth as the merchant rushed away on

his own affairs. He cast a word at the departing man, "Thanks for the news."

The merchant waved and kept going.

"Everyone's on their own, I suppose." Apeth beckoned Athson after him. "We'd best speak with Marston, if he's around."

Athson veered toward the counters. "I need supplies. You watch the mule for me. I've no news for Marston, except the obvious and my own."

"What's this?" Marston stepped out of the crowd.

Athson sighed. Another delay in his quest for his mother. He needed to gather supplies and push east faster than these empty conversations allowed.

The tall elf eyed Athson, his pointed ears almost erect like Spark's. "I guess you'll join the guards protecting travelers evacuating to Auguron City?"

That reminded Athson of his invisible dog, and he glanced around for the mountain hound, catching sight of his fur through the bustling crowd near the mule. Maybe the mule was safe with the dog.

He opened his mouth to answer Marston's question, but Apeth spoke first.

"We've news from further east."

Marston's blue eyes fixed on the Withling. "Don't I know you?"

Apeth Stellin shrugged and tilted his head so his hat brim partially hid his face. "I pass through here on occasion. But I've had the recent acquaintance of this ranger. We were attacked by several troll scouts as we came east."

People milling nearby paused a moment at this news and then re-doubled their efforts to obtain supplies, their shouts louder.

Marston groaned. "As if we didn't have enough trouble getting these people served and moving." The crowd pressed around them, and the elf beckoned them away from the counters. "Come, let me hear your tale. I'm commanding auxiliaries to supplement the few hundred rangers left to guard the road."

Athson cast a hungry eye at the counters as they followed Marston into a quieter section of the station. Here a few rangers readied their gear at a cluster of dining tables. Athson needed to leave fast to head east, and now he needed to escape Marston's notice. He eyed Apeth, who ignored him. "Great. I'll never get moving now."

Marston turned to them and slapped Athson on the shoulder. "Good to see you made it. Hastra claimed you were coming soon." He eyed the Bow of Hart with arched eyebrows but said nothing of the relic, obvious by its white color.

Athson's jaw worked a moment. "What? How did she get here?" She'd been prisoner in Rok, with his mother.

"Yeah, came through a few days earlier with that bunch you left with months ago."

Athson found a bench and sat as he gaped at the elf. "They're alive?" He stared at his hands a moment and then raised his gaze to Marston. "Who was with her?"

Marston paused. "She said you'd been separated. You thought they were dead? None of them said much about where they'd been. But everyone was with her except you. That Grendonese woman claimed her white horse and—"

Athson leaped to his feet. "Limbreth? That can't be." But he'd dreamed of her giving him something, light. He paced away as confusion settled in his mind. He returned to face Marston. "All of them, you said. They were well?"

Marston nodded and glanced at Apeth before he looked Athson in the eyes. "Yes. Even Limbreth. I'd remember her anywhere, the Silver Lady. Anyway, they left with the main part of the garrison several days back for the landings on the river. A man and a woman arrived in the evening and had a private meeting with Hastra, after which there was some argument among the whole lot of them. Oh, and Hastra's bunch returned with a middle-aged woman who—"

Athson gasped, and his gaze raced in every direction. *That can't be.* But Hastra had escaped Rok. "Who was the woman? Did she have brown hair going gray?" He searched his memory of the brief glimpse of his mother he'd received when Corgren threatened his captive mother and Hastra, revealing them through that spell. "She—she had crow's feet wrinkles at her eyes." He latched onto the features he remembered. "She would look like me."

"Yes, that's her. Called her Danilla." Marston grabbed Athson. "Is she your mother? I remember when they found you years ago. I thought you were an orphan."

Tears welled in Athson's eyes as he sat down hard. He wiped his face with his palms. His voice was husky. "Uh, yes. Apparently, she was held captive in Rok. My father—Corgren had him. He died on the Funnel with me just a few weeks back. How did Hastra get my mother free? And this far so fast?" It was a miracle. But then, she was a Withling. He glanced at Apeth, who ignored him. Apeth knew something. He turned his gaze back to Marston. "Can we catch them at the landings?"

Marston shook his head and spoke with a softer tone. "They're several days ahead, Athson. Your best chance is to try one of the landings farther west, but they'll go faster."

"Where can I get supplies? I need to go."

"Hold on—we'll need every hand we can to get this mob west without trolls catching them."

Athson displayed his bow in one hand. It actually worked, at least normally. He'd used up the last of his arrows shooting attacking trolls several days earlier. "You can guess what this is if Hastra's told you something. I can see it in your eyes. I can't let it be taken."

Marston spread his hands and leaned closer, his voice

lowered. "I understand it's important. But we need to protect people too. Make sure there are no thieves and thugs in among them."

Athson paced a moment and then faced Marston. "Sure, I'll help guard against the latter, but I need to travel as fast as I can rather than stand rearguard. Can I get supplies?"

Marston watched Athson, then glanced at Apeth. "Sure, I can issue you some supplies. That quiver's empty, so get some arrows too. I'll get you assigned with the next group of guards going out with travelers. They'll have a wagon of supplies and work to keep people from squabbling and stealing." The elf chuckled. "I don't know which will be worse, panicked merchants or the trolls. It's good to see you. And equally good to know your mother is alive and well. Let me issue some orders." He strode away, called for another of his auxiliaries, and issued commands.

Apeth sat and sighed his weariness away. "Well, you changed your mind fast. Told you to come this way. West was your path all along."

Athson leaned forward, placing his hands on his knees, his face square in Apeth's. "You knew about Hastra and my mother all along, didn't you?"

The old Withling smiled and Marston suddenly found something elsewhere to issue instructions. "Hastra actually made the same mistake you did." He lowered his voice and glanced at the other elven rangers preparing nearby them. "Thought I was Eloch, like you."

"You mean you were with her?"

"Helped the two of them escape."

Athson grabbed Apeth by the lapels of his coat. "Why didn't you tell me? Did you—" He choked back a sob. "Did you know about Limbreth and others being alive?" How? His face twitched with relief. His friends were alive. Limbreth was alive.

Apeth easily pried Athson's hands loose. "I get around, Athson. I've helped you more than once since Chokkra, Hastra too. You know what it's like to be a Withling. I can't tell you everything. I didn't know about Limbreth or the others until now, except for your dream."

"But why not?"

Apeth invited Athson to sit beside him

Athson's suddenly weak knees led him to the bench. "Well, out with it."

Apeth leaned close, his voice low. "Look, I meant no harm, but you were set on your own course. I couldn't tell you, because your choices are your own. You're supposed to become a Withling. No, let me finish." Apeth raised a hand to silence Athson's disagreement. "You have the talent, but you must come to trust Eloch yourself. You had to find out things beyond you for yourself. Athson, you've been caught in this familial curse your whole life. You have to learn to ignore it as a Withling, trust Eloch, and make his path your own. That's why you had to find out now and I had to remain silent. The question lies before you. Will you serve Eloch as a Withling?" Apeth's gaze searched Athson's. "You have the gift already. You just need to trust and choose to do Eloch's will rather than follow your own cursed way. You've been given other gifts to help you along."

Athson looked away. "You mean I might have known sooner except for my own hard-headedness?" He looked back to Apeth.

The Withling shrugged and pushed his hat back. "I can't say that for sure. But that curse sure ties you up on knots. Those fits you had and all that. You've believed a lot of negative ideas for so long."

The bow leaned against Athson. His hands trembled as he grasped it. "Does this work?"

"Likely so, put to the proper use." Apeth tapped Athson's

sword sheath with a fingernail. "This works, doesn't it? It's blessed of Eloch."

The sword worked, and there was no denying it now that Athson knew the truth of it. So the bow would work, and he'd just made all the wrong choices at the Funnel. And Limbreth still lived, beyond all his hopes. How could he have acted differently at the Funnel? By listening. He'd learned to listen to what? His heart, regarding instructions about the sword. No, it was Eloch's voice speaking to him. He glanced at Apeth. The old Withling was correct, much as Athson hated to admit it. Athson had been acting like a Withling at times, hearing instructions to use the sword and experiencing dreams. If only this curse hadn't distracted him so much.

Then the truth flooded his understanding. He'd been pulled by that curse to all the wrong decisions much of his life, certainly since Eagle's Aerie. The fits affected him until the blessed sword came into his possession. He chuckled against the tremble in his body. One good decision there. Had he been listening then, acting like a Withling?

But there was more, he realized. He'd thought he didn't need Withlings and Eloch. He'd thought Eloch didn't help him at all. He had fallen into believing that Eloch did nothing for him, added nothing to his life. But Eloch had helped all this time. If he'd just listened, there would have been answers. There were answers anyway. His mother had been helped. The others were safe. It was his cursed stubbornness and wrong decisions that led to so many problems, though he doubted there wouldn't have been troubles along the way.

Athson swallowed hard and blinked a sidelong gaze at Apeth Stellin. "Will it mean the curse is gone? What do I do to become—" He glanced around at the others in the room and leaned closer to Apeth. "To become a Withling?"

"Good to hear you're getting it now." The Withling patted Athson's leg. "I don't think that curse will be lifted just yet. But you have that sword. Use it often, and just listen. Learn to listen, and then act the best you can with the instructions you understand. The more you do that, speak and act according to what you hear of Eloch, the more you'll see and understand. But you'll battle that curse for now, I think." He shrugged. "Doesn't matter if you can hear, though. Other than that, I'll give you a blessing."

Athson chuckled. "What now, a special set of words or a prayer?"

Apeth paused and considered that. "I'll ask you a few questions and offer the blessing. But first, let me go check on that mule. You watch our things, and I'll be back. We'll find a quiet place without distractions." The Withling stood and battled his way out of the station to check the mule.

At a touch to his sword-hilt, deep calm entered Athson's thoughts. It was the correct decision. He'd be a Withling. He'd do what was necessary with the Bow of Hart.

∾

CORGREN STOOD over his maps of Auguron lying on the carved, wooden table, information gleaned from his long time disguised as Domikyas the Rokan trader. Thank the Great One he no longer wore that magical disguise. Within this northernmost ranger fort saved from fire, Corgren chose comfortable quarters furnished with a proper bed with a feathered mattress and woolen blankets from which to direct his troll army, even to the smallest of scouts. His back knotted with residual pain from his wound even seated in the padded chair and elven officer left behind—curse that traitor. But then, a traitor ever acted the traitor. He smiled With magic now flowing better from Magdronu, Corgren traveled often to gather reports from his far-ranging troll army.

He moved pieces on his map. The elves fled on the river

and sought to protect fleeing travelers on their road. He shrugged. No matter. He'd burn every station on the way to Auguron City, every farm and every little hamlet. The smoke of his—Magdronu's—ravaging hordes signaled eventual triumph for them.

Light flashed at Corgren's finger. Three for urgent, but not the color of Magdronu. Paugren called. Corgren spoke the word of acknowledgment but not that for communication. Let Paugren, who possessed a limited supply of blood on his mission, hold the spell if he needed to speak. Instead, he dropped the coins of the houses of Hart into the bowl in slow succession. Let Paugren wait as Corgren had waited in anguish until their magic was restored. He smiled. He dropped the last of the coins, and spoke the spell, each word pronounced with distinct care.

Pale blue light flared over the bowl, and Paugren's drawn face flickered in its center. The magic wasn't as strong as before but soon would be. *"Brother, you have news?"*

Paugren frowned. *"Do you punish me for your previous suffering? It was not my fault you—"*

"You can quibble all you like, since you hold the spell, Paugren." Corgren schooled his face to an even stare.

His brother swallowed his anger. *"We've spotted the Withling and Athson. They travel with the elven guards to quell thieves and quarrels on the road. It seems fear among the defenseless drains resources from the rangers and causes trouble."*

"I would think you know what to do, then. There'll be fewer to stop you."

Sweat beaded Paugren's face in the spell's pallid light, but he managed a smile of invitation. *"We'll let them spread out on the trail, then strike at night. We'll make the Withling's death look like brigands."* He cocked his head. *"Perhaps you'd like to be there when we kill this one. He's advising Athson, teaching him Withling secrets."*

Corgren stroked his bearded chin. *"Perhaps I might. My*

primary duties are with this grand army of ours, but a little diversion might keep things interesting."

"Cass and I will contact you when the time is right." Paugren closed the spell.

Corgren appreciated the brevity. The longer the communication, the more likely was their discovery. But with their newly restored lines of magic, they could afford a few luxuries as they carried out their missions for their Master. He smiled. And there would only be more magic available with the new shrine, though Paugren's mission delayed that somewhat.

Eyes traveling across the maps, Corgren chuckled. They had the luxury of time. Victory was inevitable.

~

MAGDRONU-AS-GWELD GAZED into the reflection of sky mirrored in the rippling river water. He'd chosen a barge filled with rangers for his part of the ruse. He suppressed a chuckle at the thought. He bore a fake arrow in his quiver, wrapped in cloth. Far too obvious for their needs, but certainly something to bring pause to any attacker. Far too easy to discard as the real White Arrow.

He closed his eyes and let the breeze brush across his face, yearning to fly as himself rather than float on this barge. Magdronu-as-Gweld opened his eyes to the forest drifting by. The quiet talk among the elves was a welcome change to the foolishness of the group with which he'd traveled for months. *Especially that oafish giant.* He'd chosen separation from them for some solitude while he toyed with them over the arrow.

Magdronu-as-Gweld waved to the familiar figures of the dwarves and Ralda, who traveled in the second barge from the one he occupied. They bore an arrow each, wrapped in cloth. As any if them would be trusted with such an item. The others waved in return.

Magdronu-as-Gweld sneered inwardly. Those three were more likely to drop the White Arrow in the river than protect it.

Beyond that floated one of the smaller boats in this pitiful fleet. There the other two Withlings and Danilla each carried their own fake arrows. And even farther down the line of boats and barges, Hastra and Limbreth traveled in a larger hauler mostly carrying what travelers and merchants fit aboard. Crewmen poled and steered each vessel but mostly let them drift on the current of the river.

His companions signaled often among themselves that all was well. They'd set up a series of signals based on ranger hand-signs so they could communicate anything amiss. So far, Magdronu allowed nothing. But he'd soon let the Bane make several "failed" attempts at the arrow. Best to let them think the ruse had worked.

When night fell and most of his fellow rangers had settled for the night after a meal from their rations, Magdronu called to the Bane. *'Come'*.

The creature glided over the surface of the river in the shadows of the night. The rangers slept with only a few guards set, thinking themselves safe on the river as they outdistanced the troll army. The Bane slipped over the rail of the barge as Magdronu waited, feigning rest, the fake arrow where the Bane could easily steal it.

'Take the covered arrow.' He needed witnesses.

The Bane grasped the arrow and withdrew it from Magdronu-as-Gweld's quiver.

The whisper of cloth against the arrows and quiver stood out in the silence. Magdronu-as-Gweld grunted and gasped. "Help, something's aboard!"

The Bane fled overboard and glided away.

Magdronu-as-Gweld pointed to it. "There!" He set an arrow to string and released it at the Bane.

Rangers clamored at Magdronu-as-Gweld's warning. Some loosed arrows too. An officer approached and questioned Magdronu-as-Gweld. "What was that?"

Magdronu-as-Gweld leaned over the edge of the barge's rail. The Bane slipped into the shadows of the riverbank. "Something that has haunted the trail of my companions and I for months. We feared it might appear. But I doubt it will trouble us again."

"Why?"

Magdronu-as-Gweld turned to the officer's concerned face. "Because it knows what I carried wasn't what it sought."

He withheld a laugh. He had his witnesses, and the others would be concerned. But he'd lull them with false security regardless.

CHAPTER NINE

Athson and Apeth left with the next squad of guards to escort travelers, though they had barely rested. The hum of anxiety at Marston's Station faded as the group put distance behind them. Athson sighed. He and Apeth had found no time for the Withling's blessing. It would have to wait until they stopped. Urgency to get moving superseded the prayer. Athson and Apeth needed to catch up to their companions if possible. Athson slouched in the saddle of the horse provided by the rangers. It would be quieter at a camp than at the station.

Beside him rode Apeth on the mule. Spark trotted in and out of the forest and among the travelers, who dragged their feet.

Athson leaned toward Apeth. "You'd think the trolls were weeks away."

The Withling merely grunted and scratched his side absently.

By Athson's count, there were at least seventy-five merchants and other travelers in this group of fleeing evacuees. He snorted to himself. Four rangers, including him—and two recovering from injuries sustained in accidents during the garrison evacuations—were not nearly enough to hold back a big fight among them, let alone intimidate any brigands operating on the road. If any trolls scouted this far ahead of the invading army, they'd certainly lose people. He shook his head and twisted in the saddle. Nothing on the road behind them.

How was he supposed to learn anything about being Withling while guarding a caravan? He doubted his decision after the shock of the news from Marston and the hasty departure settled into the plodding pace. He touched his sword, and the doubt faded. *Interesting.*

Letting his horse drift to the rear of the line of travelers, Athson faded farther back. They needed someone watching for anything amiss approaching from the east. He had just the idea for that, and he'd try it, now that he'd agreed to become a Withling. Doubt or not, he'd do something. Maybe it was Eloch's leading.

"Hey, Spark."

The mountain hound trotted close by Athson's horse and flicked its eyes his way. The dog's dark back and brown underbelly coat shimmered even in the late afternoon daylight.

"Anything watching us from close by?" Why not talk to him more?

Spark offered no sign of anything nearby, and his tail didn't wag. It did sometimes when asked a question, as Athson remembered. But Spark just trotted along the road without any apparent care, panting like any dog.

"Well, how about you follow farther back and bark if you spot anything?" Athson didn't know if it would work.

Spark wagged his tail and slowed until he was several hundred paces behind Athson's horse.

"Hmm, that worked." He should have gotten Spark involved in things much sooner. Better now than never.

When the merchants called for a halt far too early, Athson

sighed and instructed Spark to circle the area. The mountain hound trotted away, and Athson spotted him go past several times after he dismounted next to Apeth where the Withling had set their part of the camp away from the others.

The Withling started building a fire. "You having second thoughts?"

Athson settled his gear, careful to keep the Bow of Hart within reach. "I did, but I took your advice about making choices."

A little flame danced to life in the kindling, and Apeth carefully added more sticks and then larger pieces of wood. "What's that?"

"I grasped my sword, and the doubt went away."

Apeth nodded approval. "A good start. Stop listening to the wrong things. Won't be so easy for you all the time, though."

Athson sat at the growing campfire and warmed his hands. There was no snow here, but the late winter still brought a deep evening chill. "I'm also trying something else." He watched Spark circle by in the nearby forest.

Apeth added more wood to the fire and coughed as the smoke blew in his face. He waved a hand to clear it away. "Uh, have a care what you say. You don't have that much experience yet."

"Nothing like that. I've only heard Eloch when I hold the sword. It's about Spark.

Apeth nodded and fanned the smoke with his hat.

"Well, since we're so thin on guards, I set him to guarding behind us this afternoon and walking circuit of this camp."

The old Withling chuckled. "Wise, I'd say. I doubt you'll wear him thin any time soon. Let's eat, and we'll get down to our business, shall we?"

They ate rations from Marston and then watched the fire in silence. Smoke curled into the mostly bare limbs that swayed in the evening breeze. Spark slipped by again. Amazing—the dog did precisely as he asked. He snorted. All the times he and Gweld had argued about Spark, and now he'd set the dog to work. The elf would ask if he needed more Soul's Ease if he knew.

Apeth stirred. "What's so funny?"

Athson stared at the fire. "Just that my friend, Gweld, never believed Spark was real."

"Really?" The Withling sat up.

"Really. Always said I needed Soul's Ease to stop my hallucinations."

Apeth tilted his head. "I guess elves aren't always as thoughtful."

Athson brushed crumbs from his lap. "He just remembers what I was like with my fits. The sword helped me with those, though. I gave up the medicine, and Spark is there even when I touch the sword."

The Withling inhaled and yawned. "Those fits were from the curse. Spark's not."

Athson's brow furrowed. "I hadn't thought of that."

Silence passed for a while as the last rays of daylight succumbed to night. Apeth stirred from his thoughts and rubbed his hands together, extending them toward the campfire. "So you're going to be a Withling?"

"I guess so." Athson shrugged and scratched his ear. "I'm starting to act more and more like one. You said so yourself."

Apeth nodded and stared into the flames beneath his hands. "Will you follow Eloch's instructions the best you can, even to stay your hand or not speak, though you do not understand why?"

Athson sat up straighter and squared his shoulders. "Yes, I will."

"Will you help others in need as often as you can?"

"Yes, I will." Athson furrowed his brow again. Didn't he do

that already, as a ranger? Perhaps Apeth meant more than being a ranger. He scratched at his cheek in consideration.

"Do you forsake your own interests for those of serving Eloch as a Withling?" Apeth fixed his gaze on Athson.

Athson held his own gaze steady under the old Withling's unyielding stare. He swallowed. This was it. Committing to something beyond himself, beyond doing what he wanted. He'd done that plenty over this journey. How often had he chafed at Hastra? He realized how selfish he'd been all too often. What must his other companions think of him?

He cleared his throat. "Yes, I will do that."

There, he'd agreed, and now it was done. No more acting petulant. That was what he'd been often enough. Maybe it was the curse, maybe not, but he was determined to learn another way.

Apeth stood, edged around the fire, and touched Athson with his forefingers. "May Eloch dwell with you and guide in peace, no matter the troubles that surround. May you come to know his presence, hear his voice, and take action accordingly. May you be a balm to others in need." He withdrew back to his bedroll. "There, it's done."

Athson was a Withling. He didn't feel any different, but somehow he felt like a weight had lifted from his shoulders, from his thoughts. "Now what?"

The other Withling drew his blanket over himself. "Now I get some sleep while you stand watch."

"Spark can do that, I think."

"Oh yeah. Well, get some sleep, then."

∽

RALDA STOOD at the front of the boat. He'd forgotten what they called it, but *front* wasn't the right word. Funny how these boats had such odd names for their parts. Ralda watched for any signal from Gweld. These hand-signs were different from his people's. So simple, these motions. They conveyed nothing of emotion, color, or anything else.

The boat rocked slightly under Ralda's feet and left him only mildly unsettled. The first day was different, though. He had stumbled everywhere and almost fallen over the side. His head felt funny, and his stomach flopped some. He rubbed his belly. Thankfully that had passed.

His brow furrowed. Gweld bothered Ralda for some reason. Something was different about the elf since—he thought back— since Ezhandun at least. No, it was further back, but Ralda wasn't sure how far. But leaving Ezhandun had bothered him. That odd look from Gweld still puzzled Ralda.

Just before they'd left, he'd rested in the dwarven barracks and fallen asleep. Gweld had frowned at him over by the mirror. At the time, Ralda just thought he'd surprised the elf, but there was more in that passing expression. Something of— he tapped his cheek with a finger in thought—hate? No, not that. Malevolence. That fit better. Very odd for Gweld, who was respectful to everyone.

Movement from the barge ahead drew Ralda's attention. Gweld signaled, and Ralda squinted to see the gestures. *Arrow gone, Bane came.* Ralda's eyebrows climbed his forehead. So the Bane could get at them on the water like this? Not good.

Ralda turned and found Makwi, who stretched and yawned. "Makwi."

The dwarven champion moved near Ralda. "Good morning. Something from Gweld?"

"He hand-talk. Bane take his arrow." Ralda added with his hands that the encounter on a boat among so many elven rangers surprised him.

Makwi crossed his arms and gazed ahead. "Didn't think

that Bane could get at us so easily on the river. It's faster, but we are limited in movement. Did you answer his signal?"

"No. Gweld just pass it over."

"Well, you answer him, and I'll pass it along to the others behind us as soon as I see them." Makwi turned for the back of the boat.

Ralda turned forward again. There was a name for the back end of the boat too, but he'd forgotten that as well. He replied to Gweld, *"We'll pass the news along. When did it happen?"*

The elf replied that the Bane came in the night, and Ralda acknowledged the message. He told Tordug, who relayed the information to Makwi.

Ralda kept his watch for more word from Gweld. He steadied himself as the boat rolled beneath his feet. Odd that it should go after Gweld, who made no real effort to hide the disguised arrow.

Ralda scratched the back of his neck, and a memory came to mind. Back at Ezhandun, Gweld's reflection in the mirror had been odd. There had been light like fire in his eyes before he turned to Ralda. Back then, Ralda had dismissed it as light from a candle in the room. But he'd never seen light reflected like that. It came from Gweld's eyes. At least that was what Ralda thought. And Gweld had been odd in the Troll Heaths and even since then. Maybe it was just that little memory that disturbed Ralda for no reason. He glanced the elf's way. There was no further signal.

Ralda rubbed his chin, and his stomach rumbled. Best get some food. Maybe he should ask Hastra about his concerns. He shrugged. Probably not. He wasn't sure of what he'd seen. He left the rail and went in search of some food.

CHAPTER TEN

More groups of panicked travelers joined Athson's caravan by noon the next day. He eyed them at Spark's first signal, then rode back to question them. He found no rangers to guard them, and they'd been harried by a few lone ne'er-do-wells along the way. But the group of more than forty people included a few guards hired by merchants and other men experienced with weapons who had driven the thieves away in the night.

It was only a matter of time before the single thieves banded together and attacked. Too bad there weren't enough rangers to patrol the road and put down such roving bands. He shrugged. But then, the thieves had few places to hide from the trolls other than the city. Thieves would be turned away if identified and forced farther west or south. Those who kept traveling beyond the city would prove troublesome to other refugees traveling further too.

Two people, a man and a woman, cloaked in chestnut brown wandered past Athson, their hoods pulled over their heads. Were they troublemakers? There was nothing he could do unless they stole something. The two travelers weren't well-equipped and likely didn't have much food. They'd look for handouts from the rangers. Athson fingered his sword as he rode, hoping for insight, and left the bow mostly covered from prying eyes. He decided those two cloaked travelers would likely find aid with his fellow rangers if they weren't quarrelsome. Regardless, they bore watching.

Apeth eyed a few of the travelers but never reacted to them. The Withling otherwise ignored the added number of people. When he caught sight of Athson watching him with a questioning lift of his brow, Apeth just shrugged and rode the mule in silence.

Athson sighed. It was a long road, and some of these people would likely stop off at different places and linger, joining later groups. They'd probably have several hundred before they reached Auguron City. He yawned as the last of the new travelers melded into the current group, leaving him alone at the rear. He glanced at Spark.

The mountain hound sat farther back in the road.

Athson motioned for the dog to follow. Odd that he'd stop like that. He shouldn't get tired. Was there someone who bothered Spark? Athson eyed the mass of travelers, now mingled together. It was hard to tell them apart.

Apeth drifted back to Athson. "Something bothering you?"

Athson scratched the back of his neck with a frown. "Just wary of these new people. Spark's acting odd." Maybe he needed a few Withling tips. "What about learning to, you know, do things? Like a Withling."

Apeth snorted. "That's right, I did mention I'd train you earlier today. But there are no tricks or shortcuts to the training. You have to listen to Eloch, and that's no easy task when you first start."

People chattered ahead of them, and Athson extended his hand, palm up, toward the refugees under his care. "So I can't just, uh, somehow know there's trouble in this lot ahead of us?"

The old Withling shook his head with a frown and closed his eyes for a moment, then fixed his gaze on Athson. "I can't even do that. Sure, I might get an impression to handle an issue that's coming, but just knowing people's intentions is not part of being a Withling. It's about listening to Eloch and acting accordingly. If Eloch is saying to do something, then it needs doing for his purpose. But we're not about tricks or miracles just because, or else it would be magic. And we're mystics."

"Do I need to learn prayers or something?" This was not what Athson had thought it would be like. Listening, knowing what to do, sounded nothing like what he'd witnessed Hastra, Howart, Zelma, or Apeth do. A flush of heated irritation rose on his face.

"Don't let it irritate you." Apeth sighed. "It's simple, and it's not. Being a Withling is about serving and listening." He raised an index finger in the air. "The trick is learning—accepting, actually—that your mind is not as disciplined as you think. Learning to be attuned to the spiritual, to Eloch, teaches you much. When to speak and when to be silent. When to act and when to refrain. It is in that discipline that miracles are demonstrated. If you don't know when and how to do it, how will you know what to do? Are you going to just think you must do something and learn by trial and error? That's mostly failing, and you'll do plenty of that. Don't be irritated, Athson. Touch that blessed sword and learn to recognize when you are being affected. At least in that, you thwart the curse and learn to know your own thoughts from the curse."

Athson touched his sword and gaped. That was a simple lesson, but he'd never noticed his ire growing into anger over nothing. So that was the curse and how it played him. He cleared his throat. "I guess you're right. I'll have to remember that."

"Don't just remember—pay attention to your own thoughts. Know when they wander from attentiveness, when that curse sets you on evil's path and off that of being a Withling." Apeth steered the mule around a rut.

Athson rode on in silence for a few minutes. He turned back to Spark, who followed with seeming alertness. "How do I listen to Eloch? I've heard nothing like what you or Hastra talk about." He waved his hand at Spark. "How do I know what Spark really knows about things?"

Apeth turned in his saddle and looked behind them, though there was nothing for him to see. "As to your dog, that's something people have reported at times in the past. Usually it's a person. That you see an animal like a dog means it's an image you trust." He eyed Athson without turning his head much. "You must like dogs, eh?"

"Well, yeah. Had them around Depenburgh when I was a kid."

"Anyway, that's a guardian spirit. I suppose many have one, but this one seems to do a lot for you. Likely about that, uh, foretelling."

A young woman ahead of them removed a rock from their shoe, and they paused their discussion. For some reason, Apeth liked his anonymity more than Hastra. The young woman finished with her shoe and ran to catch her father, who Athson knew was a merchant.

Apeth coughed into his hand to get Athson's attention. "Anyway, listening is just what I said. But you don't start with important things, at least not usually. Sometimes that happens, but mostly you just learn to hear small things. Once you have learned to hear about little things, then you begin to hear about much more."

Athson rubbed his cheek where his beard had started growing again since leaving Marston's Station. "What little things?"

The elder Withling shrugged and pointed to the young woman who had stopped for her shoe. "Small kindnesses are a start. What if you'd been instructed to help with her shoe? You might not know why, but you do it because it's what's needed and you give it. Learn to give what's needed, and you'll see what you need given."

Athson's eyebrows climbed his forehead in reaction. "I just do nice things, and I'll hear Eloch speak and get good things back as a result?"

Apeth waved his hand and shook his head. "No, no, no. Nothing of the sort. This isn't spells or controlling Eloch with your behavior. It's being part of the saying, living it. 'What is needed is given.' Learn to hear Eloch's purpose, beginning with trivial things, and you'll go far as a Withling." He shrugged. "It's as simple and as hard as that. You want to think I'm being mysterious or talking in circles. Be faithful in small things, and you'll be given bigger tasks. Until you can hear about little things, you don't even know what to do. You'll have to know your own thoughts to hear from outside yourself, from Eloch."

Athson rode his horse in silence. Listen. That was all? Thoughts whirled through his mind. Where was Limbreth? How had she survived? What was he to do with the bow? Then there were all the noises and signs of the forest he had been trained to note. He did that without thinking and reacted to them. The forest informed him of his surroundings. His head hurt at trying to sift his thoughts constantly. Training. Apeth was just teaching him concepts. He already knew how to focus on the forest and know things from it.

"Is it like what I know as a ranger? I can spot all kinds of information around me that other people are ignorant of."

"I suppose you listen to the forest and know what's going on around you. A good merchant, let's say a horse trader, learns to know when he's about to be cheated. He can spot the signs. It becomes almost an instinct." Apeth wiggled his fingers at the side of his head. "Almost no thought, just reaction to information. It's a similar thing. Learn to listen for Eloch like you listen to the birds twitter. Know what's you and what's not. Want some help getting started?"

"Uh, sure? I suppose." Suddenly, Athson remembered his father teaching him the bow or Heth showing him how to track. "Yes, that would be helpful."

They rode in silence for a while. Ahead, a gaunt man with a bald head and a long beard laughed at some jest but stepped on a rock oddly and twisted his ankle. He fell hard with a cry and a wince. His friends laughed and walked on, jeering about walking it off.

Athson glanced at Apeth, who nodded. Athson steered toward the traveler, dismounted, and offered his hand. "You need help?"

Through his grimace, the man nodded. "Don't think I broke nothing. Just hurts bad."

Athson pulled the other man to his feet and dusted off his back.

The fellow started walking but winced again and ground his teeth through the pain. "Twisted it good."

Athson glanced to the side of the road and glimpsed a forked limb lying on the ground. It looked sturdy. He walked over and picked it up. "Here, give this a try."

The man took the branch and hobbled a few steps with it, then declared it helpful. He started to move on but paused, then turned to Athson. "My thanks. Can't waste time on this road injured if trolls are coming."

"You're welcome. I'd let you ride my horse, but I'm on duty with the rangers." Athson climbed back on his horse and waited for the man to walk out of earshot. He leaned over to Apeth where he sat astride the mule. "Like that?"

Apeth chuckled. "Something like that, I suppose. But I heard nothing about you doing all that. You just needed to show kindness."

"So, a trick?" His ire rose, heating his cheeks. *Nope, grab the sword. Learn something here.* He touched his sword-hilt, and his anger subsided. "I don't understand."

The Withling grinned. "It's simple. You heard nothing, and I heard nothing from Eloch about helping that man. Therefore, it wasn't Eloch. See what it means not to hear?"

Athson rubbed his chin. "I guess."

"Anyway, there is a bit of a lesson in it otherwise."

"What's that?"

"Oftentimes, it's good to just be kind regardless. Refrain only when instructed." Apeth shrugged. "At those times, it may be another's time to help. Withlings have often learned to hear Eloch by just dedicating themselves to simple actions like this one, since it's what he likes. Simple obedience to the general rule of kindness will take you far." Apeth gathered his reins in one hand. "Speaking of which, I'm restrained from healing right now, since I'm supposed to lie low. However..." He kicked the mule and rode off, tossing a final word to Athson. "Better get going before the trolls catch us."

Athson kicked his horse into motion, and Spark trotted alongside him.

Ahead, Apeth rode up to the man who had fallen and stopped within earshot of Athson. "Here, ride my mule this afternoon, and I'll walk with you." The Withling winked at Athson and mouthed, *That's what I heard for me.* He pointed at his chest and started off with the man, talking with him. The two of them chatted and laughed throughout the afternoon.

Meanwhile, Athson tried listening to his thoughts. He had a lot of them to sift. Then he laughed. It would, indeed, be a long journey to the city with lots of little accidents in need of attending. Maybe others would take heed and learn kindness in the midst of their fear. Perhaps they might hear just because he was learning.

∽

Days of riding and "listening" consumed Athson. Some days he thought he heard something, and others just seemed like an exercise in frustration that left him with a headache.

Rumor of trolls faded over the miles, and with them the fear. The ninth day out from Marston's Station, Athson rode his horse with one thought nagging his mind like scavengers around a carcass. The people around him idled and laughed as if ravaging hordes of trolls were a distant, harmless tale. He adjusted the reins in his grip. Maybe he'd been too long in the wilderness with trolls as an ever-present danger. But the trolls still marched west, and the forgotten danger bothered him.

"What's got you knotted up now?" Apeth rode the mule beside Athson. He had reclaimed his mule after the injured man awakened the next morning with a foot suddenly well enough to walk on. The Withling only replied when Athson queried him about it that some miracles needed less fanfare.

"Nothing." Athson checked himself. No sense in sulking like normal. He grabbed his sword, and the sulking, nagging feeling lifted. Yep, that was the curse. He was learning, albeit slowly, to check all such negative thoughts. "Actually, I think these folks are taking all this too easily. There are real trolls coming this way. I know they shouldn't live in fear, but they need to travel faster than they are." Other groups had joined them over the last few days, so they traveled even more slowly.

Apeth considered Athson's thoughts. "I don't think that horde will go fast enough. They have to forage. But yes, more people need to take it seriously. They will in time. Some will stop, thinking they have plenty of time, and then run for it when smoke drifts on the eastern sky."

Athson gazed at the sky over his shoulder. Nothing yet. "I know what will do it for some of them. Lukey's Post. It's not but a few days west, the way we're traveling. Just seeing what trolls did there will remind many here to get moving."

The Withling offered Athson a grin. "Just remember, you're

used to traveling long days both mounted and afoot. Most of these people are used to slower paces."

Athson sniffed. "That won't help them when troll scouts come tracking their heels." He sat atop his horse in silence for some minutes. "Anyway, I've been thinking about something else." And it was much clearer with the sword in hand, sheathed though it was. "There's a couple who likely needs some rations from the ranger wagon. They've been with us over a week, and they don't seem to have much."

Apeth's sidelong glance drew Athson's attention. "Maybe you're hearing something."

"You think it's what I've been trying to hear all along?" Athson failed to restrain his enthusiasm.

"Maybe. You have to learn that for yourself." Apeth offered one of his noncommittal shrugs. "You thinking anything else?"

Athson thought a moment and rolled his tongue around his cheek. "Might need to say something like a blessing when I give them the food."

"Then it could well be from Eloch." Apeth hesitated, and Athson guessed he was watching him grasp the sword-hilt. "You learning anything there with that sword?"

"Yep. Learned a lot, I guess." He scratched the back of his head and wondered how much to say. *Stop hiding things. He's teaching you, and you're a Withling now.* He wanted to cross his arms and grind his teeth. Instead, he worked his jaw a moment, like he was loosening his muscles. "I've learned several times that my moods are the curse. Just now I was sulking when you asked about me. Touched it, and the feeling left. I don't think I do it enough, so I guess I need to learn to know what's me and what's the curse. Maybe I'll hear more that way."

The elder Withling rode a for several long moments. "I guess that's right. That sword is a bit of a shortcut for you to learn your own thoughts better. But then, not many live under the curse you have. You'll still have the same amount to learn. The more you give yourself time to listen, the more you'll learn the difference."

Athson grimaced and slouched. That was disappointing. He'd heard one thing in nine days. Maybe. He arched an eyebrow. He still clutched the hilt, so that was his own line of thinking. Maybe he'd clutch the weapon all day in the saddle. He might learn more from it that way. It would be like the makeshift crutch he'd given that man on the road a week earlier. "Um, Apeth?"

"Hmm?" The old man stirred from nodding with the rhythm of his mule's gait.

"Maybe what I did with that crutch was something for me." When Apeth looked his way, Athson met his gaze. "You know, maybe that was to tell me to use this sword as a crutch, because it's what I need now."

Apeth rubbed his neck and scratched behind his ear. "Could well be. Sounds about right." He chuckled. "Took you about a week to figure that out. I've seen some learning the way of Withlings go far longer."

Athson looked at the sun shining through the bare limbs overhead. He smiled, and an odd excitement set his heart racing. That made two. And one on his first lesson.

Apeth spat to the side and then shrugged. "You know, Eloch sometimes makes something out of nothing, and you never see it coming at the time, but only later when you look back. Remembering something is a good teaching too. The why of something can become clear. Keep working at it."

They rode on in silence after that.

Evening found Athson strangely exhilarated at the prospect of doing something for the couple he'd seen arrive in their group with little in their possession. How had they been eating well since? Or sleeping? Maybe it was the kindness of others on the road. He walked toward the wagon where the elves guarded the supplies and made their meal.

Minith arched her brow at seeing him. "You still with us? I haven't seen you in two days."

Elves and their dry wit. Athson shook his head. "It took me that long to catch up to this slow-moving wagon train."

The rangers snickered, and Minith answered, "Yes, they are slow."

Athson nodded farther west. "When they see that Lukey's is burnt out, I think they'll have a reminder to move along."

Minith motioned to the other elves. "We thought so too." She paused. "Guess we should have seen this coming after those trolls raided this far west last fall. I heard they were west of the city then."

Athson leaned against the wagon and propped his head in his hand. "Yeah, I was there. Almost got me and Gweld once."

"Yes." She cocked her head. "Strange, that." She eyed the Bow of Hart. "I've heard a rumor there's some Withling prophecy caught up in this. You've been with Hastra. What do you say?"

He shrugged. "It's trolls, so Magdronu is mixed up in it, you can bet. But she had us looking for something he wants." This was getting too close for him to discuss much further. "Anyway, I just came to—"

Minith lifted her head toward the darkening eastern sky and pointed. "That wandering star is a sign, if anything is." She looked at Athson. "I wouldn't think a Withling would bring trouble on us like this, so I hope it's worth it." She coughed and resumed sharpening her ranger long-knife. "Anyway, what did you come for?"

Athson glanced into the wagon. "Just some rations."

Minith motioned toward the crates half-opened at the rear of the wagon. "Get what you need. I guess you're feeding that old man too?"

As he grabbed an armload of rations, Athson grinned. "Yes, he's with me. And yes, he's part of all that's going on. And yes, so am I."

The elven ranger's eyes narrowed in answer, and one of the others spat in the fire. Minith stirred and stood. She walked to the wagon and removed a few more rations. "If I guess right, then what is needed must be given."

Athson nodded without saying more. They knew what Apeth was, if not who. He took two steps down the road.

"Athson."

He turned to Minith, who walked closer to him.

She ran her hand along the Bow of Hart. "I'm not sure what this is, but don't worry about the trolls coming just because of you or Withlings or anything else. They've been aiming this way for decades, and we've known it." She glanced over her shoulder. "Nobody blames anyone for it. It's just the way of that wizard and the dragon." She stared into his face for several long moments.

"I guess so. Thanks for, uh, everything." He left and stopped by the fire kindled by Apeth. He looked at the rations. That thought had bothered him for several weeks. He, and the bow, had brought this on everyone. But he knew it wasn't really true. It was just Magdronu, his way, as Minith had said.

Athson grabbed several ration packages and stood. "Guess I better get this done. Don't know what I'll say, though."

Apeth swallowed what he'd been eating. "Just say what you know should be said. Nothing more, nothing less. You'll be fine."

Athson's hands shook as he left in search of the couple. The paper-wrapped rations crackled in his grasp. *Easy, take a deep breath.* Where was Spark? Then he remembered he had the mountain hound circling the camp again. How could he forget? Just nervous about this visit to strangers, though he didn't know why. Athson wove between campfires and peered at the people gathered around them. He didn't much like talking to strangers most times, but this was just handing people some food. Where were they? He supposed this was just a new process to learn as a Withling. He didn't want to fail. How could he? Those two had to be around here somewhere. They never camped with other people. Private, he supposed. Athson pulled up short at the thought. He didn't want to intrude, to presume anything. Sudden sweat beaded his brow and trickled along his spine under his shirt. He took a deep breath and went ahead. He had to do this.

A few campfires later, he found them. He cleared his throat and approached slowly. "Uh, good evening."

The man ducked his hood-covered head. "Good evening, uh, ranger."

The woman stared at the fire, her head down and hooded too. "Hello, ranger. What can we do for you?" Her eyes glittered in the light of the campfire when she lifted her gaze, though she hardly moved her head.

Athson hesitated. They were so stiff, like they feared him. He must be intruding. "I'm Athson. I have a few extra rations and thought you might want them." What did he need to tell them? Nothing special came to mind. He almost tossed the rations toward them and rushed back to Apeth. His cheeks flushed warm.

"Oh, uh, thank you." The woman rose, her head still down and her movements stiff.

How oddly they behaved. Was he that scary? He gave her the rations. "Don't worry too much about trolls. We need to keep moving, but they're still days behind us, and there are other travelers farther back."

The woman sat with the packets of food in her hands, unmoving. Neither one gave their name. Athson fidgeted with his shirt and cloak. "Uh, well, that's not much. No fancy wine to be had on the road, or much fresh bread." He motioned toward the rations. "Those will keep you going, though." He almost turned and left but paused. "If you follow Eloch, you will be blessed."

If anything, the man and woman stiffened at his words.

Athson offered an odd, half-wave in the firelight. "Well, time to get back to my fire. Good evening."

"Thank you for your kind words and deeds." The woman's voice held a tense but uncertain tone.

With a nod and a quick glance, Athson caught sight of the woman's hands clenched around the food, trembling in some effort. "You're welcome."

He left with a quick step and felt exhausted by the effort. How silly of him to feel that way. It wasn't much to give some food to people and speak some encouragement. He took a deep breath, and on his exhale realized his stomach had stopped fluttering. He stumbled among the trees, feeling a sudden weakness, and rested a hand on his sword-pommel. The edgy weakness cleared.

He'd done it, though he didn't know why. He hoped his words were correct. Athson halted. His weakness had cleared? So maybe the curse had halted him from acting kind? Over his shoulder, Athson beheld the pair huddled at their fire. Certainty gathered and settled in his mind like a flock of birds to a tree. They'd needed the food and the words. He didn't know why, but he'd have to live with not knowing until it was revealed.

Athson heard the man speak lowly, "I don't know about you, but I'm weary of these things. Doing what we do."

Athson half-turned and observed the woman nod and her shoulders shake. Her answer was soft but tremulous. "I do as well. Can we turn from it?"

The man touched her hand and said, "I don't know if we can. We'll do this one thing, because we must. Then maybe we'll go to Auguron City and it will be better, easier."

The woman sigh. "He can do it when he comes."

Athson sighed. So they were in some predicament. His gift was necessary. He squared his shoulders and headed for his camp and Apeth. "What is needed is given." He'd done what was needed, given what was needed with actions and words. Distant thunder rumbled overhead with the promise of storms to come. He wondered what those two were discussing. He shrugged. It was none of his business.

CHAPTER ELEVEN

Days passed on the boat, and the tension of guarding the arrow weighed on Limbreth's mind like a pending avalanche. Doubt often settled like ice and pressed on her. When it worried her the most, she stole away to the little cabin she shared with Hastra, removed the arrow and stared at it in awe. It gleamed white, though its brightness faded some each day.

Limbreth stared at the arrow now. She caressed the shaft, the pale feathers, and peace filled her from the belly up, ending with a surge of her heart. She covered her mouth and restrained the laughter—holy joy, Hastra termed it. Though this joy overcame her, Limbreth considered it more of a bother. Her odd laughter over this arrow left her feeling almost crazed in some way. But it lightened the load, and she needed that today.

Three more times, the Bane had stolen fake arrows from the others, according to their reports. Limbreth embraced the arrow. She had to protect it, with her life if necessary.

The door to the hold opened and footsteps scuffed on the creaky steps. Limbreth re-wrapped the arrow and stowed it in her pack. *Don't let anyone see it.* She stood and drew a sword, waiting by the door. When the door opened and Hastra peered inside, her apprehension displayed on her face, Limbreth exhaled and sheathed her sword. "Good, it's you."

Hastra pushed into the little room of wooden bunks normally meant for crewmen. "You need to keep that hidden more."

Limbreth's jaw tightened. She needed to see it, feel the encouragement from it. But Hastra was right. "I was just, uh, checking on it."

Hastra sat on the lower bunk. "Rain's settled in for the day." Thunder rumbled and lightning cracked in the distance outside the hull. "We best stay below and dry."

Limbreth sat beside the old woman and sighed. "Great, nothing to do but stare at walls instead of the river and the banks." Her world shrank further, and with it her concern. "Wish there was something to read."

The Withling snapped her fingers. "I have my Book of Prophecies. You can listen to me awhile."

Limbreth resisted rolling her eyes and moved for the door but hesitated. What about the arrow? "You going to be here awhile?"

"Don't want to listen?" Hastra flipped through her book, found a spot, and ran her hands over the page.

"Uh, not really. Not now. I can't stand the waiting, the confinement aboard this boat. I need something to do." Limbreth crossed her arms. She could practice with her swords, but there was no room for that below the deck, and out in the rain it would be slick.

"The crewmen have games to pass the time when they're off duty." Hastra peered at Limbreth over the top of her book. "But you'd need money."

Limbreth sniffed. "Not wasting my time, or my few coins, on that." Sword practice in the rain it was. She grabbed her cloak. Good footwork on a rolling boat and slick deck seemed like a good way to keep sharp. Footing was always important in a fight. She opened the door and fixed her gaze on her pack, then Hastra. "Watch that. I'll be back."

Swords drawn, Limbreth climbed the steps to the broad deck, where crewmen worked their duties amid a steady shower that soaked the wood underfoot as well as the tarps covering crates of goods and supplies. At the prow, a crewman spotted the river while several stood ready with poles should another vessel drift near. The captain, an elf with extensive experience on the river, steered the boat in the river channel.

Limbreth paused for several moments and stared into the rainy mist that hid the riverbanks in a shroud of mist. The Bane lingered out there, waiting. Eventually, it would come for her arrow just like the others'. Her grip tightened on her swords. She'd be ready.

She stepped away from doorway and slowly worked through her practice exercises, concentrating on her footwork. She slipped a few times, then continued or re-started her practice. Beneath her cloak, she worked up a sweat, even in the chill rain. As she practiced her moves faster, she gained confidence in her footing, her swords weaving cuts and parries as she turned.

Upon completion, Limbreth lifted her swords in salute at her face. On the surface of the blades, wet with raindrops, she glimpsed a reflection beyond the captain and the wheel. She gasped at the chill along her spine. She stared a moment, then whirled, her swords on-guard.

Nothing stood beyond the captain, who saw her expression and glanced over his shoulder. Beyond the elf at the wheel, nothing but river and rain was in sight.

Limbreth peeked around the tarped crates behind the captain, her eyes narrowed. Nothing there. But she'd seen the Bane. It wasn't her imagination. The Bane knew her location.

Limbreth opened the hatch, clattered below decks, and stalked to her door, swords still on-guard. She could only stab in this confined space. With a swift turn at the knob, she leapt into the room and found only Hastra with her book.

The Withling startled from her read—or had she been sleeping?—her eyes wide. "What's wrong?"

Limbreth shut the door and pulled off her soaked cloak, then hung it on a door peg. "The Bane. I saw it on the bow. I did a salute and caught sight of its reflection in the blades. But it was gone when I turned. The captain jumped like a startled cat."

Hastra closed her book and got to her feet. "You're sure? Everyone else has seen it but us. We've kept low until now. I felt nothing."

Limbreth nodded. "I'm sure. I've had too many encounters with it not to know when it's been around. We've got to do something."

The Withling opened the door and checked the passage beyond. "Nothing there. It must have come and gone fast." She snapped her fingers for emphasis.

"Yes, that fast." Limbreth puffed her cheeks as she exhaled, her heart thumping. How could she get rid of it? Tordug had thrown it down a mountainside. "Maybe we can push it overboard if necessary."

Hastra shook her head. "After what you told us of your fight in the mountains, I doubt it would help much. I should be led to deal with it somehow, if it comes to it. We've not yet met." Hastra lifted her chin. "I look forward to chasing it away, if given to me."

Limbreth peered at the old woman, her puffy cheeks flushed with expectation of a confrontation. She knew better than to laugh at the Withling, but Limbreth wondered what Hastra could do. "It's coming, and I won't be unprepared." But when it came, it could slip in without her reaction. Gweld never knew it had entered past him while on guard in the mountains. But she'd do what she could. "We'll warn the rangers aboard that there might be trouble."

"We can have a watch set, though I doubt it will do any good."

Limbreth wiped rain from her swords. "It's better than nothing. We've nowhere to go but with the river."

Hastra drummed her fingers on a cheek. "I know, let's hide it somewhere." She cast her gaze around the room in search of a likely place. "We should have done that already."

"No, it stays with me. I'll sleep with it." Limbreth sheathed her swords and checked her pack. She wanted to see the White Arrow. But not now. "Let's rig the door somehow while we sleep. Something that rattles if it's opened."

They tied tin cups and silverware so they bumped each other with dull *clinks*. Limbreth surveyed their work once completed. No much, but the best available warning. She shivered. The Bane had entered and grabbed her that night in the shelter, and she had hardly stirred from sleep. With a slight twist of her head and thin grimace toward Hastra, she nodded. "Better than nothing."

After that, they set a watch and brought food for each other from the crowded mess. Hastra spoke to the elven sergeant aboard and asked his assistance in standing guard with an explanation of the situation without mentioning the White Arrow.

Meanwhile, Limbreth's gut twisted in knots during the following days as she awaited the certain appearance of the Bane in her room.

∽

Limbreth lay each night after that with the cloth-wrapped arrow clutched to her bosom with one hand and a sword in another. Her other sword lay ready should she need it. But two nights passed without any jangle of their warning at the door. Limbreth slept little at night and sat with the arrow during the day. She thumbed through Hastra's book once when alone but found nothing of interest. Why Hastra kept its contents so closely guarded, she didn't know. Most of what she glimpsed pertained to events long over.

The third night, she lay awake, her brow furrowed. She yawned repeatedly, but sleep eluded her. The rain had passed that day, and the sky cleared just after dinner when she strolled the deck to stretch her legs while Hastra guarded the arrow. The Bane either waited on them to slip up or something else. She released her breath in a long sigh. At least it no longer sought to capture her. Hostages meant nothing to Corgren. For now. If he lived.

A yawn dragged Limbreth toward sleep. She rolled over and cradled the arrow close in her arms. Her grip loosened on both sword and arrow. She jerked awake once, then another time, and adjusted her clasp of her weapon and charge each time. Hastra snored softly, and Limbreth's eyes dropped until she slept.

A distant clang sounded through Limbreth's slumber. She clawed for awareness, and her eyes fluttered. The room glowed softly a moment and then faded. She rolled over, and her sword clattered on the wooden floor.

"Limbreth, the arrow in the hall." Hastra scrambled from her bunk and stumbled.

Limbreth bolted up in her bunk atop Hastra's. A scream escaped her lips. The White Arrow was gone. She rolled from the bunk and landed in a crouch. She gathered her swords and leapt through the door.

The White Arrow glowed in a nimbus beyond the silhouette of a cloaked form that filled the passage at the steps to the deck.

"No! You can't have it!" Limbreth roared along the hallway.

The Bane slipped up the stairs to the deck.

Limbreth stormed after the creature. Hastra shouted wordlessly after her. Upon the deck, the Bane swirled toward the port rail and the river. Limbreth dropped her swords, jumped onto some crates, and snagged the feathered end of the White Arrow in her left hand. She landed awkwardly but retained her grasp.

The Bane yanked the arrow, but Limbreth held fast.

She laughed in the glow of the arrow. "You won't break my grip!" She yanked back on the arrow. "You can't have it." She kicked at the Bane.

The creature reached for Limbreth, and she dodged its freezing touch. She needed a sword. Foolish to have dropped them. They danced with the arrow between them.

Hastra shouted, "Limbreth, don't!"

"What?"

The Bane lurched and dragged Limbreth around. She fell against the deck rail with a grunt and rolled over the side. A snap quivered up her arm before she smacked into the water and coldness embraced her.

CHAPTER TWELVE

Magdronu's wings unfolded from Corgren as the traveling spell ended, and he stepped across dry leaves. He traveled now more than ever, splitting time between command of the trolls, overseeing the new shrine hidden within the city, and oversight of Paugren. This latter task Corgren considered but a formality while his brother and Cass worked their way closer to their prey. Where were they? He stepped through frozen leaves. Maybe he should have brought some trolls for this. But they couldn't steal the bow, unlike the arrow. The bow had to be given.

Two figures rose out of the shadows, and Corgren's hand drifted to his dagger.

"Easy, brother." Paugren leaned closer. "Come by the fire. You won't stand out."

Cass hesitated. "Pull your hood up so no one recognizes you."

Corgren arched an eyebrow and ran his tongue across his front teeth. Cass bothered him. But why? She and her sisters were sly, but something else about her troubled him this night. He followed his brother and Cass to a campfire and sat without warming his hands. He glanced about. Other campfires lay near, though none too close at hand. Still, he leaned close to his companions for the evening—at least for a while. "What's the plan, then? I'll see this done and report it to the master."

Cass touched his leg. "You'll do it." She looked at Paugren and back to Corgren. "We're the distraction. The ranger brings rations each night."

Corgren shook his head. "The dirty work for me? I don't mind, but this is all you're doing for this assignment?"

Paugren extended his hands toward the fire. "We're to keep watch over the other one."

"You'll go help with the shrine." Corgren pointed at each of them for emphasis.

Cass and Paugren exchanged glances before his brother spoke. "Plans have changed. We'll make sure he gets to the master first, then the shrine."

Cass flashed a smile, visible in the firelight beneath her hood. "There's plenty of time for the shrine."

Paugren pointed and leaned forward. "He's coming. Time for you to go. Do it clean and fast. Run back this way first. We'll feign stopping you. They aren't far, just over there between those two trees. Wait until he returns, then run this way. When she screams, cast the spell in those shadows there." Paugren pointed to the deeper darkness at a thicket.

Corgren grimaced. "You owe me, brother, for doing your job. I'll not waste more time on you. I've much more to do." He stood and walked into the night, making a wide circuit of his targeted campfire. These worthless refugees only prolonged their plight by fleeing. He drew closer, crouched in the underbrush, and watched the old man at the fire. So, that was him. Not much of a challenge. Just don't give him a chance.

∞

The rangers led the growing party of idling refugees past Lukey's, which stood as a charred testament to the coming doom in the east. Minith let the rumor spread that the destroyed post was from a troll raid, and Athson spoke no reassuring words to the alarmed people around him. Some disbelieved the story and claimed it was an accident, but others claimed they'd traveled this way in recent months and knew it to be so.

A few continued the dispute. Athson rode among them and drew their attention. "I was here the day after. It was trolls." He glanced at the building ruins. "That's just a touch of what they'll do. My village was destroyed by them when I was a lad."

After that, the pace picked up considerably, though some still loitered. The rangers started before dawn and ended just at dusk, and more people followed than days earlier. With more leagues under their feet, Athson's worry faded, though he handled his sword far more often, working to listen for Eloch. All he felt was the urge to help that couple more.

Athson lounged by the fire one night after he ate his fill. He took rations to his new friends each evening now. They never refused but never conversed much. They seemed a little less shy than that first night, and he thought they appreciated the food and his blessing. He'd seen them on the road with a faster step for several days, so he supposed they hadn't been eating that well after all.

He yawned, the travel catching up to him at last. "I reckon we've got three or four more days to Huffer's Post." He looked forward to seeing the dwarf and his wife, whom Hastra had healed of an arrow wound. He shook his head at the memory. It had been several long months since then. Hard traveling flooded his thoughts. He'd come far. He stretched the stiffness from his limbs.

Apeth nodded and muttered to himself first, then to

Athson. "Remember what I said." He pointed a finger at Athson.

"Which topic? You say lots of things." Athson grabbed a couple packages of food and stood.

The Withling motioned him closer and held up one finger. "First, you keep listening. Second, anything happens to me, you ride and keep that bow safe."

Athson mock-saluted with a grin. He started away, but as an after-thought he carried the bow with him.

As he trudged through the trees and searched for his friends, Athson also looked for Spark. The camp was much larger now. He must be way on the other side somewhere. Athson halted and searched for familiar shapes in their dark cloaks. There were three people at one fire, or he would have gone there. But then one rose and stalked into the darkness. Athson watched a moment or two to confirm the man and woman he'd been helping were at that fire. Assured he'd chosen correctly, Athson walked toward the fire. The third figure had moved with a familiar gait. He shook his head—there were lots of people on the road. But the recognition nagged him still as he edged into the firelight, the food in his hands.

"Good evening. Thought you two would like a bit more food tonight."

The woman moved less stiffly as she took the rations from Athson. She practically whispered, "Thank you, ranger."

"Eloch's blessing for you." Athson paused a moment, but neither spoke a reply. Some of the shyest people he'd ever seen. He wondered where they were from. He scratched the back of his head and turned away, then back. "Look, if you need something else, just let me know. I'll do what I can. Blankets, maybe?"

The man and woman exchanged glances, and she spoke for

them again. "Thank you, but we have our cloaks to keep us warm. Perhaps others need blankets."

Athson nodded and offered an awkward wave. "Sleep well." He turned toward his own encampment.

Someone shouted in the night.

∼

CORGREN WAS the dragon's hand this night. *Strike the blow and remove this thorny threat.* His shoulders tensed for action as he stepped into the light of the Withling's campfire.

"Can you spare some food?" Corgren asked. "My family, we don't have enough for the trip."

The old man reached for wrapped rations like those Athson gave nightly to Paugren and Cass. The foolish ranger fed his enemies. The Withling paused and peered into Corgren's hood-darkened face with a squint. "Don't I know you?"

Corgren edged closer, his left hand extended. "I don't think so." He couldn't keep the hard edge from the tone of his voice as his other hand drifted toward his waist.

The Withling pointed at him. "I recognize your voice from long ago. At Withling's Watch. You're Corgren!" The old man scrambled for his feet.

Corgren snatched his Wolfshead dagger free and grabbed the Withling by the shirt, pulling him forward. He stabbed the old man in the shoulder.

The injured Withling fell with a bellow of pain. Corgren twisted the knife. "Rotten Withling!"

He yanked the dagger from the wound and charged back toward Paugren's campsite. *Remember the plan.* He brushed past Athson. Corgren could have killed the ranger, but then what of the bow and giving it to Magdronu?

Paugren and Cass feigned trying to stop Corgren as they

fell to his shoves. He sang out the traveling spell, and Magdronu's wings enfolded him. He escaped across the Auguron Forest to his troll army.

~

ATHSON HALTED at the sound of a scuffle and searched the surrounding campfires. It sounded directly ahead of him. "Apeth!" He rushed forward, his sword half-drawn.

Someone rushed past him, and he turned to follow.

"Athson." Apeth's voice sounded weak.

Athson forgot about the fleeing person and lunged for the encampment. He found the Withling lying in his own blood, trembling with shock.

"Went that way." Apeth motioned vaguely the way Athson had come.

Shouts erupted in the night. Athson searched the darkness but saw nothing. Voices called, and others joined the commotion.

"Here, let me help you." Athson laid an old shirt on the wound and pressed it.

"Remember what I said." Apeth's voice trailed into a whisper.

"Apeth, stay with me." The shirt did nothing to staunch the wound high on his chest. Blood gathered in Athson's hands. Not again. He blinked and saw his father slipping away. This was an artery. He pressed harder.

"Can't help me." Apeth shook his head. "Listen."

"I can say a prayer. Tell me how." Athson's mind raced. He grabbed his sword from where he'd dropped it. He shut his eyes and listened. Nothing. He held his breath. *Eloch, where are you? Tell me what to do.* Nothing but more blood answered Athson when he opened his eyes. Of course, these daggers dripped pain with the blood. No surviving those without a

Withl— He was a Withling. Why couldn't he hear Eloch in this?

Apeth shook his head. "Murder. Dagger. Rokan." He winced but his brow furrowed in effort, and his eyes rolled to Athson. "Corgren."

Athson ground his teeth. "Corgren! Of course, he survived."

Apeth grabbed Athson's hand. He held it while he spoke, his eyes wide with effort. "Ride!" His lips trembled and his face shook. "Ride. The bow." He reached for it, and Athson put it in his hands. "Remember. Not. For. Him." He pointed at Athson with weak emphasis. "You. You, you, for you."

The Withling's voice faded, and he slumped onto the ground. Athson pressed on the wound. Apeth ceased moving at all, his eyes open to the night sky. His grip fell limp in Athson's hand.

Athson slammed a fist into the dirt and sat back on his heels. This wasn't right, wasn't fair. Eloch left him alone. His chin dropped to his chest, and a ragged sigh escaped his throat. It shook his body. How could this happen now? He had so much to learn. Apeth had done so much, lived so long. But Athson had drawn him into the open. Athson was a target, watched by Magdronu's forces. They wanted Athson isolated. He stood and gazed at Apeth. That was why the old Withling wanted him to ride on. To get away from Rokan spies. He wanted to run immediately, but there was a grave to dig.

∽

LIMBRETH GULPED water and thrashed in the river, expecting to slam into a rock. *No, that was the Funnel.* She gripped the White Arrow in her hand and kicked to the surface. The Bane kept throwing her into water. She was getting tired of that. The boat drifted away.

Crewmen and rangers waved torches across the water from the deck. "Overboard!" they shouted across the water.

"Here!" Limbreth waved her hands, one still holding the arrow. "I'm over here." She thrashed and splashed for emphasis until they tossed a rope from the bow. She grabbed the life-line, and they hauled her aboard the boat.

Hastra grabbed her face. "Are you well? Did it harm you?"

Limbreth laughed. "I got it back. I got it!" She waved her left hand in Hastra's field of vision.

The Withling fell on her backside amid the spreading water from Limbreth and gasped, her eyes wide. She clamped one hand over her mouth and pointed.

Limbreth's laughter died as she glimpsed her death-grip hand frozen around the arrow shaft. It was broken halfway along the length. She wailed. "No! It's still got the other half!" She stood and searched the darkness for the Bane, and crewmen and rangers had to hold her back from falling into the river again.

The captain approached and bellowed, "What's going on? What's all this commotion?"

Limbreth shook the broken arrow toward him. "It's broken!"

The captain gazed at everyone else in the sudden silence. "All this about an arrow?"

"Uh, you looking for this?" One of the crewmen stooped farther down the deck and approached with what he'd retrieved. "Saw that thing drop this. Then it went over and just slid across the river." He motioned with his flattened hand across the water and shivered. "Creepy, that."

Limbreth snatched the other half of the arrow from the crewman and held the pieces in each hand. She whirled to Hastra. "Do something! You can mend it with a prayer."

Hastra shook her head. "I've got nothing."

The Withling's face was stricken with terror. Limbreth

grasped both halves of the arrow to one hand and grabbed Hastra's shoulder. "Don't just sit there. Pray!"

Hastra took the pieces and lowered her face, and all fell silent. She raised her face after a few moments, now composed but tense. "I'm sorry. There's nothing for me. Perhaps Zelma or Howart can."

"What's wrong with you? You've always got the answers."

Hastra handed the pieces back to Limbreth. "It's not about answers. Perhaps it will be mended in due time. Either that, or..." She looked toward the darkened riverbank, then lifted her gaze to the sky. "It's still there."

Limbreth gaped at the night sky. "The sign. It still means something, then?

Hastra watched Limbreth a moment, her lip trembling. "It means we go on. As long as it's there, we have something to do, broken arrow or not."

"What does it mean if no one can mend the Arrow?" Limbreth raised the pieces high overhead.

"I don't know. Maybe..." Hastra slouched. "Maybe the prophecy is thwarted." She glanced at Limbreth sidelong.

Limbreth whirled and strode to the prow. Her shoulders shook with a sudden sob. What had she done? She never should have taken the arrow. It wasn't meant for her to keep for Athson. She'd failed him, failed the prophecy, failed everyone. Including Hastra. That mattered to her. She admitted that much to herself. What the old woman thought of her mattered as much as everything else. She gazed at the broken arrow in her hand, the holy light gone from the pieces. They were worthless. Limbreth stretched her arm behind her.

Hastra grabbed her arm. "Don't."

Limbreth pulled away and swore. "They're worthless now. It's over." Tears came. All the travel, the sacrifice. It meant nothing. It was over with these two broken pieces of arrow.

Hastra embraced Limbreth. "Listen to me. Just listen a

moment." Limbreth grew still in the Withling's embrace, who then continued, "I've suffered losses before, but I'm still here. Eloch still had his plans. It's not over, and these may not be worthless. Who knows how Eloch will lead us from here." She took the pieces from Limbreth. "We know nothing of what this means."

Her sobbing faded, but Limbreth slouched, her energy gone. She shivered from the cold and the chill of the river. Hastra led her below to their room and helped her out of her sodden gear. She lay in the lower bunk and gathered the arrow pieces from where Hastra had set them.

"Hastra?"

"What, my dear?" The Withling's voice sounded husky, less energetic than Limbreth ever remembered.

"The Bane, it won't bother us anymore. We can get this to Athson without trouble."

Hastra slowly turned and gaped at Limbreth.

CHAPTER THIRTEEN

Athson turned and found the man and woman he'd helped standing in the shadows. "Know anyone with a shovel or spade?"

The woman stammered, "He h-hit me in the face when we tried to stop him, and punched him in the nose." She pointed to the man.

Athson squinted at them. Her lip was busted and bloody, and his nose trailed blood. Athson watched them sidelong as other people crowded near. Still looking at the man and woman, he asked again, "Anybody got tools for digging?"

"I do." Someone at the back of the throng raised a hand in the shadows of night. "I'll go fetch them." Athson watched the man's head bob through the crowd as he went for his things.

"Was it thieves?" A woman, not the one Athson had visited for several nights, hugged herself, her face pale in the firelight.

Athson stepped close to her as her knees wobbled. Other people nearby caught her as she collapsed. He glanced at his hands, covered in Apeth's blood. He motioned to the couple he'd been feeding. "They were knocked down by the killer."

The low voice of a dwarf rumbled out of the crowd. "He get anything?"

Athson almost ran his bloody fingers through his hair, then thought better of it. He shook his head. "Don't know. This man has traveled with me for weeks. He didn't have much."

He squinted at his "friends" as they edged back into the crowd. A few people asked after them and offered a cloth to wipe the blood from their faces. Athson retrieved his sword and sheathed it.

A figure in dark clothing left their campfire.

Now that was from Eloch. Why not a prayer to save Apeth Stellin? Still, Athson had seen something familiar in that mysterious figure's stride, the set of the shoulders, the angle of the neck—even if they were cloaked and hooded. Athson glanced back at Apeth. Killed by a Rokan dagger? That too was familiar. It had to be Corgren, just like Apeth said. He clenched his jaw. Corgren needed dealing with.

Minith arrived, and Athson told her what had happened. She backed the bystanders off and told them to keep their weapons ready. Some folks mumbled about trolls scouting the road. The elven sergeant asked several stout men and the dwarf to help with the digging, since someone had procured several tools. They all obliged, and Minith took Athson aside to clean him up after she gathered his gear, including the Bow of Hart.

"This about your mission? With the Withlings?" She pitched her voice low.

"Probably." Athson's stomach knotted. "I'm pretty sure it is. He told me it was a Rokan dagger. I've faced a certain wizard, named Corgren, who owns one."

"I see." Minith washed Athson's hands and cocked her head toward the grave being dug. "Why him?"

Athson fixed his gaze on Minith. Could he trust her? He

should. She was a ranger and an elf. Athson whispered, " Just like I told you before who he is. That's why."

Minith's eyes widened. "There are few enough of them left. Who was he?"

Athson gauged his setting. Apeth had said to ride out. "I shouldn't say. But I need to ride out in the morning. I've got to finish this." He glanced at the Bow of Hart.

Minith paused. "I see. Well, there are several merchant's guards we can depend on and several dwarves and other men who are pretty stout. We'll do well enough."

Athson nodded. "I'll see him buried first. But if I leave, much of the immediate danger leaves too. Thanks for understanding."

They buried Apeth in the morning. Athson helped cover the grave. He was doing a lot of that lately. Well, just one other, but it was starting to add up. He didn't think this was part of being a Withling. With the last shovel of dirt, he paused, sweating in the chilly morning air. Hastra and Apeth had both mentioned the slaughter at Withling's Watch centuries earlier. Maybe death was more of being a Withling than he expected, at least when Magdronu was involved. Athson returned the shovel to its owner with his thanks.

Most of the people who slept nearby left before Athson and the other few men completed the burial. Some stopped off and paid their respects, even mentioning small kindnesses done for them by Apeth. Those little tales surprised Athson, since he hadn't noticed most of them. Apeth would be missed. His stomach felt like an empty pit.

He gathered his belongings and mounted the horse but kept the mule in tow, a hard reminder of his missing friend and mentor. He caught sight of Spark nearby and motioned to him to follow. Best just trot on through, clear the crowd, and then ride hard. He'd trade the mule later for supplies.

As he passed Minith, Athson nodded to her and the other

rangers. He hated leaving this duty, but the bow was important now. His father and others had died for it. There was some reason behind all that, and Athson wasn't going to squander their sacrifices.

Athson yanked on his reins near Minith. "Do you have something I can use as a pole?"

"Yeah, got a spear here in the wagon." Minith rode over by the wagon and pulled the spear out. "Will this do?"

Athson took the pole-weapon from Minith. The haft was long and sturdy, the head still tight. "Good enough. You don't need it?"

"No, not for this kind of work. We have our bows and long-knives. Take it. You're still with the rangers."

"Thanks." He was still a ranger, he supposed. With the butt of the spear braced in his stirrup, Athson wheeled away and set out at a fast clip, the mule still trailing. He'd stow the spear with the mule later. But now he had what he needed. If everyone around him had died for a purpose, then he still carried the banner of his family's house for a purpose. He'd tie that onto the spear and furl it until he needed the banner of the ten-tines. If he was going to beat back the curse, he'd best declare his freedom from it as well as not being from a family of traitors. He set his jaw. Maybe that was something from Eloch. He didn't know but it felt right somehow.

He rode hard all day, bypassing Huffer's Post, though he hated missing the chance to see Huffer and his wife. But by the looks of it, they knew trolls were approaching in numbers, as they appeared to be selling or loading their inventory to evacuate. Athson rode on and passed the turn to the landing farther north on the river. He reined his horse to a halt and considered the road. What was needed just now?

Horses approached from the east in the distance. Spark's hackles rose, and he snarled. So not normal riders. Athson waited, letting them get closer. Best see who was following him.

They drew close and pulled their reins, slowing to a trot. They rode with their hoods fallen about their shoulders. A man and a woman, the ones he'd helped.

Athson drew his sword. Not them. He held his sword aloft until he could shout to them. "Close enough. What do you want?"

The woman urged her horse forward a few steps. "You helped us. We want to ride with you and help you in return."

Athson's horse danced beneath him. He shook his head. "I don't think so. Ride on back where you came from and return the horses."

"These are ours. We mean you no harm." She raised her hands.

"Maybe they are yours, but you're not going with me." Athson brandished his sword. "Do not try me."

The woman eyed the sword, then Athson. She swallowed and said something over her shoulder to the man. Athson doubted they were married.

Athson's hair rose like Spark's hackles. The mountain hound still snarled. Athson had a thought, but first he said, "Look, I befriended you because I was supposed to. I've offered you blessings. I suggest you take them and turn from whatever it is you're doing. But for now, you're leaving." Was he even doing this right? He missed Apeth more than ever.

"And who will make us?" the man shouted, his accent suddenly tinged with that of a Rokan.

Time to see if they knew about Spark. Athson smiled. "My friend here will do the honors. Spark! At 'em!"

The mountain hound charged. The man and the woman hesitated, but their eyes followed Spark's snarling approach. They both wheeled their horses and galloped away.

Athson whistled Spark back. Good to know he could use Spark against them. They were likely Rokan mages of some sort. The woman had recognized his sword, so she'd attacked the dwarven tower that night.

Athson eyed the landing road. Now for the decision.

Make your best choice and ride. Time's getting short.

Why he felt that, Athson didn't understand, but he turned and rode hard until dusk. Other landings remained downriver, and he was more likely to catch the fleet of river vessels carrying the bulk of the ranger garrison and his friends—not to mention his mother.

After nightfall, Athson watered the mule and the horse and let them rest awhile. But he soon mounted the mule and walked the animals into the night, leaning onto the mule's neck and dozing as he rode. Spark kept watch for him. As he nodded, Athson wondered if a mule walked faster than the current in the Auguron River. He snorted. Likely not, but at least he was moving. Just like Apeth wanted.

But Corgren was somewhere out there.

∼

HASTRA SAT AWAKE HALF the night or wandered onto the deck. The arrow lay broken in Limbreth's care. The Bane no longer pursued them. Presumably. Upon the deck, she considered the implications as the wind brushed against her face. Without interference, they'd make Auguron City without more trouble. The boat rolled in the current beneath her, and she shuffled her feet. Their entire journey shuddered beneath them if Limbreth's statement proved correct.

Less trouble suited Hastra well. The entire trip weighed on her now. How long until...? Well, not worth considering. She touched her midsection where the old wound lay hidden behind her blouse. She wasn't as young as she used to be. Less excitement suited her fading energy now. Her exhale billowed her cheeks. If she survived the confrontation to come—and there would be one—she needed retirement, or a nice long stay somewhere. Withling's Watch, perhaps. She doubted that would ever happen for her.

She found a seat on a crate, her legs worn out. Limbreth and the Bane proved far quicker than she. Weariness dragged at her daily now. Hastra cast her gaze skyward. With the arrow broken and the sign fading quickly in the sky, she needed direction. If Athson still retained the Bow of Hart, then certainly Eloch planned something with the White Arrow. All of the prophecy's elements had been presented to them already. That was no mistake. The arrow was always Eloch's provenance. She chuckled. Well, all of it really. Who was she kidding? She trusted Eloch. No sense giving up now. Not after all this time guarding, struggling, and sacrificing.

Limbreth had almost tossed the arrow in the river. Good thing Hastra stopped her. She shrugged. But then, Eloch always provided, so no use considering what had never happened.

A ranger guard walked by Hastra. "Withling, can I help you?"

"Ah, no, just thinking." She offered a wan smile in the light of a nearby lantern.

"Well, my apologies that the intruder got aboard without our notice." The ranger turned to go.

"That thing has been a bother to me for months. Someone threw it off a mountainside and still didn't kill it. Limbreth's brave but over-matched."

The ranger gaped. "Really? Off a mountainside?" He shook his head. "That's dark magic if I ever heard tell of any."

"Dark indeed. But you needn't worry about it. I doubt it will return now." She patted the ranger's arm, and he left.

She sniffed. Likely that Corgren and his lot, maybe even Magdronu, thought they'd won this contest already. Eloch could use a broken arrow if he wanted.

She chuckled and wobbled below decks, where she found Limbreth fast asleep in the top bunk. Hastra wedged her way into the lower bunk and put her hands behind her head. She stared at the upper bunk in the near darkness. Things weren't good at the moment, but they weren't hopeless. She'd been in a dungeon after being stabbed to death and still escaped. Things could always be worse. Hastra closed her eyes and went to sleep for what was left of the night.

∽

Tordug's heart sank with the morning news. The White Arrow broken in a fight with the Bane overnight. He walked away from Makwi and sat on some crates, his belly suddenly as empty as raided treasure chests. He rested his head in his hands and grimaced. What hope had they without Eloch's prophecy? Without everything they needed? Corgren's trolls marched for Auguron City, and they could easily win that fight with Magdronu's help. Tordug tried to swallow the lump in his throat.

Makwi approached and stood by him. Nearby, Ralda rumbled some song of his people.

"Pass the word to Gweld." Tordug lifted his head and stared into Makwi's eyes, where suffering mirrored his own losses. What use was serving needlessly?

Makwi clutched his shoulder. "We'll fight on, regardless."

Tordug nodded silently and swallowed hard. "That was our hope against the odds. This fight could have freed our home." It could have restored his lost honor. What was he to leave Makwi now but an empty future? Suddenly Tordug wanted to pound something, hack it with his ax.

"We'll win it back." Makwi crossed his arms and stood impassively, gazing at nothing in the distance over Tordug's shoulder.

"How? Our people are scattered across this forest, across other lands. They'll never return. Not to my banner. Ezhandun..." He trailed off into silence. They'd barely provided help. "Ezhandun proved I'll gain no help from anyone."

Makwi bent close to Tordug's face. "If no one else will, then you and I will do it. Alone. With these elves." He motioned to the rangers aboard their barge.

Tordug clutched his son's arm. He'd retained his honor, his hope, even when he lost his respect for Tordug for several years. Tordug's face trembled. "You're right. We'll fight, maybe gain some honor in the doing of it."

"More than honor. We'll retain who we are, maybe inspire others to hope."

Tordug mustered a nod. Hope. A thin glimmer of light to shine in darkness. Their home lay ruined and occupied by foul trolls. He closed his eyes. The bones of his people lay unburied. Their homes despoiled. He ground his teeth at the memory of their trek through Chokkra. He released his hold on Makwi and clenched his fists until they shook. They murdered his people on mountaintops. That memory alone raised his blood.

He lifted his gaze to Makwi. "Aye, what hope there is in our dying, we'll offer to others who might remember their own courage."

Makwi nodded, his dark beard shifting in the morning breeze. He strode away to the prow of the barge and signaled Gweld.

Tordug tugged his gray beard. Without the White Arrow, he and Makwi likely went to their deaths. They'd make them good ones, if it could help their people regain their hope. Tordug suddenly laughed in the chill morning air.

Makwi paused and grinned over his shoulder.

Tordug laughed harder. "Come, then, wizard! It's time to harvest trolls!"

CHAPTER FOURTEEN

Magdronu-as-Gweld received the news on the morning breeze. Makwi's signals told the tale he already knew. The White Arrow and Eloch's precious prophecy, nurtured so long by overused Withlings, broken in the night. He lowered his head in feigned dismay and turned from the bow of the barge. It was over before it had begun. One thing remained to ensure victory, and he'd gain the Bow of Hart with guile as necessary.

The rangers around him murmured at the signals. They knew none of the details, just that some attack on the Withling left her without a promised weapon. The elves murmured about the coming trolls, and Magdronu-as-Gweld noted their uncertainty. Their own memory of Chokkra's fall and this vague news of prophecy lost left them wondering about the fate of their own home.

But Magdronu-as-Gweld involved fate in none of his plans. Magic, brutality, cunning, but never fate. He ducked through the crowd of murmuring rangers. Rumor of the mission was known among them from months back. The sudden invasion of overwhelming forces on their meager garrison reinforced the rumor to fact. The witnessed signals hammered the last nail into their understanding. Doom approached their fair home across the vastness of Auguron's forests.

Magdronu-as-Gweld found an empty place on the barge and leaned against his raised forearm, feigning defeat and shock. *Time for a little meeting.* Magdronu inhaled and sent his summons. *'Corgren! Paugren!'* He waited as he suppressed a roar of victory. His long years of plotting and waiting neared their end. He had his enemy entrapped within his own prophecy, the weakness of mortals and holy weapons.

Corgren's presence answered, *'Master, I answer.'*

'It is done. The Bane has broken Eloch's arrow. The prophecy has failed. Is everything ready as planned?' Magdronu-as-Gweld took deep breaths.

'Master, you shall ascend and your renown will resound across Denaria! The trolls march and have put Marston's Station to the torch. All is ready in Auguron City if the shrine is completed.' Minute uncertainty edged through the spell.

Paugren's presence entered the spell, and Magdronu linked them in his mind. *'Master, I answer your summons. What is your desire?'*

'I was just reveling in our certain victory, for the arrow was broken in the night by the Bane. What of this other Withling and Athson?'

'Great one, this is wondrous news. We set the trap, and Corgren killed him without our being discovered.' Paugren paused, but greater uncertainty tinged his communication.

Magdronu-as-Gweld inhaled. No joy over their victory? Paugren was becoming weak. But he'd complete the shrine, if nothing else, and Magdronu would then determine the nature of his loyalty. *'And what of Athson?'*

'We followed him as you desired, but he guessed our intentions. He set the guardian upon us, and we fled. But he rides east hard.'

'Then he's separated. Perhaps he'll come to me. If not, I'll find him in the city and complete the plan. Then we shatter the city.' Magdronu

purred a low rumble over the spell. *'Now we need the shrine to complete the traps set for the city. Paugren, you take Cass with you to help complete the shrine, slow though it may be.'*

'Master, we depart this hour on the wings of your magic to fulfill your request.' Though Paugren suppressed his doubts, Magdronu felt the vibration along the spell.

'You harbor doubts, Paugren? Is magic not enough?' Magdronu pitched a velvet tone through the spell. Lay the trap for him if he was weak and draw him out.

Wariness crawled from Paugren. *'Magdronu, you are greatest, and I serve you. I have wearied of this contest, but I serve your wishes alone.'*

Magdronu allowed another pleased purr along the spell. *'But a while longer, and you shall have rewards and rest. But now, we press our enemy and win the age to come under my rule. Away with you both on your assignments. Nothing stands in our way.'*

In his pleased mood, Magdronu allowed the spell to close slowly. No need to force his servants now. They understood his preeminence.

He stood and frowned as Magdronu-as-Gweld. One thing remained for him to accomplish. Gain the Bow of Hart and ascend to rule of Denaria—starting with the elves of Auguron, who would soon bend their knees. The age of Eloch drew to a close.

∾

ATHSON ARRIVED at another landing road east of the hills less than a week from Auguron City. Even the mule's legs wobbled as if it carried Apeth. A mournful thought. Athson grabbed his sword and, though the grief remained the dark side of his mood departed. Good, he needed to take action, not dawdle over what he couldn't change. Perhaps he'd caught the river fleet.

"Which way? The landing road or continue west on the main road?"

The horse snorted and stomped one hoof, then stood still, waiting with its head down. Athson gripped his sword but found no guidance from that source. He sighed. It would take hours to ride north and find the river fleet. If he missed them, it was hours back.

Precious moments slipped away. Athson tucked his chin and stared at his horse's mane. The animals were exhausted. It was this one or nothing.

He released a heavy sigh and flicked the reins. "This landing or not at all until I meet them in Auguron City."

Beside him, Spark wagged his tail.

He guided the horse north for the landing as the afternoon sun lengthened. Several hours of daylight remained to reach the river in time. "Spark, watch behind." He didn't want those Rokan spies turning up again, even though he hadn't seen them for several days.

Apprehension grew in Athson's mind with each hoof-fall on the little-used road. He scratched at his chin as the horse dragged its hooves on the road. He wanted to see Limbreth. But he'd have to tell her of his failure, apologize. His heart soared a moment with exhilaration at the thought of seeing her, then dropped into a pit. She might not understand. He still had to tell her. And he longed to hold her. His heart surged again amid the doubt.

And then there was his mother. Long years of separation weighed on his mind. He had so much to say that he didn't know where to start. He'd tell her of his father's sacrifice upon the Funnel. The fact that she was free of Rok still seemed impossible. But he was a Withling, and nothing was impossible with Eloch—if it was needed.

Athson swayed in the saddle as the rhythm of the horse worked into his weariness. His head nodded more than once.

Too long in the saddle. But Apeth had been right—his instructions got Athson away from the Rokan agents. His throat constricted. He hadn't known Apeth Stellin long, but the old man's death added salt to his old wounds. Everyone died around him.

He shook himself. *Stop thinking that way.* He touched the pommel of his sword. No, everyone didn't die. His friends still lived. His mother was returned from captivity. That thought was incorrect. *Don't believe those things. Test them.* He rode on with his hand on the sword.

Long minutes passed, and Athson nodded again, almost sliding from the saddle. He jerked awake and shook his head. He pulled his water loose, unstopped the skin, and poured some over his head. In the chill, he stirred further awake. Best take advantage of it. He nudged the horse into a trot with his heels. The sooner he arrived at the landing, the better.

Dusk lay across the river when he arrived at the landing. Water coursed by under the gathering darkness. He approached the landing office and called for the attendant.

A wizened elf stuck his head out the door and spilled lamplight across the small dock. He squinted at Athson in the darkness, his sharp features suspicious. "Who is it?"

"I'm Athson, a ranger." Athson dismounted and stepped into the light.

"You're no elf, though you have the cloak of a ranger." He stepped out the door with a short spear. "Be gone if you're brigand, or I'll stick you."

Athson motioned to the river. "The eastern garrison travels to the city. Have barges been by today? Any rangers?"

The elf lowered the spear. "The eastern garrison isn't on the move. Can't be. You must be some spy."

Athson sighed. "Look, have boats been by today from upriver? There are trolls on the march west. I need to meet the garrison if possible."

The elf shook his head. "No boats." He squinted. "I've heard rumors for days about trolls coming. You say it's true?"

"Yes, lots of them are coming and—" Athson stared at the river as lights appeared around the bend. "Is that a barge?"

"Eh?" The elf turned toward the river. "Could be, at that. Might be another one coming too."

"Do you have a boat? I need to meet them." Athson led the horse and mule onto the dock.

"Hold on. What I got won't carry your animals."

Athson grabbed his gear and the Bow of Hart. "Then row me out. You can have the horse and mule as payment. You'll need them. Ride for the city, but don't leave the boat for the trolls."

"Really? I can't leave the landing unattended." The elf leaned on the haft of his spear. "This is a business, and the council wants these running."

Athson laughed. "Do as you will, then. Trolls will burn this dock and your office to the ground. They're coming to lay siege to the city. Just row me to that first barge."

The elf pointed his spear toward the oncoming craft on the river. "We don't even know if that's the garrison."

Athson started for the little boat tied at the dock. "Look, there are more of them. It's the garrison. I'll row myself if you won't, but I need to reach them." He wheeled toward the attendant. "Ranger business." He hadn't used that line in a while.

The elf sighed. "I guess you're right. My dinner will get cold, but I'll row you out. The boat belongs here." He stepped back inside the office and returned with his coat and a cap. "Best get it done so I can get back to my food."

Athson scrambled into the boat and somehow avoided falling into the river. He'd never been in something this small on water, but he found his balance and sat with his gear at his feet.

"Slide over and help me row. It'll go faster, and we'll miss the first one otherwise." The elf climbed into the boat and sat beside Athson. "Guess ranger business will pay if you are really a ranger. If not, I'll keep the animals."

"You should flee on them and sink the boat." Athson grabbed an oar.

The elf cast off from the dock and instructed him when to row so that they turned into the river. "Can't just leave because you say so. You're probably not even a ranger."

Athson grunted with each stroke. The long rides for days wore on him now. He ground his teeth with effort and set his back to the work. He had to make it, find his friends and escape any chance of being caught by Corgren or the Rokan agents. "I'm a ranger. You'll see when we get to that barge."

They pulled on the oars and rowed farther into the current, then fought it until they drew close to the barge drifting near them. The old elf hailed the barge and waved his lantern to get their attention.

"Who calls?" someone from the boat asked.

Athson looked over his shoulder, and his heart sank. Just a crewman. But then, in other lights, he glimpsed rangers in forest green gazing at them.

The landing attendant tossed a rope to the barge. "Got a man who says he's a ranger and needs to come aboard."

Crewmen hauled on the rope and pulled them close until Athson could climb aboard the taller vessel. The crewmen eyed him suspiciously. But rangers crowded close, and an officer stepped into the light. "Report, ranger."

Athson saluted. "Athson. I've been on assignment with the Withling Hastra. Another ranger was with me, Gweld. Are they aboard?"

The officer arched an eyebrow, grabbed a torch, and stepped closer. "You're him. Gweld's with us, but the others are on different boats. Come with me, and I'll explain."

"I'll be a fried fish. He is a ranger." The landing attendant chuckled. "I guess I get to keep those animals."

The officer called over the rail. "You're to head for the city without delay. Either take that boat and drift down or ride, but don't leave the boat. Take your valuables. Trolls are coming, thousands of them."

The elf in the boat gaped. "That's true?" He sat down and fumbled with the oars, then set out, rowing like trolls might be waiting on the riverbanks.

"Come with me." The officer led Athson away. They passed rows of rangers lounging on the deck among crates of supplies and goods. They crossed the barge on heavy planking and turned a corner around the compartments for the bridge and crewman's quarters, where they almost ran headlong into a ranger.

"Gweld?" Athson pulled his hood from his head.

The elf startled back in the close quarters and eyed Athson with a passing, blank gaze before his eyes widened. "Athson! How did you get here? You made it!" He grabbed Athson's hand and shook it. "I lost you in the snow storm back in the heaths and couldn't find you." He took Athson by the shoulders and looked him up and down. "You don't look any worse for the wear." He glanced at the Bow of Hart, and his eyes flashed wide for a moment. "So, you do have it?"

Athson took the elf's greeting in stride and laughed. "I made it! I've been looking for you and the others." He shouldered the Bow of Hart. "Yes, though it did me no good at the Funnel. I thought it was useless until I had to kill some trolls escaping the Troll Heaths." He leaned sideways and peered behind Gweld. "Where are the others?"

Gweld saluted the officer. "Can you excuse us, sir?"

The officer returned the ranger salute. "I was just bringing him to you. Clearly you have much to discuss." He walked away.

Athson leaned close. "Who's that?"

"That's Kuruth. Good officer. He knows some of our mission already from evacuating the garrison forts." Gweld put his arm around Athson's shoulders. "Come this way, we can talk in quiet up here." He led Athson atop the bridge cabin, and they sat with the frosty night breeze on them. "We've got a bit more privacy here. We'll catch up on the news. Tell me all that happened. We guessed some of the tale before the storm came." He glanced over Athson's gear, his eye lingering on the spear with the furled family banner lashed to it. "You have enough weapons now?"

"I guess." Athson laid the spear between him and Gweld and the Bow of Hart on the other side.

"Where'd you get the spear?" Gweld ran his hand over the furled banner.

"From some of our fellow rangers I was helping days back. I'm going to use it as my standard. That's from my family's house." He patted the spear haft. Tension eased from his shoulders. Speaking openly about it felt right. "Corgren called us traitors. We're not. A lot of people have died over this and I'm not hiding anymore. For the sake of each victim. I'll stand by this. It's for my father most of all." He rummaged in his pack and found his father's ring and the signet on the necklace. Athson put the ring on a finger and the necklace about his neck. "That makes it official, I guess."

"Inspiring." Gweld looked away, then back after a few moments. "So, tell me all that happened and I'll fill you in about the rest of us."

Athson launched into the tale upon the heights of the Funnel and related his illness and meeting Apeth Stellin. He then related their discovery of trolls on the march in numbers and their running fight with scouts as they escaped to Marston's Station. He related the tale of Apeth's death and his ride to catch them and avoid further danger from Rokan spies.

Athson gazed up at the wandering star, its tail now long and thin as it faded each night from the sky. "I think Corgren killed Apeth, but I'm not sure why." He fixed his gaze on Gweld as he ended the tale of his journey.

Gweld rubbed his chin in one hand. "That's quite a lot of news." He shook his head. "Hastra said she thought Apeth Stellin was behind the unusual help we received. It's good to know it was him, but bad that he's gone. We could have used him in what's to come." The elf frowned as he turned to Athson. "Much has happened since that wandering star appeared in the sky." He shook his head again. "And you decided to become a Withling? I never would have thought that after all your arguments with Hastra."

Athson shrugged and ran one hand across the bow he'd laid across his lap as he touched the hilt of his blessed sword. "It seemed like the best thing. I had to think about it for days on the way to Marston's. I still hesitated for several more, though I knew Apeth was right all along. I've had dreams that come true—little prophecies. I've been hearing other things too. Spark's part of that." He gazed at Gweld, his eyes narrowed. Let him challenge that with the suggestion of Soul's Ease.

Gweld scratched the back of his neck. "Guess I was wrong on that point."

With a nudge of his elbow against Gweld's arm, Athson chuckled. "Well, even you can't know everything." He paused and cast a frowning gaze about them. "So where are the others?"

"Oh, yes, that." Gweld ran his fingers through his hair. "We also found out about the trolls and warned the garrison. They evacuated, and we made our way to Marston's Station. We were met by Howart and Zelma. You know them, right?" At a nod from Athson, Gweld continued, "While I was away from my room, Hastra borrowed one of my arrows, and the

Withlings blessed it. Athson, they made the arrow of the prophecy."

"What? That I didn't know about."

"Yes, well, we decided that we'd travel with the garrison on the river and avoid attacks to get the arrow. We even split up to confuse the Bane. The others are on barges and boats farther back. I had a fake arrow, but the Bane got that pretty quickly one night." Gweld paused, his face suddenly drawn. "There's a lot to tell still."

"So Limbreth isn't on this barge? How did she survive? I thought she was dead, that I'd failed completely. How did my mother and Hastra get over the mountains?" Athson gripped Gweld's arm tightly as he asked his questions.

"That all goes back to Howart's Cave. That was a mess, I can tell you. I thought we were dead then." Gweld shook his head. "It was a miracle we all survived." The elf launched into the story and related the whirlwind that save them and how Eloch had brought Hastra and Athson's mother from Rok so that the Withling could stop the whirlwind. Gweld then related how they tried to catch Athson, but they had no horses, and Hastra led them to save Limbreth from the river, telling what he knew from Limbreth of her unlikely survival.

Athson stopped Gweld. "She said there were lights around her?"

Gweld nodded. "And the wind blew so hard she fell sideways."

"Those lights. I think that was Spark. He went over the cliff after Limbreth."

Gweld shrugged and shook his head. "My apologies, Athson. I didn't believe you about Spark, but I guess you were right all along." The elf continued the tale up to the creation of the White Arrow and Limbreth handling it first so that she succumbed to the holy awe with joyous laughter, becoming its protector.

Athson's chest swelled with pride that Limbreth carried the White Arrow of Hastra's prophecy. "You've made it this far with the arrow." He patted the Bow of Hart. "And I have this. We have what we need to fight Magdronu, I guess."

"Uh, that's not all." Gweld let out a heavy sigh. "Remember I told you how we each had disguised arrows?" At Athson's nod, the elf continued, "Well, it tried to get the real arrow from Limbreth, and it was broken."

"What?" Athson stood and paced the roof of the bridge. How could this happen? Apeth killed, and now this. He slouched and stood looking down the line of the river fleet's many lights. "How did it happen?"

Gweld stood beside Athson. "I don't know for sure. They passed the news up the line with signals a few mornings back." He paused. "Athson, I don't know what we'll do."

Athson held the Bow of Hart close. He'd distrusted it, then become a Withling and now trusted the prophecy. The arrow had come and gone without him ever seeing it.

"I don't either. I guess Limbreth can't be blamed without me around to chase off the Bane with my sword." He sniffed. "I did worse on the Funnel." He'd failed his father and Limbreth, choosing revenge over saving her. The bow could have done the job. At least, he thought so now. He had to tell her. But as for the White Arrow... He inhaled and sighed. "I don't know what will happen either." He gripped his blessed sword—it was becoming a habit to check his thoughts now, and a sudden one occurred to him. "But I do know this."

Gweld spoke into Athson's pause. "What's that?"

Athson fixed his gaze on the elf. "What is needed is given. We'll have what is needed."

CHAPTER FIFTEEN

A knock at the compartment door roused Limbreth from sleep. She reached for the arrow, but the pieces lay in her pack. No need to guard it any longer. The pit in her stomach widened. She'd eaten little and finally slept this night after several without much rest.

Hastra rolled from the bunk below Limbreth's with a groan. She muttered about her aches and the weeping keeping her awake.

Limbreth covered her mouth with her hand and stared at the knots in the wall while Hastra opened the door, letting in lantern light from the hall outside. She hadn't realized she'd kept the Withling awake with her sobs over her failure. She'd tried to keep that to herself. Limbreth sighed. She'd failed at hiding her sorrow too.

Hastra exchanged words with whoever stood at the doorway. "He's there? How? Well, if you don't know more, then I guess we'll find out when we land at the city. Thank you." The Withling shut the door.

Darkness descended in the room again, and Hastra trudged

to her bunk. "Too late," she muttered to herself as she rolled into her bunk.

Limbreth let the matter lay a moment. Maybe she'd go back to sleep. She furrowed her brow. Who was where? Who was late? Her heart thudded in her throat. She hoped it wasn't Athson. She swallowed. "Whoever came with the message woke me too. What is it?" She wanted to both see and avoid him.

Hastra hesitated in the darkness. "Guess I can't act like I'm asleep yet. Let it wait until the morning, Limbreth."

That wasn't a good answer. She rolled over, and her heart beat erratically. She dreaded finding out, but she couldn't wait. "Just tell me."

The Withling sighed. "It's Athson. He's aboard the first barge. Arrived earlier tonight. Don't know why they didn't send a message sooner than the middle of the night."

Limbreth got out of the upper bunk and walked the few paces available in the small space. "What am I to do?" All her failures haunted her mind. She'd failed that night with the Banshee. She should have been with him at the gates of Chokkra. Then there was being taken hostage. "I've failed him again. I don't want to see him."

Hastra sat up in her bunk. "You won't for several more days. But this is not your fault. I wish you'd see it. The Bane isn't something you just push overboard."

Limbreth whirled, her anger flaring. "It was my responsibility. I failed Athson just like all the other times. It's on me that the White Arrow lies in pieces, that—that—" A sudden sob choked her. "That its light is extinguished. Like that." She snapped her fingers, then huddled in the darkness as she inhaled and exhaled raggedly.

"What do you mean all the other times?"

"You set me to watch him closely, back in Auguron City. I failed him when the Banshee attacked that night."

Silence answered Limbreth.

She stepped back and leaned against the door. Hastra thought so too? She covered her mouth with one hand as she squatted, then sat on the floor in sudden tears. She had truly failed, then. She found her voice. "I should have been with him at the gates of Chokkra. Is that—is the Banshee why you wouldn't let me go then? Because I failed?"

"What?" Hastra fumbled in the darkness and lit the lamp. The light displayed her puffy eyes and disheveled hair. The Withling's face—no, her entire body—sagged as if under a weight. "That's not it at all. I was going by the certainty that only those three could escape. The Banshee had nothing to do with it. Why would you think you failed?"

Limbreth crumpled further into tears. "Because I was supposed to protect him. You said so. And then there was Chokkra. And then the Bane came at the tower, and I fled rather than stay with him. I-I should have gone with him to see Howart. He—he deserved my support then. But I stayed back, let myself be captured. I got his father killed. If I'd been free, he could have saved him at the Funnel."

Hastra crossed to her and wiped Limbreth's face. "My dear, you carry too much on your shoulders. You haven't failed him."

Limbreth shrugged Hastra's arms away. "I have. I've been a coward. With the Bane. Then I just took the White Arrow without a thought, except for him. I took it and thought I'd make up for everything. The laughter, the protectiveness I felt lent me the assurance I'd do this one thing right for Athson."

"Limbreth, you put too much on yourself. You aren't a coward. You stood up to the Bane on the Funnel and when it stole the White Arrow. You showed courage." Hastra touched Limbreth's damp cheeks and embraced her.

The sobs subsided to ragged gasps, and Limbreth viewed Hastra's face through blurring tears, the Withling's expression etched with concern. "I failed with the arrow. I cannot see him.

What will he think of me?" She rested her head against the wooden hatch. "He'll blame me, think I'm a cowardly failure."

Hastra shook her head. "No, that's not true."

"Yes, it is. We had the Bow of Hart and the arrow, prophecy fulfilled. We had what it would take to defeat Magdronu. And now we're doomed. How will Athson kill Magdronu without the White Arrow?" She covered her face with her hands.

Hastra embraced Limbreth tighter. "Limbreth, it's been a long and trying journey. You've been so brave. The dwarves think so highly of you. But you still think so little of yourself regardless of all you've done? You're being so unfair to yourself over this arrow, the banshee, and the rest. You can't know everything and do everything perfectly."

"I should have known better every single time, done better."

"Limbreth, I don't even know everything to do correctly every time. I didn't even realize who Athson's father was until Chokkra!" She dabbed Limbreth's cheeks and kissed her on the side of her head. "You can't blame yourself all the time. We fight and strive in these things, but we cannot know every single twist of events. We're supposed to be faithful. You'll see Athson when we land in the city, and he'll hear the tale of your bravery."

Limbreth shook her head. "I can't see him." She regarded Hastra for the first time in the conversation. "I won't. I'll jump in the river first. He'll—he'll think I'm the worst person. He'll never want me again. He'll think—what would he think?"

Hastra leaned away from Limbreth at arm's length. "I'll tell you what he should think."

"What's that?" Limbreth hated the hopelessness in her voice.

"That he's lucky to have traveled so far with such a courageous woman as you, someone who would stay with him no matter the odds. Limbreth, you've proven yourself worthy of his esteem so many times."

"Have I? Really?"

Hastra embraced Limbreth again. "My dear, you are just who he needs. And I don't say that lightly. If he can't see that, then he's blind. But I don't think he is."

Limbreth sniffed. "How do you know that?"

Hastra tightened her arms around Limbreth. "Because he came for you at the Funnel."

∼

CORGREN TURNED from the bridge over the Auguron River. The hex was still intact. He grinned and strode through the busy city streets, his hood pulled over his head. Now to check the rest of the traps he'd left in Auguron City.

The raucous noise of the river wharfs faded but not the general bustle. Everywhere he turned, Corgren found merchants and foreigners preparing to leave the city. His heart *thumped* with exuberance. They—he, his master, and the others —had caused all this fear and confusion. These refugees might flee now, but Magdronu's rule would soon extend over Denaria. Nothing the elves did to fortify their city would stop his trolls or Magdronu, when he was revealed.

But now for the shrine and its progress.

Corgren left the city proper and strolled out to the cemetery. He jumped the fence lest the attendant, if one remained in all the confusion and preparation for the troll invasion, spotted him. He had no proper business on these grounds. Well, he did. Just not what they thought proper. He grinned to himself. Magdronu's business.

After several turns on the paths, Corgren crossed several knolls and made his way to the back of the grounds until he found two specific graves. A whispered spell—who knew if anyone lingered close—revealed the magic remained intact. A beacon to focus magic for the new shrine. A place for blood and extending his master's power in the heart of elven territory, and right when it was most needed. He shook his head and smirked. Magdronu's plans were brilliant. The dragon had outmaneuvered Eloch and none of these elves were the wiser. He chuckled. Ath never knew where he was or why. He was blind for just this purpose.

Voices murmured in the distance and drew Corgren from his reflections. Yes, time to check on his brother and the Beleesh sisters. They had just enough magic from their master to break the laws of Auguron City with sorcery for the shrine. He walked toward the voices, clearing the thin copse of oak and beech. Looking back, he found the trees screened the activity ahead perfectly.

Corgren strode toward the four figures cloaked like storm clouds and standing on bare ground. Paugren led the sisters in the incantations, a slow task using the distant magic from the Rokan shrine. He paused and watched the four mages, his hands clasped behind his back. Good thing he traveled to Rok and ensured the sacrifices there continued. He approached his brother, who was sweating profusely with the effort of the current spell.

They stood in a square, while between them a five-pointed star glowed faintly below the winter afternoon sky. In unison, Paugren and the Beleesh sisters intoned the words of the spell in the Dragon's language, their tones and pronunciation precise, lest the spell fail and they be required to begin again— or worse. He'd seen a lesser mage in Rok once fail with the words and remembered his screams as the Dragon's green flames consumed him. But these four mages knew far more. Their hands motioned with equal precision.

At length, the spell ended, and the four mages stumbled away from their work and slouched at a nearby boulder, carved flat for sacrifices. While they'd move it with magic in the end—after it was consecrated to Magdronu—they now used it for their belongings and supplies. Corgren almost laughed at the thought that these four actually stayed in differing inns around the city. The doomed elves played host to the enemy who worked among them.

"Brother, your work goes well." Corgren strode to Paugren and halted before his breathless brother as he drank from a water-skin.

Paugren swallowed and breathed deeply several times. "The work goes faster now that there are four of us. You've seen to the sacrifices elsewhere?"

Corgren walked around the design blackened into the ground. Not yet enough magic in it to glow on its own. He whirled back to Paugren. "Indeed, I have." He stepped closer and glanced at the three Beleesh sisters. "You're all keeping quiet otherwise?" He arched an eyebrow and fixed a sidelong gaze at each of the sisters. They could be unruly when they wanted.

Esthria approached as she dabbed sweat from the brow of her beautiful, oval face. "We've behaved, Corgren."

Cass threw off her cloak and stood naked in the cold by a pile of clothes. "We've worked well into the night often. Exhaustion leads to good behavior."

Corgren arched a brow. How brazen the Beleesh sisters were now. Not so those long ago years when they'd first abandoned Eloch for Magdronu. His eyes swept along Cass's womanly curves. "Indeed. I'm sure you would do with some hard labor for once."

Esthria lifted a finger to Corgren's chin and drew his eyes back to her face, beguiling with youthful beauty. "Perhaps you can spare some time to misbehave?" She pursed her succulent lips in a seductive promise of pleasure.

Corgren snorted. Youthful the Beleesh sisters might appear

thanks to the Dragon's Blessing, but their eyes held the knowledge of centuries. He brushed her hand away. "Enough. I've come to inspect your handiwork and the bridge."

Laughter tinkled from Esthria and her sisters. "You sure, Corgren? Surely you can spare a few hours from those trolls. I imagine they can walk on their own for a while without you holding their hand. Or is that what they need? I can see it now, a long line of trolls holding hands so you can herd them across the length of the forest."

With a slow clap of his hands, he turned to Paugren. "Your humor is as sharp as ever, Esthria." To Paugren, he said, "Walk with me, brother." He cast his gaze over his shoulder to naked Cass as they walked away and raised his voice. "Put your cloak on before someone spots you and you have more work to do." To Paugren, he added, "This surprise needs to remain unseen. Are they truly staying away from any suspicious activity? No men? No spells for the fun of it?" Though effective, the sisters could be troublesome.

Paugren chuckled. "I don't know about Esthria and Ahmelia before I arrived with Cass. But they've been...sedate under my watch."

"How many days until it's finished? The trolls arrive in days, not weeks, you know." Corgren gazed at the boulder as Cass wrapped herself in her cloak.

"It will be done." Paugren waved toward the sisters. "They understand what's at stake in all this, and they welcome what's to come. With the shrine in the Drelkhaz, we'd move much faster. It will be a close thing, but it will be done as the Great One expects."

"Good. I've inspected the bridge, and my hex is still in place. With it and our other plans"—Corgren swept his arms wide to indicate the shrine under magical construction—"we'll defeat the fortifications."

Paugren smirked. "They'll be astounded."

"And they can do nothing to stop it." Corgren stepped away. "I'll see to the trolls." He winked at Paugren. "See to it you don't stop to enjoy any temptations, eh?" He arched an eyebrow.

Paugren snorted. "Not with any of those hell-cats."

Corgren spoke the words of the traveling spell, and when the darkness of the dragon's wings unfolded, he stood in his camp of trolls.

CHAPTER SIXTEEN

The constant current of the river belied the approaching danger, and Athson almost enjoyed the remaining five days to Auguron City. But the sight of the bridge overrode any thought of a pleasant return to his adoptive city, if the gathered throng of rangers from the eastern garrison ever escaped his attentions. The wooden span stretched atop thick brick supports rising from spits of natural rock further fortified by elven engineers. He marveled now at the elegantly designed braces and connections along the bridge since he'd never traveled aboard a barge from upriver.

The bridge over the river struck Athson, and tension gathered across his shoulders as if he had drawn a bow. He'd never truly considered the bridge in the defenses of the city. That vague notion of the city's defense he'd accepted as the vastness of the forest. It was a notion, he now realized with his grip on his blessed sword, born of a familial curse that left him confused and in turmoil on any number of accounts.

Athson snorted. No wonder Sarneth had assigned him to the peaceful, empty western reaches of the forest where nothing ever happened. Not until the inheritance fell into his hands, anyway. He relaxed his grip on the sword. Magdronu had been watching and waiting for years, just for a chance to take the Bow of Hart and thwart Hastra's prophecy. He shook his head and took a deep, relaxing breath. He'd been so blind to it all. But no more. If only he could hear Eloch. If only he could have saved Apeth Stellin. He stared at his feet.

"Got your gear ready?" Gweld appeared at Athson's side. "It won't be long until we arrive."

"Yes, I'm ready." And Athson was, in more ways than one. He hefted the Bow of Hart, its white wood shining even in the wan winter sunlight.

His gaze returned to the bridge as they drifted closer. Details pricked his present from the vague past, details that meant little even months ago but now meant everything in his understanding. And no less so than for the entire population of Auguron City. Five hundred paces the bridge stretched over the river between spits of rock that extended into the river. Ahead, sunlight flashed in the choppy wavelets. The river was a defense, and the bridge a weakness.

But Athson's eyes spotted, even from this distance, the preparations on the bridge. The steel and wood gates stood open, ready to seal the bridge from invading trolls, where once they'd been stored away during peace. Plates of metal now festooned the length of the bridge, which served as protection for defending archers as well as fire resistance. On the city side of the bridge, heartier defenses had likely been erected, should the bridge defenses be breached, but only as a last resort. Any true invasion across the bridge faced one detail: it was rigged to collapse if necessary. A series of levers, well-oiled and maintained, served as a system to release the span and plunge any invaders upon the bridge into the river.

For now, the gates stood ajar, allowing those who wanted to escape the coming siege access to the southern or western roads. Athson inhaled in anticipation of the coming siege. Any attempts to cross the river near the city were accounted for as well. Barges and boats such as the one he now traveled aboard would be drawn up along the city's docks and riverbanks and used to repel a river crossing with archers and rams behind portable fortifications. Higher up on the docks and banks, more screening fortifications were likely being erected by work crews, which served as additional cover for archers as well as a second line of defense for a retreat from the vessels at water-level.

Since so many elves of Auguron served among the rangers at various points of their long lives, there were plentiful reserves with experience ready to serve in the defense. Athson's chest swelled at the thought. His adopted people gathered, even now, to defend their homes from invading trolls. Corgren's army faced a daunting task with or without magic and the Dragon's aid.

The barge slid under the bridge, its shadow passing over the gathered rangers in the open hold until they cleared the span. The barge was guided out of the deeper channel with the rudder. Other crewmen used poles to ease the barge close to the dock as lines were tossed to waiting hands.

Shouts erupted from the barge and the docks as various commands and activities began or continued. Athson gathered his weapons and pack and joined the other rangers. Gangplanks banged across the breadth of space between the barge and the dock, and the rangers marched into Auguron City. Athson had come home—to war.

Upon gaining the dock, Athson ignored the shouts from officers to form up in ranks. With no assignment among these rangers, he wandered toward the trailing vessels with Gweld at his side, in search of his other friends. He raised his voice above the tumult on the docks. "Who's next?"

"Ralda and the dwarves. Look, there they are." Gweld pointed toward their friends, awaiting their turn to disembark.

Athson peered down the length of the docks. "How far back is Limbreth?"

Gweld waved his hand. "Much farther. We'll collect everyone else before they're docked, I should think. It's never this busy, so it will take time to bring all of them in."

Athson stood back with Gweld as more rangers marched off the barge. How much time had this river-fleet gained over the trolls? How many of the refugees traveling west were now caught by trolls? Smoke had sent them fleeing in haste, no doubt. Marston had likely forced people to leave several days ahead of the trolls, and the latter likely dallied as they enjoyed destroying buildings wherever there was a croft, village, or station. But Athson had little doubt Corgren kept the trolls marching on the heels of Marston's reserves, who meant to clear the road and surrounding areas of lingering disbelievers. Athson worried little for the elves and more for travelers.

Ralda gained the dock first, the gangplank creaking under his weight. The giant gathered Athson in a near-crushing hug before he stepped back with grin. "Worried for you." His hand flashed hand-talk.

Athson grinned. "It's good to see you well, Ralda. We made it back."

Tordug grasped Athson's forearm with a wide grin splitting his beard and mustache. "Lad, I thought you were gone for good." He fingered the Bow of Hart. "Glad you got it this far." He shook his head and blinked at Makwi, who stood nearby with a dour expression. "Shame about the White Arrow, though." He grinned again, but it didn't reach his eyes. "We'll make the best without it, eh? It's just one arrow, right, Makwi?"

Makwi grunted in answer and grasped forearms with Athson in greeting. A slim grin touched his face. "We'll make do with that, I guess. Could be a song in that bow of yours yet."

Athson shrugged. "We'll trust Eloch, who's gotten us this far, eh? What is needed is given."

The dwarves arched eyebrows at Athson's words. He'd never been one for avid faith. Not like them.

Tordug clapped Athson on the shoulder. "Well said. I guess the bow's grown on you. That or we'll make a dwarf out of you yet. Like that gell."

"Speaking of which, we need to move on and meet them." Gweld hefted his things after greeting their comrades, and they dodged through the crowd for the next boat.

Athson held his breath. The Withlings and his mother were aboard one of the next boats. He pushed ahead of the others, searching the following boats for sign of a familiar face. He almost missed them until he spotted tall, gaunt Howart standing with two women among the rangers and other refugees who'd gotten passage somehow. He knew Zelma immediately by her wild, red hair waving in the breeze and the crooked grin on her face. By her receding jaw he now recognized her relationship to Hastra.

Beside the two Withlings, Athson spotted a familiar face, though now worn by years of captivity. Guilt flooded his thoughts. He'd lived well and free while Rokans worked her as a slave.

Her face brightened as she spotted him. She waved and flashed a smile Athson remembered from his boyhood. He stilled his feet lest he jump aboard. The Withlings let Danilla cross ahead of them. Athson pushed the Bow of Hart into Ralda's arms, then dropped his pack and the spear as his mother faced him.

Nearby, Spark wagged his tail.

"Mother." The single word exited his lips with a bashful tone. Her face, lined with care and her dark hair now fading to gray with age, still held a touch of her younger years from his memory. He remembered the stalwart expression the last night he'd seen her when the trolls attacked but now that melted into trembling lips and a crinkled brow as tears of relief and joy suddenly burst like a summer storm on parched ground.

Danilla gathered Athson in her arms with sudden tears, and they swayed in the embrace for long silent moments. Athson reveled in his mother's arms, sniffing amid tears and ignoring his other companions, who greeted the Withlings respectfully.

He found words at last and spoke them in her ear. "I've missed you. I thought you were gone."

"I'm here, son, I'm here. I've come at last, thanks to Hastra and that other man. Is he here?" Her embrace tightened.

"No, Apeth didn't make it. Corgren killed him on the road before I made it to Gweld's barge."

Danilla wept anew. "I owe him much for freeing me."

"Mother, Father died at the Funnel after I got the bow. I tried..." His voice trailed into tears as he buried his face in her hair. "I tried so hard."

His mother found words amid her renewed sobs. "I'm sure you did, Athson. We found him in the grave. I thought I'd wept out my sorrow long since."

They finally parted enough to look each other in their tear-stained eyes. Athson wiped his cheeks and said, "Father knew you were alive. I don't know how. He told me as he died."

She wiped her face, but her lips still quivered. "I don't know how either, unless Corgren brought him to Rok and he heard my voice. I knew they'd blinded him."

Athson swallowed another sob. "Corgren gave him back one eye. He said he'd do the other if I gave him the Bow of Hart."

His mother gasped and brought one hand to her neck. "You think he saw me and I never realized it was him?"

Athson shook his head. "I don't know, but you can't worry

about it. He got free in the end. He stabbed Corgren. I'm sure he wanted to help you if he could."

She nodded wordlessly. Danilla touched her hand to her mouth at the sight of the Bow of Hart in Ralda's arms, then touched it almost reverently. "It's been a long time since I've seen this." Her eyes traveled to the spear lying at their feet with the banner furled around the haft below the spear-head. Her eyes widened. "Is that what I think it is? I've heard there was one, from your father but he knew nothing of it."

Athson squared his shoulders. "It's for everyone that died because of them. They call us traitors but I'll stand under the family's banner, declare that we're not theirs to curse and abuse any longer."

Zelma cackled. "Good to see family together at last. She talked of you the whole length of the river. That's what the banner is for by the way."

Athson wiped his face on his sleeve as he took Zelma's hand in one of his own. "Thank you for holding that inheritance so long."

Zelma blushed and fanned her face. "You're embarrassing me." Her voice, though craggy as a dwarf's with her age, somehow sounded almost girlish in response.

"And you, Howart. My thanks for holding the bow for me these past years." Athson clasped hands with the gaunt Withling, who seemed to loom over them as much as Ralda did.

"You're welcome, Athson."

Athson stepped back. The trip home and becoming a Withling had changed him. He'd greeted and thanked these Withlings and his friends in a way he'd not done in many years. He grasped the blessed sword and then adjusted his grip for reassurance. It was different just trying to live out of the shadow of the curse.

Tordug clapped his hands together. "Well, let's go find Hastra and Limbreth."

Athson collected the bow from Ralda along with his pack and the spear, and they strode down the dock, still crowded with travelers and rangers. They pushed through the seemingly endless throng, and then it seemed to part in an instant, and they found Hastra and Limbreth standing on the dock, gazing at the crowd.

Hastra strode forward the instant she spotted them and greeted Zelma, then Howart, in embraces that struck Athson as the most emotional reaction he'd ever seen from Hastra. She greeted everyone in turn, and when she came to Athson, he hugged her and said in her ear, "Thank you for everything you've ever done for me. This curse is awful and I've been horrible too often. But I've been learning."

Hastra stepped back, her face etched with suddenly rosy cheeks and a sunny smile. "My apologies as well, Athson. I've too often been bent on recovering this instead of stopping to understand." She touched the Bow of Hart in his hands almost reverently. But then she paused and gazed into his eyes with sudden amazement. "And I think we have our first new Withling in centuries." Her head turned as she searched the faces around him. "But I thought there was another Withling, perhaps Apeth Stellin? Where is he?" Sudden worry flooded her face.

Athson glanced around as the others greeted Limbreth, who'd hung back. He cleared his throat. "Uh, Apeth died. Corgren stabbed him one night on the road. Rokan agents tricked me away from him. They even tried to follow me, but I had Spark chase them off."

"Oh, I had much to thank him for." Hastra blinked away a tear. "But what's this I hear of Spark? You command him now? I doubt anyone but mages would note him."

"Uh, yeah, I suppose so." He glanced at Limbreth and her pale face, drawn with what? Apprehension? Fear? "But as I said, I've been learning. And the sword helps me clear the curse some."

"Right, well—oh, Ralda! I'm glad to see you too." The giant knelt and embraced Hastra.

As Athson stepped away from the Withling, Ralda peered around. "Me say things. Think long on big boat."

"Later, Ralda, later." Hastra patted Ralda's huge hands.

Athson approached Limbreth and spread his arms.

She hesitated a moment, then stepped into his embrace. She pressed her face into his neck. "I've missed you."

Athson wanted to hold her forever. "And I've missed you. But why the long face?"

She drew back, and he saw tears brimming in her eyes. She mustered a half-hearted smile and drew close again. "Can we talk later?"

"Yes, of course. I have so much—"

"Thanks." Limbreth withdrew again and climbed the steps toward the street.

Athson glanced at Hastra, who shrugged.

Tordug shouldered his pack. "She's thinking right. Let's find a place to bed down."

They followed Limbreth onto the street. Athson walked quickly to catch her. Did she know he'd chosen the wrong target on the Funnel? His heart lurched in his chest. Or was it about the White Arrow? "Limbreth, wait for the rest of us." He watched her walk away and wanted to hold her and tell her what he'd done, that everything would work out. If only she would wait.

Then Limbreth did stop, her posture poised as if to flee. Men on horses approached her, garbed in dark blue tabards and bearing a pair of sigils, one a leaping mountain lion and the other a fighting bear.

Athson half-turned his head to Gweld beside him. "Wonder who they are. She looks ready to run or fight."

Gweld grabbed Athson's arm. "The mountain lion is the sigil of the royal house of Grendon."

The men drew closer to Limbreth, and Athson's heart beat faster for a reason he didn't quite understand.

The man who led the cavalcade stopped in front of Limbreth and offered her a crooked smile. He looked older than Athson and Limbreth, perhaps thirty, his hair dark and curly. His dark eyes glittered as his face beamed a victorious expression. "My lady Limbreth. How good you've returned."

Limbreth stood rigid as Athson and his companions gathered around her. She answered, her voice sounding low with that dangerous tone she reserved for tense moments, "Dareth. What are you doing here?"

Dareth glanced at everyone around her. He shrugged and answered with an almost nonchalant tone, "Aside from preparing to leave this city for the trolls, I've come to collect you for our overdue wedding, which your father has so graciously agreed to host."

Limbreth gaped, her forlorn expression suddenly gone.

Athson's ears rang with sudden anger.

∾

LIMBRETH STEPPED BACK to put space between her and Dareth but bumped into Ralda, who edged away, reading her intent. Beside her, Athson's face flushed red and his jaw clenched. She didn't blame him for being angry. She'd promised him that her father's wishes and this suitor meant nothing to her. Now she was caught between them. What would Athson say? She resisted slouching. An idiotic suitor meeting the man she most likely loved but had failed repeatedly. Her stomach flopped.

Makwi stepped up beside her and chuckled. "Gotta see this. For the songs, you know."

She almost rolled her eyes. Crazy dwarf. But her nerves calmed, and her hands drifted toward her shoulders.

Dareth's eyes flicked to Makwi with a frown, and he almost said something, no doubt derisive. Limbreth really hoped he'd get his head chopped off by Makwi. But Dareth's eyes slipped back to her the moment her hands moved. "You should think before you draw swords on the king's emissary."

The soldiers behind Dareth urged their horses forward and slipped their swords free.

Limbreth drew her swords and ground her teeth. "Seriously? You'd draw on a royal princess of Grendon?"

Beside her, Makwi gaped a moment but recovered when he heard Tordug's rumble of laughter from behind. The dwarf-champion grinned. "This I have to see."

Tordug leaned between Limbreth and Makwi. "Now, Makwi, let's not join a fight that's not ours."

Makwi actually guffawed, and Dareth looked down his nose at him. "No, I'm just interested in seeing this ax-maid of the death-grip send this rabble running for their mother's aprons." He sighed. "Mounted men may actually present a challenge for a few moments—until she takes a horse from them."

Tordug laughed. "Always a joke from this one."

Athson stirred. "Tell your men to stand down or you'll all find yourselves leaving in caskets."

Dareth sneered at Limbreth's companions. "Who are these —people?" He glared at them one and all.

Limbreth laughed. "I'm sorry you've not met *my friends*. Let me introduce Tordug, Lord of Chokkra, and his champion, Makwi." The dwarves saluted sharply, dwarf-style. "Oh, I'm sure you remember Withling Hastra. And there are two other Withlings here, Zelma and Howart. As you can see, I'm not just with *people* beneath your courtesy, *Lord Dareth*. Now call your men off!"

"That depends on you, *Lady Limbreth.*"

"How's that?"

Makwi grunted. "Wish I had a chair for the front row of this show."

Dareth's horse danced beneath him, sensing his agitation. "Well, you see, as I mentioned, I've come to collect you."

"I heard that much, Dareth." She took two quick breaths through her nose to steady her icy tone. "But I left and don't want to be collected."

Dareth advanced his horse. "You don't have a choice in the matter."

Before Limbreth moved or replied, Ralda pushed forward and grabbed Dareth's horse by the bridle. The giant pointed his staff at one of the men-at-arms who advanced. "You come, I throw in river. From here. You stay." He pointed his staff successively at each man, and they drew their reins. Then Ralda leaned directly in Dareth's face. "Have respect."

Dareth's face paled. "Who is this?" He drew back from Ralda's stare into his face. He lifted his chin. "Your friends seem intent on threatening an emissary of the King of Grendon. I'll—"

"What's going on here?" Sarneth suddenly stepped into their midst with three squads of rangers at his back. "Everyone put your weapons away."

Limbreth sheathed her swords, along with everyone else. Makwi chuckled, and Sarneth eyed him.

Dareth turned to Sarneth. "I'm carrying out my sworn duty to my king by returning this errant lady to her father so we can be wed."

Limbreth crossed her arms and stood straighter. "And I'm not going. I'll stick my foot up your—"

Sarneth pointed at Limbreth. "You'll do no such thing, Princess. You're in Auguron City, and I'd rather not have another war to fight besides the trolls marching on this city.

Work out your lover's quarrel, but leave the threats and weapons out of it."

Limbreth snorted and lifted her chin at Sarneth. "Lover's quarrel? Hardly that." She motioned to Dareth. "He's a jumped-up—"

"King's emissary." Sarneth stepped further into the crowd. "You didn't inform me of who you were when you arrived with Hastra." He actually glared at the Withling. "But you'll work this out civilly in this city."

Limbreth spread her feet. Where was her horse when she needed it? "I'm not going anywhere with this man. I—"

"Uh, Lord Dareth." Everyone turned to Hastra as she stepped forward. She nodded to Limbreth. "Lady Limbreth has just returned from a long and arduous journey during which she dispatched numerous trolls alongside those of us sharing her journey. She and our whole group are weary. Would you allow Lady Limbreth to refresh herself and visit you in the morning?" Hastra glanced at Sarneth. "Say, in Captain Sarneth's receiving rooms?"

Limbreth didn't wait for Dareth's answer. "Suits me fine. C'mon, Athson." She grabbed Athson, not by the arm as if he were escorting her, but by his hand. "Let's go find something to eat before I really get rude." She strode past Dareth with Athson and straight through the column of gathered horsemen, making them shift out of formation. She was a royal princess of Grendon, after all.

Behind her, Limbreth heard Makwi laugh. "Ax-maids—you just gotta love watching them fight, with weapons or with their tongues."

Limbreth imagined the dwarf shaking his head as he set out following her. Tordug added a laugh, and she even heard Ralda's deep laugh echo along the street.

She leaned close to Athson. "I told you, didn't I?"

She just hoped she didn't eat those words.

CHAPTER SEVENTEEN

Athson and Limbreth found the Broken Bow Inn crowded with patrons. Their friends entered the tavern soon after the two of them and claimed various benches. Rangers and other citizens of Auguron City mingled with various merchants and travelers from all over Denaria. Even a few Grendonese soldiers from Dareth's contingent sat in the crowd.

The latest news and rumors floated in the chatter around Athson and Limbreth as they sat on a bench. The people around them ignored them as they received mugs of ale and wine. Limbreth perked up at the sound of nearby dwarves speaking in their tongue, while Athson listened to several rangers beside him and sipped his ale.

"Will they make it ahead of the trolls?" one of the rangers, an officer, asked of another officer.

The other officer shrugged. "Reports from Marston's auxiliaries indicate they've been successful delaying the trolls. They'll still be here within the week, though. I suspect any travelers from the east will pour into the city or just head on west or south."

Athson hoped the best for Minith and her two rangers escorting their refugees. It was a long trip, but they were sure to arrive with Marston leading some resistance. Athson sipped his ale and licked the froth from his lips. It had been too long since he'd rested like this.

Athson sat next to his mother as they piled their gear about them or on the table. The others found seats at surrounding tables. Limbreth squeezed in beside Athson on his other side. He turned to his mother. "I can't believe you're really here! There's so much we need to talk about."

Danilla kissed Athson's cheek and held his attention with a smile. "This is all beyond my hope. A true blessing of Eloch. We can speak more in a quiet place." She grabbed his hand. "For now, it's enough to have you at my side. I've returned to my boy at last."

Athson squeezed his mother's hand. "I have a home. It was my foster-parents but they died, murdered by Corgren's magic. I'll move you in there are soon as we have a chance."

"A home of my own again? How wonderful!" Danilla's face dropped, her expression suddenly drawn. "But others died and left it empty. And all the friends I ever had are gone too." Tears brimmed at her eyes. She wiped them away with a trembling smile. "But we have each other and a place to live after all the troubles."

Athson kissed his mother's hand. "It's not the same there without Heth and Cireena, my foster-parents. They would be pleased to have you. We won't have father. But we'll have what we need. We'll make a home for ourselves when this fight is over."

After a pause with Athson's mother, Limbreth nudged him in the ribs, and he turned to her. "Sorry about all that in the street. I didn't know he was coming all this way. Like I said, I don't want him. I didn't mean to drag you into the disagreement." She sipped her wine and eyed him over the rim of her cup.

Athson took a deep breath. He'd almost lost his temper back in the street. He gripped his sword, and the tension in his shoulders subsided. "I get it. I guess you made it clear when we left where we stood." Was it time to talk now? He'd let her decide.

"I did say as much to you back in Ezhandun." But her face bore an uncertain expression, almost a question as she gazed at him.

Athson rubbed his chin and searched for the right thing to say. "You backed that up in the street." He shrugged. "Good enough for me, I guess. What are you going to tell him?"

Limbreth grimaced and shrugged. "That I'm not going with him. I'll see this through with you and the others." She ended with a sharp nod.

Athson sipped his ale. As much as he could expect. He grabbed her hand and held it. They still needed that talk she wanted, whatever that was about. The White Arrow, most likely.

He motioned toward the nearby dwarves with the mug in his hand. "What are they saying?"

Limbreth leaned closer. "All dwarves are pulling out of the city and heading south. They want none of the fight, and most don't want the trouble. I guess they're more interested in their current affairs than killing trolls. A few said they'd like to stay and help, but they think it's doomed. Corgren will win, in their minds." Limbreth shook her head in disgust. "Tordug and Makwi will hear from where they're sitting. But the wandering Chokkrans have an air of defeatism and lack inspiration." She shrugged. "Well, they could do a lot, but they don't think it's their fight even if they've been living in Auguron for a while."

Athson drained his mug. "Too bad. Though I doubt Sarneth

would hire any of them either. Not his way, and likely not enough money. They've been planning for this a long time. I just hope everyone coming this way makes it or gets away otherwise."

She pointed into the crowd. "I heard someone say a few boats are heading upriver to offer stragglers a chance to head east or downriver."

He considered that and shrugged. "I suppose they can pole and row upriver after picking up passengers. But who knows how many trolls will lurk farther east, and most everything will be burned by now. Most elves would just come here anyway."

"Yeah, I guess the merchants and tradesmen from elsewhere just want to get away and do business wherever they can until this invasion blows over." Limbreth slouched with a look of unease.

Athson touched her free hand again. "Look, don't worry about what happened in the street. I know you didn't plan that. You stood up for yourself."

She responded with a half-hearted laugh. "What, Dareth? I hated making a scene, but I'm not worried about him. It's just, other things are—complicated."

"Want to talk about it now? I mean, we already declared our interest in each other before your father's emissary." Athson held his breath, as much for her reply as for the fact that he'd actually threatened his rival for Limbreth's affections, who happened to represent her father's interests.

"Not here." She frowned and drained her cup of wine.

"What about out back? Maybe there's a quiet spot somewhere." If he read her mood correctly, whatever hesitation she'd displayed back at the dock had changed with the confrontation in the street with Dareth. He offered her his best *why not* expression.

She looked around the crowded room and sighed. "I guess. No avoiding things with Dareth here. Lead the way."

They gathered her gear and walked out the back door into

the stable-yard. Outside, they found Limbreth's horse already delivered. It trotted toward her for a greeting, and she doted over the animal. "How did you get here?"

Athson scratched the back of his neck. "If I know them at all, either Hastra or Tordug got Sarneth to send it here with any others the lot of you had on the boats."

They left the horse, exited the yard, and walked down a side street until foot traffic eased to nearly empty. Athson paused between two buildings and leaned against a wall. "So what's on your mind?"

Limbreth crossed her arms and paced a few steps away then back to him, then retraced her steps several more times.

Athson sighed. "Look, we've not seen each other since Howart's cave. I know there's a lot to tell, but nothing's changed." *Or had it?* His stomach suddenly knotted. Maybe he'd have to tell her about the Funnel. Gweld thought he'd have to some time. He suddenly didn't want to talk that much. He was about to suggest they just go back inside the inn or go arrange for their rooms when Limbreth stopped in front of him and gazed at her shoes.

"Things might change." She lifted her gaze to his. "I don't know how to say it all." Her lips trembled with emotion.

He released a long, slow breath. Maybe it wasn't such a good time to talk after all. "Maybe it can wait. I mean, you're still upset about Dareth."

"It's not about him at all. It's about other things. I need to know something." She paced away again.

Athson suddenly wanted another mug of ale and a meal. But based on the flutter in his stomach, he wasn't too sure about the meal.

She returned to him. "I—I just don't know if I'm good for you, is all." She flopped her arms like wings for a moment, clearly frustrated.

She turned away with her arms crossed, but Athson drew

her back to face him, though she stood with her face downcast. "What do you mean? I've missed you so much. I was so worried for you. I thought you died at the Funnel, and then I found out you'd been to Marston's Station." He remembered how his heart had soared out of his remorse and grief at the news. "I felt so—"

Limbreth kissed him suddenly.

"What was that for?"

"You don't like it?" She gazed at him through her eyelashes, her face slightly lowered and her expression blank.

She expected something, he knew that. "Well, yeah, but you just said you didn't know if I wanted you. What's that all about?"

Limbreth closed her eyes and pressed her lips tightly together. "It's just that, I seem to keep failing you."

His brow furrowed in confusion. "What do you mean? You've been on the journey every step. You want to stay for this fight. I don't understand."

A thin smile crawled onto her face. "Hastra said you should be glad you had me along."

"I am." He certainly was. "You've put up with a lot out of me."

"I kissed you because you're glad to have me along."

He sighed. This was confusing. "Then why are you upset?"

Her face scrunched like she experienced sudden pain. "I just keep failing. Like with the banshee."

"That again? We settled that long ago, back in Chokkra. I really meant it that I don't blame you for any of it." Why was she still on that? He watched her as she struggled with her next statements.

"I'm not what everyone thinks I am." She paused and watched her words sink into his understanding. "Makwi talked like I was a hero back on the street."

Athson snorted. "If you're not, then you're the closest thing to it I've ever seen."

Limbreth shook her head. "No, I'm not. I'm a coward."

He groaned. "How could you think that?"

"It's true. And not just that, but I keep making mistakes that put us in danger." She crossed her arms.

Athson hugged her with her arms still crossed. "The whole journey was dangerous. I made plenty of mistakes too, but we made it."

She squirmed free of his embrace and held up one finger. "First, back at Nazh-akun, when they attacked the tower, I ran instead of staying with you. The Bane was near, and I ran. Like a coward."

She'd run then? "I thought you just went with your assigned group to escape. But it doesn't matter, we all had to leave. And the Bane isn't something you can defeat."

She motioned to the blessed sword on Athson's hip. "You have that, and I could have stayed. I panicked and ran after the others when I wanted to stay."

"Limbreth, you aren't a coward. You've stood up to the Bane. I saw that much on the Funnel. You struggled then. Word has it you fought it on the boat."

"And that leads to other things." She held up a second finger. "I should have gone with you to see Howart, because you had the sword. You said you'd watch after me with the Bane loose. We knew they were coming, but I stayed back instead of staying with you and going ahead. Instead, I got captured. Otherwise, you—we—might have saved your father."

Athson sighed. It could have been different. Maybe. Maybe not. "I don't think you're being fair to yourself. I don't think worse of you."

"Then there's the next part." She held up a third finger. "I had the White Arrow. I was holding it for you. But I got it broken before you ever even knew about it." She spread her hands, palms up, at her waist. "So there. I've failed you, and I don't know why I should even be around with that record of failure."

He hugged her again. "Oh, Limbreth. I do want you around, and you're not as much trouble as you think. Eloch will do something about the arrow." Her arms wrapped around his waist. "You think no one else has made mistakes these last months?" He swallowed a sudden lump in his throat. Best tell her now. "I've made them too. I—I chose poorly on the Funnel. I had a shot at the Bane. But Corgren threatened my mother and I—I wanted revenge so badly. I tried to kill him instead."

They stood in silence for long moments in their embrace.

Then Limbreth stirred in his arms. She pulled back from him. Her eyes narrowed with a question. "You what?"

His heart pounded in his ears at the tone of her question. "I shot at Corgren in revenge when I should have tried for the Bane. I don't know if it would have done anything to help you. It didn't with Corgren." He swallowed. *Not a satisfactory answer, judging by the sudden anger in her eyes.*

Limbreth stepped back, her head cocked and an expression of confusion on her face. "You didn't try to help me? Or your father? You just tried to kill Corgren for vengeance?" She stopped speaking, her mouth opening and closing several times without words.

Athson spread his hands in explanation. "Yes, I messed up. Remember the curse? It takes over, and Corgren knew what to say to get my reaction. It was—it was my responsibility, and I failed."

Limbreth's nostrils flared with her quick breaths. Without another word, she whirled and walked away.

∼

MAGDRONU-AS-GWELD WATCHED Athson and Limbreth down the side street as he feigned getting some fresh air, his mug of ale in his hand. The conversation ebbed and flowed for several minutes. Across the distance, Magdronu sensed the apprehension in Limbreth and the confused uncertainty from Athson. *Take that advice, Athson. Tell her.*

Instead, they embraced. The ploy hadn't worked. Magdronu-as-Gweld opened the door to go back inside the inn. He'd have to try another ploy to get Athson to hand over the Bow of Hart.

Movement caught his eye. Limbreth pulled away from Athson, her posture rigid. *Interesting.* Athson followed with an imploring gesture, explaining himself. Maybe the ploy had worked. Magdronu-as-Gweld watched as Limbreth questioned Athson again. She wheeled away from him and stalked along the street, her face a mixture of anger, confusion, and shock.

Limbreth spotted Gweld and kept walking, her face set, concealing her emotions. She walked beyond view, presumably around the front of the inn.

Magdronu-as-Gweld smirked as his gaze returned to Athson, who leaned against a wall, his head pressed against his forearm. Athson pounded on the wall with the bottom of his fist. It had worked. Wedge driven between the two lovers. Now to play Athson further and seal Magdronu's control of the outcome. He'd seize victory now.

Athson grabbed his things, caught Magdronu-as-Gweld's attention, and signaled that he was going to find room at the ranger barracks. Magdronu-as-Gweld signaled he'd be along later. He sat and called to Corgren with his magic.

Corgren's presence opened to Magdronu after some minutes passed. *'Great One, I answer your summons.'*

'How far away are you?' He allowed a purr of pleasure along the spell's connection.

'We are struggling as you asked we do.' Corgren's devotion flowed across the communication spell.

'And the shrine? I've just arrived in the city today, but I don't want to give anything away by going to it—yet.'

'It progresses well enough with what magic is available. It should be ready in six days.'

Magdronu let someone pass on the back steps of the inn. Alone again, he continued, *'How soon can you arrive?'*

Corgren hesitated, no doubt considering his answer well. *'If I eliminate the resistance, we can slaughter those upon the road and be there in four days' time.'*

Magdronu-as-Gweld sipped his ale and slowly savored it. He did like some things these mortals made, after all. *'I'll have my hands on the Bow of Hart the fifth night. Spring your surprises that night, and we shall make use of the shrine the next day to seal my victory.'*

'Master, I obey. To your victory!' Magdronu-as-Gweld could almost feel Corgren's shout across the spell, though he had not the power to send such trivialities.

Magdronu let the spell close. He sipped the ale and continued to savor it as if the long journey mattered. He drained the last of the drink and shook his head. He'd better have a few more. No telling how much would be available after the next week.

Within the Broken Bow Inn, Limbreth studiously ignored Gweld from the seat she'd found near Hastra. After several more rounds, she left for a room on the second floor, her face still blank, concealing her true emotions.

Magdronu-as-Gweld drank his fill and then sauntered off in search of Athson to hear the tale of his woe with the high-minded Limbreth.

∼

HASTRA WATCHED Limbreth squirm her way across the crowded common room after she excused herself. She'd spoken hardly a word since returning alone from her foray out back with Athson. Clearly the conversation had gone poorly. What had Athson said that silenced Limbreth, his faithful support during their long journey, so thoroughly?

Zelma's eyes followed the flow of the crowd. She loved the company of people, but her long time upon Eagle's Aerie had left her shy. Not that she wasn't a bit so when they were young, but Zelma so loved hearing all the latest news. "Ooh, that's interesting, there."

Hastra arched a single eyebrow. "Which bit? I hear much."

"So do I. But some are much more important than others." She smiled almost absently and leaned closer to a conversation.

Howart shrugged at Hastra's questioning glance. Few things truly disturbed the gaunt Withling. Dire events for sure, but Zelma's little eccentricities weren't on the list.

"Sister, do tell us your interesting tidbits." Hastra drew Zelma's attention back from the chatter around them. Honestly, Hastra just wanted some rest before they considered the White Arrow and prepared for the coming conflict.

"Well—" Zelma started but then paused, a sudden smile on her face again as she listened to another conversation.

Hastra sighed. "Sister, what news did you hear?" She held Zelma's hand and squeezed it.

"Oh, yes, that." Zelma, never one to dwell in the moment, sipped her tea. "It seems that not all Rokans have left the city. A few have been spotted in the last few days. You'd think anyone from Rok would have left, suddenly being unpopular." She giggled as if the information were some pleasing little joke.

Hastra sat back and stared at her sister. Rokans in Auguron City? She tapped her lower lip. To what end? "That *is* interesting, sister. Have you heard where they've been seen?"

Zelma lifted a finger as she looked elsewhere. "I'm working

on that, but no one seems to know exactly where. It's just a rumor. Likely fourth-hand."

Hastra glanced at Howart. "What do you think?"

He rolled his eyes in thought. "Bears checking. There are so many people here. I bet they've left since that rumor started around, though. There's been so much traffic across the bridge this week, according to what I've heard."

Hastra stared into the middle distance. Still, Rokans in the city bore checking if possible. "And all the Chokkrans are leaving too." She shook her head. "Tordug won't like it much."

A moment later, Makwi rose from the bench he occupied with Tordug. The Chokkran champion sidled through the crowd and approached Hastra's table. They probably knew the news already.

"Makwi, we'd make more room if there were more chairs," Hastra said.

The dwarf cleared his throat. "May I speak with you alone?"

Limbreth was likely in her room. "Let's see if there's a room available in the hallway." Maybe the proprietor wasn't using all his dining rooms for extra customers. "I'll be back shortly. Let me know what you find out," she said to Zelma and Howart.

Makwi cleared a path through the crowded room, and Hastra followed. They found the service room, which held a spare table and a stack of chairs, empty. Hastra shut the door, and the noise of the common room faded.

Without hesitation, Makwi knelt before Hastra. "Bless me, Withling." His somber eyes fixed on her with sincerity.

She partially turned her head but left her eyes locked on Makwi. "Why ask for a blessing now?"

The dwarf lowered his head, but his whisper carried regardless. "For the coming fight."

"So you are staying?" She had wondered if they might leave. Their business was their own, and this was no different.

"Yes, we're staying. For our people. We've come too far in this not to see it through. If it means the difference between trolls and not..." Makwi shrugged. "I'll need a blessing for this fight. I, uh, we don't expect to do anything but offer our honor to our people here."

"You mean you expect to fight to the death here?" Hastra almost grabbed the dwarf by the shoulders. Were they crazy? Now she agreed with Limbreth's quiet assertions about them. How could she bless this? Her eyes narrowed. "What do you intend, Makwi?"

"I think that's my... I just think I need a blessing if I'm to stand here against the trolls."

Hastra's eyes widened, and she experienced a sudden intake of air. Her heart leapt at one word. She shifted to dwarvish and uttered the sudden words given. "May you stand when no one else can."

With those simple words, Makwi stood and offered a simple nod.

Hastra stumbled from the room and dabbed her eyes with a handkerchief. Her impression about Makwi, Tordug and Ralda returned from memory. *They would all face death again.* That blessing felt like she had said goodbye.

CHAPTER EIGHTEEN

Athson sat on a bunk in the ranger barracks. He didn't know where else to go. Limbreth had walked away from him at his confession like he'd slapped her. He grunted. Maybe he had. Emotionally.

He glanced at his things. Should he stow his pack? He had no assignment yet. He was a Withling now, though he'd heard nothing of Eloch in days. He thought. He didn't think his confession to Limbreth was from Eloch. He knew a Withling didn't lie, but never speaking those words wouldn't have been a lie.

He fumbled his belt loose and laid his sword on the bunk. Was he still a ranger? If not, where would he go? Maybe he'd wander Denaria like Hastra or find a cave like Howart. There was Heth and Cireena's home. Maybe another night.

Athson laid back on the bunk and considered things with Limbreth. Maybe she would think better of him in the morning, after some rest. He snorted at the thought. Sleep wasn't the answer to their botched relationship. Maybe Limbreth would speak to Hastra and figure it out. But the expression on her face, the shock as she pulled away, as she turned from him without a word. He'd lost her trust with his confession, and he'd never earn that again. He'd abandoned her on the Funnel, and only a miracle had saved her from certain death.

Gweld arrived later, pausing as he searched the big room and found Athson on the bunk. The elf approached and nudged him. "You want to eat something? There's food across the courtyard."

Athson grunted.

Gweld stood there a moment. "You have words with Limbreth or something after that scene in the street?"

Athson grunted again.

"You're suddenly back to the old, dour Athson?" Without an answer, the elf turned to go. "Well, I'm eating."

"I told her like you said I should." As the elf faced him, Athson gazed at Gweld. Should he blame his friend?

"And I take it the conversation didn't go well?"

"She said nothing, just walked away."

Gweld scratched the back of his neck. "Not what I thought she'd do. Maybe she'll think it through."

Athson stared at the upper bunk. "Yeah, maybe she'll talk it through with Hastra." It didn't matter. He truly was the failure Limbreth merely claimed she was. He touched his sword, and the thought didn't change. Not the curse, just his own thought. But then, he'd faced that failure on the Funnel until he'd heard the miraculous news at Marston's Station. He'd faced it then, and only his desire to see Limbreth pushed it aside, but the truth had clung to him the breadth of Auguron. He'd dreaded ever telling her this. But he'd promised to be honest with her, and he was. He sighed.

Gweld rocked his weight from foot to foot. "I don't know what to say. I thought she'd talk it through with you. Listen about the curse."

Athson sniffed. "Yeah, it was a fool's hope on my part. But better to tell her than keep that secret between us."

Gweld sat on the opposite bunk, his pack between his feet. "All this time and all her words that she'd stick by you. All her effort for the bow, and she just walked away." He shook his head.

"Gweld." Athson turned his head. "What am I supposed to do now? With the bow? I mean, this isn't anyone's fight but Auguron's."

Gweld slapped his shoulder. "Athson, Hastra got you into this, and she must have some answer for it all. We've got several days. Get some rest, eat, let Limbreth work out how she feels. The Withlings will do something. You know, what is needed is given. We'll get assignments and prepare for the defense. But me? I think I'll go eat. How about you?" He offered Athson an inviting grin and waved toward the barracks exit.

"I don't think so, not now." Athson continued to stare at the upper bunk. He needed to work out what came next, like a Withling.

"Well, I'll bring you something back." Gweld left, leaving his pack and bow on the opposite bunk.

Athson picked through the food Gweld brought back later and finally found a way to eat it all. Answers evaded him otherwise, so he went to sleep, hoping for more answers the next day, though the one thought that struck him was his mother. She must be with the Withlings. He'd talk with her in the morning, get her to the house in the trees.

But the morning brought fewer answers. Gweld returned from his early breakfast at the mess as Athson stretched, feeling like his heart resided in his toes. "Anything left?"

Gweld sat and stared at Athson. "Probably. I don't think anyone will eat much today."

Athson lifted his head, his brow furrowed at the ominous comment. "What now?"

"Marston's dead."

Athson buried his head in his hands for several moments as other rangers strolled through the bunkroom. "How?"

Gweld belted on his long knife. "I don't know much, just what the messages from the birds say, or at least, what Sarneth lets out. The trolls caught them in a sudden attack and killed a bunch of the force screening the remainder of the garrison and the auxiliaries. They're in a hasty retreat, and anyone left on the road is running for their lives."

Athson shook his head. He needed guidance from Eloch now. But he heard nothing except his own thoughts about Limbreth. He'd done her a kindness not to let her think of him as a hero when he wasn't. That hadn't done anything but visit him with misery. He still didn't know if Eloch had directed him in that or not. He tried listening, but nothing happened. He needed to talk to Hastra or one of the others.

Athson stood and belted on his sword, then grabbed the Bow of Hart and headed for the door.

Gweld called after him, "Where are you going?"

"To grab some food and then to see Hastra." Athson waved to Gweld, who offered a dismissive wave of his own. They'd meet later. No doubt Gweld would get them an assignment together.

Athson pushed through the food line, filled his pockets with what he wanted, and then left. The streets were abuzz with news as he strolled toward the Broken Bow Inn. Less than halfway there, he passed the grandest inn, the High Oaks, where foreigners with plenty of coin stayed. Outside, he spied several Grendonese soldiers. This was where Dareth was staying? Didn't surprise Athson.

But then he spotted Limbreth's horse. Saddled with her saddlebags. Athson swerved toward the soldiers. "Hey, I know this horse. Where'd you get it?"

The soldier glanced at him and grimaced. He spared a sidelong look to his fellow guard standing near several other saddled horses, one of which Athson recognized. He felt as if his heart stopped. Dareth's horse. The second soldier shrugged, and the first one said, "It's the Lady Limbreth's horse. We leave this city for the trolls and elves to fight over."

Athson stepped back. She was leaving? He turned and stared at the bustle of the crowd. Leaving? He ran his fingers through his hair and turned back to the guards. "You know where she is?" Hopefully not inside. Not with Dareth. He needed to tell her goodbye, at least.

The second guard pointed farther along the street.

Athson looked in the indicated direction. Limbreth marched along the street in her white dueling leathers and her cape from the dwarves of Ezhandun. Several soldiers followed, but they looked more like they were guarding her rather than holding her captive. Indifference defined her expression if he'd ever seen such on a face. But he knew better.

Limbreth spotted him and her gait hitched slightly, but then she recovered and marched with renewed pace. She started past him without speaking, her eyes fixed ahead of her.

"I need to talk to you." He ground his teeth. Maybe she'd misled him all this time. He rested his hand on his sword's pommel. No, he'd done this on his own.

"I've nothing to say to you. You said it all yesterday." She swept past him.

Athson snagged her arm. "At least let me say goodbye after..." He glanced at the six soldiers who suddenly crowded around him. "After all this time."

She snatched her arm away, her expression never changing. The soldiers reached for their swords, but Limbreth lifted her hand. "No need." Her eyes flicked to Athson's sword and then back to his face. "Besides, I doubt the lot of you would stand a chance against his steel." To Athson, she said, "You just said your goodbye."

He swallowed the sudden lump in his throat. "Why are you doing this? You don't want to."

Limbreth's jaw worked slightly behind her closed lips. "Leave us."

The soldiers retreated beyond the row of prepared horses and murmured among themselves, tossing dark looks toward Athson.

Limbreth grabbed his arm and steered him between her horse and Dareth's. "You know why I'm doing this, Athson." She leaned toward him like so many other times, but not with a kiss for him. "But for Spark, I'd be dead. You let me die on the Funnel. And thanks to Spark, wherever he is."

"Uh, he's right beside us."

Limbreth's expression broke with a swift, sweet smile for Spark. Then she returned her gaze to Athson, the indifferent expression back. "My—"

"He's on the other side of us."

Limbreth rolled her eyes. "Whatever, Athson. I'm tired of all the games. I worked myself into a frenzy this last week over you, and for nothing."

"But you don't want this. You don't want him." Athson slapped Dareth's horse for lack of any better representation of the man.

"That doesn't matter." Her tone took on an icy chill in the late winter morning. "My father has ordered me home, and I'm going. I'll deal with the nuptials when I get there."

He stood slack-jawed and wide-eyed a moment before he recovered. "Since when do you care if your father orders you to do anything? You traveled here and then to Chokkra and back without a care for his orders."

Limbreth lifted a hand and shoved him into Dareth's horse. "Oh, I cared. I cared to gain his respect. Just like I cared that the man I likely love and who probably loves me would—

would..." She stammered into silence, wheeled away to her horse, and leaned her head on her hands at the saddlebags.

He touched her shoulder. "Limbreth, let me—"

She shrugged his hand away and pushed him back. "Enough, Athson. I don't like this, but it has to be." She turned her head and peered at him sidelong, tears brimming in her eyes. "It's hard enough as it is." She fumbled with the buckles of her saddlebags.

Athson remembered how he'd fumbled with his saddlebags, the inheritance hidden within, when he wanted to quit Hastra's quest at Huffer's Post. He'd asked to Limbreth to go with him then. *Her eyes indicated she wanted to say 'yes' then.* But not now.

Limbreth opened the saddlebag with a sniff and rummaged through the contents until she found what she wanted. She offered her hand to him. "Here. Maybe you can use this. I don't know."

Athson glimpsed the object she held out to him. A broken arrow. The White Arrow. His eyes widened as she dumped the broken pieces in his hands. *The dream. Except then it was a shining object, and now it's a useless, broken arrow.* He recognized her gaze, her expression. *The same as the dream.* Except now he knew the meaning of her sorrow and disappointment. In him. "Not again." He stepped back into the Dareth's horse.

"Again?"

He shook his head. "Nothing. Another dream of mine coming true."

Limbreth's eyes narrowed. "Don't try to trick me into this with duty." She pointed to the arrow. "Goodbye, Athson." She walked away again, without another word.

Athson watched her go, just like in the dream.

He stood between the horses. She'd brushed him away like dust from her shoes, and in the street. Athson glanced around, but no one bothered with him standing forlorn with a broken arrow in his hands. Broken like he'd broken her trust and their relationship.

~

Hastra eased down the stairs of the Broken Bow Inn and paused as Athson entered the common room. He looked worn. His sandy hair was tousled and his clothing rumpled as if he'd slept in the street. But he carried the Bow of Hart and that sword of his. She eyed his grip on the sword. His manner seemed distant, distracted.

Athson noted her peering at him from the stairs. He shuffled his feet as if he considered leaving. Perhaps he sought Limbreth, but she'd left early after a restless night of sleep. Hastra paused. Limbreth had hardly spoken a word since leaving with Athson the day before and returning without him.

She motioned for Athson to approach her, and the old, evasive sideways slouch returned to his posture. After a moment, he shrugged one shoulder and pushed through the crowd. Hastra descended the rest of the way to the floor, her lips drawn tightly on her face. Honestly, she spent most of her time managing these two and less being a Withling. At least, it felt that way all too often.

She nodded. "You slept well?"

Athson shrugged one shoulder again. "I suppose." He scratched the back of his neck and eyed the door. "I came looking for you. Figured you'd know what to do next." He tapped the Bow of Hart, his arms slightly crossed as he did so. "About this."

Hastra ran her tongue across her lips. He doubted something. Most new Withlings did at some point, but this situation was beyond most experienced Withlings. Including her, she admitted to herself. "Good of you to seek guidance. Zelma and

Howart are in a room down the hall already." She extended her hand for him to precede her.

She followed him to an open doorway, where they found Zelma and Howart. To her slight surprise, Sarneth stood looking out the window, his hands clenched behind him. She nodded to her fellow Withlings as Athson found a seat. "Sarneth, what a pleasant surprise."

The ranger commander crossed the room to Hastra's waiting hands, which he grasped in greeting. "Hastra, we had little enough greeting yesterday. But I came to offer my thanks for diffusing yesterday's...affair in the street." He glanced at Athson with an expression bespeaking both judgment and curiosity. He cleared his throat and continued, "I also came to confer with you about the current circumstances."

"Thank you, Sarneth. I only meant to serve as always, regarding yesterday's misunderstanding." She sat at the commanding elf's offer of a chair. "I suppose the issue is being resolved?"

Athson stirred. Not surprising to Hastra, since Limbreth held the key to his heart. Athson propped his head in his hands and rocked it sideways several times but held his tongue, though not a sigh.

"I believe it is." Sarneth sat. He motioned to Athson. "I can only suppose this bow is what you mentioned last fall in this very room?"

"It is." Hastra glanced between Sarneth and Athson. "I've asked Athson here, though I didn't know you were coming, as both the bearer of the bow and as a new Withling."

Sarneth's eyebrows climbed his forehead. "What she says is true? You've chosen to become a Withling?"

Athson responded with another one-shoulder shrug, what Hastra took as his calling card for the day. "Sure, though as much called as choose. It's a long story. As long as the trip or more. Dreams and visions, you know."

Hastra nodded her agreement, as did Howart and Zelma. "That it is."

"So those were more than just trauma?" Sarneth rubbed his chin and eyed Athson as if appraising a horse or a bow.

Athson held out a hand and tipped it side to side a few times. "Some, not all. Spark's real, though."

Sarneth shot Hastra a glance.

Zelma threw her hands in the air and dropped them on the table with a soft smack. "I could have told you that." She glanced at Howart.

The gaunt Withling shrugged. "First I heard of it."

Zelma observed everyone in the room, lastly Athson. She pointed between them. "You mean he and I are the only ones who see this dog?"

Hastra chuckled. "That's no surprise, since you're the only one that sees that eagle."

Athson lifted his hand hesitantly. "Uh, I've seen it."

Sarneth snorted. "It seems more is going on than anyone in Auguron ever suspected. I'm sorry I ever doubted you, Athson."

Athson, to his credit, straightened his shoulders, possibly remembering Sarneth was a ranking officer, and saluted. But Hastra noted a lingering sense of disinterest in him nonetheless. "Thank you, sir."

Sarneth turned to Hastra, then observed the others. "Well, to the business at hand. We have trolls advancing on the city. As of my latest reports, Marston died yesterday in an ambush."

Hastra gasped and covered her mouth. Dangers abounded in these times, but she'd not foreseen this. Of course, she couldn't, but still... "He was a good man."

The elven commander slouched slightly, then recovered his air of command. "That he was, Withling. However, I must consider more than his death if we're to beat back this attack. That same ambush took out many of the remaining skirmishers. The trolls advance without much to hold them back from any refugees. They'll arrive across the river several days sooner than expected, and I cannot send enough forces to save the refugees. However, I've sent smaller boats to the nearest landing and instructions to those remaining to evacuate everyone they can. All who want to leave this city must do so within a few days or risk death on the road. I expect the main bridge traffic to grow today as many of our foreign merchants flee south or west."

Hastra watched Athson finger the Bow of Hart until he met her gaze and looked away in continued disinterest. She opened her mouth to reprimand him and then shut it with the inclination to hold back. She brushed at the wrinkles in her rough skirt. "I'm sure you must do what you must. Is there anything we can do for you?" She motioned to her fellow Withlings, including Athson, who took note and sat up straighter.

Sarneth pursed his lips. "It's hard to ignore this bow in the room and the possibility that you've brought this attack on us." He raised a hand to forestall several protests. "I know better, as do many in the city who know far less about this bow—or nothing at all. We've watched Corgren's trolls for decades and prepared. Marston knew his danger all this time. But many have seen the sign in the sky and questioned its meaning."

Hastra lifted her chin. "It is a sign of our prophecy." She laid her book on the table and flipped it open, running her hand along the page upon which she'd written the words. "All has come true. The wandering star was for his arrow, sent by his blessing at our hands." She pointed to Howart and Zelma.

Zelma nodded vigorously but bit her lower lip with apprehension.

"And you have this arrow? What is its intended use?" Sarneth pulled the book closer and inspected the passage.

Hastra opened her mouth to explain the arrow's condition and what the prophecy read, but Athson spoke first. "I do have it." He rummaged in a cloak pocket as he leaned the bow against the table and produced the broken pieces. "But I do not know how I shall use it, unless we determine something else."

Hastra gaped. Limbreth had already bestowed it upon him?

Sarneth stood, his brow pinched, and loomed over the table at the sight of the broken arrow Athson laid upon it. "What's this? A useless arrow."

Howart stood, walked over to Sarneth and placed reassuring hands upon the elven commander's shoulders. "It is the White Arrow of promise. It was broken by Magdronu's Bane. But do not lose hope in Eloch over mere tokens and their condition."

Zelma cackled softly and nodded. "True words, those."

Hastra recovered her wits. "It's true. The arrow was broken, and we have convened what Withlings remain to determine Eloch's will in fulfilling the prophecy."

Howart seated himself as Sarneth paced across the room, hands clenched behind his back once again. The gaunt Withling added, "Nothing happens by chance. It came into Limbreth's hands for its protection and presentation to the bearer of the Bow of Hart. It was broken, but Eloch foresaw it. He is not shaken by the event at all."

Athson slouched in his chair at mention of Limbreth. "What will we do? What's my part in this?"

Hastra cocked her head as she faced Athson. "The prophecy is clear that the bow is not to fall into Magdronu's hands, and you've played your part in bringing it here safely. But the words we spoke long years ago indicate the bow shall be used to thwart Magdronu's plans, to bring to naught his attempted rise to rule Denaria." She turned to Sarneth. "You've known all this time that the trolls threatened Auguron, but this is but Magdronu's first target since taking Chokkra, and he aims for all of Denaria in the end. The Bow of Hart has come here, and that is not by chance, as Howart aptly points out."

Sarneth tucked his chin in thought, then nodded, after which he lifted his gaze to those in the room. "What would you have of me, of my rangers?"

Hastra spread her hands, palms up. "You must defend your home. We've come to do what we can in your aid and that of Eloch's plan. We are at your service as much as Eloch directs us. At present"—she paused and motioned to the arrow—"we must determine Eloch's next instructions to us."

"I would have assigned Athson elsewhere, but it seems he is needed here, so I leave him in your care." Sarneth stood. "You are gracious to lend us your aid. But I fear without that arrow, it won't be enough. May Eloch guide your hands." He turned to leave. "Hastra, will you share your tale with me this evening? I'd like to know more of what we face in any way." He reached for the door, but hesitated. "Oh, and what am I supposed to do with these two dwarves who've offered their services? I can only assume they are who they claim to be?"

"They are indeed, the former ruler and champion of Chokkra. I should let them do what they do best." Hastra refrained from informing the elven commander that she'd blessed Makwi to some end over which her heart lent her misgiving. He needn't presume they were ill luck.

Sarneth opened the door. "What would that be?"

Athson stirred from his preoccupation. "They kill trolls."

"I wish I had an army of them, then." The elven commander closed the door as he left.

They sat in the room in silence after Sarneth left them, until finally Howart stirred. "I have pondered the condition of the arrow for days, but I've no leading from Eloch in the matter." He spread his hands across the table and signaled for any other input.

Zelma scratched her chin. "I've only sought these rumors

of Rokans in the city. Nothing about the arrow. We haven't even heard any rumor of Magdronu's approach."

"Indeed, sister, that would seem something upon which we might gain some inkling of what's to come." Hastra's irritation toward Athson grew at his apparent disinterest. "Athson, what of your thoughts on the matter? Did you learn enough from Apeth to listen?"

He pushed the arrow pieces farther onto the table with a grimace. "I hear nothing at present about this or anything."

Hastra's patience broke at sight of his disgust. "Athson, if you're upset with Limbreth, that's misplaced anger. Perhaps it's the curse at work. But don't blame her. As Howart said, nothing happens by accident."

Athson fixed his gaze on Hastra for a moment before his face constricted into grief. "Then I guess it's not an accident that Limbreth is leaving with Dareth and his soldiers today."

Hastra gaped. "What?" She stared at the broken arrow and almost snorted at the irony that they sat in an inn named the Broken Bow.

"She gave it to me this morning when I found her. She's leaving because of me." His eyes narrowed as he regarded Howart and Zelma. "Because I acted in revenge in attacking Corgren. Because I told her what I did."

CHAPTER NINETEEN

Limbreth rode out of Auguron City beside Dareth, her stomach knotted with anger and her mind awhirl with thoughts unspoken. She ground her teeth all the way across the bridge. She'd intended to fight, to stand with Athson. But he had betrayed her at the Funnel. When she had fought for him, tried to fix all her failures, he had betrayed her. The horses' hooves rang on the metal of the bridge.

After they'd left Auguron behind, Dareth spoke and she ignored him until he rode in silence. Let him understand now. Even if they were married, he'd never be happy with her. She wanted—well, not him. She resisted the urge to put her heels to her horse and gallop away, never to return. The one she wanted had failed her utterly, miserably. The one she despised spoke only of his favors won. Limbreth lifted her chin and rode south with the cavalcade of Grendonese soldiers, passing fleeing refugees by the hundreds.

At nightfall, Limbreth vomited her dinner behind her tent. She had abandoned her friends and all their labors. She had abandoned the gracious honor of the dwarves. She felt like she'd carried her horse all day. The steady number of dwarves who hurried on the southern road from Auguron City served as a constant reminder of her abandoned cause. She wiped her face. Why should she feel sick about it? She didn't do the abandoning at the Funnel. Her stomach roiled at all the dwarves on the road, at the thought of all their honor lost, her wasted efforts.

"Limbreth," Dareth called into her tent. He must have ducked into it. "Limbreth?" He wandered off, looking for her.

"Good." Her voice sounded as feeble as her stomach felt. A deep sigh escaped her lips as she sat against a tree. Who was she kidding? A hero? The death-grip was just something left over from an injury. Brave? Nothing but an act, mostly for herself. But she hated the thought of what awaited her in Grendon. Her lips suddenly trembled at that thought as much as at her lost honor and failures.

Limbreth buried her face in her hands. But Athson had betrayed her, thoughtlessly, carelessly. She stood, rounded her tent, and crawled into it. She lay holding her sickened stomach.

Dareth sought her again. "Limbreth, love, come have some wine and sit by the fire. Listen to the men sing songs of our home."

Anger flamed in her in an instant. She shot to her feet and yanked a sword loose, holding it at Dareth's face. "Get out. Don't come to my tent again."

He backed away, his hand raised. "Easy with that." His eyes narrowed but he left and didn't return.

She curled into a ball and lay awake most of the night. The world twisted tighter than a hangman's rope. A love lost. A wasted cause. Honor falsely earned. Betrayal heaped on her failure. An empty marriage at the end of this journey as empty as the one just completed. How stupid of Dareth to think he could marry a woman who despised him. Finally, Limbreth slept.

The next day, she rode stiffly as they passed more dwarves.

"I should think we're out of danger, if that upset you, love." Dareth offered a welcoming smile that never touched his eyes.

Limbreth's lips pursed in reaction. "I'm not your love, and I don't care about danger." She showed him the repairs in her leather armor. "I've got scars you'll never earn."

"All the fearsome things you got yourself into on that foolish journey. You'll do better, I think, with other clothes and forgetting all these troubles. We'll keep riding farther from the trolls. You'll feel better and change your mind. You'll see." Dareth watched her with empty affection.

Limbreth wanted to kick him from his horse. She bit back her snarl, stared at the road, and attempted to ignore all the dwarves clogging their progress.

"Why do you bind your hair? What are those silly things in your braids?" Dareth sounded like he was admonishing a child.

Limbreth held out her braid and leaned closer. "This one with the ax names me an ax-maid among the dwarves. I got it charging three-score or more trolls one night to save one companion. This one is for the death-grip because they had to pry a sword from my hand when it was over. This last one, the prince's crown, that's for being a royal representative. They are all earned and honored."

A few passing dwarves swore when they overheard her. Limbreth glanced their way, and they saluted her. They spoke in dwarvish, "Hail, honored one!"

Limbreth smiled, noted the trinkets in their beards for merchants, tinkers, and warriors, one an officer. She answered in dwarvish. "Well met, honored warriors. May your beards grow long and your axes never dull. May the count of your enemy dead be higher than the count of your years."

Dareth sniffed and lifted his nose. "Speaking to these people. You've learned all the wrong things on this adventure."

"Foolish words from a foolish fop." She glared at Dareth.

He lifted his hand as if to slap her.

She half-pulled her sword in a blink. "Do it, and you ride home with one hand less than when you started."

He lowered his hand. "Your father will hear of all these things."

She laughed. "I'll tell him myself."

Trying Dareth's patience proved Limbreth's only entertainment. He understood nothing. She'd been held captive by a creature beyond his reason. His threats and insults meant nothing against that or trolls' arrows in the night or soldiers fighting on a cliff road.

Limbreth looked over her shoulder, saluted the dwarf officer again, and called in dwarvish, "You are welcome to exchange the count of your enemies with me." The dwarf likely wouldn't seek her out that evening, but if he did, she'd welcome a good tale of battles fought. Her heart soared a moment. Maybe she was brave even if she returned home. She hadn't done the betraying. Nothing was on her. She told herself that all day, though she never believed it.

The dwarf found their location that evening, since the cavalcade traveled only as fast as the foot and wagon traffic. Limbreth received word from the Grendonese guardsmen, and she went to meet him. She approached the guards, who wore the Grendonese uniforms of blue with matching capes, their breastplates shining, as did their other equipment. One man addressed her with a bow. "Your highness, this dwarf says he's answering your invitation to visit you."

Limbreth almost laughed at the Grendonese ignorance of dwarven customs. "Yes, he is invited by me. He's a veteran of the Chokkran military with several honors, and I would like to speak with him."

The dwarf doffed his hat and bowed, wide-eyed. His bulbous nose bore smudges from travel on the road, while his wrinkled and worn clothing bespoke nothing of his former honor. But the knots and braids woven with trinkets indicated his honor and rank among his people. "Uh, your highness? I didn't know you were of higher station." He pointed to her braided hair. "But I see that now. If I'm a bother, I can go."

Limbreth switched to dwarvish. "Nonsense, you are not bothering when you come at my invitation. You have shown me honor by recognizing these." She pointed to her own trinkets. "I merely wanted the company of a dwarf to swap tales. I see that you bear the honor of a captain and a medal for bravery. What's your name?"

The guards observed them with sudden suspicion and muttered to each other at the foreign tongue. "Your highness, shall we turn this dwarf away?"

"No, he's to come with me." She spoke the common tongue, then switched back to dwarvish. "Please forgive the interruption. They do not know the formalities or the tongue."

The dwarf bowed as a warrior, his hands on his hips and feet shoulder width apart. "I am Erskwe of Chokkra, former captain of the Granite Brigade. My honor is offered for the tale of yours."

Limbreth resisted a smile as she sketched her own bow of rank with far more pretension. His words were a polite way of asking for proof she was who she claimed to be. "An honor to meet the captain of the Granite Brigade." She motioned to show the dwarf into the camp. "You shall have the tale of my honor with the hospitality of my fire." She switched to common tongue and addressed the guards. "He will come with me and share my meal."

The guards bowed. "As you wish, your highness."

Limbreth led Erskwe through the camp, but took care to avoid Dareth's campfire. She led the captain toward her own campfire and called for food and drink. They sat, and Limbreth returned to dwarvish. "I must apologize that I do not have beer or ale available. But such as is available, we'll share." She'd never hosted a dwarf, so it was new territory. Limbreth racked her memory of Duliwe's feast in Ezhandun. "But for now, the tale of my honor."

Erskwe's eyes narrowed at her words. "Please do." He refrained from addressing her as ax-maid just yet. He stroked his beard and took the offered bread and stew, as did Limbreth.

She decided to start with a well-known leader. "Be assured that I've been received by Duliwe of Ezhandun and his men, as well as the village, and accorded due honor."

Erskwe chuckled and stroked his beard. "How is that old crow?"

She laughed, and the knots in her stomach relaxed as she drank wine. "The old crow still flies true enough, but his beard's gray, though the weight of his people do not bow his back. But let it also be known to you, brave Erskwe, that I was named ax-maid by Makwi, champion of Chokkra, and Tordug of Chokkra. Makwi composes my verses, though the tale of them grows faster than his slow tongue can knit words."

The dwarf's eyes widened as she spoke, but he laughed at her jibe about Makwi. "He's a careful poet, that one, and his humor sourer than week-old goat's milk."

"That it is." Limbreth laughed. "But his beard his long and still dark. He's raised his ax beside my sword any number of times, as has Tordug, whose honor has risen with the company of Makwi, Hastra the Withling, and my own. Would you hear my tale, Erskwe, honored of the Granite Brigade?"

"I would." He drank his wine and tore into his bread. "I've not heard the tale of an ax-maid from her lips." His eyes flicked to her braid. "Nor have I met one with the death-grip."

Limbreth launched into her tale, beginning with following Hastra and her daring charge at Marston's Station. She recounted the number of times she'd been overcome with the death-grip and her fights with the Bane and other creatures. She made sure to emphasize Tordug's prowess and how his honor was accepted at Ezhandun, in large part because of her.

When Limbreth finished her tale, Erskwe rose to his feet and knelt. "I acknowledge your honor, ax-maid Limbreth of the death-grip, Silver Lady and protector of travelers, as well as princess of Grendon. May the tales of your scars ring around campfires long after your days have faded."

She inclined her head. Thereafter, they spoke of dwarves and his own honor, a daring charge against greater odds at the opening of the fighting that led to Chokkra's fall. The dwarf spoke of the lack of hope among his scattered people, and she listened, gathering more information about those who traveled south and whether she might help anyone along the way.

As they neared the end of their conversation, Limbreth asked, "How many of your people migrate south from the fighting?"

At mention of the trolls, Erskwe's cheeks flushed, and he clenched his jaw several times. "We are many, well over a thousand. But few wanted to stay, so those who wanted otherwise bowed to the wishes of the many, waiting for a better time to fight."

Her eyes widened at the number. "So many? I had seen many, but the count is much higher than I'd realized."

"Aye, ax-maid. We are many, but we are hopeless." He looked away and spat.

"You could have stayed and defended your new homes."

"We lack a leader to mobilize us to hope, so we flee when we should lend our arms to the troubles of Auguron City, which has harbored us in trade and goodwill." His cheeks flushed. "Why do you leave, ax-maid?"

"I am called home by my father." Her own cheeks heated. "Did you know that Makwi had come to the city?"

Erskwe shook his head. "We knew nothing of it. Some of us might have stayed for him."

She noted he mentioned nothing of Tordug. Their meal ended as they traded a few jests, and she walked him back to the guards. Afterward, she slipped into her tent and slept better, which puzzled her in the morning.

The Grendonese plodded along the rutted road with the crowds of escaping travelers. The third day out from Auguron City nagged at her mind. Dwarves crowded the road, and she passed several, who gave her avid salutes. Apparently, word got around fast, either from Erskwe or just what was overheard by his companions. She snorted. If only she could return to Auguron City with this dwarven army, ready to fight trolls. She shook her head at the thought. They didn't want to fight.

Dust kicked up from the road at a breeze that rolled along its length. Limbreth covered her face for a few moments. Overhead a hawk screamed among the treetops of leaf-barren hardwood and needle-bristled pine. The hawk's call echoed another scream—her scream—when she'd fallen from the cliff at the Funnel. She frowned. Athson had let her down.

She tugged her reins and halted her horse, her jaw slack. She'd left Auguron because of Athson. Hastra's prophecy reared out of memory. *Go and return again as if from death.* Her sudden flight felt like death. She swallowed hard.

Dwarves trudged past, and she watched them. Were they truly hopeless? Or just leaderless in their own minds?

Dareth drew close, "Are you ill?"

"No, something else." She ignored his further questions, kicked her horse into movement, then practically fell out of the saddle when she reached the group of dwarves in her haste to dismount. She chose the most senior veteran among them and leaned close to him. She pulled her braid into view. "This axmaid needs help."

The elder dwarf stroked his salt-and-pepper beard, his brows furrowed. "What can an old sergeant do for an axmaid?"

Limbreth grinned and switched to dwarvish. "I need soldiers."

"What for?" His bushy brows climbed, but she read his guess in his expression.

"For killing trolls."

The dwarf's eyes narrowed, and his companions muttered among themselves. "You're calling us to arms?"

Limbreth nodded. "I am. We march to Auguron City."

The dwarf stroked his beard. "You can prove your status among us?"

"There are two who can. One composes the verses of my deeds. Regardless, I'm going back to Auguron City." She lifted her chin. "But, if you need more now, you'll have it." She closed her fists so tightly they shook and crossed him at her chest in show of death's repose.

The old sergeant's eyes widened and the gathering dwarves who saw muttered among themselves about the sign of the death-grip.

Limbreth followed the death-grip salute by drawing a sword and flourished it with a twirl and held it on-guard like a dwarf champion and an ax-maid's salute in one, her left extended toward the dwarf's face.

The old dwarf stepped back with a gasp and the others around him uttered gasps too.

"I am Limbreth, Princess of Grendon, Maid of the Ax." She lifted her left fist to signify the hand which won her the titles near Marston's Station. "I grip death." She followed with the same words she used on Duliwe at Ezhandun. "I am the Silver Lady of Auguron and both Patroness and Protector of the Wayfarer on the Road. I stand with my honor, in place of Makwi-angk-tho, for Tordug, Lord of Chokkra. I honor him! If you want the tale of my verses, you'll have to fight trolls for it! But I go to win my honor again." She lifted her gaze to the surrounding dwarves. Perhaps more than a hundred gathered for the spectacle. "I need as many axes with me as possible. Will you come and add your honor to mine?"

The old sergeant inhaled and shouted, "I fight to the honor of Limbreth, Maid of the Ax, may her grip never fail!"

One by one, the gathered dwarves cheered, their deep voices booming along the forest road. Then, they shouted the call to arms along the road to other bands of dwarves nearby. Startled glimpses answered at first, followed by more shouts along the road.

Limbreth sheathed her sword.

Dareth stopped his horse by Limbreth and raised his voice above the din. "What are you doing? What's all this shouting?"

She never looked at Dareth. "I'm giving these dwarves hope."

The nobleman snorted with laughter. "And how are you doing that?"

She faced her would-be suitor, her stomach steadier than at any time the last few days. "By giving them a leader."

Dareth's horse dance beneath him. "Who would that be?"

Limbreth clenched her arms behind her back and faced Dareth astride his horse. "Me."

∽

ATHSON MARCHED among a troop of rangers on one of the drill grounds. It beat waiting for trolls, and he had to do something besides sulk in silence with Hastra. Eloch could speak to him anywhere, and drilling was doing something.

It didn't chase Limbreth from his mind, though.

He turned the wrong way and stepped on someone's foot. He whirled to march the correct direction. None of the elves spoke a word, but Sergeant Illeth arrived moments later. "Trolls won't wait for you to get your directions correct, ranger! Set your mind to it, or you'll find yourself in a grave all too soon!"

Athson marched ahead, his face flushed with embarrassment and his jaw clenched in anger. He'd done it again. Just kept piling mistakes on himself. But he'd joined this troop unassigned—and without Gweld—to fix things as best he could. Sarneth didn't know. At least not yet.

The troop turned on command, and Athson followed this time. He might be able to escape Hastra the rest of this day after his revelation, but she'd look for him tomorrow until she found him. He stood out here more than ever with the Bow of Hart and his blessed sword, which were definitely not ranger issue, but he might make up for all his mistakes somehow. He'd sleep in the barracks and that way might avoid his other companions.

After drilling, Athson moved his gear to another bunk and ducked Gweld's notice in the crowded mess hall. He wasn't supposed to be here, and Gweld might tell someone, and then he'd end up right back with Hastra expecting something out of him that he couldn't do. He picked at his food, his appetite gone. He'd chased Limbreth away. He was a worthless Withling.

Sergeant Illeth gripped his shoulder and leaned into his ear. "I know you're not assigned to me. I don't know what game you're playing, but keep up with the mistakes, and I'll boot you. I've training to complete and trolls due here in just a few days."

Athson glanced at the sergeant and opened his mouth but found no answer worth speaking. He nodded.

The sergeant flashed ranger hand-talk at him that he was watching Athson, his sharp elven features intent. Athson stared at the scar on the elf's pale cheek before he moved along the row of tables.

A lump rose in Athson's throat. There was no winning for him here. He shoved food into his mouth and chewed in silence. No matter what he did, Limbreth wasn't coming back. Ever. Not after finding out about his mistakes. And either

Eloch spoke to him or didn't. *Just be a ranger.* Nothing mattered but making a difference in the battle to come.

After he ate, Athson returned to his bunk and checked his pack. The inheritance lay within, the note and the banner as useless to him as the pieces of the White Arrow Limbreth had given him. He sniffed. She'd done no better than him. He stared at the arrow pieces in his pack. But then, she hadn't chosen revenge over his life. His shoulders slumped at the thought, and he shoved his pack out of the way. He lay on his bed and grappled for sleep. Tomorrow was an early day, and he needed to blend in beneath Sergeant Illeth's eye.

The next day, Athson patted himself on the back as he successfully completed the morning marches without incident. They proceeded to the archery range for practice. Limbreth's face leapt to his mind along with the memory of her kisses. Those were gone for good. He spilled his quiver of arrows, swore, and gathered them back up.

Sergeant Illeth walked past Athson with grunt and a shake of his head.

Athson stood and nocked an arrow. Best make some sure shots and avoid further attention. He let the arrow slip off his bow as he drew, then regained control of the projectile only to pluck the string. The *twang* sounded loud among the soft releases of the other rangers. His arrow missed the target entirely. Athson swore under his breath. *Focus, or you'll be sitting with Hastra in no time.* He waited for the command to draw and release again with the other rangers. At least he hit the target the second time. Better, but not good enough yet. He knew he could do far better. Good thing Gweld wasn't around, or he'd hear it from him too.

Arrows *thunked* into targets and Athson relaxed. He'd recovered his aim. The sergeant walked by and sniffed. Athson owned a reputation even among the rangers.

With a final release, Athson allowed his mind fleeting

considerations. He hated abandoning the others. Where was Ralda? What of the dwarves? He shrugged. They were probably running errands for Hastra. He'd sought his mother several times, but the Withlings kept her busy on some errand or other.

Sergeant Illeth called for flaming arrows. Athson turned to a brazier and selected a specially designed arrow. Limbreth's smiling face, her cheeks dimpled in pleasure, stepped to the forefront of his thoughts. Or how about when she'd kissed him back in Ezhandun? He clenched his jaw. She'd promised he wasn't something temporary.

Athson set his first arrow aflame and wheeled toward the firing line. His arrow brushed another ranger's sleeve, which caught fire. He dropped his arrow and helped the ranger beat the flame out before it did more harm than cause a scorch mark.

"Thanks." The other ranger's eyes narrowed.

A hand grabbed Athson by the shoulder. "That's it. You're gone." Sergeant Illeth pulled him away.

Athson rounded on the sergeant, his free hand clenched. "Hey, I can do this."

"Yeah, sure you can. But someone wants to see you." Illeth thumbed over his shoulder where Sarneth stood at the end of the line of rangers.

"I was wondering when Hastra and Sarneth would catch me." He sighed and glanced at the elf he'd almost caught on fire and then Sergeant Illeth. "Sorry for the trouble." The fire of his anger shriveled like Limbreth's admiration. He shouldered the Bow of Hart and walked toward the elven captain, fighting the slouch of his troubles all the way across the back of the range. He halted in front of Sarneth and managed a fairly crisp salute, which the captain returned. "You found me."

Sarneth sighed and shook his head. "Follow me."

Athson trailed the elven captain off the range as he held his grumbles of complaint. He just wanted to do something. Fix things and show Limbreth. She wasn't here, but she might hear about things if he used the Bow of Hart correctly. "Where are we going?"

The elf skipped a step, and Athson fell in beside him. "What are you doing out here with that bow? I thought we agreed you were assigned to Hastra."

"I wanted to use it more. It's not accurate. At least it wasn't back at..." He almost spoke the word *Funnel* but choked it back. It was useless without the White Arrow. At least against Magdronu. He thumbed over his shoulder. "Back there."

Sarneth snorted. "Yeah, that was more you than anything. Too much running through your head. You need to get that straight. Trolls will be here within a few days. But you're going to see Hastra and figure something out and get it all straightened out."

Athson's step hitched, but then he caught up to Sarneth as the captain presumably took Athson directly to Hastra. That was the nagging idea on his mind. Magdronu approached with this attack. Surely that was the case. And Athson had nothing to combat the dragon. "Have you heard any reports of the dragon with the trolls?"

"Oddly, no." Sarneth squinted one eye. "But then, he's rarely made direct appearance in the past, if memory serves. Not even at Chokkra."

"Well, that's before my time." Athson shoved a hand into a cloak pocket and fiddled with the arrow pieces. "Just wondering what to expect."

"I can't help you there, Athson. Hastra's the best person for that." They turned down the street for the Broken Bow Inn. "I don't suppose I can trust you to actually go meet her?" Sarneth shot Athson a sidelong gaze. "You're slippery and tend to get around commands. I want to make sure you make it to her even if you take me away from other duties." He wagged a finger in Athson's face while they approached the inn. "But I've got better things to do than drag you into Hastra's presence." He fingered the Bow of Hart. "This is too important to ignore, though. So do us both a favor. Do what you can to forget the girl and figure something out with Hastra. We need you, Athson."

Athson swallowed hard. "I'll do that."

He doubted he really could. Her kisses sent a flush across his cheeks, and the pit in his stomach opened. Did she really have to go and leave him without talking out his failure at the Funnel? But she had, and nothing would change that fact. He slipped through exiting rangers at the inn door and dragged his feet up the steps to the porch. Limbreth wasn't coming back. He didn't know if he'd live that down, certainly not in the days to come.

He lost his battle with his posture and slouched as he entered the inn, remembering that night when he'd arrived with her after hunting the Bane. No reason for that thing to hunt her anymore. She'd taken herself out of the fray. He sighed, unable to forget her smile or her kisses.

CHAPTER TWENTY

Dareth raised his chin and his smile failed to reach his eyes. Limbreth lifted her own chin and stared at her would-be husband.

"I think not." Dareth waved a dark-gloved hand. "Colonel Meegs, please escort the princess away while I deal with this rabble."

Murmurs rippled among the gathering dwarves at Dareth's haughty words. The colonel ordered two men to join him as he approached on horse. "Princess, if you will—"

"I will not." Limbreth drew her swords, her eyes narrowed at Dareth. "Colonel, I've known you in my father's household many years. You are subject to my command, are you not?"

The colonel hesitated, his ruddy face a sudden mask of confusion. "Princess Limbreth, let's not have a scene."

She glanced toward the colonel. His sunken cheeks twitched with the tension of a withheld command. "You will obey a member of the king's family. This man is not my husband, and though he may have brought you to Auguron to retrieve me, I am well within my rights to command you all."

She urged her horse closer to Colonel Meegs. "Or shall I show you why these dwarves answer my call to arms?"

Dareth laughed. "You foolish, willful girl. I shall be happy to take you over my knee when the time comes."

She backed her horse toward Dareth's mount. Without a word, she punched him in jaw, her hand still around a sword-hilt.

Dareth grunted and leaned away, dazed and suddenly silent.

Limbreth freed her foot from a stirrup and kicked Dareth's free. She edged her horse closer and shoved at her would-be husband with her shoulder and elbow. He fell from his horse, landing with another grunt.

The dwarves laughed at the sight.

Limbreth flashed a grin at them. Let their honor be protected. They appreciated that.

She turned to Colonel Meegs as more dwarves answered the calls from farther along the road in either direction. "You'll find my recent journeys have left me rather direct, colonel. I'm quite willing to use my weapons—very able, in fact. These dwarves are veterans of Chokkra, and they are willing to fight now, should it come to that." She pointed a sword at the colonel. "I'm quite able to take you in a moment, should I have the need."

Dareth stood and found words as he rushed around his horse and grasped at Limbreth with one hand, drawing his own sword. "You spoiled child. I'll see you horse-whipped!"

Limbreth kicked him in the chin. His knees wobbled, and he fell on his backside.

A nearby dwarf guffawed and added, "Ax-maids are rough. You sure you want this one for a wife?" The dwarves laughed again.

Dareth struggled to his feet, his sword lifted.

Limbreth twirled her own sword, snagging Dareth's

weapon with her own and disarming him. "Attack a member of Grendon's royal house again, and I'll see you hanged as a traitor, Dareth." He opened his mouth, and she held her sword at his eye. "Speak, just speak again."

He shut his mouth and his shoulders sagged. But his eyes flashed to the colonel.

"You have a choice, Dareth. Ride with me to Auguron City, or ride home under guard. Trouble me again, and I'll have you tied over a baggage horse for whichever destination I choose." She looked at the colonel. "Meegs, you have a similar choice. Ride with me to Auguron City, or answer to my father for disobeying me when I return."

The colonel fixed his dark eyes on Limbreth. "Riding for the city is death. We have but four hundred horsemen with parade lances. Those trolls will kill us all. We don't have the numbers to relieve the city of the siege. You know this."

"Indeed, I do." She motioned to the gathering dwarves. "However, these veterans would like nothing more than to kill trolls, and they are more than enough to wreak havoc among them." One of the dwarves opened his mouth to speak, but Limbreth knew what to say and spoke faster. "A dwarf doesn't count his enemies with armor but with his ax."

Dwarves roared approval and cheered. The roar filled the road around them, though none but those nearby knew the cause.

Colonel Meegs's gaze remained fixed on Limbreth. Once the uproar subsided enough, he turned his head to his nearby majors. "Gentlemen, you heard your princess. We ride for the city!"

Limbreth grinned as the dwarves hooted their delight. "Find me Erskwe and bring any other officers. I want ranks organized and scouts chosen. Gather such weapons as you have as well as rations. We march on the trolls."

Men and dwarves swirled in a rush.

The colonel joined Limbreth. "I hope you know what you're doing, princess. Or we'll never live to worry about what your father says about this."

"Well, I'm not going along with this. I'll ride south." Dareth scrambled for his horse. "Bring me guards, colonel. I'll happily tell the king of your treachery against his emissary."

"Not so fast, Dareth." Limbreth glanced at his arms. Sudden suspicion rose in her mind and she'd seen a few things among the Rokans who followed Magdronu. "First we need to check for something. Show me your bare arms."

"I'll do no such thing." Dareth lifted his foot into a stirrup.

Limbreth pointed a sword at this throat. "You seem rather anxious to leave and quick to attack your betrothed."

Dareth pushed the blade from his throat. "Nonsense! You attacked me and are forcing me to leave. What else do you want of me?"

"Remove your shirt, Dareth!" She brought her sword back to his throat before he could mount.

"I'll do no such thing!"

"Colonel, have your men strip his shirt off."

Colonel Meegs ordered some men to carry out Limbreth's orders. Dareth reached for his sword on the ground, but one of the soldiers stepped on the blade. Meegs glared at Dareth. "Let's not make this too difficult." The colonel eyed Limbreth.

She stared at the colonel without breaking her firm expression. She'd see if Dareth was loyal or not. She swallowed and narrowed her eyes. She didn't know which was better from Dareth, misguided loyalty or disloyalty.

Dareth scuffled with the soldiers, who quickly removed his cloak and drew his shirt up. "How dare you touch me. I'm noble born and cannot suffer this way. I'll have you whipped."

The shirt rose as far as Dareth's shoulders before Limbreth spotted the lower part of a tattoo. Her nostrils flared at what the symbol emblazoned on Dareth's shoulder blade meant. "The mark of Magdronu. He's no mage, but he's a spy."

A dwarf drew a knife and stepped forward. "Let me gut him."

"Hold your blade." Several emotions flared in Limbreth's thoughts, anger not the least. He'd likely been sent to drag her away. She stared at the mark on Dareth, who ceased his struggles with an expression of resignation on his face. "Colonel, I leave him in your hands to guard."

"Shall we bring him?"

She hesitated. Send him away, and he might escape. They'd never learn anything from him. "Bring him in irons and question him tonight."

Chains were brought and Dareth led away captive at the colonel's orders. When Dareth was marched to the baggage train, the colonel cocked his head. "How did you know, princess?"

Around them, dwarves formed ranks, their veterans easily remembering their past experiences. Limbreth inhaled and released a long sigh. If she didn't know better, she'd think she'd been drawn away from Auguron City. But how, and why?

She looked the colonel in the eyes and shrugged. "He's a bad actor. If he'd truly been interested in me and the place he could win, he would have spent his time wooing me. He would have pleaded with me not to waste my life. He would have been jealous of another man."

"A poor actor indeed." The colonel gazed in the direction of the baggage train. "Would you like to be present at his questioning?"

Limbreth stroked her braid in thought. "Not directly. Put him inside a tent, and I'll listen from outside." She shrugged. "I doubt he's got much to offer that we need now, but I'm certain there's much he knows about plots against Grendon."

Colonel Meegs's face paled. "I shudder to know those

secrets. But better to know the traitor's plans than be blind to them. We'll send messages if there's anything impending. I had no notion of this until now."

"He may know some details but not all." At a look from Meegs, Limbreth continued, "After many dealings with the dragon's minions and servants these last months, there's one thing I know: they don't know all. The dragon keeps his deeper schemes close to himself and maybe his mages." Her eyes narrowed as she watched a group of dwarves approach, one of them Erskwe. "At any rate, his plans appear fluid, but he has one goal, and that's his own power." She chewed her lower lip. And he'd found a way to play her out of his way. But to what end?

"You seem to have learned much on this journey of yours." Colonel Meegs flashed a wry smile at her. "Your father should know of the information you've gathered."

Limbreth glanced skyward in thought. Perhaps a message was in order. "Prepare something when we know more from Dareth. But there's much my father won't learn until I return home. Especially about my ties to dwarves."

"Indeed. I think he should be proud of you." Meegs lifted a finger. "But we yet need to survive this wild gambit of yours."

"We can turn the tide against the dragon's trolls with these dwarves." She pressed two fingers to her lips and sketched the bow of an ax-maid to the dwarven officers as they approached

The ten dwarves returned their various bows to Limbreth. Erskwe spoke for the group, "Well met and well-done, ax-maid. May your, um, braid grow to your knees."

Limbreth suppressed a grin. Best to keep it formal and proper for now. "My thanks for your aid. May your beards never be cut, nor your knots be loosened in misfortune."

The dwarves muttered their approval in dwarvish and nodded among themselves. Erskwe gazed hard at his fellow dwarves as if to emphasize that he'd been right about her. He turned his gaze upon Limbreth again and exhaled so deeply that his mustache fluttered. "We're organizing into marching lines now and gathering our weapons. We'll organize down to squads as we march and take inventory of weapons. Few carry battle-axes, but we've such arms as we carry these days."

"Good. I'd expect nothing less of solid veterans. You're hardy with your travels. Have them spar a bit each night." She lifted a finger. "But not too long. It's three days yet to Auguron City, and we want them fresh too. I suspect we'll need some guile to approach the bridge while it's under attack. But just the surprise may put these trolls in confusion."

One of the dwarves bowed. "I'm Montug, ax-maid. Trolls are rabble, but we'll need some luck to send that many in retreat."

Limbreth nodded. "That's why we need scouts. Pick your best men." Her gaze included Colonel Meegs. "We'll need to know the situation so we can plan the most confusion and thus free the rangers to help us clear the way. Confusion leads to rout. We get to choose our approach."

The dwarves muttered assent, and Meegs saluted.

Limbreth clapped her hands once. "Then we should be moving now, or Auguron City may be in flames before we can lend our aid. I'll need full reports from you all on your units as we progress."

The dwarves forestalled total organization for simple marching ranks and set out behind the Grendonese cavalry. Limbreth led her army north. Her stomach fluttered with misgiving as much as excitement. They might not reach the city in time.

Athson entered her thoughts, his bearded jaw after days on the trail that set her heart racing. She loved him. At least she thought she did. She spent far too much time thinking about him not to. She shrugged. But trust was another matter. And a question to which she had no answer. Auguron's safety meant more now, and then she could deal with Athson. She didn't know if she'd ever trust him again. She couldn't account for Athson now; she was just bringing help to Auguron City because that was the right thing to do. She couldn't let it be for Athson, no matter how much she wanted to make it about him. After all, she hadn't decided to trust him with herself. Yet.

And so Limbreth's army marched on Auguron City for more than two days until they arrived south of the city, just within a short trek and battle. Her heart sank at the reports of her scouts, but her officers looked toward her for leadership.

The night of the second day, they slept without tents in the cold of the late winter, the better to set out before dawn. She slept fitfully, butterflies rolling around her belly, and dreamed of shadow crossing Auguron's bridge.

∽

ATHSON SULKED FOR THREE DAYS, and Hastra fretted. Trolls were arriving across the river in undisciplined ranks, hooting and howling their rage. Sarneth's rescue fleet of small boats only partially worked, with some travelers and rangers able to board before pursuing trolls had attacked them. Others had swum for the safety of the boats. Many made it, and many didn't. All three days, the Withling waited for the slightest guidance from an urge about the White Arrow, but nothing pierced her growing apprehension.

Today she had requested Athson sit with her and Danilla, and Hastra now resisted an urge to scream. The bearer of the Bow of Hart sat forlorn, his mind on the departed Limbreth. She sighed. "Athson."

He didn't stir.

"Athson."

His fingers fit the pieces of the arrow together, and he frowned.

"Athson!" Hastra immediately regretted her waspish tone.

Danilla jumped where she sat in the corner doing needlework with what she'd brought along from Rok.

"What?" He twisted his head and gazed at her, his tone edged with anger.

"Why don't you go get us something to drink?" *Do something besides mope.* Her own anger flared, but she held her tongue. Just when he'd turned the corner, now this.

"Don't feel like it." His gaze returned to the broken arrow.

Danilla peered at her son but continued her needlework. He was ignoring her too, it seemed. Athson's mother shook her head slightly.

Hastra sighed and stood on wobbly knees. She was weaker every day and got no help from Athson. She paused at the door. That wasn't fair. He wasn't a trained Withling. "I'm going, then. Would you like something?"

"Uh, yeah, sure."

"Tea for me, or do you need help?" Danilla paused with her needle.

"No, I can get it." Athson said nothing else, so Hastra left and returned with an ale for him and tea for herself and Danilla. She sloshed the ale beside his hand on the table like a weary tavern maid and returned to her seat.

"Thanks." Athson hadn't noticed her shoddy delivery and ignored the mug for several minutes.

Hastra stared at him. Undone by Limbreth's repudiation of him. At least the rest of their group spent their time more wisely in the face of the impending danger from the swelling numbers of trolls across the river. The dwarves assisted Sarneth. Ralda worked on setting the defenses on the moored barges and boats. Gweld already drilled with his new unit. Even her sister and Howart sought word of the rumored Rokans in the city. But Athson sat with Hastra and mumbled about Limbreth or the Funnel.

"Why don't you do something?"

Athson lifted his gaze from the broken arrow again. "I was until you pulled me in here today. At least drilling with the rangers kept my mind busy."

Hastra snorted. "Sarneth said you stepped on feet, dropped arrows, and almost set someone's cloak aflame."

Athson sat back in his chair in the dining room of the Broken Bow Inn and stared at her. "That's why we drill."

"No, that's—"

"Are we back to squabbling, Hastra?" He stood and paced the room. "You want me to just snap my fingers and come up with an answer?" He leaned over the table from the other end and pointed to his head. "I don't hear Eloch. At least, I don't know when I do, and I've heard nothing about that." He waved his hand at the broken arrow. His face contorted. "Limbreth didn't..." He lifted his gaze to Hastra. "I'm not perfect, and she storms away and leaves me this." He grabbed the Bow of Hart and headed for the door.

Hastra snagged his arm. "I'm sorry. Let's just start over, and I'll work with you." She really needed his help. Maybe he would hear something if she didn't.

Athson pulled from her grasp and yanked the door open. But he paused in the doorway, stepped back into the room, and shut the door. He stared at the wood. "I don't know what to do, Hastra. She's gone. I failed, and I don't know what to do."

She pushed a chair out for him. Maybe he needed some guidance about being a Withling. "Sit. We'll try a few methods of training. I want to help you as much as I can."

He sat and propped his head in his hands. "I don't know anything except that none of this is for Magdronu." He lifted his head and fixed his gaze on Hastra over his fingertips, his features hidden. "That's what you keep saying, anyway. What can I do?" He set the bow on the table and slapped it. "This was no good to me at the Funnel when—when—" He swallowed and stared at the opposite wall. "When I needed it. When I didn't help—"

Hastra groaned. "Athson, this has to stop. You were better before she left, more lucid and calm. Now you're just feeling sorry for yourself. You told her the truth, and it shocked her. But you did the correct thing by speaking to her about it. You weren't perfect and you won't be. She wasn't. I'm not."

"You sound like Apeth." He rubbed his eyes with his palms. "What is wrong with me?"

"If I sound like Apeth, then what did he have you do about it?" Hastra leaned forward, her gaze intent. This was important.

Athson stood. "Look, it doesn't matter. I've driven her away, and it's all my fault."

Hastra leaned back, stood, and walked to the window. "It has to stop."

Danilla set aside her needle-work. "Athson, dear. Why don't you try writing her a letter?"

He fiddled with the pieces of the arrow. "That won't work, she's gone. For good." He sighed.

Danilla bit her lip and glanced Hastra's way before she continued, "She might not get it for a while but it will make you feel better just to tell her everything. Tell her how you feel about her. Tell her about the curse - that you didn't know about it. Tell you would never hurt her or abandon her, that you know better how to deal with it. Let her know you never wanted harm to come to her." She glanced toward Hastra.

Hastra nodded and looked back out the window.

"It won't work." Athson's chair scuffed on the floor as he got to his feet and left.

Behind Hastra, the door opened and closed. "We'll have to find another way, Danilla." She tapped her lips with a finger. "Gweld knows him best. We'll ask him to help." She spied Athson's makeshift standard leaning in the corner. "He's even forgotten that banner. He was so motivated and now he doesn't care at all. At least he took the bow and arrow."

Hastra wrote a note to Sarneth, requesting Gweld's presence. She waited, drumming her fingers on the table. She was getting too old and weak to walk across the city. Not like her sister and Howart. She gazed at the message left for her from her sister.

Found rumor of a few Shildrans and maybe one Rokan. They haven't been seen for a few days but left all day and returned well after dark. Nothing else. Still searching.

"Danilla, since Athson's not around now, could you go look for Zelma? She may need your help searching for those Shildrans." Hastra fumbled with the paper. They needed to find out if there were Rokan agents in the city or not.

Danilla stood and set the frame and pattern aside. "Anything I can help with. Do you know where they are?"

Hastra flipped over the message. "This reads the Leaky Ladle. May as well try there. I don't think that's elven owned either."

"I'll get my cloak. Perhaps someone can give me directions or one of those rangers can help." She shrugged. "Maybe I can get Athson to help me find it. I'll take this to him too." Athson's mother retrieved the spear.

Hastra snorted. "It would give him something useful to do instead of practicing his long-face."

Danilla chuckled and left the room, but in the end, she got her son to escort her around for the afternoon looking for the other Withlings.

Hastra sighed after Danilla left. There was no other news from Zelma or Howart She felt as weak as a kitten and as useless about the White Arrow as she had when she had been chained in a dark room in Withling's Watch after Corgren and Paugren killed all the other Withlings. The three of them had survived only for Eloch's will over the long centuries since then.

Blood and screams surfaced from the past. Why remember that now? Distraction?

She fidgeted in her chair and rolled her eyes toward the ceiling. *Eloch, help me.* She stared at her cold cup of tea and felt as chilled as it was. She drummed her fingers again. Where was that elf?

Gweld appeared as if Hastra had rung a bell for him. He saluted respectfully. "Hastra, I didn't know you required my service. I only just received your missive."

"Thank you as ever, Gweld." Hastra motioned to a seat at the table. "It's Athson. Have you seen him since Limbreth left?"

Gweld sighed. "I've been busy with my new assignment, but the few times I've seen him in the barracks, he's been withdrawn. Why?" The elf's face displayed concern in the twitch of his eyebrows.

"He's been inconsolable about Limbreth. He's spent most of his time blaming himself." Hastra straightened her blouse. "But I need him learning rather than pouting or whatever it is he's fallen back into these last few days. We have trolls at the gates, and something must be done about the arrow."

The elf inhaled and exhaled slowly, laced his fingers together, and rested his hands on the table. "I see. So you think I should speak to him?"

She laid her hand atop his. "Please, would you? Have a drink with him, console him. He listens to you. Get him talking or something. He needs to use the bow, and something must be done with the arrow, as you well know."

Gweld pulled free of Hastra's hand and ran the fingers of one hand through his hair. "Well, I'll do what I can. Do you know where he is? Perhaps I can get him to take ownership of his old home like he should, and we can talk alone."

"That would be something. Perhaps he'll get it out of his system. We need him ready with the bow." She inspected her cold tea cup again. "Limbreth left too fast. She should have spoken to me." She shrugged. "These young people are so tightly wound." It left her dizzy and unable to focus when she needed to. "Honestly, Athson's mood has annoyed me to distraction." She offered a smile to the elf and patted his hand. "You've been so steady these last months. Anything you can do this last time would be helpful."

∼

MAGDRONU-AS-GWELD SOUGHT out Athson in the barracks where he lay as if in some malaise. Well, he was, though it was a curse. He'd forgotten about his blessed sword. "Athson, what are you doing here? Aren't you preparing for the battle? Trolls are at the city gates."

Athson stirred. "Gweld, how have you been?"

"How have I been? There's a war on, Athson. You're needed by all. That bow is needed." Magdronu-as-Gweld feigned a friendly grin. The bow was needed. But Hastra and elves would never have its use after tonight. Corgren would see the gates opened, and Athson would give Magdronu the Bow of Hart. Victory in a single night after years beyond count trapped in Eloch's curse. "Let's eat, and we'll have a long talk. Maybe some wine will cheer your spirits." He managed to beckon to Athson without bursting into laughter and rolling his eyes. The pitiful soul fell back into his dolorous ways so easily.

"I don't know." Athson exhaled a heavy sigh. "I guess, but I'm not really hungry." He grabbed his sword and shook his head as if suddenly waking. "This has been all wrong." He frowned and gazed at Gweld for a moment. "Yes, let's eat and talk."

Magdronu-as-Gweld clapped him on the shoulder. "That's the spirit. We'll eat and visit a tavern. Maybe we can talk quietly somewhere. Hey, what about your home? It's quiet. Why aren't you staying there?"

Athson slouched but kept his hand upon the sword pommel. "I honestly don't know. I should have settled my mother there. I've ignored her too much already. Hastra's kept her busy though. I escorted her around looking for Howart and Zelma all afternoon." He grimaced and ran a hand through his hair. "I'll have to apologize to her about not getting her into that house." He motioned toward the door. "Lead on."

Magdronu-as-Gweld led Athson off to dinner and paid for it. Then they watched a few remaining foreign merchants gamble in a tavern along with their guardsmen until they latter started a brawl. They slipped out the back lest the city guard arrest them as part of it. They laughed at the fight, and Athson staggered with a bit more ale in his belly than usual. Magdronu reeled in Athson like a fish.

After a few more mugs at another tavern, Magdronu-as-Gweld slapped Athson's back. "How about we drop your gear at that home in the trees and have a talk?"

Athson shrugged and staggered to his feet. "Sure, let's get my pack and gear." He belched. "Sarneth took all my arrows after I almost burned someone else. You have any?"

Magdronu-as-Gweld guided Athson through the pipe smoke and songs toward the door. The oblivious fools sang when they should run. He grinned at Athson. "You planning to shoot tonight?"

"That bow must be good for something. Maybe a few stray shots across the bridge." He raised his hands uncertainly and frowned before he laughed. "Who cares which troll I feather!"

"Come on, let's get what you have and settle you in the house. You'll feel better. We'll have some tea and talk." Magdronu-as-Gweld led the way. He certainly couldn't let Athson near the bridge. Not at the moment. Not with Corgren at work. "Wait, the barracks is here."

Athson paused and swayed on his feet. "Nah, I want to shoot some trolls. That'll get Limbreth's blood up." He frowned. "If she ever hears about it." He choked on a sob. "What did I do, Gweld? She was the best thing I had going."

Indeed, and Magdronu had planned her removal for months. "You're right, she won't hear about your drunken exploits. Let's just get your things and go to that empty home."

Athson slouched. "What difference does it make? They're gone too." He eyed Magdronu-as-Gweld. "It's just empty."

"Hey, I'm trying to cheer you up some. Let's see about getting it ready for your mother if you want her there." Magdronu-as-Gweld tugged on Athson's sleeve, and he followed with reluctant steps.

"I don't know. Hastra's expecting me sometime. I gotta do something about this arrow."

"Not tonight. Let's get you somewhere quiet and have a chat."

Athson gazed at the darkness surrounding them. "You're right, not tonight." He sighed and came to a stop.

Magdronu-as-Gweld sighed. Maybe he'd overdone it by plying Athson with so much ale. "Just come on, and we'll sit in the quiet for a while."

They trudged along the darkened streets, lights gleaming from doorways. Above, hushed voices and movement from the high-walks in the Auguron Oaks twirled onto the street like leaves. The wind rose into a sudden breeze and blew dust in their eyes. Athson crouched and swore at the dust.

Magdronu-as-Gweld lured Athson to the barracks, and he sobered a bit as they gathered his belongings. "Sarneth doesn't want you here anyway. Maybe a bit of a change for you and Hastra will help you figure out the arrow."

Athson fumbled with his belongings and almost handed Gweld the Bow of Hart. "Here, take this." He handed Gweld the makeshift standard.

Magdronu-as-Gweld took it. He'd almost given the bow

freely. So close. He started to ask for the bow instead but shut his mouth. He'd have it soon regardless. "You ready?"

"Yeah, I think so." Athson followed Gweld back to the street, and they soon found an entry ramp to the walks in the trees. Athson stumbled and dawdled on the way onto the walks.

Magdronu-as-Gweld prodded him along. He might have to carry or push him. Whatever it took, he would have the Bow of Hart in the end.

At last, they arrived at the door. Athson searched his pockets for a key. "Don't have it."

Magdronu-as-Gweld sighed and reached around the forlorn remnants of a potted plant. "Here it is, remember?" He unlocked the door carved with the woodland scene of a stag by a lake and painted well enough to send Athson off hunting if Magdronu didn't get him through the door fast.

Athson paused, and his voice caught on sudden words. "I haven't been here since I bought that dagger. This." He reached for his Rokan dagger. "Oh, Father, you should have left it in Corgren." His eyes narrowed. "Wonder how he survived."

"I don't know, but let's go on in and light a lamp." Magdronu-as-Gweld pushed Athson indoors.

"Hope there's not blood stains on the floor." Athson stumbled in and rummaged for a lamp.

"Sarneth had that cleaned up after they investigated." Magdronu-as-Gweld dropped Athson's pack by the door and laid the spear on the floor. He narrowed his gaze as Athson left the Bow of Hart lying across a chair. *Just give it to me and this will be over.* He hung his cloak on a peg by the door. "Here, give me your cloak."

Athson inspected the home and found no blood. The familiar rooms creaked beneath their feet.

Magdronu-as-Gweld cared nothing for it but feigned otherwise. "Nothing is out of place, and the furniture is still the same." Wooden chairs carved with care along with a table stood in the kitchen. Curtains of flowers or of waterfalls, all sewn by Cireena, still covered the shuttered windows. Nothing had changed. *Just sit and talk while the tea brews.* How he'd managed patience with Athson all these years Magdronu failed to fathom. Too many wasted years. Time to end the charade tonight. Now. "Let me start the water."

Elven homes in these oaks bore water into them with sets of screws that lifted water to troughs that flowed between homes. Water even turned the elevating screws. Magdronu-as-Gweld simply let fresh water into the tank over the sink and then filled a kettle festooned with a field of flowers. He faked lighting the stove with matches and really lit the belly of the burner with his touch. Perhaps he was impatient to brew the tea.

Meanwhile, Athson traipsed through the house and inspected further. He returned and sat in an upholstered chair of green fabric with his forehead resting in his palms. "They—they cleaned it all. It looks like they still live here except for the dust."

Magdronu-as-Gweld found tea in its usual spot and prepared the cups. "Athson, they're gone. Don't dig them up tonight. This is about taking your mind off your current troubles." He sat in a matching chair while the water heated. "What did Limbreth say when she left?"

The tale of Limbreth's harsh rebuke and lost trust spilled from Athson's lips. When he finished relating the encounter, Magdronu-as-Gweld almost laughed out loud. What had this boy thought she would do with the truth? He resisted snorting in derision. Athson deserved Limbreth's reaction. His failure was born of the curse on his family, but it was still his choice.

Athson slouched in his chair, his drunken stupor wearing off. "I failed her and us. I guess I deserved that."

Magdronu-as-Gweld played his part while the water rose to

a boil. "Look, you messed up, but so did she with the arrow. And a few other things along the journey. Why not send her a message and apologize? Maybe she'll realize you're no worse than she is after a month on the road and welcome your message." He spread his hands. "Can't hurt. Remind her that you're just being truthful like a Withling." The kettle whistled. Time to take his payment. Magdronu-as-Gweld strolled to the kitchen and poured water for the tea.

Athson's voice trailed him. "Maybe you're right. But there's still this invasion."

"Yes, and you need to figure out the arrow—Limbreth's failure. Do what has to be done for the prophecy, and then she'll see you as someone she can trust again. You'll be someone who can overcome her failures and your own." Magdronu-as-Gweld withdrew a vial from a hidden pocket in his breeches and poured several drops into Athson's cup.

"I don't know. What if her father makes her marry that— that—whoever he was? What if she finds someone else she fancies?" Athson slouched further in the chair.

It didn't matter after the next several minutes. Magdronu-as-Gweld smiled while Athson fretted in his chair, oblivious to his fate at the hands of his hidden enemy. Magdronu-as-Gweld leaned over the cup, blew magic into it, and spoke soft words. The cup flared briefly, and the brew steamed in the cup, prepared for Magdronu's final grasp of the Bow of Hart and certain victory.

"Athson have a little faith in Limbreth. She's not that flighty, just angry. She'll come around. You need to work harder at being a Withling and fulfilling this prophecy. We need you. It's what we traveled all this way to do. What we all sacrificed for in the snow, in the mountains, in that swamp. Do this, and she'll change her tune. She'll see that you've changed, grown, and open her arms."

Not a chance, but Magdronu-as-Gweld loved the act up to

the very end. *Just hand the bow over.* He handed the cup to Athson, and his irritating ward of years took it without question.

Magdronu-as-Gweld offered a smile. Trust. He'd built it each day with Athson, no matter what he did wrong. All that patience paid off in this setting, in these minutes. He sipped his tea, a subtle prompt to his prey.

Athson blew on the tea and set it aside. "Look, about all that Withling stuff. I need more training. I don't hear Eloch like the others. I don't know what they—we—should do." He yawned.

Magdronu-as-Gweld inhaled and sighed. *Don't fall asleep.* Maybe he shouldn't have let Athson drink so much ale after all. "I don't know about all that. You have the bow for a reason, the arrow shouldn't be that much trouble as you all think. They blessed one. Maybe they should just bless another. After all, that wandering star is still in the sky, though it's grown fainter these last few weeks." He lifted his cup toward Athson. "Drink up while it's hot." He sipped his own.

Athson took several sips and swallowed. "I don't know if it's that easy."

Magdronu-as-Gweld waited in silence and sipped his own tea, and Athson followed his lead. How long? Soon. In mere moments, he would take the instruction, then he'd die in a heaving, frothing mess. And victory would be Magdronu's.

A yawn erupted from Athson, and his head lolled onto his shoulder. He jerked awake. "I don't feel so well."

"Drink some more tea. You probably had too much ale." Magdronu-as-Gweld drained his own cup.

Athson drank more and frowned. "I really don't feel well."

"Say, why don't you let me look at the bow awhile? Maybe I can give you some ideas about it." Magdronu-as-Gweld stared at Athson, waiting for his reaction. Was he under his suggestive control yet in the minutes before the poison killed him? "Just hand it to me, and if you feel bad, you can lie down for a while."

"I—I don't know if I should." Athson's head dipped again. He blinked and shook his head. "I really don't feel well." He clutched his stomach. "I feel sick."

Magdronu-as-Gweld stood and went to Athson. "Here, let me help you. The bow is just over on the table there. Just get it and let me see it. Then lie down." *Do it. Stop being hardheaded.*

Athson got unsteadily to his feet and struggled toward the table. He braced himself on the table as his gut seized him with the first death-pains. It passed. "You think I should? You need to see it?"

"Yes, you should. I'll figure something out while you rest."

Athson frowned a moment, then lifted the Bow of Hart. "Alright, then." He turned to Magdronu-as-Gweld, and his belly constricted again. He fell to his knees in pain. Confusion settled on his face. "You—you—why?"

Magdronu-as-Gweld extended his hand. "Just give me the bow, Athson, and it will all be well."

Athson's hands trembled. "Very well. Here you are." He extended the bow toward Magdronu-as-Gweld.

Magdronu's belly flared with the heat of victory mere steps away.

CHAPTER TWENTY-ONE

Ralda finished his work with the rangers along the bridge well after dusk. The rangers thanked him for his efforts the last few days, during which he'd lifted many pieces of the defenses into place along the bridge or the docked boats, where archers planned the defense of the city. Just this day, Sarneth had ordered the bridge gates closed and the span tightly guarded as trolls arrived in great numbers on the opposite bank. Ralda stretched, releasing tension from his shoulders. He looked forward to cracking some ogre heads if the need arose.

Sarneth met the giant at the end of the bridge. "Thank you, Ralda. You've saved us a lot of time and effort. Will you be part of the vanguard here if it comes to it?"

With a flourish of his hands, Ralda answered, "Stand here, fight troll. Hastra need, I go with her." He tapped his chest. "I fight troll." He added with his hands that he still wanted to see his home, but he missed his brother and it wasn't the same. He rubbed his hands together and waved farewell to the elven captain for the evening. He paused. "Sarneth, where Hastra?" He needed to speak with the Withling about Gweld. A subject he'd put off for too long with all his work and her schedule. The White Arrow was a priority, but Gweld left him uneasy.

"At the inn, I should think. She's been working to discover what to do about that arrow." Sarneth left, his face tense as he observed the defenses.

Ralda retrieved his staff from where he'd laid it aside that morning and set out for the Broken Bow Inn. He strolled between patches of shadow and light along the streets. On the main streets, rangers marched or carried supplies. But on side streets, muffled voices drifted from homes in the trees or taverns and inns. Yet at other streets, silence followed Ralda like the grave, and that set him into a faster pace. He'd put this off for far too long.

"Ralda!" A dwarf's voice.

He turned toward the speaker behind him. Makwi jogged along the street, his weapons bristling from his armor. The broad man approached and saluted Ralda like a dwarf. "Where are you going? I haven't seen you all day. We should stick together if they get across the bridge, since we fight together well."

Ralda's hands went into motion. "Lift on bridge. Watch troll come." His hands added that the nasty creatures were ruining the forest, and he was ready for the fight. "We fight, you, me." He patted Makwi on the shoulder. "Me talk Hastra. Go to inn. Go too?" His hands invited Makwi to come along and talk. He turned and strode on. He couldn't wait any longer. He knew it, for some reason.

"What are you going to see Hastra about?" Makwi jogged beside Ralda to keep up. "You seem in a hurry."

"Uh, got talk. Something wrong." Should he tell Makwi? He pointed to his head. "Memory follow me. She hear me on it."

"Can't wait, huh? Must be something important."

Ralda remembered to nod rather than shake his head for

yes. "Something wrong Gweld." His hands flitted that Gweld was acting strangely.

"Yeah, he's been a bit off at times but that's just concern for Athson." They rounded a corner and Makwi dodged an elven messenger. "He's calmer now that we're back here."

Ralda almost nodded his head for disagreement, then shook it. "Not right still if not right then." He stopped, stooped toward Makwi, and pointed toward his own eyes. "See eyes glow once. Ezhandun." Kralda slid away at the end of the rope in his mind. Ralda couldn't let that happen again if he knew something. Even if he slid toward his own death somehow, he had to do something.

Makwi's eyes narrowed. "What are you talking about? His eyes glowed?" The dwarf eyed the length of the street in both directions. "We can't just accuse him of something. We need to be sure."

Ralda lifted his hands to forestall the dwarf. "Go talk Hastra. She know." He wasn't cutting this rope. Not this time. *The rope slithered across the snow.* He'd say something, do something. "You go with me."

"Sure, I'll go. But let's get Tordug. He'll help us. But you must tell me all that you know while we go." Makwi adjusted his belt as he set out with Ralda again.

Ralda swallowed his frustration with his language limitations and told Makwi all the things that left him suspicious. He described as best he could seeing Gweld's eyes glowing in the mirror at Ezhandun. Makwi asked questions, and Ralda patiently answered. He talked about Gweld letting the Bane into the shelter and how he was never around for long times. He related how agitated the elf was about the bow and Athson, almost ready to fight just before they saved Limbreth from the river. "No memory he there at big wind. Where he then?"

Makwi stroked and tugged his beard all during the conversation. "You know, as much as I hate to say it, since Gweld's been with us through so much, you may be on to something. I don't remember him with us when the trolls started in on the mules. He just showed up after the whirlwind. And then there was what happened in Howart's Cave. He tried to go on past the gate after it pushed me away, and the gate threw him back. There was even a flash of light. If there's something different about Gweld in some way, maybe that's why it tossed him back." Makwi glanced to Ralda. "Let's find Tordug and tell him even if we can't find Hastra. I think we need to have a talk with Gweld. Tordug should be just up here in the ranger offices, assisting with troop plans."

Guards stopped them from entering the grounds at the ranger's complex. All the bustle confused Ralda. Makwi got a message to Tordug, and they waited for the old dwarf. Ralda fidgeted with impatience. Why not go to Hastra now? "No wait. Go Hastra. Talk."

"Just wait and let's talk this through. We don't even know where Hastra is right now." Makwi tugged his beard and his voice sounded like a growl as he spoke to the guards. "Can't you go find him?"

One of the guards regarded them. "We're on alert because of the trolls. Only ranger personnel within the area now."

Makwi pulled a crumpled paper from his pocket, smoothed it with his hands, and showed it to the guards. "We've been working with you rangers for several days. This is a pass signed by Sarneth."

The elves eyed the pass and called for an officer, who read it over and eyed Makwi and then Ralda. "I'll have to confirm this."

Makwi's face flushed. "I just need to speak with Tordug. Can you send him out?"

"I'm here." The elder dwarf stepped into the light at the gate. "What's all this about, Makwi?" He turned to the elves on guard. "Ralda and Makwi are with me. They might know something useful."

"We do." Makwi motioned to Tordug, and when the elder dwarf stepped closer, Makwi lowered his voice and spoke in Tordug's ear.

Tordug's bushy eyebrows rose, and he glanced at Ralda. "This is true?"

Ralda nodded, and his hands fluttered about the details. "We go talk Hastra."

Tordug glanced at the elves and then back to Ralda. "That's enough for now. Let's go and see her. I could use a break and a meal." Tordug turned to the guards. "Let them know inside that I'll be back later. I don't know when." He exhaled a heavy sigh and stroked his beard. "Let's go." He led Ralda and Makwi away. When they got out of earshot, Tordug murmured to both of them. "Best not to talk about Gweld around the elves. He's popular, especially since he got back from our trip. Tell me more, though." His brow furrowed with a frown. "We don't need any of this now."

They discussed Ralda's information, and Makwi added his own as they traversed the distance to the Broken Bow Inn in hope of finding Hastra.

Tordug paused away from the inn and anyone listening. "I wish you'd said something much sooner, Ralda."

Ralda shrugged. "Say to Hastra off boat. She busy. Me busy. Talk now. Think days. Not want say bad about Gweld, so me think long."

Makwi chewed on one side of his mustache a moment. "Yeah, you did the right thing. Best not to falsely accuse someone, especially since it's Gweld. But you're right, he's never around sometimes, often when it matters or something unusual happens like at that shelter with Limbreth."

Tordug turned for the steps and the door to the inn. "Well, let's go see Hastra. She'll know what to do, if anyone. She probably needs something else to think about besides that arrow and Athson. He's been trouble since Limbreth left."

The dwarves clomped up the steps, and Ralda took one stride to reach the porch, its boards groaning beneath him. He eyed the door with a groan himself. Low doors and only slightly higher ceilings bothered him. He stooped and felt like he held his breath as he squeezed into the crush of bodies and noise of chatter inside. Better than that Troll Neath or one of the dwarven shelters in the mountains, at least. But they needed a quiet spot to speak with Hastra.

Eyes followed Ralda across the room, and he heard people speak of his presence and wonder about more giants. His snort sounded loud in the room regardless of the noise. His people wintered much farther away than the trolls marched. It was just him, and people should know better than to dream false hopes. Others around him muttered about the dwarves leaving along with the Grendonese.

Makwi started up the stairs, but Ralda checked the dining room Hastra now used as an office of sorts. She sat in a chair with a slight snore escaping her lips. Ralda whistled for Makwi as Tordug entered the room. Hastra stirred awake at his whistle, but Ralda waited for Makwi's response. The dwarf peeked over the rail on the stair. "She here." Makwi clattered after them into the room.

"Nice to see you all." Hastra's weary gaze took them in for a moment. She rubbed her upper abdomen as if in discomfort and straightened her blouse. "But by your faces, this looks serious."

"Withling, Ralda has been thinking about some incidents from our trip, and he thinks you should hear them." Tordug sat by Hastra and motioned to Ralda.

"That's right, you wanted to speak when we arrived. I'm sorry, Ralda, but this arrow and Athson have been on my mind. Not to mention these rumors of Rokans in the city." She patted Ralda's cheek as he went to one knee near her. "Go ahead and tell me."

The room cramped Ralda, and sudden sweat beaded his forehead. He longed for open lands. At least they'd been through some of those on their travels. He liked the mountains, though they reminded him of when Kralda died.

He told Hastra of his misgivings from what he'd seen. Makwi added his own observations. All the while, Hastra's eyebrows rose and fell either one at a time or together. She listened to their whole tale without comment, and when they were done, she turned to Tordug. "What do you think?"

Tordug scratched at his beard while he bared his teeth. "I don't like what I hear. I wish we had noticed this sooner, but we were just concerned with living through each day most of the time. The thing with the eyes bothers me. Same with the incident in Howart's Cave." He shook his head. "I don't remember Gweld being around when that whirlwind struck or just before it." He paused and grunted, twisting his head in thought. "He scouted an awful lot. It seemed good at the time, but with all this, something seems off. What do you think, Withling?"

Hastra pursed her lips. "I'm puzzled enough to speak with him about it." She sat up straight, her eyes wide. "I've asked him to have a good talk with Athson tonight. It's a perfect opportunity for him if he's really up to something." She rubbed her chin and pointed a finger toward Ralda. "Now that you mention it, his watch was always when something happened with the Bane." Her gaze encompassed them all. "We need to find them if we can."

Ralda offered his steady hand to the Withling as she stood with a grunt. "Where they go?"

"We can start with the ranger barracks." Hastra motioned to them all. "Lead on. I'm not too fast at the moment. Seem to be off more these days." She shrugged one shoulder. "Bad time for it. Tordug, can they spare you?"

"They can. That bow is important, and we can't let a spy gain possession of it." Tordug steadied Hastra with his hands. "Let's go find them if we can. I hope nothing's amiss."

Ralda squeezed out the door and cleared a path for a quick exit. He wanted out of the small space, but Athson meeting alone with Gweld worried him. In his memory, the cut rope hissed across the snow and ice as Kralda fell to his death. He'd grab that rope for Athson now if he could.

∾

HASTRA TOTTERED AS FAST as she could after the giant and Makwi. Tordug stayed back with her, sensing her weakness. She hated her weariness just when events called for her the most. Her gaze swept the shadows along the street. With trolls across the river and Corgren's likely presence as well as the possibility of Gweld being a spy, they could be none too careful. And then there was the rumor of Rokans in the city.

She halted. "Tordug, please go leave word with the innkeeper that I've gone searching for Athson. Just in case Zelma, Howart, or Danilla come looking for me." Of course they'd turn up something with all of this upset.

Tordug trotted back toward the inn with a nod.

"Makwi, Ralda, wait for me." Hastra gathered her energy and marched toward the giant and the dwarf as they waited. Her breath dragged at the fast walking. "I've sent Tordug to leave word about me for Athson's mother or the other Withlings if they return. It could be important if Gweld is up to something. I might need them too."

Makwi guided Hastra by the elbow. "Are you not well, Withling? You seem weak lately."

Hastra sighed. "Just old, I suppose. Long trip wearing on me." A Withling in service far too long.

Tordug soon returned from the inn as they reached the

ranger compound once again. The rangers let them past the gates with hardly a word exchanged. Tordug sniffed. "Much better this time. Had some trouble getting Makwi and Ralda in earlier. It delayed us."

Hastra halted. Delayed? The guards saw everyone, and Gweld was well-known among rangers, if not Athson. "Tordug, can you ask after Gweld's movements this evening? They're sure to remember him. We'll check inside for anything." If only the Bow of Hart lay with Athson's belongings. He'd had it earlier, but maybe it was here, even though she never saw him without it.

Within the barracks, rangers either slept or stood talking in groups. Makwi soon discovered where Athson slept but didn't find him. Makwi checked under the bunk. "Don't see anything here of his. Wonder where he went with his things?"

An elf on a nearby bunk rolled over with a sigh. "Don't suppose I'll sleep much before an attack." He seemed annoyed. "Athson came by for his things with Gweld. One of them said something about his house."

Hastra frowned. "Whose house?"

"Athson's. Must be from Heth and his wife."

"Quickly, we must go." She hobbled away. A sudden pit opened within her with an urge: save Athson.

They met Tordug at the door. "They said the two of them came and went several times tonight, the last time with Athson's things."

Hastra picked up her pace. She needed all her strength and more. They passed the guards and left the compound. "I visited the home once. I think I can find it. We must hurry."

"No good?" Ralda's fingers fluttered in the shadows of the street.

"I don't think so. You all have weapons? Good. I didn't know." She glanced toward the giant. "How I wish I'd spoken with you before today, Ralda. I feel Athson may be in danger.

Evil was done at that house and it may be used again. Why didn't I think of it? Magdronu marks places for return with spells." She slowed at a sudden thought. "Oh, of course, that's where they'll find them."

Makwi drew his ax. "You want me to head somewhere else?"

"No. Come with me. You may be needed if Gweld is far more dangerous than appearances. I should have realized what was going on earlier and sent the others directly where their search likely leads. I'll speak with them later." Hastra quickened her pace until they arrived at a ramp into the homes among the trees. "This one, I think." She climbed far too slowly and wanted to send the others to the house, but they didn't know where to go.

The walk groaned and swayed under Ralda, and Hastra stumbled, slowing her progress. She mumbled under her breath, but the giant had his uses, for which she was thankful.

She peered ahead and slowed. "There, I think it's the third down. There's a light inside. Makwi, go check if the door bears the scene of a stag at a lake. Beautiful carving and even better painting."

Makwi crept ahead of them and checked the door. He nodded and waved them forward. They approached, and the dwarf motioned for silence as he whispered, "I hear voices, listen."

They edged toward the door and heard from within, "Just give it to me, Athson, then rest."

"That's Gweld's voice." Makwi reached for the door, then shook his head and mouthed the word *locked*.

Hastra stepped aside. Time for one of Ralda's uses. "Kick it in, Ralda."

The giant kicked the door with the bottom of his foot, strong as a horse. The door splintered and opened crookedly on his hinges.

Gweld turned his head and gazed at Hastra, his face constricted into a snarl. Hastra stepped into the doorway. Gweld stood facing Athson, his back to them and his hand stretched toward the young man. One glance at Athson's vacant expression, and Hastra knew some potion had been used on him. The Archer stooped as if sick, his face pale but his arms extending the Bow of Hart toward Gweld.

Hastra reached out with her hand. "Don't do it, Athson. It's a trick."

She gasped. Gweld's eyes were glowing. But even worse, his pupils were horizontal slits like an animal's. "You're not an elf."

A voice rumbled from Gweld, deep and resonant. "No, I'm not, Hastra. And you're too late!"

CHAPTER TWENTY-TWO

Hastra took another tottering step into the room as Gweld reached for the Bow of Hart. "You will be still!" Her voice rang with sudden authority not her own.

Gweld turned slowly toward her, his eyes alight with flames. He cocked his head. "Who are you to command *me*?"

"I am a servant of the most holy Eloch. You shall not have it or him!"

The elf, if such he was, laughed. His mouth opened, and heat burst into the room.

Hastra extended a hand almost on instinct as much as insight.

Flame spewed from Gweld's mouth.

"Be gone!" Her shout met the flame at her hand and suppressed it.

Gweld closed his mouth and glared at her. Suddenly, he ran for the shuttered window, spewing flame on the furniture as he went. He leapt through window in a crash, his dive carrying him over the walk. Darkness, blacker than the night, enfolded the elf as he fell. In an instant, tattered wings unfolded and bore, not an elf, but a beast of black scales into the sky, trailing a tail that flicked like a cat's. It roared in its passing, tearing limbs like a gale. The house shuddered in his escape.

"Quickly, the flames!" Hastra directed the others toward the sudden fire. She limped, gasping, to Athson's side.

The dwarves and Ralda quickly beat out the fire on the floor, but the chairs still burned. Ralda heaved them out the ruined window with a shout of warning toward the street below, where Hastra presumed they would burned to charred heaps.

She inspected Athson as he swayed on his feet, the Bow of Hart still in one hand. A spasm wrenched his body, and he collapsed. His eyes rolled to Hastra's face. "What was that?"

"That was Magdronu." She touched Athson and murmured a prayer. In an instant, understanding lit her mind like a beacon. Poison. Not good in her weakness.

"Why didn't he kill us?"

"His power must be limited here for some reason." Hastra checked for Athson's heartbeat.

Tordug knelt beside her. "We'll call for help, carry him to the elven healers."

Voices called outside the home. Makwi called for help as Ralda stomped on smoking embers in the floor.

Hastra shook her head. "There's no time. I must do it." She looked Tordug in the eye. "I may not survive this. I must take the poison into myself with this healing, and I'm not as strong as when I did it at Huffer's Post. It's what took my strength then."

"Don't. Wait. Maybe the healers have an antidote." Tordug withheld her gently.

"There's no time. He'll die, and all will be lost. I must." She grabbed Tordug's hand. "He was with us all along. He could have taken the bow at any time. He had to be given it. Did you see how he demanded it?"

"How long has he been disguised?"

She shrugged. "Who can say? But don't deter me. I must act now. What is needed is given." She turned toward Athson, who spasmed on the floor with a wild roll of his eyes. That was her fate now. But she'd escaped death years ago. If this was her final service, then so be it. "Tordug, give my sister my love. Remind Athson the bow is not for him." She jerked her head toward the destroyed window.

"Withling, you are truly a servant."

She looked at Tordug and found tears streaming into his beard. She managed a smile. "May your honor tower like the mountains of your home, Tordug."

Tordug smiled through his beard and his tears, his eyes squinted almost shut as he nodded.

Ralda and Makwi loomed over them. She nodded to the dwarf and the giant. "You've both been just what was needed these last months."

She turned back to Athson, who spasmed, the beginning of froth in the corners of his mouth. With more certainty than at any other moment she had known as a Withling, she laid a hand on Athson's stomach and head and uttered her unknown prayers to Eloch. Her voice rose and fell with sudden cadence as her awareness floated on the euphoria of doing Eloch's will. That wouldn't last.

Below her, Athson's eyes widened and his lips formed the word *no*.

Hastra continued her prayer, her awareness drawn into Athson's body, seeking the essence of the poison. Magic, dark and venomous, rose in resistance, flaring like flame, the fire of Magdronu. The essence roared in her ears, but she hid in her prayer and sought the essence with her words. Her utterances reached for the poison and the magic alike. Beneath her hands, it siphoned from Athson's body. She lifted her hands away from him, and the glow of magic followed, wisps alight with darkness rose into her hands and her body.

The poisoned rippled through Hastra and struck her body like a hammer. She prayed on, unwilling to let it beat her into silence. *Complete it.* Her body trembled with effort at the sudden, deeper weakness that filled her. The ruined organ of her heart protected her from the certain effect of it racing away. But, the poison drained her. She must finish. Her voice faltered and drifted into a hoarse mumble, though she still prayed.

At last the poison streams left Athson entirely. She fell silent, and her body slumped beside Athson. A spasm rocked her gut. She blinked at the other person in the room. She hadn't noticed him before. She must be seeing things as her body hastened toward death.

His blue eyes glittered in the light beneath a floppy hat as he smiled. "Well done, Hastra."

~

ATHSON STIRRED, sat up and wiped spittle on his sleeve. "What happened? I remember Gweld jumping through the window." He almost slumped to the floor, but Ralda, who knelt beside him, steadied him.

"It wasn't Gweld. It was Magdronu. Come for the bow." Tordug wiped tears from his eyes. "He poisoned you, Athson. He's been in disguise." He shrugged. "Who knows how long he's been this way?"

Hastra stirred beside Athson. "Ath-son."

Athson gaped at her. "She healed me? Gweld? He was Magdronu?" His enemy played his friend. For how long? His head spun anew.

Makwi crouched nearby and nodded. "She did. Drew it out of you with her prayers. I don't think she'll survive it this time.

And it was Magdronu who tried to kill you, played Gweld. He had us all fooled it seems."

Athson leaned over Hastra. She had sacrificed herself for him. She knew better than him what need to be done. "Hastra, tell me what to do, what to say. I don't hear him yet."

The old Withling's face constricted with the pain of a spasm, and frothy spittle formed at the corners of her mouth. She shook her head, and her eyes rolled. She motioned weakly at the dwarves and Ralda. "Bless."

Athson nodded as sudden tears blurred his vision. "I'm sorry, Hastra. I've been nothing but trouble for you since we met. I've been so hard on you. I'm sorry. We could have done it if not for me. Please, tell me what to do."

"Arrow." Her body spasmed again, and she grimaced until the pain passed.

Athson handed her the arrow pieces from his pocket. She kissed them.

Nothing happened. He fit the pieces together, but they were still just pieces. He watched her face. No more miracles from Hastra.

Her lips formed barely audible words as her eyes widened, and she gasped. "Bow. Not. For. Him." She shook her head feebly and clutched at Athson's sleeve.

"I know, I won't give it up." Tears welled in his eyes and dribbled on his cheeks. Gweld his enemy. His true friend all along had been Hastra and he'd pushed her away. The rotten curse misled him at every turn.

"Not for him."

He shook his head. "It's not for him."

Hastra's body slumped and spasmed. She gasped again, her eyes wide. "Limbreth. Go." Her throat and jaw worked to form words, but no others passed her lips. Only the noise of gagging in the froth.

Ralda rolled Hastra over as her body spasmed a few last

times. Then she lay still, her eyes staring at nothing as the life faded from them.

Athson slapped the floor with his palm. "I've been such a fool."

He grabbed the hilt of his sword and lifted his head, eyes closed. Images of Gweld passed through his memory. How the elf led him around, coaxed him into things, taught him more of weapons or woodsman-ship. But there were other details, like his denial of Spark's existence. Athson opened his eyes and found the mountain hound sitting nearby. The medicine Gweld —no, Magdronu—had pushed on him eased his fits but hid all his true visions and dreams, kept him in the dark. The darkness beneath his dragon's wings. It hid the real world from Athson until Hastra and Limbreth and the others came. But still, Magdronu exerted control. The curse, he certainly manipulated that. He'd done that these last days as Athson had languished in his depression. How long since he'd sought the truth of things from his blessed sword? All this time, Magdronu had played the part of Gweld in order to lure Athson into giving him the Bow of Hart with threats, tricks, and poison. He'd hidden squarely under Athson's nose. Everyone's nose. Hastra, Sarneth, everyone. Understanding flooded Athson in a flash of memories.

Gweld—Magdronu—on the trail to Ezhandun, working against Athson, trying to convince him he needed Soul's Ease, that Spark wasn't real. Athson's stomach roiled, but not from poison. He'd sent Corgren that night to threaten his father as a hostage. Magdronu was there when they escaped. He'd ordered all of them taken hostage for the Bow of Hart. He'd been in the cave when Athson got the bow from Howart, and had taken Limbreth then. Athson uttered a wordless shout of anger and frustration and slapped the floor again, his body wracked with sudden sobs. He'd followed Magdronu's advice— his will—and driven Limbreth away, just to throw Athson off when he needed to do something with the White Arrow. Athson gasped and gaped at the broken arrow lying on the floor. It had come from Gweld's quiver.

Voices from outside broke Athson's stream of bitter memories. One rose in concern above the others, one that Athson knew. Zelma.

He stood as the Withling pushed past the people crowded at the door. She uttered a wail of despair and collapsed beside her sister.

Howart entered the room, paused, and then knelt beside the weeping Zelma. He turned to them. "How?"

Makwi explained in his terse manner. Athson stumbled across the room, thankful for Makwi's detachment in these moments of harsh truth. The Bow of Hart lay on the floor beside Hastra with the arrow nearby.

Tordug approached. "Maybe we should go?"

Howart lifted his head at the question, his sunken-eyed gaze oozing sorrow. "We can handle this for now."

Athson squeezed Zelma's shoulder before he gathered his things. "She gave her life for my own."

Zelma nodded wordlessly amid her tears.

Makwi tapped Tordug, Ralda, and Athson each on the shoulder and thumbed over his shoulder to the door. His look was drawn and his eyes misty in the light. "Uh, we've gotta talk."

Athson paused. What should he do? Makwi was right, they needed to talk. Things needed their attention. But Hastra had died. What would she want? She had given him instructions. He glanced Tordug's way, and the elder dwarf motioned to him. Athson sighed and followed them through the press of people at the door.

They tramped to the street, where someone had doused the burning chairs. Glass, broken limbs, and other debris littered the street. Above them, Athson glimpsed stars where the dragon had escaped through the treetops. They gathered at the side of the street, well away from the growing crowd.

Makwi crossed his arms. "Not a pretty death."

"Aye, but an honorable one." Tordug scrubbed at his damp cheeks. "She may have died, but we need to take action now." He peered at each of them, holding their attention a moment. He cleared his throat and ran his fingers through his gray hair, pacing a few steps away and back while Athson and his other companions shuffled their feet uncertainly. "This is tough, but Hastra and I talked about this on the trail. I guess this is no different. She told us things before she saved you, Athson. We need to think this through before we take action."

"Gweld knew almost everything about the defenses here and elsewhere." Athson crossed his arms, then lifted one hand to support his chin. "We can assume Magdronu has plans to cross the river, maybe even tonight."

Tordug nodded, his eyes averted in thought. He smacked his head. "Hastra said it made sense he chose the house. Evil had been done there previously. She implied there was more to consider. Athson, what other places did things occur?"

Athson's mind churned, remembering Hastra's last moments. She wanted his companions blessed. He supposed he could do that. Where else had evil been done? He inhaled deeply and exhaled slowly. He wished Limbreth were still here, just because he needed her. He snapped his fingers and pointed at Tordug. "I met Limbreth in the cemetery when she followed the Bane there. I was at the gravesites for Heth and Cireena. The Bane could have done anything when we didn't see it."

"Fine, so we need to know if there's anything magical there for some reason."

Makwi waved his hands. "Wait just a minute. We need to make sure things are secure too. What about the bridge?"

"We need to inform Sarneth of this news and have more

rangers sent to the waterfront." Tordug shuffled his feet as if to go, but then spoke again. "But I know the most about the troop assignments and guards for the gate, since I've consulted on the plans."

Athson pointed to Makwi. "You go see Sarneth and tell him all that's happened and that we need more people at the gates in case there are deeper plans there."

Makwi shrugged to Tordug. "I am faster than you. I can cover the distance faster."

Tordug nodded. "Aye, you go. Let's hope the guards let you in now."

Makwi turned to go. "Oh, they'll let me through." He shot them all a wolfish grin.

"Wait." Athson grabbed Makwi's shoulder. "Hastra said to bless you all. I don't really know what to do, but I'll do it." He offered a one shoulder shrug. "Since I'm a Withling."

Makwi grinned again. "Already got mine from her days ago, the night we arrived. I'm gone. The sooner I get troops gathered, the better." He waved to them and trotted down the street as rangers rounded a nearby corner to check the disturbance.

Athson turned back to Ralda and Tordug. "Right, then, I'll bless you both. Then Ralda and I will check the cemetery." He pointed to Ralda, who nodded.

The other two waited, watching Athson. He placed a hand on Tordug's shoulder. "Uh, Eloch bless you, Tordug." On a whim, he pulled his Rokan dagger and offered it to the dwarf. "I feel like I'm supposed to give this to you. It was used here, but its curse is broken. It almost killed Corgren. Maybe Eloch has placed some virtue in it you may need."

Tordug accepted the weapon. "Thank you, Athson." He slapped Athson's shoulder. "You've come a long way lately, lad." He nodded to Ralda and shook the giant's massive hand. "If anything happens, I want you both to know that no dwarf could expect better companions on the trail." He left at a trot in the direction of the bridge.

Athson turned to Ralda and grabbed his forearm. What should he say now? Maybe he had heard something from Eloch for Tordug. Why not for Hastra? He shook his head with a grimace. He couldn't guess about the past. He grabbed his sword.

"Ralda, we've come a long way since you charged those trolls. Eloch bless you. I know how you've grieved for your brother for a long time. Know that I consider you a brother. Eloch go with you."

Ralda nodded, and for once his hands remained still. Finally, the giant cleared his throat. "Hastra say watch you. I watch you for trip."

Athson's jaw worked for a moment. "She put Limbreth to watching me too. I guess I needed a couple of people keeping an eye on me, then." He still had that help, even with Limbreth gone. "Well, I guess we should go check things out."

"Hold on." Howart's voice halted him. The gaunt Withling approached with Zelma, whose face was drawn into a mask of unreadable emotion. She scrubbed her damp cheeks. Howart pointed toward the house above them. "The rangers asked us some questions, but you need to give the rest of the answers."

Athson scuffed his feet and set his hands to his hips as he glanced at his feet. He needed to go with Ralda. But the rangers needed the news from him about Gweld. "Right, I'll stay a while. Ralda, take the road out there. It's two turns past to the north, after you enter by the main gate. Then you go over a few rises. There's a stand of trees where they are." He pointed a finger at the giant. "But come back if you spot something, and I'll come help."

Ralda nodded and took off at a run without another word.

"He's in hurry." Howart watched the giant disappear into the shadows along the street.

"Yeah, let me see the rangers." Athson paused. "Where's my mother?" He hadn't seen her since yesterday morning.

Howart cocked his head. "We've been looking for some Rokans and tracked them down. We got word of Hastra at the inn, and Danilla stayed in case someone came back. We set out in search of Hastra with our news, heard the commotion, and came here."

Athson tilted his head and held his breath. "What news do you have?" His heart fluttered.

"Those Rokans aren't what we thought at all."

"How so?"

Zelma's voice sounded weak in all the noise. "When we realized there were actually three Shildrans, I finally realized who they might be. We tracked them down to separate inns and confirmed their descriptions. It's the Beleesh sisters for sure. Former Withlings who turned to Magdronu back at Withling's Watch."

"I don't know of them. What would they be doing here?" Athson's apprehension rose. He'd just sent Ralda off to the wrong place after all.

Howart glanced at Zelma before he continued their story. "From the other description, the last person is a man from Rok."

Athson groaned. "Not Corgren?"

"No, his brother, Paugren." Howart frowned and chewed the inside of his cheek. "They are all mages. They would be here secretly to create something magical. Like a shrine. We know they've been going just out of the city, but not where."

Athson swore. "I just sent Ralda to check the cemetery. Were they going north?"

"Why check the cemetery?"

With a glance to Zelma, Athson answered, "Because Hastra told Tordug it made sense that Magdronu used this house tonight, since the Bane attacked there months ago. It's my stepparents, they're buried out in the cemetery, killed by the Bane with a Rokan dagger, one I'd bought off a merchant. Then Limbreth later followed the Bane into the cemetery, where we met. We think it did something there that Magdronu could use now."

Howart stared at Zelma. "Sounds like they're making a new shrine in a quiet place." He faced Athson. "They can focus magic with blood and provide easy magic for themselves. They can use it to work against the rangers."

Athson gaped. "We need to go there."

Howart exhaled, blowing out his sunken cheeks. "Sure wish we had Hastra now."

"Why?"

"We're three against four."

Athson's heart sank to his feet. "And I'm not trained." He arched an eyebrow and tilted his head slightly. "But with Ralda we have four. Maybe that's enough."

Howart glanced at Zelma, who shrugged. "It's something. Better than nothing."

Zelma frowned out of the mass of wild, red hair that blew across her face. "Four aren't enough since the dragon is out. But I want to take them on anyway. For Hastra." By her expression, Athson thought she might break into tears again. "I want them now." She smiled at Athson. "You know any Withling hymns?"

"Uh, no. Why?"

She sighed. "Hastra taught you nothing these last few days. Not even Apeth over the weeks you were on the road?"

"No. I don't understand."

Howart gripped Athson's shoulder and turned him toward the direction Ralda had gone. "It's one way to nullify magic. Looks like you're in for a quick lesson while we take a walk tonight." He peered into the sky. "Morning, that is. It's well after midnight now."

Athson went with the other Withlings. They were several blocks away when he remembered the rangers back at the ruined house with Hastra's body. "Uh, we forgot about the rangers. Maybe we should have taken them with us."

Howart kept walking. "They have enough information and promised to take excellent care of Hastra for us while we went looking for magical trouble."

"Well, I did forget about the spear with that banner. I might need that." Athson offered an apologetic half-smile.

Howart turned around with a sigh. "Fine, I'll get the spear. And tell the officer where we're going, maybe they can send a few squads later - just in case." The gaunt Withling's long legs carried him away quickly.

Athson scratched the back of his head and scrunched his face into another apologetic expression. "One more thing..."

Zelma rolled her eyes in the light of a roadside lamp. "Always something with you. What now?"

With a shrug and a flip of his hands skyward, Athson said, "I don't sing so well."

CHAPTER TWENTY-THREE

Corgren stood in his tent at the bowl, the blood of a captured elf brimming in it. Much blood was needed for this large a reach. He spoke the incantation, his hands lifting toward the bridge that spanned the Auguron River as his sleeves receded to his elbows. Time for the scheduled trick as he activated the hidden hexes along the bridge.

His words passed his lips, as a low susurration. Corgren's murmurs, pitched in a hypnotic tone, crossed the distance toward the bridge at a crawl, dark against the night like a blanket. Too bad he couldn't put the whole city under the spell. But that required far more power than he possessed even from Magdronu. He continued the murmur of the spell as it reached the bridge gates and slipped through the narrow creases between the gates and fixtures that held them in place.

With eyes closed, as if he too slept, Corgren peered along his spell as it passed among the gathered archers who guarded the bridge from his invading trolls. The unseen shadow of his magic words flowed like viscous water along the bridge and touched each hex until it stretched across the length of the bridge and beyond to the guards gathered around the far gate, then farther up the street.

When the spell reached all the hexes he'd set while in the city months ago, hexes that had waited inert for this spell, Corgren paused. He smiled, his sight along the length of the spell taking in all the guards within his reach, even the patrols several hundred paces along the street beyond the far gates. He slowly closed his hands into fists. "Esko sulumbar mei-notchiskra." His spell activated the awaiting hexes hidden since disguised spying as Domikyas in the city.

Hastra had taken out the one he'd left to delay them. But she'd never seen past the distraction. A long problem of hers. Myopia born of her limited faith.

He smiled as the elven rangers slumped or collapsed into sleep. His smile deepened. They'd soon die at the hands of his trolls without a fight. *Too easy.* The spell spread among the rangers, and they drooped into sleep before they could react or give the alarm. Hundreds fell asleep as one.

Corgren slipped his Wolfshead dagger into the sheath at his belt. Now for the next stage of the plan. Once Magdronu succeeded in his attempt for the Bow of Hart, they would break all resistance. He strode toward the bridge gates, his assault force of trolls, all wearing soft-soled boots, slipped among the trees and approached the bridge behind Corgren.

The trolls crouched as they approached lest watchmen along the waterfront spot them and sound the alarm. His minions knew their place and the plan, and that any deviation merited swift death. They even held their breathing low in the silence along the river and the bridge.

Corgren spoke another spell and kissed his hands and then touched his feet. He turned to the bridge gates and climbed them with ease, a shadow sliding along the length of the steel-plated wood. He dropped silently onto the bridge beyond the gates. With another whispered spell, the locks for the levers released, and he slowly opened all of the mechanisms. Then, with quiet care, he removed the bars and left the gate.

Behind Corgren, the trolls awaited his signal until the very last moment, lest their presence be given away before they captured the length of the bridge. He half-grinned. The very security of the bridge would conceal and protect his forces as they crossed for the attack. Nothing of Sarneth's plans accounted for Corgren's actions this night. He climbed the far gates, where the rangers on guard slouched in their magically-induced slumber. He observed the fruit of his magical efforts along the street. Nothing moved.

The whisper of the unlocking spell freed the levers, and Corgren released them all. He had lifted all but two bars free when a sound disturbed the surrounding silence in which the slumbering rangers uttered not even a stray snore. Corgren froze and gazed over his shoulder. Someone moved along the street, and he withheld his signal, a spell to whisper in the ears of his initial assault force.

With a tug at his hood, Corgren slipped into the shadows among the sleeping guards and waited. A lone figure approached with care, discovered the guards asleep, then inspected the gates. He whispered the commanding spell to his waiting trolls. They would begin crossing the bridge while he handled this last obstacle silently.

He drew his dagger and stepped from the darkness into the lamplight. He grinned. It was a stone-rat dwarf. He restrained the sudden urge for laughter and attacked.

~

TORDUG TROTTED along Auguron's streets, where some places bore no traffic at all due to the hour. Weariness pulled his mind toward sleep, his feet lagging in response. He'd sleep later, though, and he hoped he found nothing amiss at the bridge. He yawned.

He turned along the broad street toward the river. His boots smacked against the paving stones in the silence, but he passed a few patrols out on this street and saw others on the side streets. That was good. Still, he needed to check.

The jolt of his strides dug up old memories. *He ran through the tunnels of Chokkra, heading toward the sounds of battle. The boom of dwarven voices singing as they killed or fell. He had to bring support. The dwarves of a few tattered squads would do little. They lost ground at each turn. Cursed Rokans marched in and overwhelmed their thin forces at the eastern gates. They broke his honor as well as his troops. He must drive them...*

But that was long ago, and his honor had been ruined well before this night. He'd sought honor in killing trolls wherever he found them. No one knew of his years of wandering, each hunt undertaken without word to his people. They had abandoned him long ago, and a few trolls here and there did nothing, even with Makwi's help once his son had finally returned to him. Tordug grunted. Makwi had agreed to hunt trolls because he needed to do something, but they kept their distance as father and son. It grieved Tordug the most, to withhold his honor from his son. Yet Makwi remained the revered champion, bearing his own legacy rather than Tordug's wagonload of dishonor.

The gates stood in partial shadow in the distance, a few lamps still burning. Tordug slowed. With the light and distance, he glimpsed nothing definitive ahead. But his sense of his surroundings slowed him further with suspicion knotting in his belly. He slipped into the shadows along the edge of the street. There were no patrols nearby. His eyes narrowed, and he crept along the street toward the bridge gates.

The silence left him on edge. It wasn't the guarded silence of men on night duty. That always bore the occasional cough or murmur. This silence disturbed him with its emptiness, a blanket like a fog of sleep. His eyes drooped, and Tordug pinched himself. *Stay awake.* He passed storefronts, goods displayed in shadow, but ignored them.

Tordug approached closer to the bridge, still shambling in the shadows, flitting between pools of light. He squinted. No one moved near the gates. He paused and waited. Guards should be patroling in front of the gates of steel-plated wood. He knew from the designs Sarneth had shown him that levered mechanisms sent lock-bolts half the length of an elven forearm between the gates into metal-sheathed recesses. Each of the gates locked into the bridge timbers with bolts thrust into steel-sheathed holes. Dwarves couldn't have fashioned the gates any better to fit so tightly together. A key, held by the captain of the watch, locked the mechanisms, while three steel-covered arms of wood barred the gates further.

Even if the elves allowed an enemy through the far gates, which were designed the same way, they could use levers while retreating to drop sections of the bridge to stop troops. Tordug paused and stroked his beard, his gaze shifting from point to point at the bridge. They held the bridge between the gates with archers hidden behind steel-plated walls set into place along the length of the bridge. An easy retreat when the far gates fell if they dropped sections of the bridge. Tordug edged forward and crouched. The rangers kept the release levers and mechanism for the bridge sections well-maintained. They'd planned for the trolls for decades. Now that the rangers needed the defenses, one thing troubled Tordug. The lack of soldiers guarding the gates.

He edged forward and tripped but recovered his balance with a soft grunt. He felt at the sidewalk and grasped legs. He peered into the shadows and glimpsed the dim forms of a patrol. Asleep? He nudged several elves. Not even a grunt in response. Tordug knelt beside several elves and felt for a pulse.

Alive, but so asleep that he couldn't rouse them. He stood and tugged his beard. It had to be magic. His shoulders tensed, but he trotted forward. He passed more rangers collapsed in lumps. Not good at all. Were the guards on the bridge asleep too?

At the gates, Tordug nudged the guards repeatedly, but none of them stirred. He slid aside a steel plate covering a viewport in one of the gates. Guards slouched in slumber along the length of the bridge. Tordug's stomach flopped. He stood alone at the undefended gates of Auguron City. Makwi had better get here with support very soon.

A whisper from the shadows stiffened Tordug's spine. Someone hid nearby.

He squinted at movement at the far gate. They opened, and his eyes widened. Trolls crept through the far gates, one an ogre with a massive cudgel over his shoulder. Kobolds and goblins slipped among the rangers and slit their throats.

With his fingers, Tordug felt along the shadow of the gate. He must secure it until Sarneth sent replacements. He rubbed the back of his neck, and his chest tightened. Only two bars still lay across the gates. He felt for the levers on the gate and found them all unlocked and their mechanisms thrown open. He wheeled about and sought the captain of the gate. He needed the key.

A figure rose out of the shadows. A voice he knew hissed, "Time to die, stone-rat."

Tordug shouted the alarm. He was too late!

Trolls charged on the bridge. Rangers shouted from their posts on the riverfront.

Tordug snatched at the haft of his battle-ax, but his opponent kicked it from his hands before he could heft the weapon. It clattered to the street, breaking the silence. Tordug backed away from his attacker and threw the levers to lock the bolts into the ground for one of the gates. He dove for the levers to lock the other gate. His attacker swept a dagger toward

Tordug's eyes, and he ducked. His fingers closed on one lever, and he half-pulled it closed before the hooded figure shoved him away.

"I know you, stone-rat. You're Tordug." A soft chuckle escaped the attacker's lips as he tugged his hood from his head.

"Corgren!"

Tordug snatched the dagger given to him by Athson and threw himself at the wizard with a shout. He stepped inside a thrust from Corgren and blocked the blade with his forearm against the wizard's wrist. But Corgren dodged Tordug's stab and kicked at his feet. Tordug leapt the kick and Corgren withdrew. Tordug reached for a lever to lock more of the gate, but Corgren slashed the bracer on his forearm and sliced his hand.

Moments passed like hours as Tordug strove with Corgren, each of them reaching for levers to lock or unlock the gates. Corgren out-reached Tordug but the dwarf depended on his compact strength, even with just a dagger. Choices danced in his mind, force his way past Corgren's defenses or draw the wizard toward him. Corgren feinted but seemed confused by Tordug's keen reflexes and strength. Best not let him use magic. Tordug sang in dwarvish and chose.

Tordug charged into the taller man, ducked under Corgren's reach and forced the wizard from the gates. He thrust the knife but Corgren leapt back.

Tordug grimaced through his beard as shouts drew nearer along the docks. "They'll kill you if I don't, wizard."

Weight pressed against the gates as the trolls beyond pushed at them, thinking Corgren had already completed his task.

Corgren's eyes narrowed as he lunged back at the gates, and stabbed upward.

Tordug stepped back. The point missed his chest and tangled into his beard. He flinched his chin from the point. A feint ending at his throat, no doubt. Tordug snatched at Corgren's wrist where the blade tangled in his beard.

Trolls pounded on the gate, and the half-unsecured one sagged against the thrusts of the ogre's strength. The two lower bars groaned at the force of the torsion. The long, slender arm of a hobgoblin reached for a bar.

Tordug thrust his dagger at Corgren, who twisted aside. Tordug maintained his grip on Corgren's wrist and followed with another stab, then another. The wizard grunted as the blade stabbed him in the upper left chest, and he fell, pulling Tordug on top of him. Tordug bobbed his head away from the Corgren's attempted slash.

Over them, the hobgoblin yanked one bar free of the unlocked gate, and the trolls pushed all the harder. The remaining bar squealed as the wood within the steel cracked and the metal bent.

Corgren spit blood in Tordug's eyes. Tordug shoved the dagger deeper, and Corgren screamed and thrashed. Tordug rolled away and found his battle-ax. He lifted the weapon overhead.

Corgren cringed, and his jaw twitched as he attempted to speak.

"No!" Not a spell. Tordug slammed the ax into Corgren's face, and the wizard ceased his struggles. The body twitched in death as Tordug stepped on his chest and worked the battle-ax free. Tordug lifted his face to the sky and roared his exultation. Dead! The enemy of his people. His enemy. His chest heaved as the weight of his past failure lifted.

The gates creaked.

Tordug hefted his ax. He'd hesitated in victory too long.

The gate swung wide and knocked Tordug over. He grabbed for his ax-haft. The ogre squeezed through the gate and smashed Tordug in the side with its cudgel. Tordug yelled as pain caressed his hip and ribs like an avalanche. He gripped his ax with suddenly feeble strength. Above him, the ogre loomed and grinned, thick fangs dripping drool. Tordug gasped, and pain gripped him tighter. His body trembled with the message of failure as the ogre lifted its cudgel again.

A shout rolled like thunder, and something like lightning flashed in Tordug's vision. Ogre blood spurted on him. One ax-blade rose away, and a smaller hand-ax chopped the ogre's neck. The creature fell in spasming death, an arm flung across Tordug and pinning him in further anguish. Tordug squinted through his pain as a figure leapt onto the massive carcass blocking the single open gate.

Axes slashed through milling trolls, who fell back at the attack, then countered. The defender smashed two bugbears in succession with crushing blows to their chests. He glanced at Tordug with a grim grin, then faced the trolls crowding against the bodies of the big trolls blocking their attack in the gateway.

"THIS. IS. MY. BRIDGE!" Makwi's bellow echoed across the river, and he sang the dwarven battle song of life and death. The rhythm of his singing matched the rise and fall of his axes amid the snarls of trolls and the clash of weapons.

Tordug managed a grin at the sight of Makwi, his champion, *his son,* as he stood alone, defending the bridge gates against a horde of trolls. Tordug sang along with Makwi, his voice frail with pain and drowned out by the clash of weapons. The feeling in his legs faded. He coughed blood. The ogre must have crushed something vital.

Rangers shouted and crowded about the gates. Gray light grew around them. In the distance, a bugle echoed across the river. Weapons clashed louder, and the sound of Makwi's bellow rang out. Instead of trolls overrunning the gates, rangers pushed the other way. Someone dragged open the other gate, and more rangers rushed along the bridge.

Sarneth's face peered at Tordug, concern etched on the elven captain's features. He turned and waved his hand. "Over here, quickly!" He knelt and squeezed Tordug's shoulder. "Well done!"

Tordug winced in pain as hands grabbed him. His voice faded. He'd still been singing. Then vision and sound faded with a gasp.

~

LIMBRETH SLEPT little before the approach to Auguron City. She rose and met her makeshift staff of officers for their reports.

"Our scouts killed many trolls in the forest at our approach." Erskwe leaned over their dirt map. "I've been forward, and there are many trolls massed at the river, but well back from the bridge." He looked up. "For now."

"What plan do you suggest, colonel?" Limbreth watched the Grendonese cavalry officer's face in the dim light of their circle. With but a few hours before dawn, they'd roused their army for a predawn maneuver into position along the road. Their scouts had ranged all night, dispatching troll scouts and patrols to improve their chances at a surprise attack.

Colonel Meegs squatted and observed the map, his hand supporting his chin of gray whiskers. Without lifting his head, he gazed at Limbreth. "Our fastest route is by the road. If they haven't barricaded it, we'll go far more quickly."

All eyes shifted back to Erskwe. "They've not blocked the road that we can see."

The colonel leaned over their map and pointed. "With so few of us, we must charge directly at the bridge and hope to weaken the siege there so the elves can attack across it. We'll need to alert them we're there with bugles. We'll charge along the road until we reach the clearing closer to the bridge and then shift to a narrow wedge for the charge. The dwarves come in behind, and we'll chop through and hope for the best."

Limbreth leaned forward. "And if we don't get the elves to counter our attack?" She needed to reach Athson and the others.

"Then we'll be encircled." The colonel shrugged. They'd be massacred without a corresponding attack from the rangers.

Erskwe lifted one finger. "Don't use the bugles too soon. We need the surprise, since we'll be charging among them. They'll scatter before they rally, and we can pierce their ranks deeper. We call with bugles just before we clash nearest the bridges for the most effect. If the trolls attack at dawn, it will be so loud that they won't realize we're there until you sound the bugles."

The colonel nodded. "It could work." He stood. "This is unlike any attack I've led. Anything could happen."

Limbreth considered the stick drawings of the troops. "Draw all foot units close together. The first two companies follow the horses. Remaining companies cover our flanks, odd numbered units left and even numbers right. We push for the bridge without stopping. Everyone keeps moving. We kill and advance. There's no retreat." She glanced around the gathered officers. The Grendonese looked uncommitted. "This is not our city, not our fight. But it will be our fight. Maybe not this year but the next. If the trolls take Auguron, they'll sweep south toward Grendon, and Rok can attack from the east. We stop them now, and we avoid a war we can't win later."

Grendonese faces nodded, grim understanding in their eyes.

Limbreth stood and brushed dirt from her hands. "Then we march for the city. Rations eaten as we go. Silence among the ranks. Just scouts in threes to kill all they find."

The army of dwarves and Grendonese cavalry set out soon after, moving with care in the dark hours before dawn. The march dragged on longer than Limbreth anticipated, but when they reached their destination along the slope of the road down to the river half a league away, her heart raced anew.

The march hadn't really been that long. Her eyes took in the mass of shapes below, silhouetted in what light shined from city. Sudden doubt gripped her at the thrill of her heart. If they couldn't make...

Her eyes narrowed as she stared at what lay ahead and they waited for the gray brim of dawn to light their attack. Was Athson worth this? She didn't trust him, certainly not yet. But he had confessed his error to her rather than hide it like so much else. She was no better and had failed too. She pursed her lips at the uncomfortable reminder. She may have done her best and failed, but failures they all remained.

Her horse stirred beneath her. Truthfully, this wasn't just for Athson. He needed support. The elves did. Perhaps they'd stop Magdronu. But she also did it for unsuspecting Grendon. Her stomach flipped and knotted. Then there was that prophecy from Hastra. *Go and return as if from death again.* Like at the Funnel. If this didn't count, she didn't know what would. She inhaled with sudden certainty.

The merest pearling of dawn lit the road along the slope. The colonel nodded to Limbreth and led his command along the road, toward the clearing of the forest. She followed closely with dwarves right behind.

Their line paused as shouts echoed along the river near the city. Were they discovered? Limbreth hesitated. The sound of a low bellow followed by rhythmic singing rose in the distance. A dwarven fighting song. She kicked her heels into her horse's sides and rode forward. A mass of shouts now rose across the river.

Limbreth found Colonel Meegs and hissed, "We ride. That was a dwarf singing a fighting song."

The colonel nodded as the grays of early dawn brightened further, and he led the horsemen ahead. Limbreth waited and followed their line, since she had no lance for the charge. She fell in with the dwarves, and the pace rose.

Sounds of fighting echoed from the bridge as they encountered the rear forces of trolls. They rode down trolls in the road and slashed at others within reach. Surprised trolls fell out of their way. The clearing came, and the Grendonese cavalry spread into a tight wedge formation and gathered speed, riding through the encampment as they speared trolls and trampled them beneath their horses.

Limbreth led the dwarves behind the charge. She glanced left and right as dwarven ranks fanned out on their flanks. Still they uttered not a word but fought in swift clashes as they rushed for the bridge.

Ahead, the Grendonese horsemen slowed in the press of trolls closer to bridge, and the dwarves filled in behind with a clash of weapons as the trolls gathered near the river turned to meet the surprise foe behind them. Trolls scattered and they rode farther, but the ranks of horses broke into smaller clashes among the responding trolls.

Where was the bugle? Limbreth urged her horse forward and dwarves followed her, slashing with weapons as they went. Limbreth hewed at several hobgoblins in passing. Ahead, a horseman fought alone, and she saw trolls drag him off his horse. Limbreth's eyes widened. He had no lance. It was the bugler. She galloped to his aid and stabbed a bugbear in the neck before he could strike with a tulwar. Three dwarves charged into the throng of trolls before they attacked the bugler and cut them down.

Limbreth paused over the pale-faced man. "Blow it!"

He snatched the instrument from the ground, put it to his lips, and blew the signal with all he had.

Trolls swarmed around them, mingling with horses and dwarves. Shouts rose from Limbreth's troops at the bugle's call. The bugler found his feet and kept blowing as he drew his sword. They pressed toward the bridge.

Hands grabbed Limbreth and dragged her from the saddle.

She rolled and slashed as she fell and landed on the packed dirt of the road. She screamed at the trolls and slashed at bellies as she regained her feet. She found herself surrounded as she whirled and parried strokes. She could see nothing of the bridge for the mass of trolls. Dying suddenly seemed more likely than returning as if from death.

And then the bugle call ended with an uncertain note.

CHAPTER TWENTY-FOUR

Either it was farther to the cemetery than Athson remembered, or he was tired. But then, he'd been poisoned recently. He walked with the other two Withlings for what seemed like hours, and it was now either very late or very early. By the look of the stars, he guessed very early.

He yawned. "Let me get this straight. You sing to stop magic?" How was he supposed to learn these old hymns—in a different language, no less—let alone help battle four mages? Spark ranged ahead of them.

"Not exactly." Howart's long strides carried him with seemingly boundless energy. "It runs on the principle of 'what is needed is given.' We sing in praise to Eloch, and magic is nullified as necessary. My leading is that we sing and stop—or at least slow down—the magic being used to create the shrine for Magdronu to funnel more power to them. With that much localized magic available, they can destroy enough of the elven forces on this side of the river that they cannot hold against the trolls. We need to find a way to stop that."

Athson gazed toward the early morning sky. "Ralda and I can attack." He lifted the Bow of Hart. "I have this, if it counts for something."

Zelma smoothed her unruly hair from her drawn face. "That's meant to fight the dragon, I'd think. Maybe his mages."

Athson considered Zelma's words. How had she made it this far in her grief? "I do have this blessed sword. I've stopped mage-fire with it."

Howart almost skipped a step. "That's better than nothing, but perhaps you can learn the songs."

"I don't have time. We're here, and it's not terribly far now." They slipped through the closed cemetery gate and turned down a side lane. "We'll need silence, I think, so we can surprise them. Maybe we can determine what they're doing."

Howart spread his arms to stop Zelma and Athson. "Something's coming."

Athson drew his sword. But the large figure exiting the trees moved with a familiar stride. "It's Ralda."

They waited, and the giant walked up to them. He nodded, and his fingers flicked in the darkness. "Withlings. Find mages. Beyond graves. Ralda watch. Mages do magic. No dragon come." He shook his head. "Yet." He beckoned them, and Athson followed with the other Withlings.

"Ralda, could you see if they have some pattern on the ground? Is it flat rock, or is there a stone?" Howart whispered as they traversed the cemetery, wary of discovery.

Ralda spread his arms wide. "Big stone. Mages stand in square." He motioned all around him, his hands twisting. "Glow on them. No move. Stone no with them."

Zelma looked confused, and Athson explained. "He means the mages are doing magic, judging by the glow around them. The stone is very big, but it's not between them. I'd guess it's off to the side, Ralda?"

The giant nodded. "Side. Yes."

"That's interesting." Howart scratched his chin as they continued. "If I remember from what I've seen before—and I've stopped a few of these shrines in the past—they need to move the stone among them for sacrifices. If they have a stone already, they don't need to do that, just hallow it to Magdronu's use. That still takes magic, but less of it, as well as time."

Athson sighed. Howart shared more knowledge than Hastra. "You seem ready with all this information."

Howart grinned at Athson. "Hastra was tight-lipped. But I am speaking now because there is need."

Zelma grunted but said nothing as she walked with her head down. "We need to see what's there, though, Howart."

"True, but perhaps we can slow them enough to do harm to the shrine." He shrugged. "We'll see what Eloch desires when we get there."

Athson pointed them on the side lane, and they turned toward the graves of Heth and Cireena. "We'll be in sight of it soon enough."

Nobody had known what Eloch desired about the White Arrow all week. Athson shoved his hand into his cloak pocket and touched the broken arrow. He'd heard nothing at all about anything. He exhaled slowly. Well, maybe giving the Rokan dagger to Tordug was one thing. But still...

They crossed over two rises, and the stand of trees rose like huge specters to the left. Athson led them among the trees, where they spied the mages at their secret work. Three women and one man stood in the corners of a square, a green nimbus of light around them. By the glow of their spell, Athson observed connecting symbols around them, all within the defined square. A massive, pale stone stood off to the side, near some thickets.

Howart closed his eyes and knelt in the leaves. Zelma

followed his lead, and they both whispered prayers. Feeling like an untrained outsider, Athson followed their lead though he didn't know the prayer. He laid the broken arrow among them just in case it was needed. Ralda continued standing lookout. Spark sat and watched.

After several minutes, Howart whispered, "I'll sing against Paugren's magic."

Zelma murmured, "Cass. I hear she's uncertain."

Athson squinted at the other Withlings, who peered at him with expectation. He touched the sword-hilt. The stone weighed on his mind, growing larger in his thoughts. *Break it with judgment.* He inhaled suddenly. "The stone should be broken. It's been left there for headstones, so it won't be used for evil." He glanced at Howart and Zelma. "I'll use my sword on it." He didn't know what that would do, but that's what he knew to do.

The other Withlings nodded without question. Curious that they trusted an untrained Withling, but Athson accepted that. What else were they going to do without more help? And none other was coming.

They rose as one, but Athson took the lead. "You're sure they can't move?"

Howart scratched his head. "Pretty sure. From what I've learned, spells require precise movement and intonation, or the practitioner risks injury or death. If they move while performing something of this power, they could die."

Athson brushed hair from his eyes. It had been too long since it was cut. He banished the odd thought. "Well, let's creep down there. Stay behind me, and if they attack, I'll fend it off. If they don't, take them on. Ralda, you go around and get behind them and attack from the thickets as necessary." Withling or not, Athson didn't want to take chances with these mages. He'd seen them in action. He looked at his spear, then unfurled the banner. "Ralda, you've been with me since that day at the Fallendrill River. Would you carry my family banner?"

"Yes." Ralda's hand-talk was hidden in the darkness. "Carry for you. Show them."

"That's what I need. It's to declare my freedom from their oppression of my family and others, declare their crimes." Athson shifted the banner to the far end of the haft from the spear-head. "There. At a good time, drive the spear in the ground so the banner shows. We'll wait here a while, but don't take too long. Dawn's close."

Ralda nodded and motioned something with his hands Athson couldn't see. "Be well, Withling Athson. You walk many step, come here, now."

"Thanks." Being called a Withling by Ralda made his decision weeks earlier seem official. He seemed to be acting according to Eloch's wishes. At least sometimes. He paused, then spoke to Ralda again, "May your grief fade like mist in the morning sun."

The giant suddenly embraced Athson. "You brother now. I carry banner for you, for Kralda. I go, fight for you." Ralda released Athson and set out, first heading back the way they had come. Athson spotted him turn north beyond the first rise toward the west and disappear. They waited a while in silence, but then they all three moved at the same time, as if prompted for the same reason. It was time. Athson drew his sword and carried the Bow of Hart in the other, then led the way down the slope toward the mages.

Athson glanced toward Spark, intending to command him alongside, but the mountain hound loped away east, his hackles raised. He opened his mouth but thought better of calling him back. He'd kill their surprise. With his hackles up, Spark was surely after something else.

As they approached the mages, Athson heard their spell, spoken in unison. *What a harsh language.* The mages facing them watched their approach, though they made no move to protect themselves. Athson walked faster. What if their spell ended? He ignored that deadly idea.

Howart approached the man, Paugren. The gaunt Withling stood at his side and began a hymn.

Athson skirted the square and headed for the large stone while Zelma stopped by one of the women and added her voice to Howart's song. As Athson made his way around the square, the murmur of two voices in the spell stopped. He glanced at the mages as he walked around the design on the ground. Paugren and the woman no longer spoke the spell, though the nimbus of it covered them. They grimaced their frustration at Howart and Zelma, who continued singing. The other two mages bore strained expressions, their shoulders slumped as if they bore a weight. *Good.*

Athson approached the stone and lifted his blade.

"Don't do that."

He knew that voice. *Gweld.* He did it anyway. Athson slammed the edge of judgment on the stone. Light flared with a rush of sound like an enormous wind, and a torrent of green light burst in a whirl from the massive stone until it cracked and crumbled into many pieces.

"You only delay me for a while, Athson. Even with only two active mages, they are but minutes away from activating the shrine. After I repair that stone. You cannot stop what is to come."

Athson faced Gweld—no, Magdronu—across the design and the mages. "You've failed."

Magdronu smiled diffidently. "Have I?" He pointed to Athson. "Have you repaired that arrow meant for me? No?" He spread his hand, palms up. "Then what will you do to stop me? Even now, my trolls have taken the bridge and will kill all the rangers in Auguron City."

Athson's back stiffened. "Lies. You've told me nothing but lies for years." He walked toward Magdronu and, on an impulse, dragged the sword blade through the glowing design on the ground. Sparks flared across each line.

Magdronu's lip curled on one side in a snarl. His eyes glowed, and his voice dropped to a growl. "Don't try to stop me." He motioned. "Now, take him."

Athson whirled as a shadow rushed him. He fell and rolled with his sword over his head. In that moment, he glimpsed the sheen of light in the east, and then finished his roll away from the Bane.

A snarl broke from the thickets to the east. Spark leapt into the glowing design as the Bane reached for Athson. The mountain hound charged into the cursed creature and knocked it down. The Bane squirmed oddly to escape, but Spark bounded on top of it and, with what could only be assumed was its throat in his jaws, dragged it out of square as if it weighed nothing. Athson remembered Tordug recounting barely lifting it over a rock wall to pitch down a mountainside in the Drelkhaz.

Fire laced across the ground in his peripheral vision, and Athson rolled and caught it on the flat of his blessed sword's blade. Magdronu spewed more flame, but the blade snuffed it. Athson stood amid the attack and held his sword forward until it ended.

Magdronu paced sideways, and Athson moved opposite, as if they were about to duel. They circled until the broken stone lay at Magdronu's back. Athson crouched and waited for the attack.

A thought surged in Athson's mind. "How long have you deceived me as Gweld? Since he fell at the Fallendrill River?"

A snicker escaped from Magdronu's lips and it abruptly expanded into a laugh of several moments. "You're a fool, Athson. I was ever at your side before that, watching, waiting for my time to steer you into gaining the bow so I could trick you into giving it to me." His smile faded. "I've used this elven form for a very long time and no one has suspected my true identity." He paced several times and his eyes narrowed. "Do you truly believe that a great elf would tolerate you and your frequent mistakes? Do you actually believe you know as much as me, have as much skill as I do? Are you really even close to my equal with a bow?" His expression turned serious. "You're nothing but an orphan that I needed to stop Eloch's plans and further my own. Nothing more, nothing less." Magdronu flashed his teeth in a mirthless grin. "And now I have you, traitor. Son of traitors. Over your blood and that of the elves, I'll establish my rise to rule over Denaria."

A lump of emotion rose in Athson's throat. Just as he feared. Magdronu had played him for years while holding his parents as future hostages. His face flushed with the heat of sudden anger. But it faded in a moment with the presence of the blessed sword in his hands. "So, I have the truth at last."

"Yes, I've been the shadow over your life, stalking you since Corgren lost you at the Funnel. We would have had it then with you as a hostage." The mirthless grin returned.

Athson staggered back. Of course, they always leveraged what they wanted. If he hadn't escaped. If Spark hadn't led him free, the bow would have fallen into Magdronu's hands long ago.

It's not for him. Athson's eyes narrowed at the thought. It wasn't for Magdronu? Surely it was meant to kill him. *It's not for* him. Athson gaped and blinked. Not for Magdronu? Then who? *Break his curse.* Athson stared at the length of his sword where the runes glimmered in the rising light of sunrise. Its name was Cursebreaker. Hastra had told him that the morning they left. *Traitors deserve death. Curses should be broken.* Athson gaped again. Not only had he heard Eloch quite clearly, he also knew what he had to do with the Bow of Hart *and* the White Arrow.

At that moment, Ralda charged from the thickets beyond Magdronu, snatching up a massive piece of the stone. The giant grimaced at the jagged weight raised over his head as he finished his charge at Magdronu.

Athson lifted his arm, still holding the Bow of Hart, a futile motion meant to halt Ralda, who never checked his attack.

∽

RALDA WAITED and watched from the dark cover of the thickets as Athson and the other Withlings mounted their assault on Magdronu's mages. Athson broke the sacrificial stone against Magdronu's wishes and then faced him.

He almost rushed the Bane as it attacked, but Athson escaped, and something threw the creature to the ground and dragged it out of the area of the spell. Ralda watched the Bane thrash, unable to rise, while Magdronu prepared to attack Athson again. He tore his gaze from the Bane, and before him, Magdronu stood with his back to Ralda.

Athson couldn't beat the dragon. He needed help. In his head, Ralda watched the rope slide away and Kralda fall to his death. The act of cutting the rope had saved Ralda, but he carried the weight of living as guilt and grief. He stared at the false form of the elf in the growing light of dawn. He needed to do something. His eyes beheld the broken stone, pale in the growing light of the new morning.

Ralda charged from hiding, the thickets parted before his strength like smoke. He dropped the spear and his staff, then grasped the piece of rock he gauged best for his attack, raising it over his head. Too late, Athson waved him off.

Ralda slammed the rock onto Magdronu, who fell, crushed beneath the rock.

Chest heaving, Ralda bent over his stricken enemy and grinned at Athson. Moments of silence passed. Strained expressions fluttered across the faces of the mages. Howart and Zelma sang on, undeterred by the events. The Bane flopped in whatever grasp of Eloch's doing held that creature.

Ralda retrieved the spear where he'd dropped it and jammed the point into the ground. The slight morning breeze rustled the banner at the end of the haft.

The giant left the spear in the ground, snatched his staff and walked toward Athson who stared at him wide-eyed, passing Magdronu's prone body.

At Ralda's feet, Magdronu stirred. His legs twitched and his arms flexed. Ralda backed away, his eyes wide and his grin of triumph sliding away.

Magdronu shot off the ground from beneath the rock, which flew sideways. Ralda watched as the form of the elf flamed for a moment in his rising. Smoke formed around him and then solidified into wings. The black head, with rippling horns and maw of fangs as long as swords, transformed at the end of an elongated neck. The dragon's body and legs formed out of the ashen cloud, covered in glimmering, black scales. Its feet ended in hooked claws longer than a spear-head. Magdronu's tail flicked the air with roused anger as he glared at the giant.

Ralda hefted his staff as Magdronu transformed into his dragon shape. The dragon flapped its wings, rising into the air and then dove at Ralda, who stood his ground and rolled away at the last moment. But as he regained his feet, the dragon's tail slapped into his legs.

The dragon roared in its passing. Magdronu soared overhead, tattered wings snapping in the morning air.

Ralda's legs snapped beneath him. He roared in pain and fell onto his back, writhing. He'd never gotten a chance to land a blow on the dragon. One thought glimmered in his mind. If he hadn't cut the rope, he would have gone over the cliff with Kralda and never been here.

Magdronu wheeled and descended on Ralda again, one clawed foot extended.

Ralda tried to swing his staff in defense. He missed.

The claw raked his torso and his blood sprayed.

Ralda laid breathless like he'd fallen into the chasm from his memory with his brother.

~

ATHSON WATCHED the short fight helplessly. Magdronu dove on Ralda and scored his body with his clawed foot. The giant screamed as blood sprayed into the air, the dragon's claws trailing more gore in his wake.

Athson rushed to Ralda and gaped at the giant's broken and torn body. He knelt. *Tell me what to do.* Nothing arrived in his mind.

Magdronu spoke from across the growing shrine, once again in Gweld's form. His eyes flicked to the spear and the banner that flapped fitfully on the breeze in the growing light of morning. "You hope in a dead house of traitors? You dare to defy me with this banner? You are mine. The arrow is broken and the prophecy stopped. That banner is truly pointless."

"No, it's not." Athson stood and eased close to the spear and the displayed banner of the ten tined antlers and the bow. "As I said that night on the river-barge, I declare my freedom from you. You enslaved my family centuries ago and slaves cannot be traitors. I'm not. But I'm free of your deceptions." If he died it would be standing in the truth.

Again, Magdronu's mirthless grin spread on his face. "As you wish, Athson. Sometimes I like to toy with my prey or I would have killed you already. So, you have two choices, Athson. Trade blows with me, or I kill these others."

Heat rose around Athson. Sweat beaded on his brow. Above his head, the banner smoked at the edges in a sudden smolder as did the grass around them.

"I'll burn you all unless you cross blades with me. Just for my satisfaction." Magdronu's eyes glowed, rimmed with fire.

Choices? Not two but three. What about Ralda? Athson eased to his feet into a fighting stance as sudden anger rose like fire in his chest. He lifted the blessed sword. Magdronu charged, his simple ranger's long-knife on guard.

Athson hesitated an instant before the blades met. This was the wrong choice. He parried the attack, but Magdronu twisted and turned his blade. The blessed sword flew from his numb fingers and landed, point in the ground, a dozen paces away, where it rocked with its momentum.

Athson backed away from his enemy. He rushed his sword, but Magdronu followed his sideways move and feinted at him with a mocking grin.

"We're at our end, it seems." Magdronu stood in a casual stance, almost daring Athson to make his move.

"I know what you want." He shook the Bow of Hart, unused in his grip until that moment. "This. You can have it and go your own way. Here..." He pulled the broken arrow from his pocket and flung the pieces at Magdronu's feet. "That's useless, and the bow never worked right." At least he didn't think so. He hoped not.

Howart paused in his singing, and Paugren rejoined the spell. "Athson, don't. It's not for him."

"I know, Howart. Just see to Ralda when this is done. I

don't know how this works out." Athson chanced a glance at the gaunt Withling, who nodded and cocked his head sideways.

Athson flung the Bow of Hart at Magdronu's feet.

Magdronu shook with deep, rumbling laughter. "At last. I've won!"

Athson's stomach turned over. Certainty that he'd done the right thing fled his mind. He'd probably messed up completely this time.

~

LIMBRETH WHIRLED, slashed, and parried. A sword tip slashed her calf, and she grunted. She stabbed a goblin in the throat and spit out a word to her horse to attack. The animal neighed and reared, front hooves pawing the air and several troll skulls. Limbreth ducked past her horse.

"Rally to the ax-maid!" A single voice rose from nearby, and dozens answered amid the clash of weapons. And then a song formed along with dwarven ranks.

Trolls charged Limbreth. Her horse kicked and reared. She parried an attacking hobgoblin's sword and stabbed it in the gut, then slashed its throat. Dark blood sprayed. She parried and whirled from a kobold's lightning-fast stab, her second sword slamming into its collarbone, which audibly cracked. The troll squealed as a dwarf hacked it in the back.

Dwarves flooded the area around Limbreth, and trolls fell dead to hammers, long-knives, and hand-axes.

Limbreth called off her horse and mounted as the dwarves defended her in those spare moments. She guided her horse with her knees and wheeled toward the bridge. She pointed one sword in that direction. "Form up! We fight to the bridge!"

The melee grew vicious as the trolls around them counterattacked. Colonel Meegs and the Grendonese cavalry fought in a dwindling knot, but they edged toward the bridge. Around Limbreth, dwarven companies held their flanks.

The dwarves fought to form a wall of defense and marched toward the bridge. Hundreds had fallen, but more still stood against the trolls.

"The bridge!" Colonel Meegs's voice rose over the noise of the fighting.

Limbreth's head whirled, and she glimpsed hundreds of trolls fleeing the bridge, followed by a stream of rangers led by a single dwarf. Limbreth laid about herself with renewed vigor and a shout of glee. "They're coming!"

The dwarves sang of reaping their foes in a deadly harvest, and she joined the song. Her grip locked and she didn't care as she slashed from her horse.

Rangers flooded the field as the trolls milled in sudden confusion, then broke and ran. Colonel Meegs quickly re-formed his surviving command and mounted a charge after the rout. Arrows sang from elven bows, dropping trolls as they fled. And the dwarves sang on as they engaged those bands of stubborn trolls that rallied around ogres and bugbears. The dwarves hewed into the greater trolls and felled them like trees. Limbreth raced around them and cut down any escaping goblins. Dwarves held no mercy for trolls, and neither did she.

Officers called to re-form their ranks as the surviving trolls fled into the forest. The rangers advanced in disciplined ranks, still releasing arrows. Meanwhile the Grendonese cavalry swept east along the road and trampled any resistance before them. Limbreth called for an officer.

"Here, ax-maid!" Erskwe stepped forward at attention, blood streaming from a cut along his scalp.

Limbreth gave him a stern look. "That's going to make one ugly scar."

Erskwe flashed a grin. "Better than yours, ax-maid."

"I'll show you mine if you show me yours." They both

laughed a moment. "Form up a guard for the bridge. It may be a while before the rangers return with defense on their minds."

Erskwe saluted and called for dwarves to form ranks. More than half formed up around Limbreth while the rest swept the field for surviving trolls or their fallen comrades.

She rethought her command. "Just a hundred for now, let the rest search among the wounded."

Erskwe called out a hundred dwarves and marched them behind Limbreth toward the bridge. She approached the gates and found one figure sitting on a makeshift chair.

Makwi hawked and spat as she approached, his ax laid across his knees. "I suppose this means another verse, ax-maid." His eyes narrowed.

"Only if you don't short me words, Makwi." She wiped each sword and sheathed them.

Makwi snorted as if unimpressed. "Guess you want to cross my bridge."

The dwarves behind Limbreth guffawed.

"What's the toll?" she asked.

Makwi's gaze swept the scene of dead trolls around them. "Oh, I think you've paid the toll for yourself and that lot behind you several times over."

She laughed and worry for her friends returned. "Where are the others? You seen them? Tordug?" She left the other names hanging between them. "Are they chasing trolls?"

One of Makwi's eyes narrowed as both filled with tears. "Tordug's dead. Defended the yonder gates alone and killed Corgren."

Limbreth gasped in spite of being among dwarves, and her troop murmured among themselves.

Erskwe shouted, "Honor to Tordug, Ruler of Chokkra and wizard-slayer!"

Limbreth's head turned at the shout and the sound of her troop of dwarves as they took a knee. The honor lasted several moments, until Erskwe ordered them to their feet. Tordug had won back his honor.

Tears dribbled down her cheeks as she faced her dour comrade. When she spoke again, her voice sounded husky in her ears. "And the others?" *Please not Athson.*

Makwi then spoke in his terse way about all that had befallen their group. Limbreth wondered as he spoke how he'd ever compose verses for her. Her tears fell faster at word of Hastra dying to save Athson, but she truly gaped at the news that Gweld was really Magdronu. She recovered her wits, and her anger rose at the betrayal. Athson's enemy among them all this time, his friend for years.

"Where has Athson gone?"

"He thought they might build a shrine in the cemetery. Don't know where, though." Makwi scratched at his bearded cheek.

Limbreth gasped. "I know. I'm going."

"Want me to go?"

She wagged her head. "You see to your father." She could speak of that now that Tordug had won his honor back. "Erskwe!"

"Ax-maid!"

"I leave you in the worthy command of Makwi, champion of Chokkra and its heir."

She urged her mount across the bridge with a final salute to Makwi. The horse wove among the bodies of trolls and elves. At the gates, she found they'd pulled the ogre mentioned by Makwi out of the way. She found the bodies of the dead and wounded laid out along the street and caught sight of a gray beard. She paused and gazed at his face in death. He'd been like a father to her. She hoped he was proud of her today, but knew he would be. His beard needed re-braiding to display his honor. She'd leave that to Makwi. However, she dismounted, took a knee, and said, "Honor to Tordug, ruler of Chokkra and wizard-slayer."

Nearby, Limbreth found Corgren's body laid out. She spat on him and called an elf over. She pointed at the wizard. "That's Corgren the wizard. He has no honor here. Remove his body and dispose of it how you will."

With those words, Limbreth reined her horse around and rode through the city for its cemetery, where many of the honored dead would soon rest. If Athson was able to defeat Magdronu with the Bow of Hart and the White Arrow.

CHAPTER TWENTY-FIVE

Athson backed away from Magdronu, his hands raised. Could he make a dive for the sword? "You have what you want. Leave Auguron alone. It's not worth all this. The bow doesn't work, and the arrow is broken."

Magdronu laughed and snatched the Bow of Hart and the arrow pieces from the grass. "You're a bigger fool than I marked you for, Athson. You gave it without a fight, without bargaining." He shook his head and offered an all-too-familiar smile. "So often you've thought me your friend and ally. To think a mighty elf of age and wisdom would bother with a troubled, bothersome kid. Such foolish thinking."

"Others with good hearts bothered with me. Heth, Cireena, Sarneth." Athson backed farther away but ground his teeth. *Easy, follow blessing, not anger.* He angled for the sword. It was his only chance to defeat the bow.

Magdronu fit the arrow pieces together in one hand. "The arrow is not so broken." He stared at Athson with a mocking grin so discordant with past memory as the "elf's" hand glowed green. He released his grip and held the arrow out for Athson to see. The arrow glimmered white. "See, the power of magic, straight and unbroken." Magdronu nocked the arrow to the ancient bowstring. "And you always thought you were a hair better than me with the bow?" The dragon-as-elf wagged his head with another grin of mockery. "Never the truth there, either."

He drew back the arrow and released it as if an afterthought.

Athson dove for the sword. The arrow glowed white as it curved toward him and pierced him above the heart.

Athson fell well short of the blessed sword. Pain shot through him, and he groaned. He touched the wound with both hands and drew them back covered with blood thick like wine. *Just like the wine sloshed on my hands in Howart's Cave.* More visions coming true. He put pressure on the wound and stretched for the sword.

Magdronu cocked his head. "Now you try to fight? Foolish. That arrow is well placed to let you bleed out slowly, painfully."

Athson grimaced at the pain. His strength waned, and his breath sounded ragged in his ears. He rolled his eyes. Ralda lay on the other side of the marked shrine, his chest no longer rising with breath. No help there. Athson flopped his head toward his other companions. The Withlings withheld Paugren and one of the Beleesh sisters with their song. The others could do nothing or risk the searing power of the magic.

Howart shook his head, reading Athson's thought. "If we release them, they operate the shrine. Why did you do it? It's not for him."

"Not for him." Athson's voice croaked, and weakness grasped his limbs ever tighter. His body shook. "Spark."

The guardian spirit growled where it held the Bane by the throat.

Athson watched Magdronu through fluttering eyes. The arrow was for him, for his family's curse and betrayals. But the sword was blessed. And he couldn't reach it. His eyes drifted skyward, and his family's banner flitted in the breeze. *Another vision fulfilled.* Smoke drifted from the old cloth as it still smoldered in Magdronu's heated presence. Sweat poured from Athson. He was out of friends and help. He chuckled. "What is needed..."

Magdronu leaned closer and laughed. "That's it, die with your faith in Eloch. But he can't help you now either. You chose poorly, Athson. And now you pay for your family in blood."

The thrum of hooves vibrated on the ground and pounded in Athson's ears. He turned his head, his eyes hardly open, and gasped while blood pulsed around the arrow.

Magdronu stood. "Ah, pointless help at the last moment. And you'll never guess who it is." He drew his elven long-knife and faced a charging white horse.

∼

LIMBRETH RODE through the Auguron City graveyard, a wide expanse mostly unused, since elves lived so long. If Magdronu and his mages were making a shrine there, it had to be in a quiet place where they could work undisturbed. The Bane had led her there once.

She sat up in the saddle and almost reined her horse to a halt. The Bane. It had marked the place for future use on that visit. She guided the horse along a lane that led deeper into copses interspersed with open fields. She avoided graves and headed in the general direction toward her first meeting with Athson. The vague notion of direction from that misty afternoon strained her memory. She kicked her heels into her horse's flanks, and the animal snorted in weary response but gained speed along the even lane.

The white horse crested a knoll, and a wide expanse opened below Limbreth. Figures stood among the trees in a wide circle. The little-used gate stood beyond, among the edge of trees marking the cemetery grounds. In moments, Limbreth and her horse passed the graves of Athson's foster-parents and, as she drew closer, her breath caught in her throat. Two figures were down in the glade. The others stood motionless. What were they doing?

She approached at a gallop and drew her swords. Quick glances informed her that the Withlings were engaged with two mages, leaving two others busy. Gweld stood with—her heart sank. He bore the Bow of Hart. The larger of the two on the ground, that was Ralda. She forced her sorrow and dismay away at the realization of who the other person on the ground was. Athson lay, feebly struggling, pierced with an arrow. How could that be? For an instant, fear surged through her, followed by anger.

The horse entered the glade, and Limbreth screamed her fury. *Protect Athson.* She guided her horse toward Gweld and attacked in a crazed charge.

The elf turned and waited in her horse's path. At the last moment, he leapt aside. His elven long-knife struck Limbreth's swords like lightning in a less than a blink. She reeled at the force of the blows, and her swords flew from her hands. She rolled off her horse, cartwheeled off her feet, and landed hard on her left arm. Numbness and sharp pain flashed up her arm. She scrambled to her feet and backed away from Gweld, who advanced with his elven long-knife held on-guard.

A mocking smile, an unfamiliar expression, spread across Gweld's familiar face. "I see Dareth failed me. Something to deal with later. And, really, Limbreth, this isn't Marston's Station, and I'm not a pack of unreliable trolls."

She squinted at her swords lying on the ground. She lunged for them, but Gweld leaped between her and the weapons. She pulled a belt knife and danced on the balls of her feet.

"Not a good choice, Limbreth. Don't remember when we

first met? I know far more moves than you'll ever learn. I disarmed Athson without a thought, and you as well." Gweld motioned behind Limbreth. "And he'll die in moments, so say your goodbyes while you can."

Limbreth adjusted her stance and turned her head so she had both the elf—dragon, whatever—and Athson in her peripheral sight. Athson croaked something.

"You'll not have him. The prophecy will take you." She edged toward Athson.

The downed ranger's words touched her ears. "Not for him. Need sword."

Limbreth whistled to her horse. Time to change the balance. The white warhorse responded and lunged at Gweld.

The elf half-wheeled toward the approaching horse and opened his mouth. Flame spewed at the animal. Limbreth's horse squealed, reared on hind legs, and surged from the glade. It almost ran into one of the mages, a woman, but veered from the green nimbus around her at the last moment. The mage never moved.

Gweld grimaced at Limbreth. "You delay me with your antics but not the outcome. Death comes for him now, and all help is accounted for." He motioned to the occupied Withlings and the Bane, which lay on the ground with an unseen force withholding it.

Limbreth eyed her surroundings for the first time. Spark. That must be Spark holding the Bane down. She'd not noticed it in the shade of the tree. She eased away from Gweld— Magdronu in truth, then, after that fiery display. "You'll not have him. The prophecy will take you."

Magdronu laughed. "Really? All is in my favor now."

Limbreth shook her head. "Your armies have lost. Corgren is dead at the hands of Tordug. Fitting, now that I think of it."

At the shrine, the male mage groaned. "Corgren dead?"

Gweld's eyes never left Limbreth, but he spoke to the mage. "Just finish your incantation, Paugren."

So, the brother, he looked like Corgren. Limbreth flexed her hand. "I will defend Athson with my life. Your armies will not have Auguron this day either." She'd save Athson yet. Surely there was time. There were Withlings here to help.

Magdronu motioned with the bow. "Your little games as an ax-maid of the death-grip won't help you. It's just an old injury, nothing more. Those fool dwarves know nothing and speak of empty valor. Such will your efforts be today, Limbreth." Magdronu advanced a few steps.

Limbreth backed toward Athson. Her foot kicked something. She glanced down and snatched up Athson's blessed sword. She grinned. "The balance shifts. Your fire is of no use against this blade." She'd defend Athson now. The blade's edges flashed blue and red, and its runes shined in the sunlight. Limbreth switched her stance and nudged Athson behind her with a boot. She drew the sword back low behind her leg, ready to sweep it upward against any attack from Magdronu. Her grip locked with a jolt of pain. "The grip is on me, dragon. You'll not disarm me again."

Magdronu hefted the elven long-knife and opened his mouth. Flame gathered in the depths of his throat.

The Bane sat up.

Limbreth gasped and her eyebrows climbed. What? Something dragged the sword behind her, not around to block Magdronu's fire.

~

ATHSON'S SWORD gleamed in his face. He reached for it. *Break the curse.* His hand missed twice, but he grasped it on the third try. The flat of the blade, he needed that. He pulled the blade with the last of his fading strength.

Magdronu opened his mouth wide. Heat glowed behind his teeth.

Spark released the Bane and raced toward Magdronu. Limbreth gasped, but she didn't release the blessed sword.

Athson twisted the blade and aimed the flat toward the arrow. The arrow's vanes wagged with the movement of his chest as he gasped for breath. Darkness ringed his vision. He tugged the blade again and tapped the arrow.

The arrow and the blessed sword flashed with white light in Athson's eyes. Something howled. Was it him? He released the blade, and his hand flopped across his stomach. An immense weight lifted from his mind. Athson had never known it existed.

Spark leapt between them and Magdronu, his momentum carrying him past the line of attack where none ever arrived. Athson squinted. The arrow was gone, but the pain of his wound remained, and his breath faded.

Magdronu writhed on the ground and howled in agony. The elven figure crouched on hands and knees, then bounded impossibly high into the air. Magdronu whirled into a black knot with a roar. Wings unfurled as the horned and scaled dragon stretched higher past the treetops, clawing at the air.

Athson watched as the dragon strained for the heights of the sky with agonized roars and fled on the winds. "Pain. The broken curse brought him anguish."

~

Limbreth covered her face as dust rose in the frantic escape of the dragon. She coughed, then whirled at Athson's muttered words.

The Bane thrashed into ash.

The man, he must be Paugren, slumped to his knees in agony, his voice choked with grief. "Corgren! I got you into this and he's gotten you killed." He looked to the nearest woman who trembled and shrank from Zelma's singing. "I'll never follow the Dragon again."

At his words, the other two women shrieked and shifted their hands to cast spells.

Limbreth raised Athson's sword. He'd blocked magical attacks before, back in the mountains. She hoped she could as well.

But one of the remaining sisters waved her hands and backed away. "Esthria, that dog's after me! Help!" But she spoke a few words of a spell and disappeared in cloudy embrace of dragon's wings.

The remaining mage grimaced. "You first, Paugren. For your treachery now. Then these others."

"No! Esthria, don't! It's over!" The woman nearest Paugren lunged between him and her attacking sister as Esthria released flames meant for Paugren.

The flames slammed the defending woman to the ground and engulfed her in hungry tongues of heat.

"Cass! You fool! What have you done?" Esthria stood with shock etched on her face.

Paugren lunged to put out the flames with his cloak but they singed his face and hands in the effort as Cass screamed.

Limbreth advanced toward Esthria, the blessed sword raised to fend off magic.

Esthria retreated, "Stay away or I'll kill you!" She lifted her hands but in that instant, she whirled and danced away from something unseen.

Limbreth paused. Spark. It had to be him.

Esthria screeched a few words and cast a baleful glance to Limbreth and the others as the magical wings of her spell closed around her and whisked her to some distant locale.

Limbreth sighed and lowered the sword. She turned to the scene of the charred mage, Paugren attempting to help and Athson lying upon the ground. So fast did those flames consume her. But Limbreth recovered her wits and scrambled to Athson's aid.

"I've got the giant." Howart rushed to Ralda, who lay unmoving.

Beneath Limbreth, Athson lifted one hand, his eyes barely open. She grabbed his hand and knelt over him. "Help!"

Zelma crouched and began a prayer. She kept praying even after Athson's grip loosened in Limbreth's hands and his eyes closed. Zelma never stopped praying, her voice rising and falling, until Athson gasped and his eyes fluttered open.

Limbreth had seen Hastra draw someone back from the doors of death at Huffer's Post, but she still gaped at the work of a Withling. She stared at Zelma.

The red-haired Withling sighed and sniffed. "That's twice today already, Athson. Don't make it a third." She wiped her cheeks. "I don't know how Hastra put up with you so long, but you might just be worth the trouble."

He chuckled weakly. "Just glad Limbreth got me the sword."

At her sudden tears, Limbreth wiped her cheeks and nose with her sleeve. She laid the sword aside. "How did you know?"

"Eloch. Maybe Hastra. Or Apeth." He stared at the morning sky. "Apeth and Hastra both reminded me the arrow wasn't for Magdronu before they died. Maybe they realized it was for me and just didn't have the breath to say it. I realized it when Eloch spoke to me and I heard. My family were avowed to Magdronu and broke their vow." He swallowed, his voice still weak. "They deserved death as traitors. Their curse was mine. The arrow was for me. But I was given the sword, Cursebreaker, to overcome the curse. It broke Magdronu, though. All his broken magic is agony to him and his followers."

"Will he die?" Limbreth's awe of Zelma's miracle faded, and her heart slowed in her chest. What would she do with

Athson now? Did she trust him? She didn't know, but he lived still.

Zelma shrugged.

Howart approached, his face downcast. "Magdronu will retreat to wherever he wills, lick his wounds, and seek to regroup."

"Ralda?" Athson pushed his way up and collapsed, his face pale.

Howart shook his head with a frown. "He was dead when I got to him. Wouldn't come back no matter how I prayed."

Athson groaned. "Oh no. He just wanted to make sure no one else died when he could help."

Tears welled anew in Limbreth's eyes, and a sob shook her body. "I guess he's with his brother now. Did all he could."

"Shame he had to fight Magdronu to see his brother." Athson took a deep breath. "I tried to wave him off." He peered intently at Limbreth. "Hey, you came back for me."

Limbreth nodded through a fresh wave of tears and sniffed. "I did." She still didn't know why, but she had done it. And good thing too.

"Magdronu said his trolls were taking the bridge." Athson held her hand and squeezed.

"No." Limbreth shook her head. "Tordug killed Corgren and held the gates until Makwi came and took the bridge back with the rangers. That's when I arrived with the Grendonese cavalry and what dwarves I had rounded up on the road."

Athson's eyes flared wide. "You brought an army?"

"I guess I did." She shrugged, and then her thoughts formed into certainty. "I did. We relieved the bridge, and the rangers came across and routed the trolls. Tordug died, but he won back his honor."

Athson flopped an arm over his eyes. "Not him too!" He released a ragged sigh. "It's just three left, then, that set out form Marston's Station last fall. Four, counting Magdronu. But he doesn't count."

Limbreth shook her head and pushed her braid over her shoulder and out of Athson's face. "No, he doesn't count." Her heart wrenched for Athson, betrayed by an enemy who had falsely befriended him for years and played his curse against him. It had almost killed him several times, not to mention her.

"What of the Bane?" Athson lifted his head to search the area with his gaze. "Spark had him. There's Spark." He pointed, his arm drifted with weakness.

Limbreth shrugged. "Gone with Magdronu, faded to ash." She looked to Zelma. "But how?"

Zelma sniffed and wiped her nose on her sleeve. "I don't know for sure. Perhaps it was tied to Athson's curse somehow, maybe fed off it."

Howart cleared this throat. "Uh, what do we do with this one? Cass is dead and Paugren's burned?" He stood near the disconsolate wizard.

Nearby, Paugren wept for his dead brother and his wounds. "You have nothing to fear from me. I'm done with Magdronu even if it kills me. I'm done." He grimaced at his pain or Cass who lay seared to death, maybe both. "Why did she do that?"

Limbreth looked to Athson, Zelma, and Howart in turn, until Zelma spoke up with a sigh. "We'll hold him in the city and let Eloch inform us what to do." She eyed Howart. "He deserves much for his crimes over the years."

The gaunt Withling nodded.

Zelma stood and so did Limbreth, but Athson couldn't make it off the ground. Limbreth offered her hand to pull him up.

He shook his head. "I think I'll need a cart. My head's spinning, and I'm done fighting my head." His hand found the blessed sword, and with it, he found the strength to rise to his feet and lean on Limbreth. He offered a tremulous smile at the sight of Ralda and shook his head, slumped, then fought his way to his feet. "I guess we better go get help and find my mother."

Limbreth called to her horse which returned nervously while Zelma gathered the spear with Athson's family banner.

Athson made it as far as the graves of Heth and Cireena, where Limbreth had met him. She stayed with him as he sat against a tree and waited for Howart and Zelma to bring help. Limbreth sat beside him and held his hand. When a cart rolled into sight with Howard, Zelma and his mother aboard. A troop of rangers following with arrows nocked on their bowstrings.

Athson turned to Limbreth. "I'm sorry I didn't fight for you at the Funnel. I know you don't know what to do about me, but thanks for coming back." He leaned into her and released an exhausted sigh.

Limbreth kissed him and said, "No, I don't know what to do about you, but I want to find out. And you're welcome."

He grinned at the sun and struggled to his feet with Limbreth's help. He hugged his mother when the cart arrived, and they rode back to the city. Along the way, he gazed at the sky, then Limbreth, and said, "I've never seen such a colorful sky. Now I know why." He touched the tear in his ranger-green shirt. "It's all gone. It's all gone. That curse."

He smiled and slept peacefully on the short ride.

EPILOGUE

The following weeks both drifted like a leaf on the wind and raced by like her horse in a cavalry charge for Limbreth. Athson soon regained his strength and began his courtship with sincere apology and discussion. Yet other necessities required their attention as the dead were buried.

Since he claimed a brotherhood with Athson, Ralda was buried in a plot near Heth and Cireena with honors and ceremony by the elves for his ill-fated stand against Magdronu. Messages of the news were sent to Ralda's people. Athson wrote the words for his head-stone, "A faithful friend and brother."

Limbreth's heart threatened to seize as the Withlings completed a simple ceremony of prayer to Eloch.

Athson walked with her from the fresh mound of soil and watched his feet. At last, he said, "I never had a brother and now I've lost one. I understand Ralda's struggle."

Grief froze any words of comfort on Limbreth's tongue so she held Athson's hand.

Dwarves constructed a memorial tomb for Tordug near the

bridge, his deeds and honor as "wizard-slayer" chiseled into the stone. Limbreth took part in the burial ceremony after some coaching from the dwarves. She saluted as an ax-maid with the death grip but her hands trembled less from effort and more from withheld sobs. Afterward, she left with Athson and said, "I'll treasure my real father from now on. I've lost someone like a father and I dread the death of my own and regret my angry words with him all the more."

Athson stretched his arm over her shoulders and gathered her close as she walked in a grim daze to The Broken Bow Inn where she remembered Tordug with a toast of ale with Makwi and other dwarves.

The elves honored Hastra with a long procession, at the end of which her burial concluded by Ralda, her head-stone reading, "What was needed, was given." With this last burial, neither Limbreth nor Athson spoke any words for a long while as they stood near grieving Zelma who knelt by the fresh grave.

After a time, Zelma found words, "She was the best of us, I think. She bore the burden personally for all those who died at Withling's Watch. She foresaw it in a vision. I think it haunted her and drove her all the long years since."

Later, Limbreth ate with Athson at a small gathering hosted by Sarneth. She barely tasted what she ate but paused at a sudden thought. "Odd that our first meeting was where so much happened, where our friends have been buried."

Athson shook his head. "Not odd, just the right time or else we would never have gone there at the end to stop Magdronu. The place was planned even then." He didn't eat much either and soon left with Limbreth.

With each burial of a companion, grief and pride mingled in Limbreth's thoughts. But with the end of sorrowful tasks and the arrival of early spring, the immediate grief dwindled to a gray sadness in the background of Limbreth's mind and her sleep improved. She noted even

Zelma's drawn expression softened and her reddened eyes were less of a frequent sight.

Athson grew warmer as he moved his mother into the previous home of Heth and Cireena for those weeks of recovery. There, he welcomed Howart and Zelma who offered training to him as a Withling. After some weeks, the three Withlings concluded as one, much to Limbreth's surprise, that their path lay in Hart where they intended breaking Rok's power and that of Magdronu's cult. Likewise, they recruited, Enlath the ranger weapons-smith, into their order and planned to rebuild their old home far away after they settled the old feuds between Hart and Rok into which Magdronu rooted his cult.

As Limbreth observed a change in Athson, her fondness for him grew, yet her misgiving lingered with the memory of her fall at the Funnel. When the day of his departure arrived, she rose in the dim light of morning to say her farewells to him, the other Withlings and Danilla, her heart heavy as she chose another path with the homeward bound Grendonese guard.

Limbreth arrived in the yard behind the ranger stables and kicked the dirt at their feet where she and Athson stood in the lingering morning dusk. Her breath caught at a lump in her throat. She brushed a stray strand of hair over her ear and lowered her gaze. "I'm still not sure how I feel after everything."

Athson touched her cheek and drew her gaze to his. "I understand your hesitance. But you did ride through an army of trolls to get to me."

"I did do that, didn't I?" She smiled, laughed, and added, "Makwi will be composing that verse for a long time."

Athson laughed too. Their laughter faded after a moment. "Look, the point is, my failure at the Funnel is my own, part of a bigger scheme of shadow in my life that no longer exists. You came back for a reason, though."

Her mixed feelings still fluttered in her head no matter what her ride into battle meant. "You need to go, if you're to start east with that troop of dwarves. I'll work through it." It was a long ride to Grendon. "I still need to answer to my father." Her stomach suddenly felt like she'd eaten nothing for breakfast. But it was a long ride, and facing her father lay weeks away. "I'm not sure what to tell him about me, who I am now, or about you."

Athson took her hand and caressed it. "Tell him you're an Ax-Maid of Chokkra with the death-grip." He ran a finger along her braid and the trinkets woven there. "Show him these. You have an honor guard of dwarves and an offer of alliance from the new ruler of that kingdom. You bring him influence and trade. Show him you're not the youthful, angry person who left in the night. Show him your strength."

Limbreth nodded. "Yes, there's that." And it was all true, she wasn't the same girl who ran from her father's house. She took a deep breath. She was far stronger than she'd assumed she was those long months ago.

Athson kissed her hand. "Let the songs of your deeds be sung by the dwarves. Show him you are the Silver Lady. Be those things."

She gazed at Athson through a sudden swell of tears. "What should I be? What should I do?" Emptiness formed in her like a sob lodged in her breast at sudden grief and loneliness for her companions both dead and alive. They were leaving and she was going her own way home.

He smiled and brushed tears from her cheek with his hand. "Be yourself. Do what you must."

"Do what he wants?" Her lips trembled. Mixed feelings about Athson, his failure to save her, fluttered within her like butterflies. But she did want him despite the doubts. "What do I tell him?" She wrapped her arms around Athson's neck. "I don't know what I want."

"But it's not simply what he wants."

"True."

"It's a long trip. Tell him what *you* want when you get there."

"And if I still don't know what I want?" Tell her father *what* about a husband?

Athson rested his forehead against hers. "Tell him someone will come in due time to ask for your hand. Maybe from east over the mountains. From Hart. Perhaps by then you'll know what you want."

Limbreth sucked at her teeth. "Yeah, maybe I'll have put the Funnel behind me by then." She did want Athson, and she drew him into a tight embrace. But his admission that he'd failed her, chosen revenge when she needed him, haunted her still. Yet she'd also ridden back for him and the others. She kissed Athson through her uncertain tears and the clouds of doubt parted for a moment.

She drew back from the kiss, their foreheads still touching. "I'll tell him all of that. I'll be who I've become, and he'll have to accept it. I'll tell him I'm waiting for a certain someone to come and show me who he truly is. I'm willing to wait for that." Of that, Limbreth was certain. "Now you go and follow Eloch's bidding where you must, and come to me when it's time."

Athson breathed in her ear. "When it's time, then."

~

ATHSON RELEASED Limbreth as regret pecked in his heart. She had to leave, to return to her home and answer the summons, Dareth's treason notwithstanding. But he had another calling leading him. That way drew him east. He crossed the corral hand in hand with Limbreth and stood beside his horse. The early morning breeze lifted the scent of spring from the forest.

Others stood ready, some old companions for farewells, and some new companions for travel. So few remained from that first farewell to Sarneth, who stood in the mingled group.

Words caught in Athson's throat, a hitch of emotion over the missing faces. Ralda, come to work out his grief for his brother, now gone without seeing the plains of his home again. Tordug lay entombed on elven land, his honor regained in his death and that of his foe. Hastra lay near the giant, now free of the burden of her labors for Eloch, the promise of prophecy completed. Gweld no longer his disguised friend, the bane of them all, but Athson most of all. Just three of them remained: Makwi to rule Chokkra; Limbreth, who would return to her father; and Athson.

The way lay before Athson with new companions, his path to restore the order of Withlings with Howart and Zelma. The future of Hart still balanced on his Withling insight. Magdronu may be weakened, but he still controlled Rok and Hart and many worshipers. Athson's broken family curse left him free, and others whom he didn't know needed his leadership to be set free as well.

His mother sat astride a horse already. In the growing light, her impatience for the road ahead lay across her face in the growing light of the dawn. "Ready now?"

Athson nodded. He glanced over his shoulder at Limbreth, who stood back a few paces. His road lay in Eloch's care, but he'd go to her in the end. His heart thrummed with that soaring thought. He swallowed. "Yes."

Sarneth offered his hand with a smile. "I can't say you haven't been interesting among us, Athson. Some say you drew Magdronu's ire upon us, but he coveted the forest for many years, with or without you and the bow."

Athson took his former commander's hand. "Thank you for everything you've ever done. I wish—" His voice, suddenly laden with husky emotion, faltered a moment. "I wish you and all who still live my best. I wish Heth and Cireena still lived. They cared for me so long when I had nothing else."

Sarneth saluted, and Athson answered. "I'm sorry we harbored traitors during that time who killed them and others so needlessly in their lust for power."

Makwi stepped forward and offered his hand, his face as solemn as Athson had ever seen it. "Withling, I guess this is goodbye for now. I've doubted you often but you and the bow have offered Chokkra a new start we never expected."

Athson took the dwarf's hand and shook it. "I'm sorry for the doubt and trouble along the way. It took me a long time to see through it all clearly."

Makwi flashed a rare grin. "They hail me as king because that fog lifted. I've sent a call to our scattered people to come and re-build Chokkra."

"Blessings upon you and your people, Makwi." Athson smiled. "The bow got you your home back as well as a bridge with some verses to be sung soon." Sarneth had named the bridge, "Makwi's Bridge" for his stand against the trolls. "May the tale of your scars and your honor be sung at the hearth for many years."

"You've learned something useful along the way, I see." Makwi winked at Limbreth as he spoke to Athson. "But you are kind in blessing, Athson."

Athson nodded and stepped close to the others. Howart and Zelma stood by their horses. "Ready?"

Howart offered a lopsided grin. "Been ready for a long time to set things right. We'll start with the order and Hart at the same time."

Zelma let out a cackle. "Sister would set out for just one, no matter the sacrifice."

Paugren's horse danced as he held Athson's charred banner aloft in his hands, scarred while trying to save Cass. He glanced at Athson, an unreadable expression on his burned face. "I'll pay for our deeds after we set things as right as possible in the order, Hart, and Rok. The other Beleesh sisters will come around, maybe."

Athson looked to his mother, who arched a single eyebrow. She'd expressed her misgivings already regarding the former wizard. Her mistrust wouldn't likely diminish, certainly not while he remained unpunished. But Athson couldn't refuse Paugren the chance to undo his wrongs before he suffered any punishment.

He scratched the back of his neck. It wouldn't be easy on the road with his mother, Howart, and Zelma doubtful of Paugren. He sighed. He didn't much trust him either, but Eloch had led him to let the scarred former wizard ride with him. Athson shook his head and mounted his horse. None of it was a small task, with or without the recalcitrant Withling among them. But he'd chosen it.

With final farewells, they trotted from the yard. Spark slipped ahead along the still-dark street. Athson turned in his saddle, and there stood Limbreth beside Makwi in the gate. She raised a hand to him, and he saluted them both as a dwarf.

They soon crossed "Makwi's Bridge" and turned east upon the road. The scars of the trolls, their carcasses burned weeks ago, but their damage on this side of the river, as well as the battle fought, lingering yet in the refuse to be burned. The elves would hunt trolls in the forest for months to come and defend the roads from raids by their dwindling numbers for years to come.

Then, Athson rode ahead, his destiny much more than the strung Bow of Hart slung across his shoulders. With the other Withlings, his mother, Spark, and his sword, he'd do his best to restore the Order of Withlings and return to Limbreth. He would show her who he was not by his deeds but by his heart for Eloch and her. He smiled.

His mother leaned close. "What's on your mind?"

Athson took a deep breath, his heart lighter than at any time he could remember in his life. "Destiny is now, and it's a good day to ride through it."

THE END

DEAR READER

Dear Reader, I hope you enjoyed The White Arrow, Book Three of The Bow of Hart Saga. The end of the series came all too soon but I have many other books in the works. Many readers have written me asking, "Will there be another book to the series?" Well, be sure to stay tuned, because, while I'm working on several other books, I might just come back to Denaria in the future. As I've written The Bow of Hart Saga, I've gotten many wonderful reviews and ratings from fans thanking me for the book. Some had opinions about all the events in the book and asked what would happen next. As an author, I love feedback. Undoubtedly, you're the reason I've been able to finish the series. So, tell me what you liked, what you loved, even what you hated. I'd love to hear from you. You can write me at ph@phsolomon.com and visit me on the web at www.phsolomon.com. Finally, I need to ask a favor. If you're so inclined, I'd love it if you would post a review of The White Arrow. Loved it, hated it— I'd just like to hear your feedback. Reviews can be tough to come by these days, and you, the reader, have the power to make or break a book. If you have the time, here's a link to the book page. Thank you so much for reading The White Arrow and for spending time with me.

In gratitude,

P. H. Solomon

If you've enjoyed reading the other books in The Bow of Hart Saga, you can subscribe to my newsletter for more information about my other books, fun updates about the series and news about upcoming releases. Click here to subscribe and receive a gift.

THE CHANGELING INCIDENT
PREQUEL TO THE ORDER OF THE DARK ROSE

The Cursed Mage Case Files, Book 1

Mandlefred "Manny" Mandeheim is on the trail of some smugglers with his team of spy-mages. Can he catch them before they disappear with unknown magic contraband?

The cacophony of protesters assaulted Mandlefred Mandeheim's ears as he rounded the corner of the block alongside the Turoqan Temple. The knot of people shouted disapproval into the air and waved signs or gestured rudely to no one in particular. He glanced over his shoulder a moment in consideration. He just passed through the boundary a spell of silence.

Someone in the crowd, powerful enough to cover the expanse of Henefrin Square along the side of the temple, stood among the protesters.

The noise disrupted magic communication for Mandlefred.

An angry man shoved him. "Get out of the way, bum!"

Mandlefred almost laughed. Odd how the protesters voiced their anger about abuses, then acted abusive to him. Angry crowds seldom lived up to their standards in his observation. With a few side-steps, he grabbed a magic particle that glimmered in his face. He grinned as he hunched in his destitute's disguise, shook the magic like a bug in his fist, then held it to his ear.

Edvard's confident tone reported, "The apples are falling in the basket."

Mandlefred capered about among the crowd, bumped a few people, and scampered away as they kicked or shoved at him. His half-crazed act worked better than a charm, literally. He dodged among the throng. The protest might devolve into a riot, always a possibility, but then he bore no responsibility for it, not being an organizer. He swatted several wisps of magic from his face, then grabbed another particle - they weren't uncommon in Cal Rindon with all the mage technology.

Nothing of the protest surprised him, of course. This bit of mayhem covered his operation neatly, including the number of city guard squads he needed on hand some blocks away in the warehouse district. Manny blended in with the protesters as he edged his way among them toward the temple door. He waved a fist and shouted as he pushed through the milling throng, "Down with torturers!"

Nearby, a broad chested fellow with a short red beard and balding head shouted with red-faced fury, "Down with Sniffers!"

Others shouted and shook signs that bore variations of phrases like, "No more torture." More signs of hateful slogans about the city guard and the young Empress of the Gallantean Empire. The capital city of the empire roiled with unrest from various sources.

Manny shook his fist in the air, cavorted with a wild laugh to act his part as a loosely hinged street-dweller, then added a few curse words as he matched shouts with the crowd and he neared the door. The turn-out impressed him. At least five hundred people massed in the square grounds as the city guard stood back lest violence erupt. Public opinion of the youthful ruler, Empress Elevenya I, of but twenty years of age, swayed toward a label of too weak for governing the empire. Popular sentiment demanded the Privy Council exert more control and oversight over the government. Manny knew the idea to be planted but not the source. Yet.

"Sniffers can die!"

"Torture Uberman!"

Manny snorted at the irony. The angry cries for violence countered the reason for the protest. Someone hired the rowdier participants and charged them with shouting the outlandish statements. Others in the crowd took up the shouts without a thought, caring little that it smacked of the very thing the protested.

As he wove among the crowd, Manny considered the cause of their unrest. One recent outrage involved the sniffers, the common name for the imperial spy agency, now beset with the scandal of a traitor whose crimes also included torturing citizens of Gallantea for information. An inconvenience for determining the depth of the betrayal since former Agent Uberman revealed nothing of the extent of his crimes other than what the agency discovered already. Someone used the scandal for furious effect and covered their involvement. The unknown source exerted the will of a foreign power, no doubt.

Manny deftly removed a wand as he stood at the locked side-door of the temple. With a few muttered words of mage-talk for throwing a lock open, he flicked his thumb on the switch that activated the spell. In answer, a sheen of white light glowed around the keyhole. He stood close enough to both block the sight and hear the click of the lock, the latter even with the clamor at his back. With a twist of the knob, and another muttered word of a spell, Manny hid his movement with the slight visual distortion of illusion. Manny pulled the door ajar far enough for entry and slipped into the temple.

The consecrated holy ground snuffed out the illusion's distortion. Manny closed the door and locked it behind him. His quick action muffled the racket behind the wooden door to a low roar as he strode into the confines of the temple, headed for the small chapel on the far side.

No one pounded on the door in response to his action, so Manny assumed his activity remained noticed when he closed the door as his spell died. Nothing surprised him about the effects of the consecrated ground. Holy edifices of Turoq and Durasim counteracted magic, one of the rare places anyone might expect such an outcome. He chose this location to wait as his team's report for such a reason. That fact, and he studied the nullification principles of the religion's consecration ritual. Best place possible for him as he awaited the time of a nearby meeting with Adrienne, his strike leader.

In a silent corner, Manny dropped his threadbare bag of belongings, those on the top consistent with his disguise as a homeless man. In moments, he peeled the knotted false beard from his face, then wiped his skin clear of the painted distortions and the dirt. He removed his long duster turned inside out and festooned with false tears for just such a disguise. Next, he pulled off the dirty shirt which revealed one beneath it, all nice and clean in contrast. Last, he pulled false pant-legs from his real ones, then wiped his shoes clean. After stuffing the disguise into his old bag, he brushed his dark hair straight with his fingers.

"Callusta." Manny's command, followed by a touch of his utility wand - he preferred the more modern term, caster - the old bag shrank in his grasp to a manageable size which he stuffed into a pocket. The stench faded from his nose. All done with the disguise and he learned a few details about the operation outside even if he ran his own elsewhere for other reasons.

He crossed the main temple sanctuary for the smaller. He passed the front rows of comfortable pews of dark wood where a few faithful parishioners of Turoq prayed. Candles glowed along the walls, lit by the frequent supplicants, and added light from the those that hung from the ceiling. Manny shook his head. No maged-lights here since magic never worked in this properly consecrated house of worship.

Within the small chapel, candles burned in a profusion from hanging stands and rows along cabinet tops along the walls. High-back benches lined the floor where a single old woman sat in a profusion of dark cloth that made up her cloak and dress. He imagined the woman as flower bloom faded into decay. Manny stepped past her, intent upon studying his religious tome for clues about the power of its prayers which nullified magic.

"Can you assist the left-handed miller's daughter?" The whispered question the woman, her voice raspy and uneven with age, halted Manny.

"Light sings at funerals." He intoned the coded response, curious as to the identification of the agent who addressed him. Manny sat behind her and opened his book to prayers and played the part of a parishioner.

The elderly woman turned her head and he saw clearly beneath her hood, the wisps of straight, gray hair. Her face bore wrinkles worn into the skin by decades of care and her nose arched prominently. The chin pointed with equal prominence toward the floor. With voice still low as if in prayer, but changed and clear, she said, "Like my disguise, Manny?"

The familiar voice of Manny's lover and team-lead, Adrienne, halted his affectation of murmured prayer. "It's very effective for one without magic."

"I can't change that fast for our little fun today. It's magic." She giggled softly.

Manny almost choked. "This consecrated holy-ground. Even I can't do magic here."

"Hmm, well, I found a way, so it's not so properly consecrated. Maybe you should try hard, love. Like this morning."

More information about *The Changeling Incident* can be found at https://phsolomon.com/cursed-mage/.

COMING FALL OF 2020

The Order of the Dark Rose
The Cursed Mage Case Files, Book 1
By
P. H. Solomon
(Artwork pending)
The Disgraced Sniffer
Proposition from a Stranger

Speaking with a wall never entered my mind when I rolled out of my cot that morning. Fate twisted around oddities as I strolled along the street, its name forgotten to me now. Oddities. I once knew such things like I knew magic. Everyone did. We used it in our technology. Commonplace wonders excited everyone, but few know it. Five years after talking to the strangest oddity, I know that I don't know magic.

My desperation gripped me at the time, the door of another writing house job having been shut in my face – quite literally. I leaned against a wall and tipped my hat over my face.

"Excuse me, but could you step aside?"

The voice spoke from the wall. I jumped aside and gaped as I face the brick wall of a building like any other in Cal Rindon.

"Hey, just lean back a step either way. Don't look so surprised, act natural. I don't want anyone to know I'm here." The wall spoke to me in a most casual way, the tone intelligent and alert.

"I must've drunk too much of something fermented incorrectly." With a rub of my neck, I shoved my hands in my pants pockets and took a stride.

A hand grabbed my shoulder. "Hold on. You can stay. You were just leaning on me and blocked my view."

A glance at my shoulder and I tensed to spring. The wall grew a brick-colored hand that grasped me tightly. My heart surged.

"Don't make a scene. Calm down. Just step aside." The arm, also brick-like and attached to the hand, pulled me aside.

I stumbled aside with a sudden numbness in my thoughts. A wall talked to me and then grabbed me. What had I imbibed the night before that? My off behavior certainly lost me that job. "Who? What are you?"

"A man like you. Haven't you seen magic? You know, illusion?" The hand let go me and smoothed the wrinkles from my coat. "Anyway, I didn't mean to startle you. I just need a clear view."

"Uh, of what?"

The hand withdrew into the wall. Magic? It ran the trams and lit rooms these days. But illusion? Someone part of a wall? "That private post over there, across the street. Someone might come today that I want know more about."

"Who are you?"

The wall sighed. "Hold on. Follow me over to that basement stairwell."

A glance in either direction revealed the sight of the suggested destination. I hesitated.

The sound of footsteps touched my ear, heading for the stairs, then paused. "Well, aren't you coming?" Shoe-soles clomping on the pavement resumed.

I followed, dragging my on worn shoes along the sidewalk and followed the walking wall. Curiosity gripped my imagination at the thought of taking a walk with a wall, gaining a new friend. Surely, something affected my mind that morning.

Shoes scuffed on the steps and stopped at the bottom of the stairwell. Or so I thought in my addled state of mind. A leg distended from the wall, followed by the rest of a body. I beheld a vagrant slouched in the basement stairwell of a nameless building beneath the slate gray sky in the crisp chill of late Fall that pierced my overcoat and clothing with a sudden gust of wind.

With a frown, I turned away as my face heated with embarrassment and leaned my back against the wall. I sighed as I glanced over the want-ads for writers, my singular talent being words. But both women and the writing houses wanted little to do with a pitiful fellow such as I. Best I look for a job. The paper rattled in my hands as the wind whispered along the street and stirred the actual mists rising from the sewers, mists that half and secure the streets at times. The vagrant played some trick on me, threw his voice or knew some minor beguiling spell. But I knew nothing of magic in that degree. Not that day.

"You looking for a job?" The voice of the beggar in the stairwell sounded clear in the crisp air. Not drunk and that was a wonder. Same voice

"Yes, if you must know. How'd you guess?" My back to the vagrant, I half turned my head to my shoulder as I addressed him. "How did you do that? And why?"

"Heard your stomach grumble from half a block away. And you leaned on me. No trick, at least, nothing aimed your way."

"Hah! Did you now?" I pressed a hand to my stomach. That loud? My legs wobbled a bit since I'd only eaten a few meager bites of gruel at a charity line that morning. That last fruitless effort at a job left my stomach emptier still with my coin running thin. I sighed. A few more day jobs to earn scant coin appealed only for the food and a barren room in the building full of grasping laborers who drank, gambled their wages and brawled half the night. It was a wonder I was still alive. I carried all my needful possessions on my person regardless, since I often found my door ajar in the room searched for valuables. "What are you doing, then, if not trying to pick pockets from hiding in whatever illusion spell you used? You didn't hear my stomach and you know nothing about me."

"Your pants are crisply pressed but the cuffs are worn. Your shoes are shined with a thin coat of spit-and-ink. You carry your belongings in your pockets as if always on the move." The vagrant stirred in the stairwell behind me.

Who was this odd street cat? He noticed everything about me in the spare moments I'd paused near his perch. "What of it, then?" I rolled my paper, slapped it in my other hand and turned to leave for my next stop. A position undoubtedly filled. Honestly, did I smell so much? I checked my clothing.

A jingle caught my attention from the stairwell. "I've a bit of corn for an easy job if you've a mind for it. Simple. Easy. Enough to fill your belly for a week or so."

My consideration of the vagrant's small purse consisted of a snatch-and-run, so low were my spirits to consider theft in that moment. But the thought skipped my mind as I peered at the figure hunched below me. Behind the smudges of dirt on his hands and face lay a keen face, hidden from casual inspection. Without a doubt, the downcast mien hid far more than a passing glance might discern about this man.

He jingled his purse again. "It's a simple job and a sharp fellow such as yourself can perform it without trouble."

I crossed my arms and assumed an air of command which one tried to take with street dwellers. My own stomach rumbled and betrayed my play for control of the situation. "Where'd you get that money? Steal it from someone?" I turned to go to my next employment possibility.

"Suit yourself. I'll find another man for the job. Hope you eat tonight." The muffled jingle of coin ceased behind me.

I drew to a sudden halt and wheeled toward him. Best hear

him out. The stop for the job would wait. Likely filled anyway. "What you want done and how much?"

"I'm man with long sideburns and wearing a black overcoat will arrive in a few minutes at that private post – shop. You'll wait in that alley until I give the signal, then you will stroll into the shop." He lifted a finger. "Mind you, stroll into the shop."

"Yes, stroll in, then what? Attempt a robbery? I hardly think that wise with a witness. I'm not up for illegalities." I wasn't interested in crime, regardless of my stray thought mere moments earlier at the noise of clinking coin. My eyes strayed along the street. The chance of a good meal for several days sounded better than starving on the street. I wasn't close to that. Yet. I did need the money.

"Hardly that. You wait for the man to do his business. Make note of what he does and says. Once he's finished, ask for a package for Mr. Blickens. The clerk will have it. I'll meet you around the corner there." The stranger pointed for the next corner in the direction I had originally intended. He spread his hands, palms up. "See? Simple. Three silvers for your time and trouble and the information about the man."

"Who is this man? Why do you want to know about him?" A few people, bundled against the cold, strolled by and my odd benefactor slouched deeper into the stairwell.

After they passed, he looked me in the eye. "No questions. Not here. If you're in, then head for that alley. He'll be along in a few minutes."

I crossed my arms again and tapped a foot. It could be trouble and more of that I didn't need. "What's in the package?"

He shrugged. "Useless trinkets."

"I see." Now I lifted a finger in warning. "There better not be city guards waiting around that corner or in the shop. I'll tell them about you fast."

Now it was the stranger's turn to chuckle. "You can be sure

I'm not with them, nor have anything to do with what interests them. They'll not help me in this matter."

I opened my mouth with more questions.

The vagrant forestalled me with a wave of his hand and the purse in his grasp. "I'm in disguise. That man might recognize me anyway. But I need the information. Are you in? If not, I'll wait for another day."

I clenched and unclenched my jaw a moment. "You have the claim ticket?"

He reached between the bars of the handrail and handed me that parcel identifier. I took the slip of paper and headed for the alley indicated and stood with my shoulder braced against the corner, out of sight of the street. The paper scrounged earlier in the morning hid my lower face without blocking the view of my accomplice. If this went wrong, I'd disappear down the alley without possibility of recognition. Without enough money for a tram ride or a maged steam-carriage, I'd have to walk fast and take other alleys but I didn't intend to be caught in an illicit scheme. Months of living in my rat-infested building left me with plenty of tales of witnessed crimes committed by teams of tricksters.

My eyes strayed to the page headline: Sniffers Still in Turmoil after Accident. I scanned the article a moment until motion grabbed my attention. My newfound accomplice signaled from deep in his hole, his face barely visible but his hands pointed along the street, though no doubt hidden from view of his marked man.

I sighed and stepped onto the sidewalk and affected my best casual stroll past a tailor's shop, then a cobbler before I reached the private post shop. I glanced at the ticket, then at the address as if confirming my location. With a nod to myself, I opened the door to the clang of a bell and entered into a small room with the counter. Various supplies and flowers which a man wishing to buy for a lady's favor or to affix to his lapel lay in easy reach for waiting package claimants. I queued behind my man and waited for the others ahead of him to conclude their business. He did indeed wear a dark overcoat and his lamb-chop sideburns stood out from his ears distinctly. I observed his salt-and-pepper hair between his collar and his rounder hat.

So fixated was I on the stranger, I almost missed listening to the clerk as he waited on him. "How may I help you today?"

The clerk a balding man with reading glasses on the end of his bulbous nose, brushed loose hair along the side of his head and flicked his gaze at me as I strode to the counter and feigned interest in the flowers. Among the variety within the floral display was that of a rose so dark as to be almost black.

"You have a package for me, I believe." The voice of my marked man sounded deep in the suddenly quiet little front room and carried what struck me as dangerous confidence. Besides his bushy sideburns, his pale, shaved face bore unremarkable features: a common nose, eyes dark but not piercing, his chin neither protruding nor recessed. Likewise, his cheeks appeared none too prominent nor his lips neither full nor thin. One would never remember him from a crowd. He tilted his head toward me slightly, as if to hide his plainness in embarrassment.

"Yes, your ticket, please." The clerk wiggled his fingers in anticipation over his running list of ticket numbers that matched to his temporary bins in the backroom. He flashed a quick smile my way as if to instruct me to patience for his service.

I shifted my eyes to my own business as my mark slid a ticket onto the counter. Except it wasn't a ticket and my averted gaze almost missed it entirely: a card with a darkened image printed on it.

The clerk covered the offered image so quickly I never glimpsed it. The balding man's face paled in a sudden sheen of perspiration which gleamed on his head in the light of maged lamps. He ducked his head and his hands trembled as he turned from the counter. "I'll just be a moment." His throat worked as he swallowed and he ducked into the backroom.

I tapped my foot with a sigh. "Seems a tad slow. Maybe a little peaked, don't you think?"

The other fellow tipped his hat toward me in the barest of greeting. "Oh, I think he's more of the skittish type."

Silence followed between us as a clock ticked on the wall. I returned my attention to the various other merchandise until the clerk returned, his hands still atremble as he carried three flowers in a narrow vase. One was a bright red tulise, the second a yellow caranelle and the third none other than the deep crimson rose.

The deep voiced fellow received the flowers without a word.

"I say, what variety of rose is that? Never seen one like it before." I spoke as the man turned and I got a good look at the vase and flowers.

My erstwhile employer's mystery man turned to go without answering the question except with another tug of his hat and the thinnest of smiles. "Good day." The flash of his dark eyes and his tone meant I should leave him alone. He left and strode away in the opposite direction from which he'd arrived at a quick clip.

"May I help you?" A flush spread across the clerk's chubby cheeks.

I pointed to the nearby black roses that numbered less than a dozen at a guess. "What were these? Out of curiosity." I offered a smile of the clerk peered at me in silence for several moments.

The clerk's fingers drummed on his list of numbers. He cleared his throat. "Actually, they're maringias, not a rose. A bit rare but I've a few clients who have me stock them for special requests. Not for sale, just show, you see?"

"Of course." I edged along the counter away from the flowers and offered the ticket to earn my pay. "Here for a package."

Stubby fingers snatched the ticket and the clerk frowned as he read the numbers through the glasses perched on the end of his short nose, then he glanced at me. "Expecting a different man for this one."

With a lift of my chin, I answered, "I'm his agent."

"Of course, not seen you before is all."

Most people used younger men than I for their deliveries and pickups. I certainly didn't look the part. "Well, I'm new to the job so I'm just getting around to some of the shops."

"Certainly. Just be a moment." The clerk consulted his list again and left the counter to me.

My gaze traveled along the list and spied only numbers. My eyelids narrowed. No names, so who was he expecting?

A moment later, the clerk returned with a small box marked with the handling instructions. "There you go. Anything else today?" He waved a hand at the flowers. "Perhaps a flower?"

"Not today. I'm afraid I must move along on my rounds." I tipped my hat in farewell and exited the post shop, then casually strode toward my rendezvous with my secretive employer. After a short walk to the proscribed side-street, box in hand, I turned left at the corner, then almost halted at the sight before me. A man stood reading a paper near the alley entrance instead of the vagrant who hired me. I reached the alley and peeked along its dank length as several people strode past us. Perhaps he hid in another basement stairwell. I approached the nearest set of steps and found no one there. Befuddled, I glanced along the alley in both directions.

"There you are." I turned to the familiar voice of the vagrant but beheld the face of the newspaper reading man.

My jaw worked at the change of appearance. No longer did my secretive employer wear a dingy, threadbare coat with stained shirt and patched-kneed trousers. Nor was his face smudged with ash any longer. Instead, he wore a proper suit of gray cloth and his face bore no marks of rough living. "But how did you...?" I pointed to his face and attire.

"Changed, of course." He held his paper behind his back. "Best not to be recognized." He glanced at the box in my hands and he pointed to it without touching the package. "You were given this?"

I glanced at the package in my hand and offered it to him, expecting my pay. "Yes."

"That won't do. Please follow me if you will." He strode along the alley.

"But, what about –?"

"Quickly. You don't want to be caught with that box in hand. Trust me." The gray-suited man strode to the second basement stairwell and clattered down the length of steps where he whispered and thrust the door ajar. "In here."

Look for release news about The Order of the Dark Rose at https://phsolomon.com/cursed-mage/

ABOUT THE AUTHOR

P. H. Solomon lives in the greater Birmingham, AL area where he strongly dislikes yard work and sanding the deck rail. However, he performs these duties to maintain a nice home for his loved ones as well as the family's German Shepherds. In his spare time, P. H. rides herd as a Computer Whisperer on large computers called servers (harmonica not required). Additionally, he enjoys reading, running, most sports and fantasy football. Having a degree in Anthropology, he also has a wide array of more "serious" interests in addition to working regularly to hone his writing. His first novel, The Bow of Destiny was named 2016 Book of the Year by Fantasia Reviews and is the first book of The Bow of Hart Saga. The sequel novel, An Arrow Against the Wind, was released in April of 2017. The third book of the series, The White Arrow, is due to be released during the Fall of 2017. P. H. Solomon also authored the award winning short story, The Black Bag, which won best published short story at SCWC 2012. P. H. is also a member of Science Fiction and Fantasy Writers of America (SFWA).

Join P. H. Solomon's social circle: https://phsolomon.com/

Thank you for reading The White Arrow and all of The Bow of Hart Saga. If you liked the book, please leave a rating and a review after advancing to the next page.

Made in the USA
Columbia, SC
13 July 2023